# RIVER
## OF LIES

B.C. Blues Crime
*Cold Girl*
*Undertow*
*Creep*
*Flights and Falls*
*River of Lies*

# RIVER OF LIES

## B.C. BLUES CRIME

## R.M. GREENAWAY

DUNDURN
TORONTO

Publisher: Scott Fraser | Editor: Allister Thompson
Cover designer: Laura Boyle
Cover image: woman: shutterstock.com/goffkein.pro; river: DannyPSL
Printer: Marquis Book Printing Inc.

Library and Archives Canada Cataloguing in Publication

Title: River of lies / R.M. Greenaway.
Names: Greenaway, R.M., author.
Series: Greenaway, R.M. B.C. blues crime novel.
Description: Series statement: B.C. blues crime
Identifiers: Canadiana (print) 20190144548 | Canadiana (ebook) 20190144556 | ISBN 9781459741539 (softcover) | ISBN 9781459741546 (PDF) | ISBN 9781459741553 (EPUB)
Classification: LCC PS8613.R4285 R59 2020 | DDC C813/.6—dc23

We acknowledge the support of the Canada Council for the Arts and the Ontario Arts Council for our publishing program. We also acknowledge the financial support of the Government of Ontario, through the Ontario Book Publishing Tax Credit and Ontario Creates, and the Government of Canada.

Care has been taken to trace the ownership of copyright material used in this book. The author and the publisher welcome any information enabling them to rectify any references or credits in subsequent editions.

The publisher is not responsible for websites or their content unless they are owned by the publisher.

Printed and bound in Canada.

VISIT US AT

 dundurn.com |  @dundurnpress | dundurnpress |  dundurnpress

Dundurn
3 Church Street, Suite 500
Toronto, Ontario, Canada
M5E 1M2

To Joyce, with gratitude

# ONE

# THE JANITOR

*February 1*

TASHA LOOKED AT the toes of her new boots and worried. Her workday was done. She had pushed open the school's service door, checked outside, and shut it again with a shiver. Indoors was all brightness and warmth, but outside 'twas definitely *a dark and stormy night*.

Shouldn't have changed from her grubby work shoes into these beauties till she got to Shaun's apartment. The school's parking lot would be riddled with puddles, and the boots were special; over-the-knee burnished-gold faux suede. The fabric wouldn't take mud well.

She had chosen to wear the new boots for Shaun, along with her favourite slinky dress. She wanted to show up at his doorstep looking like a princess, not an off-duty janitor. Because it was February, the month of romance, and he was going out of his way to make her feel special. Only the first of the month and he'd already dropped off a sparkly, heart-smothered Hallmark card. No, appearing at his doorstep in sloppy work clothes was not an option.

She blew out a breath. Tonight would be their fourth date, and she expected there would be sex involved. Like last time, what he had called *dynamite*, and what she called painful. Shaun was a tad too big for her, when it came to sex.

She thought about the card he'd given her. Her friends said it was charming, and she supposed it was. She wondered if he would carry out his threat of delivering a pre–Valentine's Day card every day till the fourteenth, a sort of twelve-days-of-Christmas shtick.

Honestly.

They were both in their midthirties, hardly kids anymore. She hoped that in the long run she would get used to his charm and that their relationship would build into something solid. Her parents were looking at her with that loud, unspoken question, *Why are you still single*? Same question from her friends. Same question from herself, really, because she wanted a husband and lots of kids, and none of that would drop out of the blue if she didn't do her bit.

She pushed the service door open farther and took another peek at the sky. The rain had stopped, and she decided that instead of changing back to her runners, she would simply avoid the puddles, walk with care. She left the warmth and safety of the school and took her first tentative steps across the asphalt. So far so good — the basketball courtyard was fairly smooth and puddle-free.

But ahead stretched the chain-link fence that separated finished ground from unfinished, and that's where it was going to get gross.

Under lamplight a new worry sprang on her, more serious than the fear of muddy boots — the sense that she was being followed.

Tasha wasn't easily frightened. Always aware, always prepared, that was the key to survival. She glanced over her shoulder, then did an about-face and stopped. Over by the school's main entrance, had something just moved, sliding behind one of the support posts? She sniffed, wrinkled her nose, caught the faintest whiff of burning marijuana.

Just some kids. They hung out under the shelter there, sneaking smokes, craving danger, as kids will do. Even at this time of night and in this horrible weather.

She went on her way, thinking she actually wouldn't mind a bit of danger herself. Not a huge amount, just enough to give her something to tell Shaun, 'cause sex and food, that's all he seemed to care about, and not necessarily in that order. Spin up a tale, start a conversation, mix it up a bit. She was already framing the narrative as she reached the gate to the gravel parking lot. She saw it was polka-dotted with puddles, worse than she expected. It wasn't a big school, not a huge parking area, space enough for maybe fifty cars. Of course there weren't fifty cars here at this time of night. Just two.

Two?

Hers and who else's?

A long black sedan. Unoccupied. It was parked near the rear entrance that led to the school's lower level. She had been the only one on the premises, she was quite sure. No office lights burned, no late meetings underway. But a staff member might have left their car, got a ride with somebody. Teachers drank a lot, she'd been told. Maybe someone had decided they'd pick up their wheels in the morning. She gave one more look around before setting foot on the gravel. At the far end of the lot and all along one side was a smudge of forest. A little scary.

*Careful what you wish for.*

She had her keys in hand, in readiness to beep open the doors, and thought about her best friend's self-defence tip. *Hold your keys like this, pointy ends out, not a bad set of brass knuckles in a pinch.* Second line of defence of course was the Toyota's alarm button, which she sometimes set off by mistake, making herself and everyone around her jump.

*This creepy guy was following me,* her exciting story would go. *I had to outrun him. Barely made it to my car. Luckily I set my key alarm going and he ran off.*

Silly to spook herself like this. She was now moving forward, stop and go, tippy-toeing around bodies of mud-grey water. Heavy winter rains had flooded the lot and the puddles spread out, broad and gleaming. Behind her the chain-link gave a metallic shiver. She could hear traffic. She could see the lights of houses in the distance. A far cry from solitude, but in a way she might as well be on Mars.

The school entranceway looked so distant now. Nobody creeping or crawling about. She laughed aloud at her own tall tale of danger, faced her car once more and stopped. She peered through the darkness, not believing her eyes. Only a stone's throw away now she saw the front right tire was flat. Flat as a pancake.

"Oh, for fuck's sake," she cried.

"Hey, what's up?" somebody called out.

She whirled. A twitch of her fingers set off the fob alarm and the car's horn went mad, *onn-onn-onn*. She yanked the keys from her pocket and pressed the red button. Silence, except the soft whish of the wind playing around her ears.

"Sorry," she said. The pounding of her heart slowed, and she smiled at the man. He hadn't been inside the black car, so must have come up from behind her. If he'd been a stranger she'd be busy forming her brass knuckles. But she recognized him. He was a nice guy. They had exchanged friendly hellos in the halls.

She snugged her coat around her tighter, hugged her handbag. The wind was awful, trying to knock her sideways. Her neck felt cold and vulnerable. She beeped open her car to grab a scarf off the passenger seat. Slammed the door shut and said, "Whatcha doing here this time of night?"

"Had to pick up something. Papers. You know."

He must have arrived as she left, dashed in, grabbed the docket he held under his arm.

He wasn't as tall as Shaun. Older than Shaun, more serious. Not bad looking. She'd seen him in the halls. What did he teach? Something interesting, like science or social studies, she'd bet. Was he single?

She focused on the flat tire. He followed the direction of her stare and pulled a clownish face of horror. Just being funny. Kind of corny, but it made her laugh.

Laughing felt good. She always laughed at Shaun's jokes, but sometimes it took effort.

She wondered if this teacher's life was as humdrum as hers, that a flat tire late at night was the most excitement he'd had in a while. Maybe this chance encounter would lead to a conversation, then to friendship, then to something valuable.

Unlikely, but things like that did happen, didn't they?

"So," he said, done being funny. "Sabotage, or bad luck?"

"I'm guessing sabotage. I know who did it, too. And I bet I know why."

He raised his brows at that. "No kidding? Tell me all about it. But first let's get going on this flat of yours. Got a spare?"

# TWO

# VALENTINE

*February 2*

THE DEAD WOMAN was in her thirties, Dion guessed. She had dark skin and black hair and was of Asian or Middle Eastern descent. She lay on her side, supported against chain-link in the rear parking lot of Riverside Secondary, and since that was likely her car over there, the dark grey Toyota with a flat tire, and there were water stains on her boots and up her fawn, toggle-buttoned overcoat, he could play out the events in his mind. At least in theory.

He turned off his flashlight. Early morning light was now seeping through the clouds and the scene was gently lit. He passed his thoughts on to his superior, Constable David Leith, who stood a few feet away and seemed to be thinking. Or trying to stay awake.

"She made it to her car …" Dion said. He glanced over his shoulder toward the lone vehicle. Too far across the lot to make out its details from here, but they remained clear in his mind. Against the car's rear panel leaned a spare tire. The trunk hatch was lowered but not secured. "Saw she had a flat. Was approached by a man. Maybe someone offering help."

He flipped through the usual considerations of intention, chance meetings, opportunity versus planning. He raised his brows at a new thought and relayed this to Leith as well. "He deliberately flattened her tire in advance, maybe. To trap her. Let out the air, lay in wait, rushed to her rescue. Right?"

"Right." Leith spoke automatically, showing no signs of absorption. He was still gazing at the dead woman with what looked like puzzled pity slanting his brow. He roused himself to make a suggestion of his own, proof that he'd been listening after all. "Or put a hole in it. The tire."

"I didn't see any puncture marks. If he'd put a blade through it, or if she'd driven over a nail, you'd see the gash."

"No, you wouldn't," Leith said. "We've all had flats. Have you ever seen an obvious puncture mark when you caught a flat, even if you drove over a nail?" He seemed to grow impatient. "If you're thinking sabotage, why would the guy bother fiddling with those little cap things to let out the air? He'd just jab it with something. A penknife. That's what I'd use."

Within the framework of the scene as he saw it, Dion didn't agree with the penknife idea. Probably hadn't been an ambush. Probably just a ruse gone wrong. The assailant had wanted a chance to bump into the woman, not wreck her car. But none of it mattered now, and he said so with a word. "Anyway …"

"Sure," Leith agreed, still impatient. "You have an end to your story?"

"It turned ugly. She ran. Aimed for the gate …"

There was an opening in the chain-link only a metre from the soles of the dead woman's boots. Both men looked at the opening, which allowed access between the well-lit school grounds and the relative darkness of the parking lot. Her head was faced in the opposite direction of the gateway, toward the thick and tangled greenbelt that backed the school. The orientation of her head and feet probably meant nothing.

"But he caught her," Dion said. "Maybe was dragging her toward the woods. She fought it."

He leaned in for a closer look at the victim. Her up-turned face was veiled in black hair, and only a glimmer of her open eyes shone through. He couldn't see enough of those eyes to check for signs of trauma. There was no blood visible on her clothes or the ground around her. Her clothes looked intact. Cause of death was a mystery. Unable to make an educated guess, he straightened and made an uneducated one. "He strangled her. It didn't go how he wanted. Maybe he was expecting her to play along. She didn't. It went too far. He took off and is lying low now. I hope she scratched him good. Or bit him."

"That would be a blessing," Leith agreed. "But you know, Cal, Forensics get paid for a reason. And it's important to keep an open mind rather than leaping to all kinds of conclusions, which they'll probably just nix once they get their lights and their ... what do you call 'em ... Hemastix out. For all we know she had a heart attack. It happens."

Dion nodded. He studied the unpaved parking lot. It had been contaminated by early morning staff, but minimally. The first contaminator had been the middle-aged female science teacher, obviously not the killer, who had discovered the body and made the 911 call. She knew the dead woman was one of the janitors, but didn't know her name. Following her call came the fire service, always the fastest to a scene, then a police unit along with basic life support paramedics, then himself and Leith, with the Serious Crimes Unit.

The deceased lay as found. First responders had not touched her beyond checking for breathing and pulse. She was cold. Stiffening. Well beyond help. The area had been cordoned off. Dion's own sedan, and Leith's, and the vehicles of any subsequent attendees on scene were on the other side of the grounds, keeping traffic around the body to a minimum and leaving the lot all but empty.

The lot had drainage problems, Dion saw. It was polka-dotted with pools of every size, now reflecting heavy clouds, dusky blue. He turned his attention back to the dark-haired young woman, thought about natural causes, and dismissed them. "Somebody she knew, trusted."

"How d'you figure?"

Some days Leith was a good detective; other days like molasses.

"Because she ran," Dion said.

Leith's only response was a narrowing of the eyes.

"She ran from her car," Dion clarified. "Across the parking lot, which we know 'cause of the splashes on her coat. See?"

The side of her light brown coat that had made contact with the ground was soggy, wicking up moisture, saturated almost to blackness, but the uppermost flap was patchily dry, and the dry parts — about knee height — showed clear splash patterns. Much like Dion had noticed on his own overcoat a time or two over the years, when forced to run through puddles. It didn't take a splash-pattern analyst to get that freebie.

Leith's eyes were still narrowed. He said, "Aside from the fact that I don't know how that says she knew and trusted her attacker, aside from that, she could have run *toward* the car, trying to escape, and was cut off and ran back to the gate. Or was pulled."

"Her spare tire is out. She was by her car when the trouble started."

"Hmm, right," Leith said. "Maybe."

Though Dion had made his point, he was already losing faith in the scenario that had snapped in so clearly. It always happened this way; intuition would whisper in his ear till he focused on the message. He got out his notebook to jot down a few key points before they escaped him. Leith took advantage of the silence to continue studying the scene.

They'd get the janitor's work schedule, Dion knew. But for now he could assume that the victim had been attacked at night, and would have been the last to leave the school, so hers would have been the only car on the lot — unless her assailant's vehicle had been there as well. For now, the vital info of whether or not the assailant's vehicle was there was only clutter.

He wrote down one thought. *Schedule?* Then another. *Driver door unlocked. Keys?*

She'd been at her car, had opened the driver's door, opened the trunk, gotten out the spare. Why had she run from the safety of her car, partway through changing the tire? If she felt threatened, why not jump inside and lock the doors?

How did it go, then? She walks up to her car, sees the flat tire, says, *Oh fuck.* Maybe her assailant had walked with her, or maybe he'd arrived after. The trunk was popped, the spare tire out. Even a slight woman like her could haul out a tire and change it, but it wouldn't be easy. And with her fine clothes, in the dark and cold and wet of the night. Wouldn't she call BCAA? Or a friend?

No, he was pretty sure a Good Samaritan had come along and helped her with the tire. They had interacted. Hadn't gotten as far as fishing out the tire iron. Somewhere along the way she got scared and ran. Again, the fresh splashes on her coat.

There were myriad other possibilities to what had happened here last night, a blitz attack as she changed her tire being a solid one. But the Good Samaritan theory was top of the stack, for Dion. He tried to explain his thought process to Leith, but the coroner arrived and the conversation was put on hold. Then Forensics started to filter in, and Leith's phone began buzzing. Dion was summoned over to the dead woman's car to look underneath it, as a Forensics member had seen a set of keys. The keys were photographed *in situ*, then pulled out for inspection. Dion and the Forensics member agreed the Toyota's key fob looked abused. Stepped on, maybe. Neither its locks nor its alarm worked. Dion made his way back to Leith, who was done with his phone and was looking around for him.

"Her keys were under the car," Dion told him. "The car key's damaged. Should make sure the residents around here are canvassed about hearing a panic alarm."

"While you were gone I got her name and nailed down our first lead," Leith told him. The words were smug but his expression wasn't.

"How'd you do that?"

"Doc found her handbag under her body. Cellphone, wallet. ID in the wallet says Nashwa Aziz. Then there's this." Leith held up a plastic bag containing an open Valentine's Day card. The front of the card was a glittery, commercial product, red and gold, and it had clearly been tampered with. Its pre-printed "Be My Valentine" was altered with felt pen to say "Be My *Pre*-Valentine." Bunch of exclamation marks added on, too. Turning the bag over, Dion saw the inside of the card was inscribed "To Tasha, from Shaun."

"Her phone's locked," Leith said. "But it rang, and I answered. It was a guy named Shaun, and he's willing to talk. Let's go see what he has to say."

\* \* \*

The prime-suspect alarm bells went off in Leith's head as the apartment door opened and he got his first look at Shaun. The boyfriend of Nashwa Aziz was a large, scowling individual with fiery red hair who demanded to see first Leith's ID, then Dion's. He asked what this was about, and when told that Leith would rather talk to him inside, he led the way into his small studio apartment, ushering them through to the living room. The place was spiffy, Leith saw. Neatly minimal, sparkling clean, colour coordinated. Shaun was watching him closely — maybe cagily — as he took in the details of the place.

Leith gave him what he hoped was an appreciative nod. The dining room table, easily within line of sight from where he stood, was nicely set for two. Big bouquet of roses as a centrepiece, candlesticks and wine goblets, cloth serviettes, the works.

Once they were seated, Leith broke the news. He did so kindly, even as he analyzed Shaun's reaction. Their prime suspect listened, transitioning through surprise, shock, grief. None of it seemed feigned to Leith. Shaun's large head bowed and swung side to side. He said it was horrible, so horrible, and he was sorry, so sorry. He then seemed to run out of reaction. Dry-eyed, he looked from Leith to Dion and asked who had done this terrible thing.

Leith told him the investigation was just getting underway, and he didn't have any answers yet. Sorry. He asked Shaun what Tasha was like, as a person, and waited as the man scowled in thought. "I dunno," Shaun said. "I guess … sexy?"

"Sexy," Leith echoed.

"To tell the truth, I don't know her too well. We've only been dating about a month." Shaun had flushed pink from throat to temple and was steadily pulverizing a palm with a fist. Leith was starting to see past his first impression of the boyfriend as a killer — the prime suspect no longer prime. His bulk was intimidating on nothing more than a physical level, and the murderous scowling was only the natural folds of an oversized face working through emotions. "But it was good," Shaun went on. "We clicked, you know. Lotta fun. She was willing to experiment. I'm divorced, right?"

Leith got the non sequitur. He gestured at the dining room table. "Expecting company?"

Shaun shook his head. "That was for Tasha. She was supposed to come over after work, about eleven o'clock. Which is late for dinner, but I was planning on putting out something light, romantic. Chicken. With lentils, butternut squash, all cooked in Marsala wine. Valentine's Day is coming up, so we wanted to get in gear, you know. Practice run for the big day." He seemed to recall that the date would never happen, let alone the meal. He scowled and wagged his head again. "Poor girl. Poor, beautiful girl."

Dion said, "Yesterday was February first. Bit soon for getting in gear, isn't it?"

Shaun's eyes were wet now. He sat up straight and said with some anger, "Whatever works, right? With a girl like Tasha, I wanted to do it right." He looked toward the dining room table, the roses that weren't looking so fresh. "What I didn't take into account is Marsala chicken is kind of a time-sensitive meal," he muttered. "Wasn't sure when exactly she'd arrive, and I didn't want to stick it in the oven too soon, dry it out. So I prepped what I could, then figured when she showed up I'd throw it all in the pan — little extra marinating never hurts — and back in for half an hour, which means we wouldn't be eating till midnight, so that was kind of a bad choice on my part."

"But she didn't show up," Leith reminded him.

"I know. I'm sorry. I'm an asshole. There's a whole lot of stuff I don't understand in life, but I understand food. It's my comfort blanket."

"Weren't you worried when she didn't show up?"

"Didn't show up, didn't call, didn't text. Didn't answer my texts, didn't answer my calls. I was super disappointed with her for that. But now I know why. Sure, maybe I'd have gone out there if I knew where she worked. But all I know is she cleans buildings somewhere. But you don't always *know* a person, right? Maybe she dumped me. Maybe she's unreliable. Or forgetful. Should I have called the cops? Maybe. But you wouldn't do anything. I know for a fact you dudes don't go rushing out when a lady's late for dinner. Anyway, I sealed up the food as best I could, had a sandwich, and I guess I fell asleep."

"What were your plans for the actual big day?" Dion asked.

Shaun studied him for a moment, as if weighing his answer before giving it. "You know what gnocchi is?"

Leith tuned out as Dion and the foodie talked about the menu, from appies to main course, that Shaun had planned for Valentine's Day. The conversation seemed to bring him comfort. Leith checked his calendar on his iPhone to see what day of the week February 14 fell on, thinking about his wife, Alison.

"… and you *don't* want to do that to brisket," Shaun finished. He covered his large face with his large hands.

"It's okay, I get it," Leith told him. "It's just another way of coping with bad news."

Shaun saw them to the door. Leith thanked him for his help and said they might be talking further. As he steered their unmarked west on the Dollarton, he mused aloud that Shaun wasn't the killing type, and whoever they were looking for was still out there.

Dion didn't bother agreeing.

"Speaking of Valentine's Day," Leith said. "How's it going with Kate?"

"It's going okay," Dion said. He sounded guardedly optimistic. "We're getting along. It's almost like we never broke up."

"You two have a lot of history."

"Tons. I'm going to take her out dancing, on Valentine's Day. Make it special."

Over their time working together, Dion shifted gears often, in Leith's eyes. Like an antsy motorist on the freeway. Moody, sharp, sometimes cheerful, but always cautious. He hoped Dion's reunion with his ex-girlfriend Kate would turn out well. Little else good was happening in the man's complicated life.

Leith was one of only two members of the North Vancouver RCMP who knew how complicated Dion's life really was. The other was their boss, Sergeant Mike Bosko. Last summer Bosko had looped Leith into a case he was running off the record, so to speak, and told him Dion could be guilty of a crime, and quite likely the crime was murder.

How ironic, if true — and by now Leith was almost sure it was — that a criminal was working, badge and all, in a cop-shop. A desperado hiding in plain sight.

But it wouldn't last. From what Leith knew of the latest developments in the case, witnesses were surfacing, and the desperado in the passenger seat beside him was fast running out of luck.

# THREE

# SILENCE

*February 5*

AS THE FOURTH DAY wound down and the case room began to clear of team members, Leith stood looking at the main evidence board, arms crossed, hoping for some last-minute inspiration. The death of Tasha Aziz was not going to be the quick wrap he had looked forward to. Cause of death was internal bleeding. Not strangulation, as Dion had guessed, but abdominal trauma. Whatever the young woman had been struck with, it was fairly acute and had been delivered with speed. Suggestions were a pry bar, tire iron, hammer.

He looked at the preliminary coroner's report. One blow had done it. One strike with an object that had departed with the killer, no doubt, and Tasha had been left in a puddle to die. She had not been sexually assaulted or injured in any other way. And if she had managed to scratch or bite her attacker, she hadn't gathered enough DNA for the team to work with.

No tips had come in on the tip-line. No witnesses had stepped forward. No surveillance footage from the school or any adjacent businesses had given a good outline of the perpetrator, at least on first viewing.

The video was being gone through again, almost frame by frame this time, by Leith's favourite teammate, Constable JD Temple. But as she'd reported at the meeting that had just disbanded, there were no breakthroughs yet.

JD was gone now, too, and besides Leith, only Dion and Mike Bosko remained. Bosko had asked Dion to stay and go over the thoughts he had outlined not so clearly in his last report, and the two men were referencing the scene photographs from Riverside Secondary pinned to a separate board as they talked.

Leith was free to leave, but he chose to hang back and listen. No longer on the Tasha Aziz case, but the Cal Dion case, and his studying of the main board was just an excuse to stay.

One ear tuned in on their conversation, he thought about bad choices. Like taking on the Dion case. Agreeing to be Bosko's spy had been a mistake, and he should have known better. But one of Bosko's skills was gentle persuasion. *Not an open file,* he'd said over coffee that summer morning, when Dion had been not much more than a stranger to Leith. *Nothing formal. I don't even know the nature of the crime, if a crime is what it is. Just keep an eye on him for me, would you, Dave? As much for his own good as ours.*

"... so as I told David that night ..." Dion was telling Bosko.

The two were talking about splash patterns as they studied the photographs of Tasha in the parking lot. Leith didn't need to listen. He'd heard it all before. He continued to study the case board and tuned out again.

The very good reason he shouldn't have taken on the case was a comradeship was bound to develop. And it had, to a point. Even if Dion continued to call Leith *David*. Not *Dave* like everyone else on the planet did. It was a distancing tactic, a refusal to become work buddies. A time or two Leith had tried to retaliate, using *Calvin* instead of *Cal* like everyone else on the planet did. But Calvin had not seemed to care, and the distance had only grown. And distance was probably wise, in the circumstances, because friendship between enemies was a bad idea.

He heard the meeting close down. Bosko thanked Dion, and Dion picked up his coffee cup and said good night. As the door closed behind him, Leith said, "Still nothing?"

Bosko was tall, fair, and heavy-set. He was young for his rank, a year younger than Leith, who was forty-three. Though Bosko came across as placid and abstracted, maybe even dim, he was far from it. He was sharp. Probably the sharpest man Leith knew.

"Not a peep," Bosko said.

He and Leith were both talking about the same silence. The witness who was supposed to light the fuse under Dion's ass hadn't been at the appointed place at the appointed time. The hour had come and gone, and she hadn't shown, hadn't called back.

"So what d'you think stopped her?" Leith said.

Bosko said nothing as he gathered papers together in a folder. He tucked the folder under his arm, looked at Leith, and with a kind of pure gravity that was unlike him, said, "Frankly, that bit has me worried."

* * *

Dion was at Rainey's with the crew after hours. Kate was at his side, and he was feeling good. He'd been with Kate for years, before the crash. After the crash he'd locked her out of his life, and when he'd finally come to his senses, he didn't think she'd want him back. But she did! They'd been talking it over, lately. Resolving things, getting back to where they'd been before. She said she still loved him. In a different way, maybe a deeper way. Even after all he'd been through.

She only knew a fraction of what he'd been through, and if he had his way, she'd never find out the rest. That he had killed a man, that night in Surrey. That his trouble had doubled when he'd noticed a girl watching him from the hillside above. The girl had been straddling a dirt bike. As he caught sight of her — she had pink hair, a detail he'd never forget — she had kick-started her machine, spat gravel, taken off. He had jumped in his car, Looch Ferraro beside him, and raced out of the gravel pit and toward the highway, hoping to cut her off.

Instead he'd collided with a sports car and ended up in a coma. And Looch had ended up dead.

He took a swig of beer and placed a possessive arm across Kate's shoulders. His job right now was proving to her that he'd come full circle, that he was fine, that they were one, and that he'd never turn his back on her again. Part of the plan was becoming the guy he once was, and that meant breaking out of his shell, shifting back to loud and funny. Getting drunk with old friends was a great start, he felt — and so far so good. The pub was as bright and warm around him as the night outside was dark and cold. The crew was all here, except David Leith. He wished Leith was here to see this, he and Kate jammed up against each other. He was proud of Kate, though he understood so little about her world. She taught at the Vancouver School of Art, and the works she created — oversized collages — were up in galleries. They were starting to sell, too. He'd never know why, as they looked to him like recycle-bin-meets-canvas. But he would learn. He'd figure out what art was, what turned her on. He'd get on her level and cement their bond.

He was saying something loud and funny when Mike Bosko put in one of his rare appearances at Rainey's, joining the crew at their table.

Bosko took a chair, smiling hello.

Dion raised his glass. The sight of Bosko usually got his defences up — that man was too smart, a danger zone — but today he wasn't worried. He was buzzed, happy, and Kate was beside him. He was invincible.

Bosko's smile broadened as he noticed her, and Dion had to shout over the hubbub to make introductions. Bosko reached over to shake her hand, adding an exclamation. "Kate Ballentyne! Hey, are those your collages all over the news?"

She was surprised to be recognized. And delighted. Dion was glad he'd paid attention when she'd shown him the article from the Arts and Entertainment pages of last week's paper, a piece about her artwork on display in a Granville gallery. "Give him one of your cards," he told her.

She gave Bosko her card, and Bosko seemed about to remark on it, but the server arrived to take his order. He ordered an IPA, and asked the off-duty constable beside him, Niko Shiomi, if he could get her another of whatever she was drinking, as her glass appeared to be low. She said yes, and thanked him. The server went off with the order and Bosko asked the constable how her ribs were feeling. She said they were a whole lot better than yesterday.

Dion knew about Shiomi's bruised ribs. She had taken a fall last month on the job, and was on light duties till she healed up. Shiomi was pretty, and Dion was maybe working too hard not to look her way, because a devoted boyfriend doesn't eye other women. Next to Shiomi sat Corporal Doug Paley, anything but pretty. Sean Urbanski was at the end of the table, texting somebody, Jimmy Torr beside him. Kitty-corner to Dion sat JD Temple. JD was tall and rake-skinny. Like a model but without the allure, he sometimes thought. She had short black hair and narrow eyes that said *Keep out and piss off*, and she seemed to be listening to the conversation that Kate and Bosko had fallen into. Art talk.

The art talk was drummed out by pub noise, and Dion gave up trying to hear. He saw something snarky in JD's expression and questioned her with a glare. *What's your issue?* No answer from JD, but Niko Shiomi was watching him as she sipped the last of her cocktail. She gave him a crooked half smile. He didn't know what the smile meant, and to avoid having to answer, he returned his gaze to Kate. Doug Paley stood and with hand on heart said, "Good night, good night! Parting is such sweet sorrow, that I shall say good night till it be morrow."

Paley wasn't leaving, just heading to the men's room. Leith arrived as Paley left, and Dion regretted that he had removed his arm from around Kate's shoulder. Bosko noted Leith's appearance and said, "Well, hey. Pull up a chair."

Leith was a family man — he had a wife and small daughter at home — and like Bosko rarely showed up for drinks after work. But he slung into the last available seat as if he was there to stay, saying the hostess had wanted to lodge a complaint of public disturbance, and who should he be arresting?

The staff knew this table of cops well, and staff complaints about the cops' behaviour was a running joke. Some of the crew answered Leith's question by pointing at the guilty party, JD. Earlier she had been laughing wildly about something not funny, slapping the table and breaking into song. She was a moody cop, Dion knew, but when she let loose, she didn't hold back.

She defended herself, indicating Dion with her thumb. "I was so thrilled they're getting back together that I had to sing out loud. What's publicly disturbing about a love song?"

Paley was back in his chair with a fresh pint, telling JD, "You singing 'Up Where We Belong' is about as disturbing as it gets, girl."

A stranger approached their table. She had been doing the rounds of the bar, selling something. She flapped a leaflet at the crew and said the tickets were for a Valentine's Day dance at the Eagles hall. Singles were twenty-five and couples' tickets were going for forty. Some great door prizes, lotta fun, proceeds toward MS research, anybody want one?

Dion was the first to pull out his wallet. He bought a couples' ticket for himself and Kate, and then got a third for JD, to get back at her for mocking him. JD didn't *do* dances.

JD folded the ticket he tossed at her. "Nice. This is going straight into the compost bin when I get home."

"No, it's not," he told her. "You're so cheap you'll show up for the free food." He leaned sideways to kiss Kate, then had trouble getting the dance tickets into his wallet, which he found funny. Others had their wallets out. Sean Urbanski bought a couples' ticket. Paley did the same. Leith and Jimmy Torr both demurred. After Niko Shiomi bought a single, Torr changed his mind and bought one as well, and on second thought, reminded by his colleagues about his wife, Tina, changed it to a couples'. Finally Bosko purchased a ticket, and the fundraiser thanked them all, hoped they'd enjoy the dance, and moved on.

Nobody at the table would enjoy the dance, Dion knew, because they had no intention of going. They were all just showing off to each other, donating to MS research. Anyway, his plans for Valentine's Day were a lot hotter. He would take Kate for dinner somewhere classy, then they'd go clubbing on Richards, across the bridge. And when she was having the time of her life, just burning with desire, he would ask her to marry him.

# FOUR

## LUNA MAE

*February 6*

IT WAS SUNDAY, nine thirty at night, and Leith was driving a police SUV out to Riverside Drive — past the school where Tasha Aziz had been murdered — his eyes straining against the darkness and rain. This was a new case, a child gone missing from her crib. She was just over a year old, only thirteen months, which meant she'd probably got her walking legs on.

"Kids of that age have amazing roving powers," Leith told his passenger. Dion was making notes and listening for dispatcher updates. "And they're quick. Soon as they find their feet, they put 'em to good use, believe me."

Leith knew about the roving powers of kids of that age because his own had been through the phase not long ago. He'd had to chase Izzy too often across park lawns and malls. She was now three and walking about like a miniature adult, but he recalled well her less predictable trajectories.

The mobility of those powerful little legs had led to arguments between him and Alison. "You gotta keep your eye on them full-time," he'd told her a few more times than he should have needed to. He said more or less the same to Dion now, adding, "It's a house on Riverside Drive, so it'll be big. Tons of hiding spaces. They're probably discovering her as we speak."

Dion was young and didn't have kids, so he couldn't get the full 3-D, blood-turning-to-ice shock of finding an empty space where a child should have been. Only a father or mother could know the feeling.

Proving that he didn't, Dion suggested the parents would hardly call 911 without first thoroughly searching the place, would they?

"Of course they'd call 911 before a thorough search," Leith said. He heard the snappiness in his own words. A red light forced him to stop, and his fingers did a jig on the steering wheel. "Happens all the time. Panic, imagination kicks in, call the cops. Then find the kid dozing in some unlikely cubbyhole, search called off. Happy ending."

He was so fervently hoping for that kind of ending to this call-out that he began to wonder about his fitness for serious crimes, where most roads lead to grief. Maybe he should aim for something less gut-wrenching, more blue-collar, maybe commercial. Maybe he should take a course, start keeping an eye on transfer options.

He fell silent for the rest of the drive. It was a road he wasn't really familiar with, though Tasha had put it on his radar. There were some nice houses along here, he noticed.

Respectfully spaced homes, with the occasional side street leading to woodsy roundabouts. Lot of rainforest still, but mankind was definitely moving in, displacing big old trees with brand-new homes and three-car garages.

The address turned out to be on the river side of Riverside Drive. There was an open gate, then a short broad driveway dipping down toward what looked like a cedar-planked hobbit-hole, but the space was clogged with vehicles, civilian and unmarked police sedans, obliging Leith to bypass the home and carry on, looking for a spot curbside.

"Search party already?" Dion remarked.

"Who knows."

They walked back toward the house. Even from the outside, even in the darkness, the building seemed to radiate anxious energy. Up close it continued to look like a small cabin, but Leith suspected it was tiered downslope, and its interior would turn out to be spacious and complex. JD met them at the door, confirmed the child was still missing, and led the way inside.

They walked into pandemonium.

Leith had been to countless crime scenes over the years, but this was new: unbridled chaos set in an upscale home, everyone decked out in fine clothes. There was mud on some of those fine clothes, but no blood that he could see. No signs of trouble except the people themselves, milling, shouting, fussing. Hard to count the moving targets, but he hazarded about six adults, not including police.

"They were celebrating a birthday," JD explained. "A dinner party for one of the homeowners, I think."

The chaos was understandable. With so much at stake, these people would continue to search even when all the obvious places had been gone over. Going up and down stairs, opening and closing doors, calling out the baby's name. Luna Mae, shortened to Luna. Clearly, this wasn't shaping up to be the Case of the Kid in the Cubbyhole. Leith stood in the open concept living room/dining room area while Dion talked to JD and others already on scene. JD was giving Dion a rundown of who here was who, while uniformed constables Ken Poole and Ken's trainee, Niko Shiomi, worked at calming the party-goers.

Leith took in what he could of the home. He had guessed right about the tiering and the expansive interior. It was solidly constructed, of course — all houses cantilevered over cliffs needed to be feats of engineering — beautifully furnished and decorated, buffed to a sheen. He could smell exotic cooking. Indian spices, though the crowd appeared Caucasian. Evidence of a feast, dining table cluttered with used dishes, leftovers going cold on serving plates, wine-stained tablecloth. A near-empty whisky decanter on a serving trolley had its stopper off. A few smudgy looking hardball glasses sat abandoned.

The floor-to-ceiling windows along the far wall were shrouded in damask. Once pulled open they would no doubt give a fall-away view on the Seymour River tumbling below. The lights were on full now, but probably would have been softer during dinner, lit by the chandelier Leith saw above. There would have been music playing then. Jazz, he would bet.

A house full of well-to-do people enjoying a good meal in an ordinary house, in a safe, quiet, woodsy neighbourhood that would hold no attraction for burglars, vagrants, or meth-heads. A place filled with light and noise. How could a child disappear from a safe bubble like this?

Not a stranger, but someone known to the family?

He didn't dwell on the thought. Unlike Dion, who jumped to conclusions and then battled them to death, Leith preferred to assume nothing. Always be ready for a twist.

In the living room he found Dion and JD restoring order, organizing bodies into corners or adjoining rooms for questioning. Others from the detachment were arriving, called in to clamp down on the scene, corral witnesses, prevent further loss of evidence. Though with so many present, with every inch of the place trodden upon and touched by multiple hands and feet in the first moments of panic, Leith knew it was going to be a nightmare for the fingerprint team.

Dion said to him, "That's the mother, Gemma Vale."

Leith looked across the room. Visible from where he stood was a breakfast nook, and at the table a plump woman sat shuddering and clutching at her short dark hair. She was being watched over by Niko Shiomi. "Vale," he said. "But the child's surname is Garland." Not unusual, these days, but enough to make him wonder how this family was structured.

Dion said he didn't know the fine details yet. "The bedrooms are all downstairs," he continued. "Including the child's room. The window was locked, but they discovered the sliding door at the back of the house wasn't.

The door looks onto a patio and has access to the street through a narrow path that goes alongside the house."

"No video surveillance, no alarms?"

"No CCTV, and they only set the alarm when they're out. There's a baby monitor set up in the kitchen, live-feed, but nobody was keeping an eye on the screen. They were eating dinner, talking. Music and all that. Whatever happened down there, they missed it."

"Both Gemma and Perry Vale thought the sliding door was locked," JD added. "But both agree the mechanism can be screwy. Sometimes you think it's clicked, but it hasn't. At this time of year it's mostly kept shut. Hasn't been used since Gemma aired the place last weekend. She's not a hundred percent sure she double-checked that it was secured since then."

Dion nodded. "Gemma says she knows who took Luna Mae, but nobody else here seems to agree."

"She's blaming her ex," JD said. "Zachary Garland. That's him over there. He's denied it."

So the family structure was starting to come together. Leith looked at Zachary Garland while Dion answered a call. The call was brief, and Dion relayed what he'd been told. "Forensics are setting up. Haven't found anything of interest on the patio or pathway out back. There are fences along both sides, but none at the rear. And there's a trail leading down to the river, also accessible from the downstairs sliding door. Unlikely, but somebody could have approached from the river. Might have taken her down there, too."

JD didn't think so. "It's the first place these people checked. I think pretty well everybody at the party except Gemma climbed up and down that trail at some point. Or down and up. Once you get to the river there's really nowhere to go. Bit of beach, but no escape. Not without a kayak or unless you're up for some heavy-duty bushwhacking."

"Why didn't Gemma go down with the other searchers?" Leith asked.

"Probably 'cause she fixed the blame on her ex. We've had to keep those two from each other's throats. And let's hope she's right," she added.

Leith nodded. A custodial kidnapping was the best-case scenario; the child spirited away, but safe and warm and soon to be found.

"We're down at the river's edge," JD continued. "Looking through the bushes. We're bringing in a drone to scan upriver and down, but it'll be dark by the time that's set up, so won't be much good till morning."

Dion referred to his notebook and pointed out the civilians in attendance for Leith's benefit. There were two couples, the invited guests, along with Gemma Vale's grey-haired husband, Perry Vale. There was also the man JD had pointed out, Zachary Garland, the ex, the child's father, who visibly didn't belong in this posh crowd. He wore a dark jogger's outfit, hood thrown back. He was maybe thirty-five, handsome, buzz cut, intense. He seemed to be bouncing on the balls of his feet as he argued with a Forensics member about the need to get past and go downstairs. He appeared ready to clock the officer with one hovering fist, and Leith watched him with interest. If Garland was the abductor, he was doing a good job of diverting suspicion.

But the big picture was fairly simple so far. This was a fractured family, and baby Luna Mae was in the middle. Now Luna Mae was missing and the exes were mustering for battle.

"Somebody better heel that guy," he said.

JD went to back up the Forensics member, while Leith signalled to Dion what was next on their agenda. Time to speak with the missing child's mother, Gemma Vale.

# FIVE

# HE SAID, SHE SAID

GEMMA VALE WORE a dark blue cocktail dress and an oversized cardigan that didn't seem to match. She sat crumpled at the table, staring dull-eyed at its surface and sucking in too much air. She didn't look up as Leith took the chair across from her. He nodded at Dion to join them and keep notes, then did his best to calm the woman before she hyperventilated. "Mrs. Vale," he said. "It's okay. We'll find your daughter."

It was the kind of empty promise he'd become good at delivering, though in truth nothing was okay, and there existed the stark potential the daughter would never be found. But he had to say something, anything, to keep her present, to get from her what she knew, and move forward.

Gemma must have registered his promise. He could see her forcing herself to slow her breathing. He told her he was recording the conversation, and unsurprisingly she appeared not to give a damn. But she did sit straighter with a nod of understanding.

She was between thirty and forty, he guessed — some years younger than her grey-haired husband. Her chestnut-brown hair was shiny, and her skin was smooth and slightly tanned. On an ordinary day she would be pretty.

"Tell me what happened tonight, Gemma," he said. "I know you've already told Constable Temple, but once more, please."

She examined the tissue she was holding, wild-eyed and blind. She lifted her face and spoke in a controlled whisper. "We were having a nice dinner. I had put Luna to bed. *He* came over."

"Who came over?" Leith cut in. Though he knew. The stress of hatred she put on the pronoun said it all.

"Zach. He came over to make my life hell because of some stupid thing, and insisted he go downstairs and say good night to her. To Luna. I let him do it. Then he and I went outside to talk it over, or fight, more like, while our guests listened, which was embarrassing for me, and worse for Perry. Zach took off, not without using some very foul fucking language, and he must have unlocked the window or sliding door when I wasn't looking — earlier, I mean — and he came back while we were eating dinner and took her."

Leith had seen a framed photo of the child, Luna. Lovely girl with soft ginger hair swirling over her brow, smiling her blue-eyed squint at the camera and showing off her first miniature teeth. Luna had just learned to walk, one of the guests had mentioned.

He wondered if Luna was as thrilled as Izzy had been on first discovering the joys of perambulation. Within the space of two weeks his daughter had gone from wobbly tottering to pounding back and forth like a crazed robot on overdrive. But in Luna's case, the ability to open doors and run away would still be a few years down the road.

He waited as the stricken mother vented a string of *Oh my god*s, then asked her to tell him more about Zachary Garland and why she thought he was responsible.

She crossed her arms and let out a shuddery breath. "He's petitioned the court to be allowed to move to P.E.I. and take Luna with him. Can you imagine even thinking for one fraction of a second of taking a one-year-old six thousand kilometres from her mother? He won't win, and he knows it, but he just wants to make my life as miserable as he possibly can till his funds run out. He wants to kill me with ulcers. That fucker."

She was starting to gulp in air again. There was a fiery glow in her cheeks, and her eyes shone with an emotion that Leith saw as somewhat removed from the situation. She was distancing herself, refusing to believe the worst. She was in shock. He said, "Gemma, Zachary's right here. He says he didn't take Luna, and we'd better focus on other possibilities right now. Okay?"

Her voice lifted and soared. "The other possibility is he called his bimbo, Chelsea Fuck-Me-Standing Romanov, to come and get Luna, and they're halfway to Mexico by now, which I've told you people fifty fucking times, and nobody seems to be checking it out."

Dion said, "That's being followed up right now, Mrs. Vale."

She stared at him, distracted. She seemed to mellow. She managed a weak smile before bursting into a flood of apologies. "I know you're working hard, all of you," she finished, staring at Leith. "But I just don't understand why you can't find her."

She whimpered and appeared to zone out. Eyes closed, she whispered the name of her missing child under her breath, as if she was there in her arms.

Leith wondered if Gemma had self-medicated somewhere between calling the police and now, and if the meds were kicking in. He prompted her gently. "You were having a party. What's the occasion?"

She seemed to swim out of her haze to explain. "Perry's birthday. My husband. Just a quiet dinner get-together. They're Perry's friends, not mine. We've only been married three months, and I'm just getting to know his circle." She gestured widely toward her new husband, and Leith looked across the room to give Perry Vale another study.

The man stood by the damask curtains with head bowed. Maybe he was crying. Maybe crying over Luna. He was somewhere in his late fifties, lean but with a paunch, neat grey hair shorn close and thinning on top. Constable Shiomi stood near Perry, tasked with watching over him.

"What does Perry do for a living?" Leith asked Gemma.

"He's an engineer. He makes sure bridges don't fall down."

"And yourself?"

"These days I'm a stay-at-home mom."

"And on other days?"

"In my past, you mean? Before I met Perry? I was a hostess."

The person who greets people entering a restaurant, Leith supposed. He asked the stay-at-home mom to recount her day, and she did her best. She didn't have Luna last night, she told him. Because Zachary had her. It was his weekend, which he got twice a month. In the baby's absence, Gemma had served a light breakfast. After breakfast Perry left for a few hours to see a sick friend in West Van. Meanwhile, Gemma had done a grocery run, then got busy with dinner prep and cleaning, delivered the kids around —

"Kids?" Leith interrupted.

"Our other children, Viviani and Tiago. Well, Vivi and Tia, we call them. They're Zach's kids, really. Actually, his brother's kids, but that's a long story. I've known them since they were little, though, so they're like my own." She glanced at Leith as if he might challenge the assertion. Which he didn't. "They're with us this week," she went on. "But since we were having an adult dinner party, they were spending the night with friends down the road. That's where they are now. Vivi's nine. She's having a sleepover at Alexa's on Bow Crescent. Tia's fifteen. He's staying with Oliver down the road here, just before Grantham."

Leith hoped the cast of characters wasn't going to get a whole lot more complicated. He had written the main points in his notebook. A nine-year-old and a fifteen-year-old. The latter especially could be interesting. "Have you called Vivi and Tia? Maybe one of them dropped by this evening and took Luna."

Gemma stared at him. "Why would they do that?"

"Decided to take her out to play, maybe? Or as a prank?"

She shook her head. "That's insane. Neither of them would do any such thing."

He nodded at her to go on. It took her a moment to get back on track after his ridiculous question. "Like I said, Zachary gets Luna every other weekend. Picks her up Saturday morning, brings her back on Sunday at two. Which he did today."

"He brought her over at two this afternoon?"

"More or less."

"Any trouble with the handover?"

"No more than usual."

"What's usual?"

"We tend to discuss what we could do better next time. That's all. Little things."

She sounded stiff now. The armour was back on. She frowned, maybe recollecting the *little things* she and her ex tended to discuss, before carrying on. The Latimers had arrived punctually at 6:00 p.m., she told Leith. The Becks about fifteen minutes later. Everyone admired Luna, and around 6:30 Gemma had taken the child down to bed, as Luna seemed tired out by all the excitement and was getting cranky.

"Normal cranky?" Leith asked.

"Yes, normal cranky," Gemma said. "Then," she went on, through clenched teeth, "the incident."

"Incident?"

"Just when I was serving dinner at seven, as I've told you, Zach came back." She had marinated the name in loathing. "He insisted on going down to kiss Luna good night. Which is not in the interim order, coming over to kiss Luna whenever he damn well feels like it. But I'm not going to make a scene, not in front of Perry's friends, am I?"

Leith was starting to withhold his sympathetic *mm-hmms*. Sympathy only fortified her anger, and he needed her to move away from accusations and get on with the facts. "Did you go downstairs with Zach when he went to kiss Luna good night?"

"Of course I did. This is my house, so my rules."

"Of course."

"I finally got rid of him, though like I said, we had words in the driveway, which everybody on the planet must have heard, and then he *apparently* drove off. Things calmed down after that. Perry was good about it, as always. He's my rock. He gave me a hug and put on some nice music, got the conversation rolling. I served dinner. Must have been about quarter after seven by then. I went to check on Luna about eight, between the main course and dessert. She was sound asleep. After dinner, about nine, we moved to the living room. The Latimers were hanging around a while longer, but the Becks had to leave. Mary Beck wanted to see Luna once more, so we went down, and that's when we found her missing."

Gone. She sagged. Maybe the unthinkable was starting to seep through the cracks in her ramparts, and she was arriving at the possibility that Zach might not be responsible. Her palms clamped over her face as if to block out the alternate theory, and behind those palms, Leith knew, the tears she had been staving off were welling into rivers.

The woman needed a break.

He called JD over to keep Gemma company, and went downstairs with Dion to look at the empty crib, and then the patio leading out into a wicked cold night.

* * *

The sliding door was being dusted for prints, and the child's bedroom was occupied with Ident officers. Dion absorbed what he could in a visual check, the layout of the place and where the exit stood relative to the nursery. While Leith continued to look around and talk to Ident, a bellow of rage vibrated down through the floorboards.

Heading upstairs, Dion found Zachary Garland skirmishing with JD and Ken Poole in the front foyer. The father no longer wanted to go downstairs to look for his baby, it seemed, but was determined to go out into the wind and rain and join the police search. JD was trying to reason with him, Constable Ken Poole was physically restraining him, and Constable Niko Shiomi was standing by, looking ready to draw her firearm.

Dion raised his voice to compete with Garland's and asked him what the problem was.

"The problem is we're in here, not out there, looking for Luna," Garland shouted. He had launched himself at Dion in a threatening move, but Poole dragged him back. Garland shook free of Poole's grip and pointed at the door. "We should be out there, not fucking around chatting like this is some kind of goddamn tea party. My daughter's missing. My wife — my ex-wife — has let her wander off, obviously, and there's a river down there, and it's fast, and I gotta get down there, like, now."

"I told you, the river is the first place that was checked," JD told him. "There are a dozen searchers down there. It's not possible that she wandered off by herself. Right? So the search is going wide and fast. And you can help us out best right now by sitting down and answering some questions. Okay?"

Deaf to reason, Garland turned to project his voice at the breakfast nook where his ex-wife still sat. "Bitch," he shouted. "You fucking bitch." And he, too, was crying. He was alarmingly red, Dion noted. Beet red, heart-attack red, snot running, choking on his words. Best to separate this guy from the others and interview him in the peace and quiet of the SUV, he decided.

He told Garland to cool it, and the man must have heard the warning in his voice, as he gave a nod of understanding. Dion shared his plan with JD, then with a reassuring pat on Garland's back, he guided him outside, past the overcrowded parking lot that the Vale driveway had become, down the road to where his police Suburban sat parked.

The fresh air from their brief walk seemed to slap some sense into Garland. He heaved himself into the passenger seat and swabbed his face with tissues from a pack Dion pulled from the glove box. With the engine started for a blast of warmth, Dion got his digital recorder out, checking its buttons in the dim console light.

"I'll tell you what happened," Garland said. "I don't know how she did it, but that bitch hid her away from me, probably hired one of Perry's rich buddies to take her over the border."

"You have a rich buddy in mind?"

"No, I don't have anyone in particular in mind. I'm just thinking."

Dion held his recorder up. "It's just for accuracy."

"Of course, go ahead. I'll co-operate a hundred percent," Garland said. "Bet she's blaming me, right? Bet she's saying I took Luna. Well, look at me." He slammed his own chest, challenging Dion to not only look at him but pat him down. "Did I take her? Does it look like I took her? Go to my place. Toss it all you want. Talk to my buddies. Talk to Chelsea. I was home all evening. There's my truck right there. Go search it."

"We did."

"Search it again. I didn't take Luna."

"I'm not saying you did," Dion said. He added a snap to the words, as Garland was the kind of witness who needed boundaries laid down. "And I'm sure Gemma isn't responsible either. So let's not waste time on this. Do you have any idea who else might have taken her?"

Garland sighed. He looked at the road ahead. Then he burst into tears.

Dion waited. Visible in the near distance was the dead-end turnaround, and from there trails rayed out into the forest and trekked up into the mountains. One trail crossed the river that supplied North Vancouver its water, the Seymour coursing along below, dam-fed and tamed, but still famous for its beauty. A vision came to him of a baby floating away, carried along on a raft of fir boughs. He was almost sure that the parents were distracted by the blame game, that what had happened to Luna Mae Garland was far more serious, that the little girl wouldn't be coming home alive. Not that he'd say so to anyone. Certainly not to Zachary Garland.

The interview had taken him nowhere. He found the button to stop recording and looked at Garland's distorted profile, ugly in grief. This was no act. And what do you say to a grown man who's crying like a child? What would Leith say?

"It's okay," he told the grieving father. "We'll find your daughter."

\* \* \*

Following her interview of Perry Vale, which seemed to confirm his wife's statement — nothing to add, nothing to take away — JD was doing her best to get the story from the dinner guests.

They were two couples in their mid- to late forties. Muddy, but otherwise clean-cut and, by all appearances, upstanding. Their names were Mary and Andy Beck and Gayle and Brodie Latimer. She was questioning them separately, and being assisted by Niko Shiomi, who was in charge of recording the conversation in both digital and written form.

JD didn't like Shiomi, and not because of Shiomi's body, which was smaller than average but perfectly sculpted, even in uniform, or her silky black hair that wisped about her heart-shaped face with the artistic simplicity of Japanese brush strokes, or the natural flush in her cheeks or shine in her onyx eyes that promised she was full of zip and sensuality. Couldn't blame a person for being born like that. No, it was her personality, and

JD had trouble putting her finger on the exact problem. Probably had something to do with Niko's manner of eye contact, which was both penetrating and circular, like she was registering the cut of your clothes and all your facial flaws instead of your spirit or intellect, and since JD's most notable physical feature was a facial flaw — a cleft-lip surgery scar, no less — this kind of unwelcome analysis drew out the lingering residues of teenaged angst in her soul.

But constables came and went, as would Niko Shiomi, and what mattered was the case at hand. "Andy and I were at Gem and Perry's wedding back in November," Mary Beck was saying. "A small affair, just ten guests, but *ooh*, the venue. It was in Hawaii." She paused and apologized; this was hardly the time or place to chat about Hawaii. "I've known Perry forever," she went on. "But Gemma not so well. I wasn't even aware of her divorce until her ex showed up here today and made all that racket. I'm talking about when he came by earlier in the evening, before the baby disappeared …"

Following Mary, Andrew Beck's story was much the same. "… This Zachary guy bangs on the door and wants to go say good night to his daughter, though it wasn't his visitation day, and you could see that Gem didn't want him barging in like this, but neither did she wish to make things worse and embarrass Perry, so she escorted the fellow downstairs …"

Gayle Latimer agreed. "You could hear them through the floor, arguing. Then they both came upstairs and went outside, and you could hear them out there going at it hammer and tongs. Poor girl. He took off, but she wasn't the same after that. It just totally trashed her night."

"What were they arguing about?"

"Well, you know, you try not to eavesdrop. We got busy making conversation."

Brodie Latimer was the most helpful of the bunch, JD discovered. Like the two other men at this party, Perry and Andrew, Brodie was also an engineer. Maybe it was his specialization, the development of surgical equipment, which made him so fabulously precise. Better yet, he was fastidious — or anal, as Niko later said. And snoopy. Seemed he had opted out of making conversation with the rest of the party and had instead perked his ear to the distant argument between Gemma and Zachary, trying to catch every word.

Brodie's snoopiness and attention to detail made him the ideal witness. He seemed able to repeat almost verbatim what he'd heard, though with the bad habit of tacking on "pardon me" whenever a blasphemy arose. Which happened a lot.

"Seriously," JD told him, on the fifth *pardon me*. "I've heard every word in the Urban Dictionary, okay? Don't worry about my ears."

"Sorry," he said. The argument he then unrolled for her was about custody orders. It was about tardiness and unreasonable conditions. He had heard "gun to the head" mentioned, but that was clearly just a metaphor. There were harsh words about showing up without warning, outside of visitation hours, money, fucking lawyers, *pardon me,* and such.

The fight lasted no more than seven minutes, then the ex left. Brodie had heard the departing squeal of tires before Gem returned. She had looked flustered but had done her best to compose herself.

"And then?" JD asked.

"And then a little while later, the baby disappeared," Brodie said.

"Which happened at nine, right?" Going by Gemma's statement.

"Between seven forty-two, give or take, when Gem last checked on her, and approximately nine oh five, when she and Mary went down," Brodie said. "That would be the window of opportunity."

"And how do you remember these times so well?" JD asked. "Like, why do you remember Gemma returning from checking on Luna at seven forty-two?"

"Nervous habit," he said, and grimaced. "I watch the clock a lot."

He did so now. The time was twelve minutes past midnight.

# SIX

# RIVERSIDE BLUES

*February 7*

THERE WAS LITTLE POINT in going to view the river, but Leith did anyway, in the dim light of morning on the day following the kidnap of Luna Mae Garland. The Vale house was now a crime scene, vacated by the family and left to Ident members to chart, photograph, dust, and explore. From its lower level exit he found the footpath that the partiers had already searched so carefully and that Ident had then scrutinized at first light. Nothing had been discovered on a physical level; now it was up to the finer art of picking up the vibes.

With vibes in mind, Leith made his way downslope through mist and bracken. "It's more of a summer footpath to the water," Perry Vale had warned him. "We don't use it in winter if we can help it. Bit slippery."

Yes, it was very fucking slippery, in fact, but with much grasping at bushes and the occasional graceless leap, Leith made it to a flat of bedrock that jutted into the Seymour. His trousers were soggy in spots and he was pretty sure he'd have one hell of a bruise on his backside from one jump that hadn't ended well.

He stood catching his breath while he took in the scenery. The river flowed by, grey-green and serene, not the crystal blue raging rapids he had imagined. But he knew from boyhood experience never to underestimate the aggression of current flow. Water meandered westward, gleaming in the hazy dawn light. Looking behind and up, he could just see fragments of the Vale house through the forest. Other than that, no evidence of humankind down here at all. He listened. No sound of traffic, either. Easy to imagine he'd been thrown back in time to the days of sabre-toothed tigers.

Eastward was a high outcropping of rock, and below the rock was a narrowing with some rapids that emptied into a belly of water that looked deep enough to be called a swimming hole.

Not at this time of year though. The water would be frigid. Divers would have to be brought in soon. Discreetly. In case a body had been weighted and tossed in.

Across the river, which spread broad as a byway, the evergreens grew tall and thick as far as Leith could see in both directions, right down to the bank. Wall-to-wall trees, moss coated and saturated. Highly unlikely that anybody fleeing the scene had crossed over and made their way through the thickets to the neighbourhood that lay unseen beyond, but the possibility would go up on the board.

Motion caught his eye. He watched as his young colleague appeared, clambering effortlessly up and over a hump of rock from the direction of the swimming hole, and came to stand beside him. Unlike Leith, Dion looked clean and unexerted. He dusted his palms, looked at Leith's clothes, and said, "You look like you've been rolling in mud."

"Where the hell did you come from?"

"There."

"I can see that. How did you get down?"

"The steps," Dion said. "You mean you took the footpath? Why?"

Leith studied the river again. It continued to tell him nothing. He said, "What d'you think, then? So far nothing forensically speaking says a stranger broke in. Zach says Gemma stashed the kid away somewhere so he couldn't take her away to P.E.I., and Gemma says Zach snuck in after she had returned to her dinner party and kidnapped her. One, the other, neither?"

"Neither," Dion said. "She couldn't have stashed the baby anywhere unless she'd gotten co-operation from the Becks and Latimers. They're not the types to throw away their lives for somebody else's custody battle. Background checks aren't going to turn up anything on them. Garland thinks she hired someone, and I guess that's a possibility. But I doubt it."

He paused to check his notebook, and tucked it away before continuing. "Garland couldn't have taken Luna with him, as the Vale guests all saw him leave empty-handed. One of the guests swears Garland left at ten after seven, actually heard his truck take off. Unless he sneaked back afterward, but I doubt he'd have had time, 'cause he was back in his apartment on Third and Forbes within twenty minutes. Taking traffic into account, even on a Sunday night, that doesn't give him any wiggle room to circle back and take the child. His arrival time has been corroborated, as he had three friends over, plus his live-in girlfriend, Chelsea Romanov. Sean and Doug arrived at Garland's apartment just before midnight and talked to Chelsea, got her statement, which agrees with Garland's. They tracked down the friends as well, and all three confirmed Garland's timeline. He had to have gone straight home from the Vales' after arguing with Gemma. We're doing background checks on these sources, and so far no flags. The story is Garland, Chelsea, and his friends were eating sandwiches, drinking beer, playing poker, and watching a game. Hockey."

He looked at Leith meaningfully before moving on. Leith had no idea what the meaning was, but didn't interrupt. "The game is why they're sure about the times," Dion went on. "Garland had gone out before it started and got back just five minutes into the first period. Then shortly after nine he got the call from Gemma accusing him of taking Luna. He wasn't sure what it was all about, but he left right away for Riverside Drive. Chelsea remained, and his friends all left pretty soon after he did, as the phone call had brought the party to an end."

He wasn't done, but seemed to have stalled. He took out his notebook for a refresher. He seemed irritated at himself for depending on his notes. Last winter he had confided in Leith that his brain was deteriorating, that he was going downhill fast, that in a year or so there'd be nothing left of his intellect.

Startling news, but then Dion — Leith had come to realize — was a bit of a hypochondriac.

"Zachary Garland —" Dion began again, notebook in pocket.

"Garland and Vale. Kind of funny, their names," Leith said. "Floral. Picturesque."

The notebook was out once more. The pages flipped noisily. Dion kept his finger on the page this time and said, "Zachary Garland's brother and sister-in-law — I can't recall their names — died in a car crash four years ago, leaving two kids behind, a boy and a girl, Tiago and Viviani. They're living with Garland right now. He's legally adopted them. He and Gemma were married at the time of adoption, of course, so she, too, is their legal guardian. She maintains visitation rights, so they stay with her for one week per month. But, you know …"

Whatever Leith was supposed to know faltered, and Dion watched a lone waterfowl with a jaunty hairdo float past downriver. "No, I don't know," Leith prompted.

Dion shrugged. "Neither do I."

Great, so they were mutually mystified by whatever it was. The duck was gone, and Dion was back in his notebook, reminding himself of where he'd left off. "Viviani and Tiago," he said. "As with Luna Mae, Zachary and Gemma share custody of them both, though without court order. It's hard to say with all that's happening with the kidnapping, but I don't get any sense of tug-of-war over the older two. They're just there. The boy is fifteen, and the girl is nine. I don't see a nine-year-old being involved in taking the baby, but the boy, Tiago, we should talk to him."

"Tiago wasn't at the house last night. He was staying with a friend, far as I understand. But we'll talk to him. We'll talk to both of them. Maybe they've seen or heard something. Anyway, thanks for the summary, Cal. Arrange for the interviews, would you? Viviani and Tiago. Oh, and Garland's girlfriend." *Chelsea Fuck-Me-Standing Romanov,* as Gemma Vale had so crudely dubbed her. "Chelsea. Let's get her in as well."

They stood a moment in silence, Leith wondering what the child Luna was going through right now, and wishing he could light a cigarette. He blamed the craving on all this raw and refreshing nature that surrounded him, for nothing went better with fresh air than a nicotine rush. But he was quitting the poison. He punched his fists in his jacket pockets and said, "This river is a lot different than the one I grew up beside."

He hadn't meant to sound melancholy. But it would always be with him. As much as he admired the coastal beauty of his new home, he missed the North Saskatchewan River. Broad and slow under big blue skies. Lots of sandbars, willows, and shrubs. He missed the openness, and frankly, sometimes the coastal rains depressed him to the point he wanted to jump in the truck and bolt east till he left the greys and greens, blacks and browns behind. Get back into the gold. Would have to drag Alison, though, away from her beloved ocean. Nope, just wasn't going to happen.

"A whole lot different," he said. "Do people swim here at all, in summer?"

"Kayak, swim, jump, sure."

"Off that rock? Looks kind of dangerous."

Dion shielded his eyes to look up. "All cliff jumps are dangerous. It won't stop them doing it, when summer hits."

These North Shore rivers had killed a lot of young people over the years, Leith knew. There were canyons, waterfalls, suspension bridges. Plenty of places to climb to, plenty of ledges to leap from. In spite of the grim signage placed by the Park Board, some with pictograms of bodies bouncing off boulders, some listing the number of deaths, youngsters continued to climb and leap. And then they'd go and post videos of themselves climbing and leaping, often set to groovy music, which brought out more daredevils who wanted to live the moment.

He could feel himself getting gloomy, and it wasn't only about Luna's disappearance or Tasha Aziz's death. It was something more personal yet somehow linked. The dangers that lurked …

He told Dion to schedule divers to search the rocky green pool they stood beside. "It's something we have to cover off." He could see that Dion had already made up his mind that the baby wasn't down here — it was written all over his annoying face. And there was something else troubling him. Something apart from the open files. Enough to make Leith ask, "What's up?"

Dion hesitated. "Brooke Zaccardi. I saw her name in the mis-per register."

Leith had seen the name, too, in his daily practice of scanning the bulletins, persons missing, persons found, warrants, breaches, wants. "Someone you know?"

"She's Looch's wife. Common-law, anyway. Widow, I mean."

Looch was the late Constable Luciano Ferraro, Dion's good friend. Ferraro had been in the passenger seat of Dion's car when it had crashed the summer before last. Dion had survived, but Ferraro had been taken away from the scene in a body bag.

Leith hadn't been local when the crash had happened. He hadn't known the pre-crash Dion, or Looch Ferraro, or anything about Ferraro's family. He could think of no response, but clearly none was expected.

The river flowed by for a moment longer before the men headed back to the steps, a long day ahead of them. "Brooke moved east after Looch died," Dion said, as they made it to the road. "I haven't seen or spoken to her since. Meant to give her a call, apologize. Doubt she'd want to hear it, though. JD says Brooke dropped by Rainey's last month for a drink. I should have been there to see her, find out how she's doing. I don't imagine it's good. And now she's disappeared."

Back at their cars, they went their own ways. Only later that night as Leith lay in bed did the conversation come back to him. The latest break in the low-profile case against Cal Dion weighed on his mind. So low profile a case that it was still only Leith and Mike Bosko doing the digging into what was looking like murder. As Bosko had said at the start, not enough proof to take it higher. But the witness coming forward in December had shifted the case into gear.

Bosko had told Leith about the break in the case, a phone call from a female witness who wanted to meet. A day or so later, Leith had stood with Dion on a rocky outcrop overlooking the Burrard Inlet and passed on the news, hoping to break him down, get a confession, end the lies, and move toward healing. Dion's response had been to look offended and call the allegation *bizarre*.

And maybe he was right. Maybe the call had been a prank, for in the end the caller had not showed up for the meeting with Bosko at the appointed time. What kept Leith awake now was a question of coincidence. Looch Ferraro was possibly Dion's partner to a murder in the valley, and now Ferraro's widow was missing.

Two women tied to Dion's past vanished without a trace. Now, what are the chances?

# SEVEN

## COLD COMFORT

*February 8*

CHELSEA ROMANOV WAS Zachary Garland's new partner. She was twenty-eight, and Leith saw that she was clearly distressed by the kidnap of Luna Mae. He also found her more even-keeled than Garland, better able to deal with stress.

She wasn't a suspect. For the night of the kidnap she had a strong alibi. All evening, she'd been in the apartment she shared with Garland. The alibi had been confirmed by Garland's two poker buddies, who came across as credible and respectable. So unless the lot of them were a pack of liars, Gemma was wrong in her accusation that Chelsea Romanov was responsible for the kidnap of Luna Mae.

Romanov now gave her more fulsome statement to Leith, with Dion sitting in. On Sunday morning she and Zach, with Luna in a stroller, had gone for a walk along the Spirit Trail. Then after lunch, his visitation time over, Zach had bundled Luna into her car seat and taken her back to Riverside Drive. Two o'clock was the drop-off time, and he'd left their apartment a bit early. Didn't want to cause a scene by being late again, because as he well knew, even five minutes past the hour drove Gemma batty.

"He was late anyway, of course," Romanov said. "He means well, but he always forgets something. I don't re-call what it was this time, but he dashed in, dashed out again, didn't quite make it there by two, and I imagine they ended up in a huge argument about it."

He had returned in an hour, and as always after a face-off with Gemma, he'd taken a while to chill. But soon enough he got into the *Hockey Night in Canada* spirit, and by the time his friends had arrived around five thirty, he was his usual happy self.

Romanov had helped Garland prepare snacks, the usual chips and dips, sandwich fixings, and beer. The guys played a round of poker before the game start-ed, but Garland remained antsy, and eventually told Romanov why. He had unfinished business with his ex, no big deal, but had to go back to Riverside Drive for an-other chat. The hockey game hadn't started yet. He ex-cused himself, said he'd return in an hour, and took off.

"He told you all this, about one last chat?" Leith asked.

"Yeah, which is probably code for wanting to get the last word in," she said. "But he was home in an hour, as promised, and everything seemed cool. He was revved about the game, and he and the guys had a good time, by the sounds of it. I just got busy cleaning up around the apartment, mostly. Headphones on."

"Hockey's not your bag?"

She almost smiled. "I prefer soccer."

So Chelsea had tightly alibied Zachary, saying he was definitely home during the kidnapper's window of opportunity. A lover's alibi can be trusted only a degree more than a mother's, Leith knew, but the hockey pals backed her up. And Chelsea struck him as honest and honourable. Her character had good bones. No criminal record and gainfully employed as an office assistant at a law firm in West Van since graduating from college. An ideal citizen.

Not that ideal citizens hadn't been found to be dirty rotten liars, but for now Leith chose to believe her. He asked her how and when had she met Zach.

"Last spring," she said. "But he was married then. Things didn't get romantic for us till the fall, after they'd split up. We'd just kind of hit it off from the start, and pretty soon I moved in. Kind of a shock to go from being a single girl to having three kids, one of them a baby in diapers, and a hubby to look after."

"I imagine so. Had your doubts some days, I bet."

"Not really. It can be a bit of a crazy household, but I adore all of them."

Again he believed her. It was the light in her eyes that only a fiend could fake.

She went on to describe how she had met Zach, a couple lessons at the gym where he worked as a trainer, learning some boxing moves. "Or call it assertiveness training if you want," she said. "We had a lot in common.

He's funny. He likes hiking, camping. He's part of a survivalist club kind of thing. So I joined up. Then when he broke up with Gemma last summer, we got more interested in each other." She shrugged to say the rest was history.

"Have any idea about what happened to Luna?" Leith asked. "Even a wild guess?"

Worry sparkled in her dark blue eyes. She seemed to consider the question long and hard before answering with a headshake. "I sure wish I did. I'm sorry. But …"

"Yes?"

"Who would take a baby except a crazy person who just wants a kid of their own?" Her hand was massaging her midriff, the place where all worry seemed to settle. "Which means she's probably okay, don't you think?"

Leith's midriff was feeling it, too, part fear for the child and her family, part fear of his own failure. "That's what we're holding on to," he admitted. The words struck him as cold comfort, but Chelsea gave him the smallest nod of appreciation.

\* \* \*

Nine-year-old Viviani sat in the glassed-off interview room, alone and waiting patiently. She was a pretty girl, Dion could see. She had a wild mass of dark, curly hair, but her face was pale. And freckled and calm. She seemed to be looking out at the world through half-closed eyes, ignoring the biscuits and 7-Up that had been placed before her.

Dion stood outside the interview room with Leith. Chelsea Romanov had given her statement, and she now waited to one side as her boyfriend, Zachary Garland, explained to Leith that Viviani and Tiago's deceased mother was Brazilian — that explained their unusual names. Garland spoke quickly, getting it over with, the tragedy that had befallen his niece and nephew. Before their parents' death in a highway collision, he said, the kids had grown up on the Seymour River side of town. So they had connections there, and that's why he had made sure they continued their schooling there. Bit of a commute from his apartment on Forbes, but he wanted at least that continuity in their lives. Hanging out with the friends they'd grown up with.

"Smart kids, both of them," Garland said, watching Viviani through the glass. His arms were crossed over his chest so tightly he seemed to be wanting to suffocate himself. "This one especially. Way too smart for me, anyway. Maybe even a genius."

Leith raised his brows. "How so?"

Dion was thinking that Garland's new girlfriend Chelsea was a dead ringer for Gemma, just a few years younger. Her grief seemed real enough, but whether it was for Luna or Zachary, he couldn't guess. If he were to bet, though, he'd say her tears were more for her boyfriend. Luna wasn't her child, and given the brief and infrequent visitation time Zachary had with Luna, Chelsea wouldn't have had much chance to bond with her.

"It's like Vivi knows stuff she shouldn't," Garland said, in answer to Leith's *How so?* "Not just math and science and all that, but, like, politics, and, you know, metaphysical stuff, stuff even adults don't understand."

"Is Tiago the same?"

"Tia? No. Smart, like I said, but pretty much a regular kid."

Garland's eyes looked rubbed raw. Dion thought he showed signs of being on some kind of sedative. No wonder, with his baby girl gone all night and half a day. He'd be facing the fact that if his ex didn't have her, a stranger did, and the chances of getting her back were getting slimmer by the minute.

Whatever the sedatives were, though, they couldn't tamp down Garland's impatience, and it now erupted in a raised voice. All these questions and pointless interviews were getting on his nerves, he complained. His mind was on Luna Mae's disappearance, and nothing else mattered, least of all his relationships or what kind of kids Viviani and Tiago were.

Leith told him a full team was on the case, round the clock. Background could be just as important as pounding the pavement, he added.

"Well, my background is clean," Garland snarled. "But how about that Perry guy? He's the big unknown, far as I'm concerned. Creepy fucking dude. Him and Gemma have only been married, what, three months? What if he did something to Luna?" A pause, then he burst out, "What if he killed her? Got rid of her? That's possible, right?"

Leith shook his head. "There were a lot of people in that house last night. Perry Vale had no opportunity to get rid of anything."

"All the same. I don't get how the law can just let one parent go and marry somebody else, and all of a sudden your own baby, not to mention your other kids, are living in a house with a stranger. It's just not right. There should be a rule against that."

"Gemma might say the same about you and Chelsea."

"That's different. She's a woman. Women don't hurt kids. Men do."

Women hurt kids all the time, Dion knew. But rarely in the way Garland meant. He didn't trust Garland, but couldn't pin down why. It wasn't the man's aggressive attitude, because Garland had every reason to be punchy at a time like this. The history run on him had turned up nothing bad. He was hard-working, a boxing and fitness coach at a club on Marine Drive, with the shoulders to prove it. He had taken on the responsibility of his dead brother's children, rented a three-bedroom apartment at no small cost. He had no criminal record or flags against him. Every reason to trust him, and still Dion didn't.

Leith had moved on, meanwhile, and was worrying aloud about the present situation, the question of two big cops interviewing one small girl. A bit much, wasn't it?

"She doesn't seem anxious," Dion said, watching Viviani through the glass.

Garland confirmed it. "Don't worry about it. She's a rock. Won't bother her."

The three of them went in, only Chelsea remaining behind. Garland sat beside Viviani. Dion sat next to Leith and observed.

Interview styles varied, he realized. But in his opinion this one, led by Leith, was overly soft-edged and roundabout, as if the kid were two years old instead of nine. And an advanced nine, at that. Was she doing okay, Leith asked. Did she know what had happened and why she was here? Did she have any idea what might have happened to little Luna?

Viviani's answers were also gentle to an extreme, Dion thought. Like a reflection of Leith's well-intentioned condescension. "I don't know who took Luna," she said. "I wasn't there, 'cause I was staying with my friend Alexa, who lives on the other side of the river."

Alexa's mom had confirmed that yes, Vivi had been there that night. No, she hadn't snuck out between seven and nine, unless she was a super ninja. The friend Alexa herself had backed it up, too, which ended that line of inquiry. The only question now was had Viviani observed anything in the days before the kidnap that might lend a clue as to what had happened.

"But I'm a seer," the girl went on. "So I might have been able to help, if I'd been there."

"A seer?" Leith asked.

Her mouth turned down, as if she didn't believe her own claim. "Tia says I am, but I don't know why, 'cause the only things I've seen are, like, totally unimportant. But he watches a lot of movies, and he thinks I'm like the kids in the movies who can see ghosts and stuff. And I've tried, sometimes, and it's like I could learn how, maybe. But so far I haven't seen anything. But if you want, I can go to Gemma's house and see if I can pick up something."

She was questioning Leith with her eyes. He told her that unfortunately the house was closed for a few days. She'd be home soon, though, he said.

"It's not home," she corrected him. "Tia and I live with Zach in town, and only visit Gemma for one week of the month. It's nice to get to stay by the river. We both have friends in the area. I'm always glad to get back to Zach's, though. But I think it's important to be able to feel at home wherever you are, and not get too attached to things or places. Or even people."

Dion agreed with Viviani. People change, or die, or disappear, so don't hang your hopes on them. But Leith looked dismayed. "Sure," he said doubtfully. "I know what you mean."

Viviani studied him for a moment. She studied Dion, too, and then gazed sideways at Zach, whose thumbs were twiddling like frantic windmills, and said to him, "Poor Luna. We'll find her soon."

She went to sit in the waiting area, and before her brother came in, Leith said to Zachary, "You're right, Vivi's a bright little girl. But a seer?"

Zachary shrugged. "Like she said, Tia's got an imagination. My brother was a smart guy, and so was his wife, so I guess they passed the genes down to the kids. Bit worried about Tia, though, frankly. A good enough guy, but his grades are dropping. And he's moody as hell."

"He's fifteen," Leith said. "Moodiness is a given."

"I know. I was fifteen myself once. But there's a limit."

Dion watched Tiago enter the room and look around unhappily. He was lanky, with the same curly dark hair as his sister. Same freckles. He had a narrow face and narrow eyes. He gave Leith a fleeting smile and took the seat offered to him. He sat squarely next to Zachary, not acknowledging him, and to Dion he appeared more troubled than moody. Or was there a difference? On a better day, though, not set against a criminal investigation, maybe he'd be more moody than troubled.

Leith asked Tia to describe his day, and the answers he got were even more economical than Vivi's. "Pal lives couple kilometres up the road," Tia said. "Oliver Walsh. Stayed over. Biked. Few games. Movie. His mom made dinner." He shrugged. "Didn't hear about Luna till morning."

"How did you hear about Luna?"

"He called," Tia said, thumb indicating Zachary.

Zachary fidgeted a moment before leaning forward to explain his son's attitude. "He's angry I didn't call him sooner." And to the boy, with a pat on the back, "Wasn't anything you could have done, kiddo."

Tia set his mouth in a hard line.

Leith said, "Could you just give me a rundown of your living arrangements, Tia? I know it's kind of complicated."

"Not complicated. We live with Zach, except one week of every month we go stay with Gemma and Perry."

"When did your week with Gemma this month start?"

"Saturday. Day before Luna went missing."

As Leith looked at a calendar to orient himself, Garland lost patience and interrupted. "You got the visitation schedule, right? I get Luna overnight every other weekend, which is not enough by any stretch. Judge says it's important for us to bond. Well, how can I bond with my baby when I only get four half days and two nights with her each month? It's hardly time to get to know her all over again each time. Gemma wants me to have even less time, some goddamn hour and a half at McDonald's or something. How am I supposed to work with that kind of person? The only fair time is equal time …"

He had stopped cold, maybe realizing this wasn't the time or place for closing submissions. Or it had hit him that *no time* was what he might end up with at the end of the day.

Leith gave Zachary a slight nod, which meant *Yeah, okay, thanks, now be quiet,* and said to Tia, "Is it tough only getting to see Luna occasionally?"

Dion saw the teen's mouth pucker. As if conflicted, Tia seemed to think over his answer. "Sure," he said, but too late, and the truth was plain to see in his hesitation: *No, she's just a boring baby, nothing to do with me, what do I care?* He dropped his lashes with a sigh.

Leith gave him a smile. "Sometimes siblings aren't much fun till they get big enough to talk to, maybe shoot marbles with, and all that good stuff, right? Or I guess you're not the marble-shooting generation."

Even if Tia didn't know what marble shooting was, he got the gist and returned Leith's smile. "Yeah, true."

"And young kids of Luna's age can be demanding. Noisy, entitled. They can be a bit of a pain, right?"

Zachary began to interrupt again, to ask where this was going, but Tia had already nodded. "Noisy, yeah. Drives you …"

*Nuts* faded away. Tia glanced at Zachary, and seemed to shift away from him slightly. Dion made a mental note of the shift, as Leith asked, "D'you have any idea at all, Tia, what happened to her?"

"No, sir."

With Tiago excused from the room, Leith said to Garland, "Sometimes it's hard to talk to kids of his age, especially in a place like this. He might be more relaxed if I spoke with him one-on-one. If he's agreeable to it. What d'you think?"

"That's not going to happen."

"It's just I get the feeling he's holding back," Leith said. "Probably nothing, but I wouldn't mind the chance to chat with him alone."

"Oh, he's holding back, all right. What he gets up to out at the river there, I don't even want to ask. Wouldn't happen under my watch, but Gemma doesn't give a shit about these two. They can run wild, stay out all night, for all she cares. He's fifteen and busy getting in trouble. Mixing with the wrong crowd, checking out girls, sniffing out the gateway drugs." Garland sat forward to project his words into Leith's face. "I tell her, keep a lid on it, Gemma. But she doesn't, because she doesn't care. She only keeps taking the kids for her one week because she has to put on her generous, loving face in front of her new yoga-mat golf-club-swinging friends, because how else you going to fit into the clique? Right? Truth is, she's thinking, *They're not my kids, they're not even my ex's kids, they're my ex's dead brother's kids, the brother I never even met.*"

"You have any hard evidence that he's doing all these things?" Leith asked. "Partying all night, taking drugs?"

"No. It's called reading between the lines."

"Which implies to me he's not ready to talk openly with you. He could be holding back something important, and that something could relate to Luna Mae."

"More likely it relates to what he gets up to at Riverside Drive. Answering your questions could end up getting him in trouble that none of us needs right now."

Garland had a point, Dion was thinking. But so did Leith, who gave it a final push. "I have no intention of digging up anything against Tia. I won't press him about drugs, drinking, or anything else. I just want to ask him about Luna, what his thoughts are, if he can help at all. And there's another thing, Zach. He's turned down grief counselling, and you as his parent are maybe too close for him to confide in. That's not your fault. Happens all the time. But he does seem closed off, to me. Troubled. Understandably so. So listen, maybe he'd be okay with talking to me about it, and maybe I could convince him to get help. Right? And yes, bottom line is whatever he has to say could land him in trouble, but only if he admits responsibility for Luna's disappearance. In which case we all need to know, don't we?"

Garland had been shaking his head through Leith's patient spiel. "I gotta protect him," he said. "If I don't, who will? Letting him talk to the cops alone — all due respect — is not what I'd call protection."

Leith nodded that he understood, and Garland departed, his big arms corralling girlfriend and kids out the door and away.

\* \* \*

"Well, so much for that," Leith said. He was at his desk, lounging in his swivel chair, and eating one of Alison's homemade, low-sugar granola bars, which he had just dishonestly described to Dion as a damn good alternative to the Coffee Crisps he liked so much. Dion was planted in the non-swivelling visitor's chair, apparently with something to say. Leith hoped whatever it was would open doors. He didn't feel the Vivi and Tia interviews had moved them ahead a jot, but maybe his more intuitive partner had caught something worth following up. "What've you got?"

"It's just a feeling," Dion said.

"Feelings are good."

"I'm wondering why Tiago's so angry at Zachary. Whatever it is, it's something to do with Luna."

The granola bar fell apart, not enough sugar to bind it, and Leith chucked the mess in the waste bin. "You think Tia suspects Zachary is behind the disappearance? Something like that?"

"Yeah, something like that."

"Or how about Tia's an angry teenager because Dad's putting his foot down about staying out late and partying? Your run-of-the-mill father-son power struggle."

Dion looked unconvinced, and tried to explain his doubts. "It's more specific than father-son conflict. Tia's a smart kid, and so is Vivi. Vivi is close to both Tia and Zachary — you can tell by how she talks about them. I'm thinking if she's got all this affection for Zachary, then Zachary must be doing something right. And Tia would get that. So whatever's bothering him, it's more about now than then."

"Because he's smart," Leith said, joining the dots.

"Smart enough to get it that Zachary's doing his best being a father to them both. And this isn't just any old day. Luna's been kidnapped. Tia would put aside their conflicts at a time like this, so whatever's got between them, it's fresh, and it's big, which means it's got to do with Luna. Like I said, just a feeling."

And a superbly nebulous one, Leith was thinking. "Then again, how much affection does Vivi feel, really? Important not to get close to people. That's a direct quote out of her mouth. Seems kind of a cold way of putting it."

"Or her way of dealing with life. She's already lost her parents. She's knows nothing lasts."

*All the same*, Leith thought, *nine-year-olds shouldn't be so philosophical.*

He tried turning the conversation to a more productive tack. "Let's get back to Tia's anger. Seems to me Zach had a perfectly good explanation for it. He says Tia's pissed off that he wasn't informed earlier that Luna was missing, when he could have pitched in and helped search. An understandable source of friction, if you ask me."

Dion hadn't asked, and didn't agree, which meant he disagreed. Leith gave up trying. All he could see in Tiago and Zachary was an ordinary father-son relationship with its ordinary father-son tensions, all set against a terrible situation. But Dion was stubborn, and when he built a theory, he stood by it. "All right, well," Leith concluded. "If Tia has something to say, and if he's as smart as we all think he is, he'll come forward on his own and tell us. Right?" He swivelled his chair to look toward the window. "You know what irks me about Zach? Him ranting about custody battles in front of Tia. Kid has to put up with that bullshit from his dad? No wonder he's angry."

"He's had to put up with the custody battle since Luna Mae was born," Dion said. "It's all just background noise to him. I get your point," he added. "But I still think whatever's bothering him is centred here." He planted his finger on the desktop, symbolizing the case they were working on. "It's about the kidnap, which means we have to talk to him alone, without Zachary hovering."

"And apparently that's not going to happen, and Zach's got every right and reason to put his foot down. I guess I'd do the same, in his shoes."

"We'll have to keep trying."

Dion rose to leave, but Leith stopped him. Asking Dion for advice was a bit like gnawing through one of Alison's granola bars, a healthy choice but a bit of a chore. "What about Viviani? Any thoughts there?"

"Bring her to the Vale residence," Dion said. "Maybe she'll walk in and *see* what happened." He was on his feet, ready to leave, and seemed to be snickering at his own reply.

Leith stared at him. "So she can see what?" he asked. Then recalled the nine-year-old's nonsense about clairvoyance, and got the joke. Not much of one, but coming from Dion it was a riot. "Oh, yes, right, ha."

He was still smiling at the great joke when Dion turned serious again and said, "David."

Leith crossed his arms. "Calvin?"

"Nothing's coming down. The witness you told me about, who's supposed to be ratting me out for something I didn't do. All I'm hearing is silence. So what happened?"

"I don't know. Maybe it was a false alarm."

Bad place to talk about such private matters, Leith realized, the heart of a police detachment thick with detectives. But there were no ears nearby, and in some ways it was safer hashing out their worries here than in the local coffee shop.

Dion stood looking thoughtful and conflicted. Finally he said, "Will you tell me if you get any updates?"

"Not sure why I should. You'll just bad-mouth the messenger."

"I won't bad-mouth you. I'll keep you in the loop."

An obscure promise, but Leith got it. If and when Dion's luck ran out, Leith would be the first to know, and he'd know all, a full confession. Not much of a bargain, from his perspective, but it was about the closest the two of them had come to an understanding. After a beat he nodded acceptance. "Okay, Cal. Will do."

\* \* \*

The weather was rotten, but Dion walked with Kate hand in hand along the sands that rimmed the restless waters of the Burrard Inlet. He could see the two of them as if from afar, and they were a beautiful couple. They were built for each other, physically and emotionally: a perfect match.

Strange, though, how seeing them from afar was better than the actual in-body experience. Seeing their hands linked was more touching than the solid feel of her palm in his, and the conversation he imagined bouncing between them sleeker, wittier, sexier.

"So d'you think she killed herself?" Kate said.

She huddled against the sharp breeze as they walked, her collar up. She was talking about Brooke's disappearance. It was news Dion had no choice but to share, because Brooke had been Kate's friend, too, up to the summer before last. What he wasn't telling her was how fairly sure he was that Brooke was the witness who had promised to come forward and turn him in for murder and who, for whatever reason, had changed her mind. None of that would he tell Kate, not in a million years.

"I don't know," he said. "I hope not. Probably she just realized she didn't want to be back here, so she took off again. Back east, probably."

He thought of how things had changed in all their lives. So suddenly, like a blackout switch. No more good times for the four of them together. Dinners, day-tripping, house parties. Hiking, biking, fighting.

The fights weren't serious, but they'd happened, mostly because he and Brooke had issues and over the years had exchanged a few nasty words. She was jealous of Looch's time, wanted him all to herself, and that was something she couldn't have. But even the bad times were good times. He tried to put himself back in the frame of mind where he'd felt integral to something close and warm. His friends were supposed to be around him forever, and life was only going to get better.

Blackout.

But crying over the past wasn't going to help. He had Kate back, a big step in the right direction. *Build it up,* he told himself. *Say something brilliant, optimistic.* What would he have done and said before the crash, when everything seemed so easy? Squeeze her hand and say whatever crossed his mind.

"It's cold," he said. He squeezed her hand. "Let's go home and fuck."

# EIGHT

## GAMES

*February 10*

DION WASN'T SURE how the conversation came to this, sitting in Oliver Walsh's living room on Riverside Drive, being told the difference between nerds and geeks. Fifteen-year-old Oliver was Tiago's friend and alibi for the night of Luna Mae Garland's disappearance. The Walsh home was only a few kilometres from the Vales', an easy bike ride away. It was a more modest house than the Vales', and on the slightly less desirable non-river side of Riverside Drive.

"Nerds can be geeks, too," Oliver was explaining. "But geeks aren't nerds, hardly. It's a thin line. I've been told I'm a nerd," he added, pointing at his own throat. "Note the bow tie."

He wasn't wearing a bow tie, but Dion got the point.

"I guess you'd say most of my friends are the same. Except Tia." Oliver was wending his way out of the abstract and back to the issue at hand, his relationship with Tiago Garland. "He's cool, which means we're not going to be hanging around much longer, you can bet on it." He ended the melancholy statement with a *so-be-it* shrug.

Dion said, "Maybe I'm not getting this, but putting yourself down like that can't be good. Maybe if you called yourself cool, you would be. You'd be cool like Tia, and you could hang around together for as long as you wanted."

Oliver looked surprised. "Who says I'm putting myself down?"

*And who said you need advice?* Dion thought, and resolved not to try it again. "So he was with you all that day. What about between seven and nine? Can you tell me what you were doing then?"

"Between those hours we were either watching a movie — it was *not* good — eating dinner, or playing *Scrabble* with my mom. That is, us against her."

"Who won?"

"My mom, as usual."

Dion grinned. "Oh. I had you pegged as a whiz at *Scrabble*."

"What, 'cause of the bow tie?"

Another short lesson on assumptions. Stick to the facts, Dion told himself. No advice, no quips. "So after losing at *Scrabble*, what did you do?"

"Tia camped out in my room. We played video games, listened to music, and talked about whatever, and eventually fell asleep. Then in the morning before heading to school his dad called — that's Zach — and we heard about Luna."

"What was Tia's reaction to the news? What did he say to you?"

"I don't recall a lot of it. He was shocked. We all were. He didn't go to school, natch, but went straight over to help out any way he could."

"So Sunday morning he came over, you said about ten. How did he seem to you then?"

"Normal. We went biking for a while, had a good time. We were going to go hike up to Mystery Lake, except then he remembered his homework. Science, not his favourite. We're in the same class, so I said no problemo, let's get this done, I'll help you. He went to get it." Oliver paused to reflect. "We didn't actually get it done, in the end. I think we got distracted, as my mom needed some groceries, so we biked to the store, picked 'em up, and by then it was too late to go to the lake, not to mention it was raining, so we stayed in after that. Should have got straight to his homework at that point, but I'd just got *Diablo III* for my birthday, and we wanted to check it out. Bad idea. The homework went on hold, like, permanently."

"*Diablo III*?"

The kid's eyes sparkled. "I'm a Barbarian."

Computer game, Dion decided. "And Tia was normal, you say?"

"I guess a little moodier than usual. More so as the day went on."

"Moody, or troubled?" Dion said, not counting on a useful answer.

Surprisingly, Oliver did have an answer. "Maybe troubled is more like it, now that you mention it."

"Do you know what he was troubled about?"

"Not really. I thought it was something to do with the party, though I'm pretty sure he'd gotten over that."

*Wild parties, gateway drugs*, Dion thought. Zachary Garland's darkest fears coming true. "What party, when?"

"January twenty-seventh. I know because my mom bought me tickets to a concert for that date, and I invited Tia, but he said he was going to check out the party. Probably more for the girls than anything."

"What was the concert?" Dion asked, if only to firm up the story, fill in the gaps.

He expected Mozart, maybe, but the group Oliver described was some kind of heavy metal roadshow Dion had never heard of. "I'm a big fan," Oliver said. He went to his desk and brought back proof of his concert attendance, a ticket stub. He had also slung an electric guitar across his chest. "Wish I could play badass guitar like those guys," he said. "But I was born with these unfortunate things." He held up both hands, splaying ten perfectly good fingers.

Dion sighed. With every word and gesture, the teenager was making sly fun of himself, along with his interviewer and all those who mocked him as an oddball.

"Where was this party? Who did he go with? What happened?"

Oliver unslung the guitar and put it aside. "I don't know what happened. Just a girl invited him to a party up in Blueridge, and he went, and later he seemed different. Like something happened, but he didn't want to say what. We didn't talk about it. If you want, I can wear a wire and ask him."

Dion wasn't sure if the offer was serious, but to be safe he assumed it was. "Thanks, but we're not at the wire-wearing stage yet. So no clue at all about what happened at the party that bothered him?"

Oliver grimaced. "Not sure, but I think it has something to do with Kyler."

"Who's that?"

"Kyler Hartshorne. I do *not* like that guy. He's trouble waiting to happen. He was at the party, too, I know 'cause Tia told me he and Kyler got into a fight over something. But he wouldn't say what. I hope you're not going to tell Tia I told you all this. Our friendship is rocky enough as it is."

When he was leaving, the name Kyler Hartshorne jotted down as an unlikely lead that had to be followed up, Dion said to Oliver, "Few days ago I heard some girls talking. They said nerds are cool. What d'you think?"

"I can live with that!" Oliver exclaimed. And curtsied.

\* \* \*

JD was at her desk, her work on the Tasha Aziz case on standby as her mind wandered back and forth, back and forth, like a lost mutt in a dark field. She was worrying about Brooke Zaccardi's disappearance. No, worse than worried, she was scared. She'd been one of the last people to see Looch Ferraro's widow alive, that's why. If she'd minded her own business like she should have, not gone out of her way to be nice to the woman, she wouldn't be in this fix now.

That's what kindness got her, in the end. Sucked into somebody else's troubles. It had started on a wet day shortly after New Year's, when she'd come upon Brooke hanging around outside the detachment looking antsy and pale, like a restless spirit trapped among the living with some kind of unfinished business. JD knew Brooke through Looch, but not well. Chancing upon Brooke like this — the first time they'd met since Looch's funeral — she'd taken pity on her, chatted with her for a moment before inviting her to Rainey's for a drink with the crew.

Brooke had agreed to go along, but only if Dion wouldn't be there. JD had promised her he wouldn't be.

Who *had* been at the bar that night? Not many, thank god. Doug Paley and Jimmy Torr, the regular regulars. Lil Hart and Ken Poole had put in brief appearances, JD recalled. But Lil had taken off before Brooke's meltdown, and Ken had clearly not been listening to any of it. Too busy talking with Torr.

As it turned out, bringing Brooke out of the rain had been a bad idea. Over the year and a half since Looch's death, she'd clearly gone nuts. Man, the things she had said that night. Things about Cal Dion.

JD knew Brooke had good reason to hate Cal. But hating Cal was like hating the black cat that crosses your path — not at all useful. He'd been driving the car that killed the man she loved, but it was a case of being in the wrong place at the wrong time, wasn't it? Dion had been driving along, obeying the law — as JD understood it — when he'd been rammed on the passenger side by a speeding sports car. Out in Surrey, known for its roads straight as runways. A bad crash, nothing left but scrap metal when the dust settled, Cal knocked out cold and Looch in the passenger seat dead on impact.

So not Cal's fault, and Brooke should know it. Yet after all this time she was still seeing red. She had made that anger clear, that night at Rainey's, going on about how Cal had killed Looch, killed Looch's family, killed her. But that wasn't all. With a few drinks inside her, Brooke had said more.

She implied that Dion had committed a crime that night in Surrey, and though her words had been mangled by emotion, JD had caught the gist. Murder. And mixed in with Brooke's anger was a kind of giddiness. About a decision she'd made to tell all she knew to Mike Bosko.

*Look at me. Tomorrow I'm going to see Sergeant Bosko, and I won't leave till he does something about this.*

Brooke's lost her beans, was all JD had thought at the time. She was playing games, making stuff up to get Cal in trouble. Revenge. But in retrospect, was that all it was?

And in the end what had happened to Brooke's promise? Had she carried out the threat and told the world? If so, the world wasn't listening. And now she was missing, and it was only a matter of time before JD and those who had last seen her would be questioned about it.

What JD needed to do was stop procrastinating and take steps. Talk to Doug, Jim, and Ken, the ones who had been at the pub that night, before they were questioned. ASAP and off the record. And why not start with now?

She found Doug Paley downstairs in the lunch room with Jim Torr. She would have preferred to talk to each man alone, but why not kill two birds with one stone? She got to the point before she had quite landed in her chair at their table. "So what's your take on Brooke?"

Paley seemed to have thought it out in advance. "Went off somewhere and combusted, I guess."

"Something wrong with that chick." Torr tapped his thick brow.

They both saw Brooke as mad, then, after her rant that night. But whether they were linking what the mad woman had said and what had ultimately happened to her, probably not. Maybe nobody would make the connection except JD. Maybe she should shut up about it, let it lie. Wait for it to disappear, like Brooke herself.

But Brooke had said things, and if Torr or Doug repeated those things to investigators, somebody was bound to dig deeper, and Cal's life might capsize.

Then again, so what? JD owed Cal nothing. Especially not this, conspiring with these guys to break the law for his sake, risking her own job. Risking Paley and Torr's while she was at it. She realized she was scowling in indecision, and that Paley and Torr were staring at her, waiting for her to come to the point.

*We have to tell the truth*, she decided. *There's nothing to discuss. I should just get up and go.* "It's coming up fast," she heard herself say instead. "Bosko's been asking questions. We're going to be pulled in, separately, and asked what happened that night. What we talked about, what she said. Right?"

Paley and Torr continued to gaze at her in silence. Torr seemed confused, but Paley didn't. Paley had arrived at this place already, she realized, and a cold shiver went through her. So what had his intentions been?

The silence stretched, and JD began to worry that she was the subject of a sting. They were waiting for her to say something incriminating. Then they'd each take an arm and drag her to barracks. But now Paley was pushing back the droopy bits of his moustache in a thoughtful way, saying, "I don't remember her saying much. She rained curses on Cal for getting Looch in trouble. I think you pointed out that Cal and Looch were both yahoos, and if they got in trouble, they did it together. She took exception to that." He shrugged. "That's about it, really. I bought her a couple drinks. Bad idea. She seemed to get kind of paranoid, then took off without so much as a have-a-nice-day. Right, Jim?"

JD could see Torr's mind turning over last month's conversation at Rainey's, getting up to speed. She could even see the moment when it occurred to him that they were cooking up something here. He crossed his hammy arms and nodded. "That's right. That's all I remember. Mostly I was talking to Ken, so I didn't hear much."

"That's how I remember it, too," JD said.

*Brilliant*, she thought. Paley's words, *seemed to get a little paranoid*, were a good way of writing off Brooke's accusation without getting specific. It covered their asses, in case the woman turned up and testified about what she had actually said that night. Then it would be her word against theirs, and unlike her, they had strength in numbers. And they were cops, and cops never lie.

"Okay," she said. Now that they had a plan, the knot in the pit of her stomach began to ease. "This conversation didn't happen, right? See you later."

She didn't linger. Next up was Ken Poole. But he worked in the busy general duties pit, and would be harder to separate out and chat up without raising eye-brows. She would have to catch him some other way.

She wasn't too worried about Poole. She recalled that as Brooke had been telling them about the murder that Dion had supposedly committed, Ken had been talking to Torr. Like Torr, Ken had always been slower on the uptake. Probably, she decided — she hoped — he had missed what Brooke had said, every damning word.

Pacified, she turned her mind back to what really mattered: find who had killed Tasha, and make him pay.

# NINE

## HARTSHORNE

THE TASHA AZIZ CASE was into its second week, and little progress had been made. In canvassing the neighbourhood, JD had spoken to a woman who reported that she'd heard something that night. She'd been putting out the garbage bins when a distant car alarm went off. Sounded like it came from the area of Riverside Secondary. But only briefly.

Another fact had emerged: Aziz's tire had been slashed, meaning quite likely her attack had been an ambush.

Over the past week JD had questioned a dozen significant witnesses, along with several dozen more who might have peripheral knowledge, Tasha's family, friends, employers, school staff, co-workers, and more. Today she was heading back to the school for a follow-up. There was a new name to check out, a local kid who attended Riverside. He was older than his classmates, as he'd failed a grade or two, and was reportedly a pack of trouble: Kyler Hartshorne.

JD hadn't met him in person — he was elusive as a bucket of eels — but from what she'd heard, he was eighteen, big-boned, full of testosterone, and knew shit about boundaries. There were two recent accusations on record against him. One was sexual assault and one was uttering threats. But both cases had gone nowhere because (a) the evidence was too thin, and (b) the complainants didn't want to push it forward. In interviewing those involved, JD had learned that Hartshorne said he would like to "fuck-kill that MILF," referring to one of his female teachers, had a locker full of revolting magazines, and plenty of violent ideations about the world at large.

*Nope, no red flags waving on this cupid*, she thought.

She stuck a mental red flag on him, hard. Hartshorne was the kind of gent who might see a woman walking across a parking lot and decide to teach her a lesson or two about respect. With a blow to the stomach? Sure, why not.

The autopsy findings pointed to a heavy, pointed instrument of some kind.

Whoever had done this, Hartshorne or otherwise, that person had rammed something into her gut and left her there to die. Slowly.

The attacker had to be caught and convicted. Just had to. Though she could already see the court case drawing out. The defence would point to the single blow. There had been no intent to kill, My Lord, ladies and gentlemen of the jury. It was momentary passion, a bad choice, maybe even a defensive manoeuvre. Almost what you might call an accident in the heat of the moment. *Maybe even Tasha's own fault.*

The defence would shoot for acquittal or, failing that, manslaughter. And maybe they'd succeed.

JD knew she was getting personal about this case, but there was no other way. She knew Tasha intimately by now, or the woman she might have been. She had checked out Tasha's Facebook page, and read her journal, and talked to those who knew her best. Tasha had made no mention of Kyler Hartshorne that JD could find. Tasha had no known enemies or secret admirers. She had a modest but healthy bank account, no criminal record, wasn't into drugs or wild parties. Her ambitions were to continue furthering her education, get work as an RN, marry, and have three kids. As one of her journal entries said, *Three kids and nine grandkids would be ideal.*

"You can't get any nicer than this person," JD had said angrily to Dion after the team briefing this morning, hoping to engage him. "And somebody comes out of the blue and kills her. For what? This proves it. There is no God." Her pulse had been revving, and she wanted to talk about what assholes men were. But Dion was assigned to the red-hot Luna Mae Garland kidnap, and hadn't been up to fielding thoughts on anything else.

Niko Shiomi was up to it, though. She not only liked the sound of her own voice, but was more than willing to talk about what assholes men were. JD had gotten to know Shiomi over the last few days. If she was to write an employee review for the woman, it would glow. Even if she didn't like her. Energetic, motivated, well-spoken, assertive, her review would say. Shiomi spoke her mind, and spoke it well. She seemed able to deal with the males on the force, gaining their respect without giving up her own — and that was something.

Unlike JD's trajectory, Shiomi's was sure to rise.

Which was fine. JD had no plans to compete with the rank-climbers of the world. The upper floors weren't where she wanted to go. She wanted to go out the door and far away. North, probably, since she preferred cold over heat. And somewhere remote, as she preferred trees over people. In a perfect world, she would blank her mind, write off her years on the force, and start over as a bush pilot.

But riding with Shiomi out to Riverside Secondary, JD began to see another side to the constable. She wasn't the perfect ten she appeared to be. Talked too much, and her slang could curdle a pirate's blood. She tended to slouch, and gossip, and dig. Though if JD knew anything about the male brass in this quasi-military institution called the RCMP, a little crudity wouldn't damage Shiomi's career. So long as she played it right, it would only help.

Shiomi had already lucked her way into the General Investigation Section by cracking a rib in an on-duty sidewalk scuffle in January. That had gotten her off street patrol and into a less physically demanding desk job while she healed. Over the last few days that had meant taking on some of the more mind-numbing tasks for the serious crime detectives. One of those tasks was taking over from JD the re-studying of the surveillance video seized in the Aziz case. There was footage from within the high school and its exterior, as well as street cams from adjacent roadways. Unfortunately, traffic was too heavy to parse out particular cars heading to and from the school parking lot, and no cameras captured traffic in and out. Shiomi had focused instead on the footage that tracked Aziz through the school corridors on her janitorial night shift, lugging buffer machines, spraying and wiping down surfaces, and finally locking up and leaving.

"She was one hell of a fabulous janitor," Shiomi had summed up for JD.

The most exciting moment in Shiomi's video-watching chore was a glitch, almost missed on her first run-through. "A glitch is what you call it when the motion detector activates and deactivates," she'd told JD. The piece of interest was from a camera that covered the front entrance of the school. A minute after Aziz had walked off camera toward the parking lot, movement had triggered the lens, briefly, and switched it off again. On careful review Shiomi had seen a shadow, barely a passing blot. Someone had entered the edge of the zone, set the camera going, trod lazily through puddles, and exited again, also in the direction of the parking lot.

The video clip had been broken down into a series of stills, enlarged and optimized, but all it said in the end was that the individual was likely an adult male with dark pants and footwear. A man in no hurry, heading toward the parking lot. Re-watching it, JD felt it was safe to say this was their first glimpse of the killer. Not much, but better than nothing. She had frozen a frame and pointed. "What's that white blob there, on his foot? Some kind of pattern on the shoe?"

"I can't even tell if that's a shoe or a boot," Shiomi had answered. "Don't know. Probably just a reflection. Or a bit of lint on the lens."

She was probably right, as the blob appeared only once before vanishing.

"Got to be the killer," Shiomi said now, as they drove toward the school, recapping their findings. She was lolling in the passenger seat, JD at the wheel, and they had fifteen minutes ahead of them in heavy traffic. "Who else would be out there, nearly midnight, early February, miserable shitty weather? Nobody's going to be making out on the steps or shooting hoops. Stalking lone females in parking lots — that's about the only attraction far as I can see. Right?"

"I dunno," JD said.

JD's bottom-line assessment of Shiomi was still dislike, and she didn't care if the woman knew it. She'd just chalk it up to envy, and maybe she was partly right.

*I wish I, too, was such a jewel.*

If Shiomi sensed that JD didn't like her, it didn't seem to bother her. Relaxed in the passenger seat, she changed the subject back to one that seemed to fascinate her. Cal Dion. "Are you going to use that dance ticket he bought for you?" she asked.

"Fuck no," JD said, baring her teeth. Even the mention of Dion's name made her heart hammer, and not in a fond way. He was an unwelcome reminder of all the bad things he had dropped on her lately, the crime he was forcing her to commit. A *Valentine's Day dance*, she thought with a snort. The ticket she had folded and forgotten. "And by the way, mention him again and I'll drop you at the next bus stop."

"I could eat him alive," Shiomi murmured.

"That's a disturbing image."

Shiomi hadn't caught JD's glance of disgust. She was looking straight ahead, lost in a daydream. "I was so hoping he was single. Like me."

"He's not."

Shiomi playfully gnashed her teeth, like a carnivore moving in for the kill. "I know he's not single, JD. Just sayin'. I'm newly liberated, which makes me dangerous."

"I bet."

"Bryce and I married right out of high school, and just split up in December. You know what that makes me?"

"Divorced."

"Untamed and hungry, and I'm on the prowl."

On some level JD had to admire Shiomi. Anyone who could mock herself with such panache got points in her book. Still, she didn't want to encourage her with feedback. It occurred to her, though, that this horny chick might sabotage Cal's hope for reconciliation with Kate. Which could be good, in the long run, because they were a lousy match. Kate needed someone with brains to make her happy, and Cal needed someone bright and funny and crazy enough to knock him out of that daze he seemed to be stuck in since the crash.

They had arrived. JD and Shiomi left the car and entered the school, where the scent hit JD like distilled misery. The day was coming to an end and the halls were mostly clear, but there was still the occasional locker door clang to accompany the institutional pong. "Let's make this quick," she said.

"Bad memories, huh?" Shiomi said. "Same here. It's like you step through the doors, and bang, you're fourteen again. Those were the toughest years, right? Bras, periods, the deathly fear of smelling bad."

JD hadn't needed much of a bra in high school. She pointed to a sign. That way to the vice-principal's office.

They were some minutes late, so the teachers would be gathered and waiting already. Before knocking on the door, JD could hear conversation within. A faint scuffling, a spike of laughter. Following her knock there was silence, then somebody called out to enter.

JD and Shiomi entered the office, and introductions were made. Present were two of Hartshorne's teachers, the school counsellor, and the vice-principal. JD informed the group that she was looking for overview info here, anything unreported regarding Hartshorne's behaviour, and access the counsellor's notes if they could be shared, if not specifically, then generally.

Unlikely, she knew, but it was worth a shot.

The science teacher spoke up. Her name was Liz Paton, and she confirmed that Hartshorne was a scary young man, but he'd never done anything in front of her that would get him expelled. "I wish he had," she said. "Done something bad enough to get him out of my classroom for good."

Math teacher Russell Singh said, "And into a life of crime? Now's the time to reach out to them, not push them away, Liz."

Paton mugged a face out of Singh's line of sight. In response to her grimace, the school counsellor, Robbie Clark, mimed a slam dunk. Singh might have sensed the insult, too, as he grew sulky and quiet. *This middle-aged bunch could use some growing up*, JD thought. She said, "So he's your classic bully, always pushing the envelope?"

"Not so much a bully," Clark said. "It's like he's got this … this …"

"Undercurrent," the vice-principal chimed in, her finger up.

"Undercurrent to his personality," Clark said, and his hands shaped what was probably supposed to be a containment vessel. "Suppressed anger."

Paton said, "And there's something wily about him."

"He's had a tough life," Singh said.

"A lot of kids have tough lives and don't turn into grade-A assholes," Paton said.

JD was most interested in what the counsellor had to say. "Whatever he's done, it's bad enough that he was sent to you three times this semester. You can at least tell me the reasons for his visits, right?"

"Attitude, mostly," Clark said. "Lack of effort, falling grades. And the last time he actually came of his own volition, just to talk. He's not so bad once you get chatting with him one-on-one."

Liz Paton snorted. "Try having tits."

"Just to talk," JD pressed the counsellor. "About what?"

"He kind of beat around the bush," Clark said. "But I think he's starting to get it, that after school is real life, and without a good job, it'll be a crappy life, so he'd better pull himself together and start getting good grades, or else he'll end up like his father, unemployed on Hastings."

The vice-principal said, "Okay, Robbie. Confidentiality, remember?"

Clark nodded. "But seriously, I don't think Kyler is as dangerous as he'd like everyone to think."

JD and Shiomi left the meeting not a lot wiser, their interest in Hartshorne waning. They were trotting along, fleeing the smelly halls, when a student flagged them to a stop and asked them breathlessly if they were police.

"How could you tell?" JD asked.

"The janitor was murdered, and you're not teachers, and you're not students, so you must be police. Plus, I saw you drive up. You drive like police."

"Well, we're police," Shiomi said, with a cheerful grin. "You have a hot tip for us? 'Cause we'll take anything we can get."

The three of them stepped into an empty classroom, and the girl turned to them with excited eyes. *A reader of detective novels*, JD thought, *eager to be part of the plot*. "So are you here about the janitor or the missing baby?" the girl said. "'Cause if it's about the baby, I know what happened."

"Uh-huh?" JD said. Far from excited, but open to offers. Many people she had talked to over the years thought they knew what happened, but didn't. And schools were fertile ground for false leads. Rumour mills, pranks. Spite ran rampant in schools, and she had seen the damage it could leave behind. Enough to leave her wary. She had her notebook out and began by getting the girl's full name. Then she asked, "What is it that happened, Megan?"

"So, I heard about this party last month," Megan said. "And I heard that they were both there, and they were talking about something. Tia and Kyler were."

"Tiago Garland? And Kyler who?"

"Kyler Hartshorne. He's in grade eleven."

"Uh-huh," JD said again, more interested now. Two boys from two different cases brought together in one sentence. "Let's hear about it."

Megan delivered the news as if it was a deliciously melting chunk of chocolate in her mouth — not somebody else's nightmare. "They were talking," she said. "Very secretly. About kidnapping the baby. And selling her. And splitting the profit. That's what I heard. I thought I should tell you."

"Who did you hear this from?"

"It's just what the kids are saying."

"What kids?"

Megan's mouth hung open. The pleasure had faded from her eyes. "Well, everyone."

Shiomi said, "Where was this party, Megan?"

"I'm pretty sure it was in Blueridge. But I couldn't tell you where exactly. I wasn't there."

JD asked the young whistle-blower a few more questions, but as expected, whatever half-truth had started the rumour was already corrupted by a few hundred filaments of gossip.

One thing came out of Megan's disclosure, though. Kyler Hartshorne could be a person of interest after all — but on a different case altogether.

* * *

JD returned to the detachment, keeping an ear out for developments in the search for Kyler Hartshorne. By day's end she had his cell number and his home address, but still no answers. He lived with his mother in the suburb of Blueridge, which was also the locale of Megan's rumoured party.

It had been a busy day. While JD and Shiomi tracked down students to question about the party, Doug Paley had driven to Blueridge and asked Kyler's mom, Millie Hartshorne, what she knew about it. She had told Paley she was pretty sure no parties had ever been held there. She didn't know anybody named Tiago or Tia Garland. Didn't even know about the baby gone missing from Riverside Drive. But Millie was also drunk out of her gourd when she said so, Paley had reported to the team. Which left the possibility open, till it could be backed up by further inquiries, that her house was the party house indeed and she simply didn't know it.

The tracking down of students had proven useful. One had told JD and Shiomi she'd heard the same rumour about a kidnap plot, and knew the gossipmonger who had started it, a shithead named Elijah. She then went about smashing Elijah's rumour to bits. The story had sprung out of nothing more than Tia and Kyler being at the same party together. It was just kids saying stuff to bug Tia, who everyone knew was sensitive.

JD was now in the process of tracking down Elijah. Meanwhile, Tia wasn't proving easy to find, either. He wasn't in town at Zach Garland's place, at the Vales' on Riverside Drive, or with his pal Oliver Walsh. And he wasn't answering his cell.

Done for the day, JD packed it in and almost headed home. Instead she drove back out to Riverside

Secondary for a bit of street-level runaround, scanning the shadows from the comfort of her police vehicle on the off-chance of finding one of her persons of interest hanging around. Tia, Kyler, or anybody who might have knowledge of the Blueridge party.

But mostly she was looking for Tia. His absence worried her. He was clearly being bullied by classmates. Accused of things, mocked. She had an idea of what kind of kid he was, from what she'd heard at briefings, seen of his photo, heard in discussions. Cool and collected, he would put on a front, keep his troubles to himself, try not to care. But those troubles would be eating at him all the same.

She knew the feeling.

Unlikely she'd find him, though. Dusk was settling in, a light rain hazing the street lamps. Nobody would be hanging out here now. As she made up her mind to call off her informal search, she caught a glimpse of movement. She braked and reversed. Sure enough, a figure cycled slowly around the corner of the building. She made a U-turn, parked in front of the school, and followed the path of the cyclist on foot.

The figure had dropped his bike and gone to stand at the far side of the basketball court, leaning against the chain-link and staring into the parking lot to more or less where Tasha Aziz had died.

JD had also seen photographs of Kyler Hartshorne, so even from this distance she could tell this slim, dark figure wasn't him. *Tiago?* She approached, calling out a friendly hello.

The young man whirled, blading his body defensively.

"It's okay!" JD's hands went up reassuringly. "Tia? Hiya. We haven't met, but I'm JD, with the North Shore RCMP. Can we talk?"

*Is everything okay?* was about all she wanted to ask, because he looked so sad. And then with any luck, she would go on to ask him about the Blueridge party, maybe get a better bead on Kyler Hartshorne, too.

She never got the chance to do any of it, as the boy sprang for his bike and took off at speed. By the time she reached her car he was gone. Where to? The Vales'?

From behind the wheel she phoned Leith to tell him about seeing Tiago, and how the kid had fled. Leith told her he'd contact Zach Garland, find out what was going on, and give her a call as soon as possible.

Minutes later, he did just that, while JD sat logging the occurrence in her notebook. Leith said, "I just talked to Zach. He's sent Tia and Vivi to stay with the Vales for a few days. Seems everyone involved was agreeable to the plan. Zach is feeling overwhelmed, needs time out, he says. I called Gemma, and she says Tia just got in and went down to his room. He seemed okay to her. Head over there, would you? Try to bring him in."

"He doesn't want to talk to me," JD said. "And I can't force him, can I?"

"Give it a shot. If not, Cal and I will head over there in the morning. That's about all we can do. No chance we'd get a warrant, with what we've got. In the meantime, don't worry. I've told Gemma and Perry to keep an eye on him."

JD did as Leith suggested, drove to the home on Riverside Drive, spoke to Gemma briefly, followed her downstairs, and knocked on Tia's door.

There was no stonewalling. He opened the door promptly. He gave JD a shamefaced smile, and he no longer struck her as sad and lost. The room behind him appeared clean and appropriate, evidence of a grounded soul, a stable mind. Music played and a computer monitor glowed.

"Sorry if I startled you at the school there," JD told him. "You're not in trouble. Why did you run? I'm not that mean looking, am I?"

"Just really don't feel like talking," he said. "I'm sorry."

"Hey, look, I know you don't feel like talking, but how about it? Promise we'll make it fast. Remember Dave Leith? It'll just be me and him, and Zach or Gemma will be there, too."

He shook his head. "I'm really, really tired. And if this is about what they're saying about me, it's not true."

Gemma now backed him up. "He's tired, officer. Leave him alone. We'll bring him down tomorrow, if it's really necessary."

JD thought about Tia losing his baby sister. And about Megan's rumour, and what the rumour had turned out to be. Just meanness. She tilted her head to look into the boy's face, searching for clues. It would be so much better if he spoke of his own volition and cleared up the story about the Blueridge party. But it wasn't in her power to twist his arm, not on the basis of a bunch of high-school innuendo.

Wherever Megan's tip was going to take them in the end — likely nowhere — they still needed to put it to him. But for now what he needed was sleep.

"Okay," she said. "We'll talk first thing in the morning. And like I said, there's nothing to worry about. All right?"

"You bet," Tia said, and gave her a small but reassuring smile. "Good night."

And he shut the door.

# TEN

## FLOWN

*February 11*

NO LONGER SEALED OFF against entry, the Vale home looked normal in the blue light of morning. *Amazing*, Leith thought, *how even tragedy gets shuffled along with time.* Dion had preceded him up the path and knocked on the door, but it was a long moment before Gemma, wrapped in a dressing gown, opened it, un-smiling, and let them in. She asked if they wanted coffee, though Leith could tell she was in no mood to play hostess. She looked rattled, upset, exhausted. More so than the last time he'd spoken to her.

But grief has an ebb and flow, hour by hour, hitting harder some days than others. This was one of those harder days, he could tell, and the question was inane in the circumstances, but he asked it all the same. "Are you all right?"

In answer she indicated the hardwood floor in the dining room as they walked in. Broken glass and spilled juice. "Dropped the jug," she whispered. She sank into one of the straight-backed chairs at the dining room table.

"Hope our knock on the door didn't startle you."

"No, no. Happened just before you arrived."

"Is Perry around?"

"Gone to work."

Dion told Gemma he would help clean up the mess, and Leith said he would go down and talk to Tia, if that was all right. He wouldn't question him till they got to the station, of course. Gemma said that was fine. Leith asked if Vivi was around as well. Gemma nodded. "Still asleep."

Having been through the house before, Leith knew its layout. He knew who slept where on the lower floor. The master bedroom, painted rainforest green by a dousing of natural light filtered through trees, was at the far end of the hall, its door ajar. The closed door still sealed off by police tape was Luna's room. Then there was Vivi's door, with Tia's opposite and offset. Both doors had plaques attached with the children's initials, a *V* and a *T* symbolic proof that they were part of the family, if not the bloodline.

Leith knocked on Tia's door. There was no answer. He called Tia's name, identified himself, asked if it was okay if they talked for a few minutes.

Silence.

He called out that he was going to open the door. When he did, the lights were off and the room was empty. Back in the hallway his heart gave a lurch, as a figure had materialized, side-lit by a wall sconce, and stood staring at him.

"Vivi," he said. "Sorry if I woke you."

"You didn't wake me. I heard something breaking."

"Your mom —" Leith corrected himself, recalling that these kids referred to Gemma and Zach by their names. "Gemma dropped a juice jug. Do you know where your brother is?"

She shook her head.

Back upstairs, with Vivi on his heels, he found Gemma and Dion cleaning up the spilled juice and last bits of glass. "He's not there," Leith told them.

Gemma dunked a wet wad of paper towels in a trash can and stared at him. "Are you sure? Maybe he's in the bathroom."

"We checked." Leith included Vivi in his answer, as the girl had deputized herself in the search for her brother.

"And I tried his phone," Vivi said. "No answer."

"Have either of you seen him this morning?" Dion asked.

Vivi shook her head. Gemma said, "No. I just assumed he was asleep."

She and Leith went out to check the garage. Tia's bicycle remained in place. They returned indoors, worries mounting.

Dion had been out on the balcony, looking down at the river. He returned indoors and shut the sliding door. "Would he have gone for a walk or run?" he asked Gemma. "Is that something he'd do?"

"Not typical. But I guess he must have."

"He likes to sleep in," Vivi offered.

Leith asked Gemma what time she'd gotten up.

"I was up at six thirty with Perry," she said. "He left at ten after seven, his usual time."

"Could Tia have slipped past you before we arrived?"

"No, not at all."

Leith frowned. "Mind calling Perry? Maybe on his way to work he spotted the boy."

She did as he asked, disconnected, and shook her head.

Dion murmured for Leith's ears only, "The river."

Not a suggestion Leith wanted to hear. The wild and rocky river in winter was not the sort of place a young man would go before daybreak and stay for over an hour. Not if he was at peace with the world.

He followed Dion down the steps that ran between this house and the neighbour's, down to the flat section of rock and the swimming hole. No sign of Tiago that Leith could see.

Dion was looking up at the woodsy outcrop from which young people liked to jump in the heat of summer. "I'll check," he said, and went to do so.

\* \* \*

There were two good spots for jumping into the river from up here, Dion knew personally, the lower jump and the higher. He stood on the brink of the lower jump and looked down. He hadn't been here as a kid. Hadn't been to North Van much at all till his career began. All he had known was Vancouver proper. Then he'd flown to Regina for police training, and his world had grown. One of the first things he'd been assigned to do when he began work in North Van was help clamp down on out-of-hand bush parties, in places like this very rock, when the water ran high and the pool lay deep, and in doing so he'd discovered the summertime thrill of cliff jumping.

After putting an end to one of the law-flaunting get-togethers and while gathering up the liquor bottles, Dion and some fellow new recruits had dared each other to return off-duty and take the leap themselves. From this very rock.

The water stirred below, emptying from river to pool, now shallow and rocky. Dion recalled the rush of stepping off, leaving gravity behind. He could hear himself whooping through the fall. He recalled the adrenalin rush, the shock of cold embracing his body, the triumph as he surfaced. He recalled climbing up for a second go.

But that was in the crackling heat of summer; this was a wet February morning, with the temperature down in the single digits and his breath puffing out white before him, and he was not looking for fun, but for a boy who was possibly in serious trouble.

No sign of him here on the lower rock. He returned to the narrow winding path that accessed the higher cliffs and was still climbing when he spotted something incongruous in the bracken near the brink. Blue jeans.

Phone out, he was already hitting the numbers and moving forward. Tiago lay in a rocky nook among moss and grasses. His eyes were closed, his skin blue and waxy. His clothes seemed to have absorbed moisture from the landscape, making him part of it. He looked as if he had sat down some hours ago for a rest, fallen asleep, and sagged sideways.

But Dion knew this kind of stillness. With the dispatcher on the line, he crouched and felt for a pulse. He saw vomit on the boy's face as he did so, a whisky bottle at his side. Tia's skin was cold and there was no detectable pulse. He stood and backed away.

First responders would be here soon. From where he stood, he could see Leith down by the river, waiting. If the news had been good, Dion would have shouted it out. Instead he used his phone.

\* \* \*

The path was narrow, the scene delicate. Being woodsy and damp, every new passage would overwrite the previous. But it couldn't be helped, Leith knew. If there was a chance of pulling Tia back, they would do it. He waited by the river as the first responders forged through the brush with their life-saving gear. They returned depressingly soon, and Leith met the lead responder on the steps to be told the obvious. There was nothing they could do.

Likely an overdose, Leith was told. Maybe alcohol poisoning, as a nearly empty 750 mL bottle of Scotch whisky had been found by the body.

He was still waiting his turn to view the scene. Dion had returned to the house to inform Gemma Vale and deal with the incoming investigators. The house would have to be cleared for the second time this week.

Leith had told Dion to be careful that Vivi didn't hear about her brother's death quite yet; he wanted to break it to her himself. It was an order that he realized could be taken as an insult, and resolved to take Dion aside later and explain. For now he stood by the river and waited for the coroner to confirm death. With nothing better to do, he huddled in his jacket — damn, it was cold down here — and theorized on what had gone so wrong in this household.

Luna disappears. A rumour spreads that Tia has something to do with it, along with a local bad boy. The rumour is all but put to rest as false. Tia is approached by JD and flees. Sometime in the night or early morning he retreats to the riverside with hard liquor and maybe other toxins in his system. Wasn't a far stretch to think Tia was haunted by guilty knowledge. But did he come down here to kill himself, or was it an accidental overdose? Or something in-between.

Coroner Jack Dadd returned from his inspection of the body. He was a heavy man in his late fifties, struggling through the bushes and across the rocks like a crashing bear. Leith watched his approach, looking forward to getting away from this cold trench and thawing out his fingers and toes. But not until he had gone up to look at Tiago himself.

Dadd told him he was sorry to confirm the young man's death. He added that the first responders' assessment was likely correct — overdose. "Strong smell of liquor, and a bottle of Glenmorangie at his side. If that bottle was full when the boy came down here, and he binged ..." Dadd shook his head.

"How much is left in the bottle, Jack?"

Dadd showed how much with thumb and finger. Barely a finger left. "Nice stuff. Pricey, but just as deadly as the worst hooch if you overdo it. Could be a bad mix of that plus something else. Blood work will tell us the rest."

The Forensics unit were going over the scene, taking pictures, looking for any obvious trace evidence that would be destroyed once the body was moved. Leith received the okay to come up, and he climbed the path to see for himself.

Tia's death was going to chase him for a long while. He had spoken to the young man just two days ago, and if he was sharper, he might have caught some warning sign. And last night, instead of dispatching JD to try to convince the boy to talk, he should have gone out himself and strong-armed the kid. Hauled him in, cuffs on, if that's what it took.

Instead he had set his phone aside, flicked off the light, and waited till morning.

He looked down at Tia. Something about his age, fifteen, made him feel weepy. And the setting, the darkness of the forest, the indifference of the flowing waters, the biting cold breeze. He dragged a palm down his face, and apologized to the boy aloud — for all the good it did.

Then he got back to work, trying to make sense of it all.

* * *

Dion was talking to Gemma. They were in her husband's study at the front of the house, with the door closed for privacy, and she was crying again, but in a shocked, dry-eyed way. She wanted Perry, and he was on his way to be with her. Leith had left the home, driving into town to notify Zachary Garland.

Gemma was in Perry's office chair, and Dion was on the leather loveseat facing her. He had taken her statement, all two lines of it. She didn't know what happened, why Tia had gone down to the river with a bottle from Perry's liquor cabinet. And yes, that particular bottle had been almost full. No, she didn't know Tiago to drink alcohol or take things without permission. If she'd had any warning, she would have done something about it.

Dion wasn't sure it was true that she was totally in the dark about Tiago's death. He felt that she wanted to tell him something — it was in the briefest hesitation that came before she shook her head. And the headshake was too vigorous, like the banishing of a thought.

Then there was the broken jug.

Earlier, while cleaning up the broken glass together, he had wondered about it. She had dropped it in the middle of the dining room floor. Why was she carrying a juice jug between fridge and dining room? Unlike in his cramped apartment, the distance between fridge and table in this luxurious home was quite a hike. With only Gemma and Perry having breakfast, wouldn't it be easier to fill two glasses and carry them to the table than go back and forth with a heavy glass pitcher?

He wondered if she had taken the jug to the middle of the floor and dropped it deliberately. There were no obstacles to trip her, no pets to dash between her feet. Was it an act of anger? Was she trying to wake Viviani?

He watched her face, lowered in profile, and saw misery. Probably the broken jug was just a broken jug, and he was looking for complications to a simple situation. Maybe the Vales drank tons of juice in the morning. Maybe they just like the look of fancy glassware on the table. Maybe it slipped because Gemma was tired, depressed, not quite rational, and exhaustion made her clumsy. His own coordination was lousy when he was feeling low.

He was also surprised that the girl hadn't come upstairs at the sound of smashing glass.

Viviani was now downstairs in her bedroom with Niko Shiomi, being insulated from the bad news. They were probably having a chat about something non-threatening till Leith could return. Viviani was probably being asked to show Niko her drawings or talk about her favourite subject in school.

Probably Viviani was guessing that something terrible had happened to Tiago.

*No, not* probably, Dion thought. Viviani had eyes and ears like anyone else. She knew a lot more than she got credit for, he would bet.

Leith hadn't said so, down at the river when dispatching Dion to break the news to Gemma, but he clearly planned to tell Viviani himself. Which made sense. Being a dad, he would know how to speak to kids. Better equipped to soften the blow. Dion had almost pointed out that of all the individuals in this family, the girl seemed to be the strongest. She wouldn't need news about her brother couched in roundabout phrases.

But maybe Leith needed to do the breaking for his own sake, if not hers.

Looking out the window, Dion watched a black car pull into the driveway fairly aggressively. Family? No, it was JD stepping out from behind the wheel of an unmarked sedan. She looked stressed, and it took him a moment to recall why. She was the one who had sent Tiago running.

He excused himself to Gemma and went to meet JD at the door. She hadn't been called out, wasn't needed, shouldn't be here, and he told her so. She begged to differ, so he took her arm and guided her away from the house, back to the side of her car.

"So I killed him, did I?" she said, when he unhanded her. "I scared the shit out of him, and he killed himself. Right?"

"Hell no," he said. "Whatever scared him, it went a whole lot deeper than you wanting to talk."

She continued to look shaky, even tearful. He began to worry. The only time he'd seen tears spring to JD's eyes was a few years back when her fuck-off finger had been caught in a slammed door. He considered hugging her, but instead gave her a symbolic embrace, fists crossed over his chest, catching her eyes, making sure she got it.

She got it but didn't seem to want it. "Why do I stay in this job?" she hissed. "It's corrosive. Half the time you can't separate what you've done right from what you've done wrong."

"Someone's got to do it."

She turned away from him and his weak clichés. She looked at the sky, and the sky seemed to comfort her. Dion knew what was going through her mind, the threat she made whenever the job depressed her. "You're not running off to fly cargo planes up north."

As she faced him again, he knew that in his attempt to be supportive he'd given himself away. He was a closet wimp, pathologically needy, afraid of change, desperate for stability. He had just let JD know how important she was to him. Now he feared she would misread that dependency as something romantic. Which it wasn't.

"Why would you care if I ran off to be a bush pilot?" she asked. "The gang's all here. Doug, Jim, Sean. And you've got Kate. What more does a guy need?"

At least he had distracted her from her feelings of guilt, but he had also distracted himself, and JD was watching him. In a low voice she said, "You better tell me. What kind of big trouble are you in, Cal? Don't say *nothing*, because something's up, and I know more than you think."

He wasn't surprised that she knew more than he thought. The kind of trouble he was in was impossible to contain, like acid leaking from a punctured barrel. He changed the subject. "What matters right now is Kyler Hartshorne. He's got footprints all over both files, and he's missing. We'd better get cracking and find this guy."

But by evening Hartshorne remained unfound. He had either left town or gone into hiding. There was a third possibility that nobody on the team would say aloud — was he another casualty of whatever was going on along Riverside Drive?

# ELEVEN

# ANIMALS

WITH TIAGO'S DEATH and Kyler Hartshorne's disappearance, all other avenues needed to be explored, and fast. JD's task was to track down and question an amorphous set of party animals about Megan's bit of gossip. Elijah had denied he'd spread a false rumour, and said he'd heard it from someone who'd heard it firsthand. He refused to say who that someone was, and unfortunately he and his friends and everyone else getting wind of the investigation were closing ranks. Nobody knew anything, and everybody pointed fingers at everybody else. The alleged source of the gossipmongering had become just another faceless ripple in a pond of lies.

With a portrait snapshot of Tasha Aziz in her wallet to renew her inspiration whenever it flagged, JD drove back to Riverside Secondary to talk to the counsellor, Robbie Clark. She figured he should best know the pulse of the school population, and might be able to tell her who did what and who was who.

She found Clark sitting in his small office looking dumbfounded. He gaped up at her as she stepped in. "I just heard about Tiago Garland," he said. "How horrible. How horribly, horribly horrible."

JD couldn't argue with the sentiment. She was still feeling the effects of her part in Tia's death — kind of a fluish funk — and being here in this puny office didn't help. She was something of a claustrophobe to start with, so this was not a happy place for her, a cubicle with its tiny window and cheery montage smothering one cinder-block wall, photographs of kids achieving things, inspirational quotes probably pulled off the internet, somebody's drawing of a cat, all overlaid with that distinctive odour of school.

She nodded bleakly. "Yes, I know."

Clark offered her the visitor's chair, and when she declined, he stood, maybe to keep them eye to eye. And they were so, almost literally, as she was tall for a woman and he was short for a man. He was clean-shaven, rotund, at least fifteen years older than JD, and his shirt had cowboy flourishes. Totally not her type, and the circumstances and setting were appalling, yet she found him … magnetic. Why? What attracts people to people? Some configuration of body and spirit that's hard to pin down.

She went so far as to wonder, *Are you single?* Nothing more than an inside joke, but she glanced at his left hand anyway, just checking. Nope, no wedding ring. This hunk was up for grabs.

"What happened?" he was asking, fingertips pressed to desktop as if to keep himself upright. "They're not releasing the details. The students are going to want to know."

"Sorry. As soon as possible we'll meet with the principal and tell her all we can." She went on to say what she was looking for, any info he had picked up in his dealings with students, even if it was just vibes. Clark disappointed her with a shake of his head. "Occasionally kids come to me voluntarily for advice. Unfortunately they rarely report that they're about to get into something risky. Wouldn't it be a perfect world if they did?"

"This party I'm talking about isn't necessarily about risk," JD said. "I'm just hoping those who were present can tell me about an argument that was overheard between Tiago and Kyler Hartshorne. Tia's sister Luna Mae's name was mentioned. She's the little Riverside girl who's gone missing."

Of course Clark knew who Luna Mae was. He grimaced his regret that he couldn't help any further. "Have you talked to Kyler?"

"We can't seem to locate him."

Clark blinked at her as the news sank in. "What's happening around here? First Tasha, then the kidnap, Tiago, and now Kyler, too?"

"Almost feels like a domino effect, doesn't it?"

Clark considered the analogy with a nod. He offered to walk the halls, talk to students, see if he could get a bead on this January party, and whatever he found out he would pass on to her right away.

"Thanks," she said, handing him her card. "That'll be awfully helpful."

As she left his office, she realized her curiosity about whether he was single was actually not completely LOL. Now, how sad was that?

\* \* \*

Outside the lobby of the North Vancouver RCMP detachment was a small outdoor plaza with benches and trees. The plaza was deserted at this time of year, February being chilly and often wet. No rain was falling this afternoon, so Dion sat on one of the benches, eating a sandwich and thinking about rings. Like the one Looch had given Brooke a few years ago, a symbol of his love. Sterling silver and engraved like that famous ring from the movie about hobbits. Magic words of foreverness forged in metal.

Why couldn't he be inventive like that?

He glanced over to see JD approaching, also with lunch. The rain had let up for a bit and the day wasn't bad, actually. They sat together and watched another high-rise going up, blocking the view, hemming the detachment in even further. She told him about her odd attraction to Robbie Clark. She said, "It's just fuckin' weird, 'cause I'm not Niko Shiomi, who wonders if every guy she looks at is single — which, by the way, she was hoping you were, *cutie pie*."

"I noticed," he said.

JD shrugged. "Maybe it's this Valentine's Day bullshit coming up, everybody going around holding hands and cooing like turtledoves. Maybe I want to give the whole togetherness thing another try. Or maybe I just want somebody to give me chocolate, too. But *him*? If you stuck his photo in front of me and asked, I would say *never in a million years*. And he'd say the same about me, except he'd say it as he ran as fast as his little legs could take him."

"I don't know where you get your negative self-image, but it's not helping any," Dion said. He told her about Oliver Walsh and his determination to be a nerd, and how that wasn't helpful in building friendships, or self-esteem, or anything else.

"Yeah, and that's not me," JD said. "I know I'm gorgeous, smart, and successful, and it's just that nobody else gets it. I don't care, though, and I value my singleness. But stay on topic. What do I see in this Clark guy? He's got the shirt, the pointy boots. All he needs is a big hat and a twang. Which would be great if we were in Claresholm, Alberta. But we're here on the raincoast. In the city. The nearest cow is miles away."

"Partly it's chemistry," Dion told her. "But mostly it's the moment. That's why you've got to be careful not to make the wrong move. You were feeling bad about Tiago, and so was Clark, and you were wishing you didn't have to go through it alone. Yet you're such a loner that you're no good at reading your own insecurities, and you mistook it for lust."

JD put down her sandwich to let out one of her abrupt, harsh laughs, sending a flock of small birds resting nearby into the sky.

Dion shrugged.

"And when did you get your shrink ticket?" JD said, still laughing. But her phone rang, and she looked at the caller ID and said, "Speak of the devil."

Dion watched her chat with the counsellor. There was nothing warm or seductive in her tone, and he doubted anything would come of her so-called attraction. Whatever she was hearing sounded positive, though, and she had her notebook out to scribble down the information. She said, "Thank you, sir. Much appreciated," and disconnected.

"My cowboy came through," she said. "Two names, first and last, with telephone numbers, of kids who might have some insight into the most awesome house parties held roundabouts lately."

"You didn't ask what he's doing Friday night."

They jostled each other. Then JD said, "Okay, damn you, what's the matter?"

He stared at her. "What? Nothing!"

"Something's the matter."

"No, it's not."

"You look green."

"I'm not," he said.

But he was. He had a diamond ring in his pocket, and in a few days he was going to ask Kate to marry him, and he had a feeling she would say yes, and they would live happily ever after. So why was his confidence drifting out of sight, bit by bit, like a swimmer caught in a riptide?

He showed JD the ring.

She studied its not-so-expensive facets and nodded knowingly. "Cold feet."

"It's nothing to do with cold feet," he said, re-pocketing the ring in its small, coffin-like blue velvet box.

"Sure it is. Don't worry. It'll pass."

He finished his sandwich, thinking it over. "I talked to Oliver Walsh again," he said. "I told him about Tiago, and he took it hard. But now that Tiago's gone, I wanted to see if he had anything more to tell me. He did. It's not much, but he said Tia gave him a hundred bucks, in twenties, the day before he died. Just out of the blue, no explanation except it was to pay off an old debt. Oliver couldn't remember any old debt, and he's not the type to forget, so he thought it was weird. Also, Tia wouldn't tell him where he got the money. He usually had ten bucks at most in his wallet."

"So, an unexpected gift. Anything else?"

"That's where it gets weirder. After Tia gave him the cash he did this." Dion forked two fingers at his own eyes, then pointed one straight at JD's face.

"I'm watching you," JD said. "So Tia's watching Oliver?"

"No. How Oliver took it was that Tia was demonstrating something. Just wouldn't say what."

"Sounds like some serious shit going on."

"But then Tia laughed, Oliver says. He described the laugh as ironic. He thinks all this weirdness has something to do with Kyler, but couldn't say what, and didn't go so far as blaming him for Tia's death. But he did say he was afraid Kyler's corrupting Tia."

"Sounds kind of nerdy."

"Being a nerd is his life's mission."

They stood, crumpling sandwich wrappings, and headed indoors. Dion went to meet with Leith about Kyler Hartshorne's ongoing no-show, while JD went to make arrangements to interview some party animals.

\* \* \*

JD had arranged interviews with the two house-party witnesses Robbie Clark had located for her. The first to arrive at the detachment was Dahlia. She was a talker.

She didn't seem to know about either Tia's death or Kyler's disappearance, and asked none of the usual questions, but rambled on as if interviews at police stations were as common as Starbucks in her life. She confirmed that she had been at the house party in mid-January. Whereabouts was it? She got on her phone and did some texting, and within minutes was able to give JD an address. Dahlia explained that the house belonged to Big Dom, who was away in Vegas, and that his son, Little Dom, who was actually a lot bigger than Big Dom, threw the party to celebrate having the place to himself for a week.

"Little Dom's proviso was that the music not bother the neighbours," Dahlia said. "And that everyone had to stay and clean up afterward."

"Were his provisos followed?" JD asked.

"Not at all. The house was quite literally trashed and we all fled to the four corners of the earth not to have to help clean up."

"Was there liquor?"

"Yes, there was liquor, because there were a few adults there. Well, people over the age of nineteen. But Dom, he's really sticky about rules, and he carded everyone to make sure nobody underage drank."

JD looked at her skeptically. "And that totally worked, of course."

"Okay, no, but it kept it to a safe level, anyway. I had, like, one shooter."

Little Dom was a worldly guy, Dahlia went on to tell JD. He had a ton of friends, both in school and out, and there were all kinds of amazing people at the party. She only knew a few to talk to, like Kyler and Rahim and a couple more names JD wrote down. Tia, she said, was a grade lower than her, and she only knew him to see him. And yes, there had been some kind of upset between Tia and Kyler at one point.

"What was the fight about, d'you know?"

"Well, I opened my ears when I heard Kyler yelling *Looney Tunes* in the poor guy's face. Like, what's that all about? I think Tia was chatting up this girl he liked, telling her about Luna, his cute little sister. You know, maybe he was trying to be the sensitive new-age kind of guy who cares about kids, because that can be very attractive to a girl, but I think it's more that he's a sensitive new-age kind of guy who cares about kids, full stop. Kyler, on the other hand, has a hate on for anybody who's nicer and better looking than him, so he butted in and started calling Tia *Tia Maria* and his sister *Looney Tunes*, and Tia called him a prick, and then they started quite literally trying to kill each other. But Little Dom — did I mention he's very big? — stepped in and told them to behave, and they did. And later I saw them by the back door talking quite friendly-like to each other — Tia and Kyler, I mean — so it couldn't actually have been much of a fight."

"And do you know what their friendlier conversation was about?"

Dahlia's brows went up. "You know, I think it was also about babies. Isn't that weird? Can't be more specific, sorry."

"Anybody else involved in that conversation?"

She nodded. "A very stoned couple with outrageously British accents, Sid and Nancy all the way. Older, definitely not from school. Dom would probably know who they are."

JD asked for Little Dom's contact info to add to her growing line of inquiry, thanked Dahlia, and welcomed in her next interviewee, Rahim.

His story wasn't the same as Dahlia's, but stories never were. The party house had been messy but never *trashed*, Rahim insisted, literally or otherwise. He and some others had returned the next day to make it spic and span, no worries.

Rahim had not noticed the British couple Dahlia had spoken of, but he did think he saw a friendly push and shove between Kyler and a smaller kid who matched the description of Tiago Garland. No, they weren't trying to kill each other. He didn't know what they were chatting about, and later they were on the back porch smoking a doobie and talking kind of seriously.

"Where did the doobie come from?" JD asked.

Rahim grew cagey and said he didn't know.

JD asked him if he knew where Kyler might be or how he could be contacted, since he wasn't at home and wasn't picking up his phone. Rahim had a suggestion. Kyler had been bragging about a girlfriend lately, Jody, who lived in West Van. He remembered her last name because it was hilarious. Groper. Jody Groper. Apparently a cougar.

When Rahim was gone JD phoned Leith to tell him about the West Van cougar, a solid lead that might just finally snare Kyler Hartshorne.

# TWELVE

# WINDFALL

JODY GROPER WAS ABOUT twenty-five, hardly what Leith would consider a cougar. But he supposed it was all relative.

Already she had two little kids. *Two.*

He sat in the dining room of her apartment, listening to the squalling of little lungs and the television babble of cartoons. The woman had asked him for five minutes so she could change the younger's diaper and get the other dressed. The five minutes gave Leith time to think about his discussion with Alison this morning. Alison had grown up with several brothers and sisters, and wanted the same experience for their three-year-old, Izzy. She had a feeling time was running out.

She was wrong about that, in Leith's opinion. They were in their midforties, and as far as he was concerned, time *had* run out. Izzy would be their only child, and they should be happy with that. But this morning she'd asked about it again. One more, then, she'd said, bargaining for a life.

This morning Leith had given in and agreed. Of course they'd try for one more. He hadn't reminded her of the two times she'd lost track of Izzy, and hadn't told her, *Only if you promise to be more vigilant.* He hadn't said any of it, and he and Ali had gotten to work at it right away, which had made him late for work.

Even now the miracle could be happening in Alison's body, he realized. Izzy could soon have a little brother or sister. He sat at Jody's dining room table and listened to the battle down the hall, imagining the joy a second child would bring to him, and trying to smile.

Jody was back with one clean and happy baby on her hip, while another ripped about the small apartment with a toy airplane. "So what can I do for you?" she asked. She sat down, bouncing baby on knee.

Leith told her he was looking for Kyler Hartshorne, and that he understood she and Kyler were close. Had Kyler been here recently?

"Yes," she said. "He left this morning, about ten. Why? What did he do?"

"Nothing that we know of. He's a possible witness, though. Do you know where he went?"

"Nope."

"Or when he's coming back?"

"Nope."

Short interview. Leith said, "He's not answering his phone."

"He turned it off last night."

"Why?"

"I don't know. Didn't want to be bothered. We were having a hoopla."

An eighteen-year-old and a cougar. Leith dearly hoped they'd used birth control, and something a little more reliable than the good old rhythm method. He said, "Maybe he forgot to turn it back on after. The phone."

"Maybe," Jody said. "And don't worry. There's no way in hell I'm going for a third."

She had read his mind, he supposed. "So, no idea where he's gone today?"

She gestured at the window. The world outside was wet and grey. She said, "With all that B.C. bud in his pocket and the inheritance from Uncle Bob, I'd say he's gone to do some serious shopping. Can never have too many black hoodies with skulls and wings all over 'em, can we?"

*Inheritance?* Leith kept the surprise off his face. To keep the fountain flowing, it sometimes helped to appear to know more than you did. "Quite a windfall, was it?"

"Quite. And the bud is personal-use possession only, by the way."

"And the inheritance, he said it was from Uncle Bob?" With the trick of inflection Leith had let her know that he considered that a bald-faced lie. The shrug she gave him said she agreed.

"Do you know the grand total?" he asked.

"Nope."

"Was it money in the bank or cash in hand?"

"Don't know."

"Why didn't he take you on this shopping spree, if that's where he went?"

She shook her head. "Babies and malls don't mix."

"With his windfall, he could have got you a babysitter."

"She's out of town."

"Pick up the paper, find another," Leith said, not sure why he was pressing this tangent.

As if she, too, was waiting for the answer, the baby on Jody's knee turned to look up at her mother's face. Jody returned the gaze, transmitting something to the child, and it was something to do with warmth and security and faith. Then she looked at Leith and said, "I'd never leave my kids with a stranger from the classifieds."

He was pleased enough to smile.

She went on, "And as for Kyler, you prob'ly have the wrong impression about us. We're not a couple. Just the occasional bouncy bed party, and then I'm happy to see the back of his saggy jeans in the morning. Like, go away. It was nice, though, that he sprang for the goodies this time, instead of mooching off me."

She flapped a hand at what she might have seen as disapproval on Leith's face at the word *goodies*. "KFC and beer," she said. "Budweiser. I had maybe two beers and one drag on his joint. And way too much fried chicken. Getting too old for the wild life."

*Too old for eighteen-year-olds, anyway*, Leith thought.

The kid with the plane whirred into his mom's lap, seeking nothing but a touch, a pat on the head to power him through, then buzzed off again.

"You think Kyler's heading back this way after the mall?" Leith said.

"Nope. I think he's heading for the Mexican border."

Was that fact or metaphor? "What makes you say that?"

"Because that's all he talks about, getting rich and taking off to Mexico. Get away from trouble, live in the sun."

*God*, Leith thought. Monitoring airports and border crossings was expensive, and the budget only stretched so far. He said, "You know about Luna Garland?"

"The little girl who went missing, yeah."

"Did Kyler mention her to you at all?"

A change had come over Jody. A tensing. Mention of the missing Luna had upset her. "No," she said. "Why?"

"It's possible he knows something. Are you thinking he knows something?"

She shook her head. "Is that what you're thinking?"

"Not sure. We'd very much like to talk to him, though. As soon as possible."

As he left, he gave her some stern last words. With no proof and no authority he couldn't force her to do anything, but he *could* sound damned serious. He told her that if Kyler showed up she shouldn't discuss this visit with him; she should just get in touch, right away. And by no means should she leave with Kyler, and more so — and he couldn't stress this enough — she should not leave her children with him. Not for a moment.

"Of course not," she said, and he knew she had gotten the message loud and clear. He could see it in her eyes. It was dawning on her that she might have been rubbing up against the very flanks of evil. "He's not stepping in this door again, promise," she said. "But if he comes by I'll call you, the second he walks away."

"Thanks." As he left, Leith looked back once more at her two little kids. *Two.*

\* \* \*

Little Dom was big. He was a recent grad of Riverside Secondary, twenty years old, six foot three or four, JD estimated, and with the looming presence of an airplane hangar. But soft-spoken. His father, who had opened the door to JD and called out to summon his son, was a pint-sized Italian Canadian with a bullhorn voice. Go figure.

JD and Little Dom sat in the privacy of a TV den, and Little Dom's eyes were huge and troubled as he waited for JD to explain why she'd tracked him down like this. His mass relaxed when he realized he wasn't in some kind of major trouble for throwing the party, and when he learned it was about the missing Luna Mae Garland, he became about the most helpful witness JD had ever had the pleasure of interviewing.

"Yeah," he said. "I don't know these guys too well, but this is what I know. This kid Kyler started beating up on this kid Tia, for some reason, and Tia's half his size, right? That's just wrong. I broke it up, and then kept an eye on them, and they seemed okay. I even saw 'em chatting and laughing it up about half an hour later, which is good. You know, parties are about having fun. I don't get it when people start getting pissy for no reason."

JD nodded in agreement. How much easier life would be if people didn't get pissy so often over nothing. She asked where he'd seen the two chatting and laughing.

"Out back, which is the only place we're allowed to smoke."

"Can you show me where?"

Little Dom gave her a tour that ended on a generous covered deck overlooking a small backyard with a dormant vegetable garden.

JD asked him if Tia and Kyler had been alone out here that night.

He shook his head. "The party crashers," he said. "Those two British people, a man and a woman. I saw 'em out here, and I went out and said, 'Sorry, do I know you folks?' And the guy said he was a friend of Kyler's, and his name was Sid, and his girlfriend was Nancy, but I think he was joking about their names. If he was, I didn't get it. Like I said, they sounded British to me."

"British," JD said. "Outrageously British?"

"I don't know what's outrageous, but definitely British."

"Party crashers, you say."

"Must be. I have no idea who they were, and I don't go around inviting strangers to my parents' house, so I told them they had to leave, and Kyler, too. And they did, shortly after that, all of 'em. A bottle of tequila also went missing, by the way."

"Did Tia leave with Kyler and the Brits?"

"No, he hung out a while, I think. I lost track of him after that."

"When you stepped out to confront them, did you hear what these four were talking about?"

"I did," Little Dom said, smiling, pleased to be helpful.

"What did you hear?" JD asked, and for some reason she imagined being swept up in Little Dom's arms and tossed on a bed to be smothered beneath his gigantic body. What was the matter with her? She was not only acting like Niko Shiomi, but outdoing her. First the middle-aged counsellor and now this huge, dark-eyed youth. Must be his smile, which was warm and firm. Like a good shoulder massage.

But the smile was gone in a wink as Little Dom sat back, suddenly indignant. "They were talking about buying and selling drugs. Would you believe it? In my parents' house. That's when I told 'em to get lost, all of 'em, and they took off after that. With the tequila."

JD was disappointed. Drugs and petty theft. She said, "Can you remember any of their conversation?"

"No, I can't," Dom said. "Except I'm pretty sure Kyler said something about ten thousand dollars. So this wasn't nickel-and-dime dealing."

"Did you hear them actually talking about drugs? Anything specific?"

"Nothing specific. I had enough on my mind, making sure everybody was having a good time and not messing up the place too much, eh? My mama, she's fussy."

JD sat for a minute mulling over his story. For all she had discovered, she hadn't discovered what mattered. What she needed was someone who had been privy to this promising new lead — Tiago, Kyler, and the mystery couple out on the back deck talking about babies and big money.

"Oh, and Caroline Brownstein," Little Dom said, and indicated a large planter at the bottom of the stairs. "She was puking into mama's chives, so I had to help her out down there."

"Sorry, what was that?" JD said.

\* \* \*

Caroline Brownstein was a small, terse college student. She told JD she'd been trying not to hurl her last meal all over Little Dom's backyard when she'd overheard a conversation between four people up on the covered deck at her back. She didn't know them, and so she didn't really pay them a whole lot of attention.

"All I know is those two Brits wanted to buy something," she said. "And the big ugly dude with the buzz cut …"

JD nodded. That would be Hartshorne, no doubt.

"… said he could get one for them for ten thousand dollars, and they were like, okay, and the skinny little dude …"

Tiago Garland.

"… was like, *sure sure,* and I don't know much after that. Oh, they said they'd need a passport, too, and the big dude said that would be an extra five. I kind of thought they were joking, but …" She paused as she seemed to hear her own words, and looked at JD with horror. "Oh wow. Don't tell me …"

"Don't tell you what, Caroline?"

"They were *wheeling and dealing that kidnapped baby*? Is that what this is all about?"

"No, that's not what this is all about," JD said. "There are a lot of holes in this case, and I'm just looking to fill 'em. That's all."

But of course it wasn't all. She didn't say so to Caroline, not wanting the news to go viral. With the girl's input, though, it was fairly good tentative guesswork. The best they had so far.

# THIRTEEN

## HOPE

LEITH WAS FRUSTRATED. JD's inquiries had been fruitful, and he now knew where the baby-bartering chatter had sprung from. But even after every party-goer had been tracked down and questioned, no witness could say definitively that there was something real behind the rumour. Nor could anybody provide the names of the British party crashers. One young person thought the van parked down the road some distance could have belonged to them. It stood out in this good neighbour-hood because it was junky. Unfortunately, that person had not taken down the van's tag number.

Somebody else had seen a couple walking away from the party toward the van, carrying a bottle of some-thing, and in every other way matching the description of the British couple. But the accent wasn't outrageously British. It sounded, well, Canadian.

But the clouds were at least starting to part, and the news could be good. If this was a case of underground baby-buying by a childless couple, it gave Luna Mae a greater chance of survival.

Better than if she'd been snatched by a random sicko, anyway.

In a late afternoon meeting Leith shared the theory with the team. Though the pile of statements before him was high, his theory was short. A couple wanted to buy a baby, and Kyler Hartshorne had conspired with Tia Garland to get them one. Tia, who had his own reasons for wishing Luna out of his life, had left the sliding door downstairs unlocked, and Kyler had slipped in and taken Luna. Kyler got paid ten thousand dollars — the so-called Uncle Bob inheritance — and had skipped the country. Tia got a share, and sick with remorse, he either deliberately or accidentally shuffled off this mortal coil.

Nobody on the team had any strong objection to the theory, though Leith noticed Dion looking less than enthused.

Dion's lack of enthusiasm rained on Leith's picnic somewhat, but he put aside his doubts and went on planning the next step. A more concerted hunt for both Kyler and the couple in the van would now get underway. Meanwhile he would take Dion on a new round of talks with Luna's estranged parents, Zachary Garland and Gemma Vale. Time to see if the new information twigged anything in their minds.

"We don't want to get their hopes up," he told Dion, when they were driving southbound, Dion at the wheel. "And we don't want them blaming Tia. But we have to see what their take is."

Dion agreed, and went on to tell Leith about his doubts regarding the baby-buying theory. It wasn't complicated. He had observed Tia in the hot seat last week, and simply didn't think he was the type. "I don't see him taking part in anything like it," he said. "Kidnapping his own baby sister." He had brought the car to a full stop for a traffic light, windshield wipers on intermittent, a river of cars ahead, red tail lights glowing in the late afternoon murk. "For what? A few dollars?"

*Only technically a sister*, Leith thought. A noisy baby, a source of trouble for Zach. Maybe she was more of an irritant for Tia. A presence he'd rather see gone. "How else do you explain the cash Tia was throwing about?"

"Hundred bucks is hardly cash."

"For him it was large," Leith said.

"That's Oliver's opinion. Maybe it was everything Tia had in his piggy bank, who knows? I can't see a smart kid like Tia breaking the law for money."

"The motive might be deeper. He resented Luna. She was noisy. He admitted that. At the same time, she got all the attention from Gemma and Zachary. He saw himself as inferior, the adopted son, where Luna Mae was blood. Or maybe switch it around; he thought he was saving her from Zach and Gemma. He thought the custody battle was tearing her apart."

Even in profile, Dion's contempt for the last suggestion showed. "And what, deliver her to a sketchy couple he'd just met at a party? No chance."

"Maybe Hartshorne had something on him. Blackmailed him into it."

"Or," Dion said, "maybe in Tia's mind the talk with the British couple at the party was a joke, but it wasn't. Maybe Kyler carried on negotiations with the two privately. He went to the Vale house, found the door open, and took Luna. Tia felt guilty afterward, because he hadn't taken the joke seriously. He should have spoken up sooner. But then it was too late to say anything, without implicating himself."

The light turned green and all the tail lights began to move. "Except no," he said, countering his own thoughts with a frown. "He'd have weighed the trouble he'd be in against the importance of finding Luna. He'd have told us on the spot. Keeping it to himself and drinking himself to death makes no sense. No sense at all."

*There you go again,* Leith thought. *Leapfrogging on your own conclusions.* Dion's conclusion in this case was the innocence of a fifteen-year-old, as if people of that age were incapable of criminal acts. "Even good kids can get themselves in unbelievable fixes, Cal," he said. "They jump off cliffs, for Pete's sake."

Dion said nothing.

They arrived at the Vale home, and Leith realized that from day one of the investigation till now, in some way Gemma Vale had filled out instead of shrunk with misery. She'd become rounder, rosier. But he wasn't surprised. How people dealt with tragedy could be unpredictable. Some lose their appetite; others eat.

The four of them took seats at the dining room table. Perry Vale served coffee and sat down next to his wife. Leith asked how Viviani was coping, and it was Perry who answered. "Not bad, actually. I think the grief counselling is helping. But she's always been a quiet little girl, kind of hard to read. We're worried, aren't we, Gem? That Vivi's talking to him, to Tia."

Gemma's nod struck Leith as distracted, not quite here. She seemed too busy fiddling with her rings to listen.

"At least we hear her kind of murmuring, in her room," Perry explained. "Or did, when she was with us. She's back with Zachary now. I'm not sure I'm comfortable with that either, but we don't have any say in the matter. In a perfect world, Gem wants full custody of Vivi. But she knows that's not going to happen."

Leith studied Gemma's face, which remained focused on her rings, then Perry's, which looked both present and haggard. "You're not comfortable with Vivi living with Zachary?"

Perry looked at Gemma. Gemma shook her head slightly, her advice to say nothing. He looked at Leith and said it anyway. "Until now Vivi had Tiago. Now she's alone with Zach. Gem was just never completely comfortable with how Zach is with Vivi. A little too ... what?" he asked Gemma.

"Touchy feely," Gemma admitted.

"So we're just not comfortable with it," Perry went on. "But Zach's really her legal guardian, more so than Gem. Gem's realizing she shouldn't jump to conclusions. At least for the time being, till things settle. But she loves Vivi like she's her own daughter. As do I. When the shock's worn off, we're going to be discussing a new visitation schedule. Week on, week off, hopefully."

Gemma had taken to cupping her face in one palm and sighing. She leaned sideways against Perry's shoulder, and his protective arm went around her, tight.

Leith asked Gemma if she had any evidence that Viviani was in danger with Zach. If she knew something, it was important to tell him.

She shook her head. "Of course not. She'll be fine with him. Zach's got a live-in girlfriend. They call that common-law, right?"

*Which proves what?* Leith thought. Nothing, just like Gemma being married to Perry proved nothing. The risk was everywhere — in the nicest of families, in church assemblies, in the dead of night or the light of day. All it took was a few moments of privacy and a bit of grooming. In his role as cop it sometimes seemed the hazard was always in the red zone when it came to children.

But he was here to share the team's theory and seek feedback. As he'd said to Dion, they mustn't raise Gemma's hopes that Luna Mae was possibly still alive, possibly sold to a childless couple in a van who were looking for an easy adoption, which in the best-case scenario could mean that the child would soon be located and brought home.

Not a great ray of hope, in his mind, and he downplayed the news as he laid it out to the Vales, where the investigation had taken them and the new questions it had opened up about Tiago's involvement. He noticed as he spoke that Gemma was staring across the table at him, her eyes growing wider with every word.

As he finished she gasped. "Wh …?"

And he watched her hopes climb faster than a monkey to the treetops.

\* \* \*

First out the door and now waiting in the SUV, Dion drummed his fingers on the steering wheel and watched Leith having a few last words with the Vales at their front door. He used the time to corral his thoughts. Strange thoughts, especially toward the end of the meeting when he'd observed the Vales soaking up the news of a possibly promising lead: Luna Mae might have been kidnapped and delivered to an unknown couple, not sucked into the scarier unknown.

Something about their reaction, though. There was a word he was looking for to describe it. What had he seen on Gemma's face as she listened, and also on Perry's? Confusion, then disbelief, then hope.. Which all made perfect sense. Yet …

Leith slid into the passenger seat and said darkly, "So that went well."

Dion backed the vehicle out of the driveway. Once on the road, heading to their next stop, Zachary Garland's apartment on Third, the word he'd been looking for popped into his mind. "It's the *ratio*," he exclaimed.

"What?"

"Gemma's reaction to what you said. Ratio-wise, it was off. The news took her off guard, but it didn't make her happy."

"Didn't make her happy? Course it did. She was ecstatic."

"Not as much as she should have been. I couldn't keep an eye on Perry so much, but with Gemma, it's like she knew what you were going to say before you said it." Seeing Leith wasn't convinced, he took it further. "I think she's involved in the abduction. We're getting closer, and that's making her sweat."

"I really don't think so, Cal," Leith said, with the patience of a Sunday-school teacher. "I know you're a hell of a perceptive guy, more so than me, but come on. There was nothing fake about her reaction. She's been through the wringer this week. And you noticed I told her not to get her hopes up. What you saw was her trying. And failing, by the way. Her hopes shot up there so fast I thought she'd hit the ceiling. So I don't know where you're getting this —"

"Hard to say, though, isn't it, with her hands all over her face? First she claps them over her mouth, then her cheeks, then her eyes. It's like she was deliberately hiding from me."

"Those are universal human reactions," Leith exclaimed. His patience had been short-lived and he was back to his irritable self, gesturing to heaven. "Haven't you ever clapped your hands to your face —"

"Not when I'm talking to two cops about a serious crime."

Leith rolled his eyes. Dion didn't see the eye roll, but could sense it, and it stung. He began to doubt his own epiphany, and already wished he could unsay what he'd said. Had he misread the woman's universal human reactions? Probably.

*I'm not a universal human, that's why*, he thought, and was flooded with self-pity. The car crash had changed the chemistry of his brain, made him weird, threw him out of alignment. Also, it had given him some contagious dark powers, such that anybody who got close to him either died or turned rotten. He should come with a package warning.

Should he advise Kate, as he gave her the ring? *With this ring I thee destroy.*

He grit his teeth. No. As long as he kept her close, she would be his cure. Already being back with her, he could feel himself getting more grounded. Day by day. Just had to stay positive and work at fixing the mess he'd made of his life.

For now, how could he fix what he'd just told Leith, stating that Gemma Vale was not a grieving mother but a liar and criminal? He couldn't. All he could do going forward was not repeat the mistake of speaking his mind without thinking it through. Better yet, not speak his mind at all. Should just shut up and follow the leader for the rest of his life.

He steered their car down Forbes, turned at Third, and found a parking spot half a block from Garland's low-rise. As they walked back to the building, Leith led a fairly one-sided conversation about the case, discussing Perry Vale's worries about Viviani living with Garland. "Might be useful to see Zach and Vivi's living arrangements, anyway."

Dion followed him into the building and up the stairs to Garland's floor. "How so?"

"Just get a feel for the father-daughter dynamics. I'm not saying there's anything to the Vales' concerns, but, you know."

No longer speaking his mind about anything, Dion only shrugged. But when the door opened and he was invited inside, he looked around the place with interest. It was a fairly large, sprawling pad. Typical family mess evident everywhere. The walls, furniture, the ambiance wouldn't betray any father-daughter secrets, but Leith was right, the interaction between the two might.

Garland was talking to Leith, excusing the mess and calling Vivi out from her room to say hi to their guests. Vivi came to stand at Garland's side, and Dion believed the Vales were wrong to be concerned. Observation and intuition told him, almost to a certainty, that this father and daughter were comfortable with each other, that there was no issue between them.

Vivi had nodded a polite hello at him, and was now levelling her serious eyes at Leith, who was just as solemnly greeting her. The two had a connection, Dion knew. Leith had been the one to break the news of Tia's death to her. She might have held it against him, seen him as a big ugly bringer of bad news, but if anything, her gaze held only empathy and understanding. As if they had both lost something special.

Dion thought about the girl losing both parents, and now her brother. He thought about Perry Vale saying he'd overheard Vivi talking to herself, and that maybe she'd been talking to Tiago. Talking to ghosts wasn't necessarily a bad thing, in his opinion. He'd had some meaningful conversations with Looch, after the crash. Lying in the recovery wing of Vancouver General, all bandages and drool, telling his closest friend what an asshole he was. Or maybe it was just the morphine talking.

Shadow boxing, really. Crazy. But it did help pass the time.

Leith was telling Garland that he had an update on Luna Mae. He asked if he and Dion could speak to him alone. Viviani listened, her eyes jumping back and forth between the adults as they spoke. Dion saw her mouth fall open as if to object. She wanted to stay, wanted to know what was going on, but Garland ushered her off to her room. He made sure her door was shut and her music was on before returning to clear the dining room table of its junk mail and other odds and ends. There was a further delay when he went off to make coffee, though Leith had told him not to worry about it.

"Sorry," Garland said, setting down cups. "Not sure I want to hear what you have to say."

While waiting for the coffee to perk, Dion had compared this home with the Vales'. Their dining room table was long and solid. He recalled its dark polished surface reflecting the modern-art chandelier above. Engineer Perry Vale made a good income, and his top-notch home showed it. The Vale house was filled with the scent of aromatherapy and rainforest. Visually clean, too, as though no children lived there.

Here at Garland's place the small table the three of them sat at was pale laminate, chipped at its corners, and above hung a Home Depot chandelier of glass and brass. There was a musty smell, like the ventilation system wasn't great. There were open cereal boxes on the counter, dishes in the sink, posters peeling off the walls, mitts and coats and an unusual amount of camping gear piled in corners.

Dion focused on the discussion as Leith gave Garland the critical update. Again, the news was downplayed, the possible kidnap scenario, the lines of inquiry that were being followed up on, the caution that it was early stages yet.

Garland's response, as Dion watched, was much like Gemma's. When he learned that his daughter had been possibly delivered alive and well to an unknown couple, he seemed shocked. Then cautiously hopeful. Then thrilled.

The short conversation was over. Out in the street Dion forgot his resolve to keep his mouth shut and gave Leith his impressions of Garland's reaction. Again, it was off, ratio-wise. There was just something not quite right, he said, trying to put it into words, Gemma's show of hope, and now Zachary's, a kind of lag, some dispro-portion of surprise versus relief.

He shouldn't have bothered.

# FOURTEEN

## DOUBLE STRANGE

TWO STRANGE THINGS happened to Dion as he was signing out for the day. The first was Ken Poole, in uniform and duty belt, stopping him for a brief chat in the main floor hallway. Or not so much a chat as a word in passing.

"Nice day, isn't it?" Poole said. "Should take a walk along the Quay tomorrow morning. Six a.m." He didn't wait for an answer but moved on.

Since the day was anything but nice, and the Quay at 6:00 a.m. would be dark and dismal, Dion stood puzzled and called out to Poole's backside, "What?"

Poole kept walking, and now Dion got it.

As he was digesting the question, suggestion, or command, his cell buzzed. It was Mike Bosko inviting him out for coffee. Something they had to discuss, serious, but not actually job related. The sergeant suggested not one of the usual cop hangouts, but a Persian cafeteria a few blocks uphill from the detachment, in say half an hour.

Dion made sure to arrive ahead of schedule. The invitation unnerved him, and he wanted time to scope out his surroundings, brace himself for whatever was coming. Inside the narrow restaurant the customers were mostly dark-skinned and speaking in a loose blend of English and Farsi. He found a seat in a corner and watched the door. Bosko arrived minutes later. He was greeted by the server and nodded at by other patrons, Dion noticed. As if he'd been here before. As if he was a regular.

"Hey, thanks for getting together on such short notice," Bosko said.

"No problem."

When they were facing each other, two cups of strong Persian coffee before them, Bosko opened with a pleasantry. "How's it going for you these days?"

Dion had overheard colleagues discussing Bosko, a man who never looked busy, never got angry, yet got things done. Bit of a mystery. JD snickered that he was an android, embedded in the North Van detachment as a CSIS experiment. Not an android, Dion thought, but definitely a spy. Worse, Dion himself was in the spy's crosshairs.

"Very good, sir," he said. He sat back with shoulders relaxed, no fear in his eyes. He knew how fearless he appeared because his mirror confirmed it, every morning as he shaved.

Bosko seemed to absorb the brief answer. Computing. Finally, he said, "You've come a long way since we first met, up in the Hazeltons. I'm impressed."

Dion's transfer to the northern half of the province after the crash was a faded memory. New Hazelton was where he had first met and worked under Bosko and

Leith. When the case that had brought them together ended, Bosko had returned to the city, Leith to his home detachment of Prince Rupert, and Dion had resigned himself to life in a small town surrounded by wilderness. But then Bosko had summoned him back to North Vancouver, to be on his team. After all this time, Dion was still trying to figure out why. "Thanks," he said. And tacked on a little white lie: "The counselling helped."

Bosko led the discussion with some small talk, weather related, then case related, before getting to the point of the meeting. "Brooke Zaccardi," he said. "Did you know she was in town?"

Dion had been expecting her name to come up, though not like this, an intimate face-to-face in a dark café. He nodded. "Doug mentioned she was in Rainey's for a visit last month."

"And then disappeared. You didn't see her, in or around that time?"

"No. She didn't get in touch."

"You didn't know of her visit?"

"Not until after."

"If you'd have known, would you have tried to see her?"

The question took Dion off guard. He thought about it, shook his head. "I don't know. Maybe."

"Any idea what could have happened to her? You're probably the closest friend she had here on the North Shore."

So Dion was being canvassed about a missing woman. But it was more than that, he realized. Brooke was connected to Looch, and Looch was connected to the night of the murder, and now Brooke had disappeared. A bunch of stepping stones that led to Dion himself, which Bosko would have figured out soon enough.

If he was in the mood to confess, Dion could have put forward his theory to Bosko, in detail. On the summer night of the murder, in the deep shadows of the gravel pit, he had seen Looch on his phone. Who would he be calling in secret? Brooke. To cry about the trouble he was in, because Looch was a coward. If he cried to Brooke, if Brooke knew what they'd done, then probably it was Brooke who had made the call and threatened to tell all. To get back at Dion, if nothing else.

Maybe Bosko knew it already. Probably he did. Probably he was here to break it to Dion over Persian coffee, away from the eyes of his colleagues, an act of mercy. Then he'd place him under arrest.

The tightness was coiling in Dion, the fear that left him cold and clammy. If he had another sip of that thick coffee he'd probably spew it all over Bosko. He left the cup alone and waited, and when the arrest didn't happen, he answered Bosko with his expertly forced calm. "Brooke and I weren't close. She's as much friends with Doug and the others as me. I have no idea what happened to her. Doug says she was acting strangely that night at Rainey's."

"Acting strangely how?" Bosko asked. "What did Doug tell you?"

What Doug Paley had said afterward was, *Hey, Cal, guess who dropped in out of nowhere last week? Brooke Fucking Zaccardi. Came to Rainey's with JD, sucked up a couple highballs, and ranted about what a bastard you are. She's hit the chemicals, man. Got the meth-face and the shakes. Skinny as a rake and looks like shit.*

"He said she wasn't looking good," Dion said. "He thinks she's doing drugs. Lost weight, not taking care of herself. I can't confirm any of it, because I wasn't there."

"Do you know who *was* there, besides Doug?"

Dion had a feeling that Bosko well knew who was there besides Doug. He'd probably already questioned those involved. Probably this was part of the test he was sure to fail.

He shook his head. "Don't know."

Bosko gave the table a light slap to signal an end to his questions. "Good enough. I'm pretty sure I've got the full list, but just checking in case I missed somebody."

Dion wondered who else was on the list, who else had heard Brooke's rant, and what the rant had been, specifically. The queasiness had passed enough that he could devote himself to his coffee, if only because not drinking was a show of weakness. Maybe it was just the extra hit of caffeine, but his heart was thudding.

"Brooke isn't our case, of course," Bosko added. He was fishing out his wallet, ready to leave. "She's got a Burnaby address. But she was here in North Van the day before she disappeared, so I'm helping out as best I can, asking around. It's not much of a lead, but anything helps."

"Wish I had something to offer," Dion said. He held up his cup to say he wasn't finished and would stay a while. Bosko gave him a smile, paid for both cups, and left.

Dion pictured Brooke's face as he had known her two summers ago. He hadn't seen her, hadn't exchanged a word with her since the crash that killed Looch. He'd heard she'd gone east, and why she was back he had no idea. He looked across the coffee shop, past the silhouettes of its patrons, through plate glass to the street, focusing on his body, his fear, his outer calm. Whatever had brought Brooke back here, whatever revenge she had planned for him, all he could do was hope she'd stay silent — even if it meant a permanent listing on the missing persons registry.

* * *

As her day ended, JD sat in her car and thought about the shoes she needed but didn't want. She put her car in gear and drove to the Park Royal Mall.

She had discovered the shoe issue this morning, while dressing for work, looking through her wardrobe, thinking about the Valentine's Day dance she wouldn't be attending, impatiently leafing through hangers of shirts, trousers, skirts, and a long-forgotten kimono. Why? Because one of these days she'd have no choice but attend some event, formal or semi, and it would be good to have something respectable to wear.

The only reasonably attractive dress she found was long-sleeved, dark grey, body-hugging, mid-thigh length. It would do at both a social gathering and a funeral, if paired with charcoal tights and strappy heels. But the only strappy heels she seemed to own were some mustard-coloured stilettos. She had untangled them, this morning, from a crate of flip-flops and old runners and dangled them in the morning light, not sure where they'd come from.

Definitely wouldn't go with charcoal tights. She needed new shoes.

She arrived at the mall in West Van, with its plethora of shoe stores, and parked her car. She didn't like malls, and shoe shopping was way up there on her list of least favourite chores. But she did her best. Store after store, all the shoes she looked at were just not her. And the ones she liked were either hazardous or uncomfortable.

She had given up on the plan and was heading back to the exit when a pair in a display case caught her eye. Wedge-style pumps, they were called. Not as strappy as she had in mind, but less tottery. A good colour, too, distressed grey on black. She might even say cute, if forced to use the word.

She went in to try them on.

While she waited for her size to be brought, she browsed the shelves. On one side of the store were women's shoes, on the other, men's. Among the men's shoes stood the masculine equivalent of stilettos: ornate cowboy boots, which made her think of Robbie Clark.

"Ma'am," the sales clerk said, holding up a box.

"One minute," JD said.

She stared at the cowboy boots, at their sassy chrome toe points. The chrome caught the store's high-watt spotlight, flashing into her eyes.

Dazzling, in more ways than one.

# FIFTEEN

# P.S. GOODBYE

HALFWAY THROUGH DINNER Leith received a call he couldn't ignore. He used the opportunity as he left the table to ask Alison a rhetorical question. "You want to bring another kid into *this* way of life?"

"One thing you don't do is waver," Alison told him, pointing her fork his way. "You already said yes, and it's going to happen, so be happy."

After putting on his coat in the hallway, he returned to apologize. She was right. With some big decisions, regret was not an option, and having a child was about as big as it got.

Driving out to Riverside Drive, he saw once again a lot of police cars outside the Vale home. Dion was already on scene, next to the graffiti-covered gateway that provided access to the steps down to the jumping rock. In the dimming light he was talking to a man who was oddly dressed in skin-tight rubber.

Leith raised a hand as he approached.

"This is Corey Bloom," Dion said. "He discovered the body."

*Bloom,* Leith thought. Garlands, Vales, and Blooms. *What's next, Twigg? Corsage? Boutonnière?* "Good evening," he said to Bloom. The odd garb, he saw now, was a wetsuit. A mostly dry wetsuit, it seemed. Bloom looked angry.

"You were, what, going for a swim?" Leith asked him.

"Whoa," Bloom said. "Another detective."

"He's a kayaker," Dion said. He gestured at a truck down the road and the bright yellow, banana-like object propped against it. "I've got his statement and he's eager to go." To Bloom he said, "Thanks for your help, Mr. Bloom. Sorry you lost your window of opportunity and couldn't get your ride in. Better luck tomorrow."

Leith now recognized the kayaker as a criminal defence lawyer he'd seen around the courthouse but had never had to face on the stand. He hoped he'd never need to; Bloom struck him as a man who'd hold a grudge.

The lawyer slopped to his truck down the block and went about wrangling his boat onto its roof rack. Leith asked Dion, "Who's in the water?"

"Pretty sure it's Kyler Hartshorne. He's been in for some hours. Maybe overnight."

The air felt heavy with pending rain. They trotted down the steps, Dion with his flashlight beaming ahead. A crew of half a dozen could be seen here and there below on the limited elbow room of the narrow beach. The steps led to the mound of bedrock stretching into the swirling grey-green water, and from there

Leith climbed with difficulty, following Dion's lead, around lapping water to a narrow strip of beach below the jumping rock, where the body lay covered by a tarp.

The tarp was pulled back and Leith looked down at the dead man's face. It was distorted, stained by lividity, swollen and eerie, but it resembled the photographs of the young man the team had been searching for. Hair, clothes, build — they all said this was Kyler Hartshorne.

Leith resisted the urge to swear at the corpse. A dead Hartshorne meant that little Luna Garland would not be found alive and well in his custody. A dead Hartshorne couldn't have the truth slapped out of him. A dead Hartshorne couldn't pay for what he'd done.

A whistle came from the jumping rock above. Leith looked up to see a constable in uniform waving down. Niko Shiomi was back on active duty. "Come take a look," she called.

Easier said than done in this vertical terrain. Leith gestured upward to the more limber Dion. "Go take a look, would you?"

* * *

Dion, standing next to Shiomi at the precipice, leaned forward and saw what she was pointing out to him. Tucked in the crag, on a flat rock and protected from weather, was a piece of lined notepaper. Weighing the paper down was a crushed-looking nylon wallet. The wallet was black, decorated with a peeling insignia of skull and crossbones.

Dion summoned an Ident member to photograph and document the note and wallet. He was aware of Shiomi's eyes on him as he worked, and also aware, with mixed emotions, that he was working to impress her. The Ident member checked the wallet and stated there was a wad of bills inside. Some twenties, fifties, and four one hundreds. Dion looked at the ID and saw it showed the face and name of Kyler Hartshorne. The other contents would be inventoried later — right now he wanted to see the most interesting bit. The note.

The Ident member opened the paper and held it out for viewing. Dion read the ballpoint scrawl, then took a snapshot with his phone. "Thanks, good find," he told Niko. He gave her a brief smile, then hurried back down the rock to show Hartshorne's final words to Leith:

*Dear Mom, I'm sorry for what I did. You've been a good mom but I've been nothing but trouble to you and you're better off with me gone. Sincerelly yours, Kyler. PS: I've left you some money to take care of things.*

"Things," Leith said. "Take care of what things? Funeral arrangements?"

"What's he *done*?" Dion added. He mentally counted up the tasks ahead of them. Hartshorne's mother, Millie, would have to be notified as soon as possible. Maybe she would be able to confirm their suspicions, maybe even provide leads to some much-needed answers. Gemma and Zachary would have to be told as well, and their hopes for Luna's safe return would be hung out to dry once more.

With a wince, he recalled his suspicions from yesterday that Gemma and Zachary hadn't responded appropriately to Leith's news. He'd be more careful with his snap judgments from now on, and doubly careful not to voice them to Leith.

The river coursed along by his feet, a deep tumult, like the havoc Kyler Hartshorne had wreaked in so many lives. Maybe Hartshorne had done an unforgivable thing, stolen a child from its crib. Maybe he felt bad enough that he'd killed himself in the end. Or that was sure to be the theory that would go up on the board.

As he read the note again, Dion had to wonder if it was really that simple.

# SIXTEEN

# LONG BLACK SEDAN

JD RETURNED TO the detachment after her shoe-shopping trip to Park Royal and accessed the school surveillance footage. She and Shiomi had edited it down to a five-second clip — Shiomi's *glitch* — that focused on the few frames where a white blob appeared on the subject's toe.

The best frames, if printed out large and placed on the wall, would be wholly uninteresting, but once set in motion, scrubbed back and forth, JD found them fascinating indeed. She didn't wait till morning but made some calls. First she talked over her discovery with Leith, who said he would join her shortly. Then she contacted Robbie Clark.

To her surprise, she was able to reach him easily. Yes, he was able and willing to come in. Yes, now, even at nearly 8:00 p.m.

"What's it all about?" he asked, over the line.

"Just come on down," JD told him. "We'll talk."

Clark arrived so fast he must have thrown on coat and boots and made a beeline straight out the door. He now sat in an interview room waiting, alone but observed through the one-way mirror. He didn't look nervous to JD. Curious and alert, but amiable as always.

But was he really so cool? His fingers and toes were taking turns betraying anxiety, softly drumming, casually tapping. He wore his usual jeans, but his footwear of choice tonight was a round-toed pair of Blundstones. No chrome, no flamboyant swirls.

Leith arrived, and he and JD watched their suspect sweat. "I'm going to hit hard on this one," JD said. "No small talk, no sympathy." It was the best approach with a guy like this, she was thinking. She was marvelling, too, that all it had taken was one sparkling boot tip for her to see right through him. She had him peeled open. She knew he was carrying a burden. Maybe she had known all along, a cue subconsciously registered, maybe converted into what she imagined was attraction.

She also believed he would be easy to crack, but it would take a firm hand. Lead him to the confessional booth and kick him inside. All she needed was for Leith to say, *Go for it.*

"If you think so," he told her. He looked far from sold. "You're sure you can do this?"

"It's what I live for."

She had shown Leith the portion of the video in question. He said it didn't look like a pointy cowboy boot to him. And that white blob wasn't necessarily the ambient light catching a steel toe. And even if it was, Robbie Clark wasn't the only man in the world who wore steel-tipped boots, and the image was a far cry from a match to the bruise on Tasha Aziz's abdomen.

But he seemed semi-convinced as he studied Clark now. JD turned her eyes to Clark as well, and guessed that he realized he was being studied, for he had ceased tapping and drumming. He had crossed his arms loosely over his chest and seemed intrigued by a poster on the wall beside him.

"D'you have anything else besides the boots?" Leith asked. "It's mighty thin, JD."

"I have more," she said. "That something special in his eyes when we talk, that *tick-tick-tick* of conflict. He knows he's paddling up shit creek. And sure, he's got a paddle, but just watch me grab it."

She grinned at her own vulgar poetry, but Leith didn't. He was a bit prissy, she knew. A bit over-religious about the RCMP's squeaky-clean corporate image. An image that had kind of lost its shine, with shame and scandals regularly hitting the news. "Well?" she said. "Do I have your blessing?"

"Do your best," he said.

JD took the chair across from Clark. He had asked on arrival what kind of trouble he was in, and she now told him. "I've got evidence you were at the school grounds, Robbie. That's why you're here. Surveillance video. It caught you. Enough to identify you. Okay?"

His eyes searched hers. Maybe he was looking for proof that this was some kind of dirty trick. But overlying his wariness JD thought she saw embarrassment. Which disturbed her. Who, having committed murder, would feel *sheepish* about it?

Setting her doubts aside, she said, "You know the school has video surveillance, right? You know where the blind spots are, and you know how to dodge 'em. Did it take a lot of practice? And how did you screw up? Puddles got in the way, you took a sidestep to avoid them, and walked into the frame by mistake? No, wait." She snapped her fingers. "You didn't sidestep anything. You splashed right through the water in your cowboy boots. Yeah, uh-huh," she said, as the truth appeared to dawn on her suspect. "Your boots are distinctive, Robert. So now you know why you're here. And I want you to come clean with me."

"No, listen. I didn't —"

"No," JD said with the kind of overblown passion she reserved for special occasions. She knew the effect this had on people. Colleagues, suspects, and family all sat up and listened when her voice went rough around the edges. "You listen to me," she snapped. "A little advice. It's true what they say, the less work you make for the system, the more understanding the system will be when it comes to trial. It could make all the difference. Right?"

He nodded like he got it.

His nod pleased her, fuelled her. She softened her tone and extended an olive branch. "I know you're a good man," she said. "A smart man. You know the line between right and wrong. You know what you did was wrong. The worst kind of wrong. You know it. Now, come on. Let's get on the road to making amends. You can't undo what's done, but you can lessen the impact. Ease the pain of the family. Okay?"

"Family?" he said. "What family?"

JD frowned at him. He was wincing. Had their lines crossed? What was she not understanding here? "Look," she said. "Robert. I'm here to find out what happened. Not judge you. I know as much as you do about the bad choices we all can make —"

His palms hit the tabletop with a loud crack.

JD blinked.

Clark took a deep breath and shouted, "Christ, is that what this is about? The janitor? Yes, I was there that night, but I didn't do anything to her. I didn't even see her. I didn't even know about her until the next day. I was there to make a pickup. No, I don't want to admit it, but if you're accusing me of murder, then I've got no choice, have I?"

"A pickup …" JD said.

"In a hidey-hole in the school's foundation. That's where Kyler leaves my stuff." He stopped a moment before moodily releasing the zinger. "My weed."

JD reconnoitred, watching him steadily. Mustn't waver. She could see where this was headed. Whether true or not, he had come up with a cover story. "Kind of a stupid place to deal drugs, isn't it?" she said. "Under the lens of the surveillance camera and at your own workplace?"

"Stupid, yes. And stupid to buy from a student, who's now got me under his thumb. It's a long and unflattering story. But it somehow just ended up this way. I'd undo it if I could, believe me. Too late. He calls the shots."

*Called*, JD mentally corrected. But Clark wasn't aware of Kyler's death. Another toppled domino, and she wasn't ready to tell him.

Clark's demeanour had altered with his confession. His gaze was steady, maybe even relieved. "I leave cash as I leave work for the day," he said. "I come back later to pick up the product. It's not a regular thing. Once in a blue moon, really."

"You pick up this product from a hidey-hole that you're going to show me shortly, right?"

"Of course. That day, the day the janitor was killed, I didn't make it back till quite late. Sure, I knew how to avoid the cameras, but nobody monitors that footage unless something happens. Just my luck something happened that night." He pinkened. "Of course, my bad luck is nothing next to hers."

"Go on."

"I picked up my pot. A dime bag. That's the largest amount I'll go for. Keep it small-scale, because I'm always planning to quit tomorrow. Which is easier said than done." He stopped cold and gave JD a morose stare. "I'm going to lose my job over this, aren't I?"

"That's not for me to say."

He shook his head, and seemed to be staring blindly into the distance. "Actually, JD, I'm not sure I care," he said, startling her with the use of her first name. "Been counselling students way too long. Time for a change, right? Maybe I'll get back in the garage. Auto body repair. Won't get the union benefits, but it's a whole lot easier to fix a dented fender than a depressed teenager."

His laugh sounded full of regret. JD continued to watch for signs that he was play-acting.

"Anyway," he went on, "I was stuffing the baggie in my pocket when I saw somebody heading to the parking lot.

I took a step closer to see who it was. Pretty sure it was Kyler, by the size and shape of him, and the way he walks. Not sure why he was hanging around, but whatever. I had no desire to talk to him. I walked back to the street, where I'd parked my car, and got out of there, like, fast."

"You didn't park in the back?"

He eyed her sharply. "No. Why would I?"

"You saw Tasha, though."

He denied it. "I did not see the janitor. I didn't know anyone was around except Kyler."

"What if someone had seen you? Hard to explain what you're doing hanging around the schoolyard at that hour."

"Had a folder of papers with me. I'd say I had to pick up something from my office."

It was all adding up to a likely story, and JD could picture Leith behind the glass, looking smug. But whatever. She was moving the case forward, if only in fits and starts. If Clark was telling the truth and was right about Kyler being in the parking lot that night, the case could be resolved. Not a good ending, as Kyler would never get the chance to voice his remorse to Tasha's family, which might help in their healing.

On the other hand, if Clark was telling the truth but was wrong about Kyler, then the killer was still an unknown, still out there.

She had to face it. Clark's presence at the scene that night, his drug use, his demeanour, it was all hot stuff, but not enough to write up a report to Crown counsel. He would remain a person of interest, but not much more. So she released him.

Leith told JD she'd done good work. She almost told him to take his condescension and go to hell. Instead, she smiled grimly and went to her desk to simmer down. She didn't sit but stood by the nearby window and stared down at the street. Movement below caught her eye, and she watched her pothead cowboy make his way along the sidewalk.

*Scurrying*, in her eyes. She saw Clark angrily remove a flyer from the windshield of a car parked curbside — a long black sedan — climb in and drive away with a squeal of tires.

# SEVENTEEN

# NOTHING BUT THE TRUTH

*February 12*

AT 6:00 A.M. THE CITY around Dion was already on the move. Traffic along Esplanade was beginning its daily beat-the-lights dance. If not for the lamp posts arching over the harbour, the area would still be pitch black.

Down at Lonsdale Quay, which had the look and feel of an enormous fish processing plant turned into a marketplace, he found only one coffee shop open. People inside were getting their morning brew to go or sitting and reading the news.

Ken Poole was one of those sitting and reading. He blended in well — middle-aged, heavy-set, going bald, and in civvies. Jeans, fleece jacket, grey plaid scarf. Dion bought a coffee and joined him at the table. Poole didn't glance over or set aside his paper. The snub didn't bother Dion. The character of their relationship had taken shape ever since the incident some years ago in Poole's apartment, when Dion was still new on the force, still learning.

He continued to view *the incident* as Poole's attempt at sexual assault, where Poole called it innocent misjudgment paired with drunken loss of inhibition. Whatever it was, it was the day Dion had found out that his supervisor, mentor — maybe even friend — was gay. But not gay in a happy way. Deep in the closet with no hope of coming out.

Aside from the incident itself, and the arguments that came afterward, Dion had nothing against Poole. He was a good cop, even if his mentoring message in Dion's first years on the force had been unwholesome. The world doesn't care about you, was Kenny's advice. So don't bother caring for the world. Take what you can when you can — and for as long as you're able to get away with it.

In a small-potatoes way, Poole had been corrupt. Maybe not so much now, but back then he'd been the cop who would lie and steal if it made his life easier. And he got away with it because of the personality he projected so well. Earnest, honest, dull.

Dion knew better. At his marrow, Poole was sly, deceitful, and sharp.

This past Christmas Dion had confronted Poole about *the incident*. All he'd accomplished was giving himself away — the fact that he was in big trouble.

Not long afterward, Poole had summoned Dion to another coffee shop in another mall for another talk. Or a warning, really. Seemed Poole had seen David Leith affixing a tracker to the wheel well of Dion's car some months back.

The news hadn't surprised Dion, but it confirmed that he couldn't trust anybody. Other than the snitch, Poole. So if Poole had something to say, he'd better listen up. Which he would do if Poole ever put down his paper and got on with it.

When the paper finally lowered, Poole gave him one of his weary stares, like a parent lecturing his disappointing offspring. "Well, Cal," he said. "You've sure fucked up, haven't you?"

Dion crossed his arms to take in Poole's revelation. He felt weirdly calm and collected. Maybe the dread that had been building for so long inside had numbed his senses. Maybe he welcomed the inevitable. "What now?" he asked, though he knew. Either the man he'd killed had been unearthed from the gravel pit, or Brooke Zaccardi had left her hiding place and was sitting down with IHIT — the RCMP's Integrated Homicide Investigative Team — to tell what she knew.

"Who did you kill?" Poole asked, his eyes flat and cold.

"Kelley Brandon Stouffer," Dion said.

The name came out of him in a muffled and distant way, as if filtered through the walls of a dream. Maybe it was a dream. Maybe Poole would now warp into a black dog and the alarm clock would buzz. But Poole remained solid and repeated the name matter-of-factly. "Stouffer," he said. "The guy who walked."

"The guy who killed his twelve-year-old stepdaughter and walked," Dion said.

"Walked right off the radar."

"That's him. We tried to monitor his movements, but lost him."

"We figured he'd hightailed it to the States," Poole said. "Where he's from."

"Yes," Dion said. He was surprised that Poole was still on top of the closed case. But some stories burned into the heart more than others, and Janine was one of those. "Kelley was the last guy we expected to see that night," he said. "Looch and me. Middle of Surrey. Couldn't believe our eyes."

"Tell me about it."

This was the conversation Dion had been having every day for a year and a half, but only in his head. He would get up to the point in the narrative that he couldn't seem to move past, and stop. Stopping wasn't an option now, though.

"It was Canada Day, and we'd been out at the Ferraros' place in Abbotsford," he told Poole. "Looch's parents', I mean. They were having a barbecue, had all their kids over. All their kids and me." His reflection in the coffee shop's window looked as deadpan as his voice. "Only Brooke wasn't there. She was away, I don't know where. At the end of the night Looch and I left. It was a warm summer night, and neither of us wanted to go straight back to North Van. So we took the long way round, through Surrey. The road was straight and dark, went on forever. Two people popped up in the headlights, a man and a girl. She was just a kid. She had a bicycle. I thought they were arguing. Looch eyed them as we drove past, and he says, 'That's fucking Stouffer, and that's Janine.'"

The words dried up in Dion's mouth. He was starting to feel shaky. He had come to the place in his thoughts where he always shut down the memories, the point he should have kept driving in a straight line, but had pulled a U-turn instead.

"Janine," Poole said. He leaned forward on his elbows, frowning. "Her ghost, you mean."

The whole world knew, the jury included, that Stouffer was guilty. He'd used a child, killed her. But with downturned eyes the jury foreman had delivered the verdict of not guilty. The Crown's case couldn't be proven. Not beyond a reasonable doubt.

The victim's family had wept — Dion had seen it for himself — and a smiling Stouffer had walked out into the rain, a free man.

"It looked like her," he said. "When we circled back the girl was gone. Just Stouffer walking up a driveway. We should have noted the address and taken off. We had no authority to lean on him. He'd been acquitted. He could chat up young girls to his heart's content. But —"

"But you two crusaders decided to unofficially tell him what's what, huh?"

"Sure. No law against that. We pulled into the driveway, got out to chat. Looch asked Stouffer what he was doing talking to kids in the middle of the night. Stouffer said it was none of our business."

"Which technically it wasn't," Poole remarked.

"Right. But if he'd treated us with respect, Ken, nothing would have happened. We'd have told him to be good, tried to get an address for our records, case closed."

"Maybe give him a piece of your mind while you're at it. Tell him he's walking sewage. Something along those lines?"

Dion opened his mouth to deny it, but he couldn't stomach the lie. "Anyway. Him and Looch started arguing. Stouffer, this guy who'd killed an innocent child in the worst way, was acting like *he* was the victim, and we were the criminals for confronting him, treading on his rights. He also kept saying he didn't do it, which is when —"

"Maybe he didn't," Poole said, coolly.

Dion stared at him. "What?"

Poole didn't bother repeating himself. He knew he'd been heard.

Dion finished the story. "Which is when Looch lost it. Slugged him. Hard. Stouffer went down in a bad way. I heard a snap. His arm, I think, because after that he couldn't use it. He's screaming in pain so loud I thought the whole neighbourhood would come running. But you know that part of Surrey, big acreages around there, lots of buffer. Seemed it was just us three on this long driveway, dark house at the end of it. Stouffer's swearing at Looch that he's going to charge him with assault, he's going to lose his job, life as he knows it is over. He pulls out his phone, and I'm seeing it all coming, 911, what's your emergency, and Looch Ferraro, best cop in the world, loses his job. Over this piece of shit? Maybe does jail time? I couldn't let that happen. I reached down, grabbed the phone off Stouffer, and now he's screaming at me, telling me I'm also going down, like I don't already know it. And he's trying to get up, so I help him. Only so I can talk to him —"

"You mean push him up against the wall."

"Garage. We were by a garage, or shed, or something. I was going to tell him what he wasn't going to do or say. But what are the chances that he'd keep his mouth shut? Even if he agrees, he's going to end up at the hospital, saying what happened. We were done, both of us. So I hit him. Wrapped my fist in something, I don't even know what, and hit him. And once I started, I couldn't stop. And I didn't stop till he was dead."

Dion took a breath. The story was done, except for the part about finding a tarp, hauling the body into the back seat of his car, and driving it to the nearby gravel pit. Poole didn't need to know all that, and Dion had run out of steam. He was exhausted. But he would feel freer now. This was where he should bow his head, and Poole would pat him on the shoulder and tell him it wasn't his fault.

It didn't happen. No weight was lifted, and he refused to bow his head. He stared at Poole with no show of remorse and Poole stared back with no show of sympathy.

"So what do I do?" Dion said. "Turn myself in, right?"

"Well, that's really the reason I wanted to meet," Poole said. "Don't go fessing up to anything just yet."

"Why not? I'm better off stepping forward. Before she does."

"Before who does?"

"Brooke," Dion said. It had come out of him in a snarl. "Fucking Looch must have called her that night and told her what we'd done. I saw him talking on his phone, and that's what he'd do, call and ask Brooke for advice. I don't know why she hasn't come forward before. But I'm putting two and two together. She's backed off, disappeared, probably afraid of what she's getting herself into, but once she's thought it over she's going to do what's right. Come out and sing. That's what you're here to tell me, right?"

"Brooke won't be stepping forward, believe me," Poole said. For some reason he'd said it in his best Godfather voice. He had a talent for voices, male or female, a throwback to better times, a party trick, mimicking Marlon Brando and other celebs for a laugh.

Even without the voice, though, it was a strange statement — that Brooke wouldn't be stepping forward. It hadn't been said like a good guess or wishful thinking. It was like he *knew*. And now Dion knew, too, and the Quay around him seemed to suddenly darken and chill. Like an ice storm was moving in. Exactly like that.

# EIGHTEEN

## DISNEYLAND

THE FIRST MESSAGE Dion received as he arrived at his desk was good news. The pair of suspects in the Luna Garland kidnap had been nabbed. Chilliwack RCMP had discovered the outrageously British couple sleeping in a van in a Walmart parking lot. Reading the report, he saw that the couple had been identified not as Sid and Nancy, but Seth Haney and Paula Vaughn. Both were native British Columbians with long but non-violent criminal records, no warrants out on them, and no fixed address.

There had been no baby found in the van with them, and no evidence of any child having been there recently — or ever. Haney and Vaughn claimed to know nothing about a Luna Garland, and stated they were travelling to Alberta to look for work in the oil fields.

They were brought to North Vancouver, and by mid-morning Dion had arranged to speak to each of them in turn. First up was Seth. He was older than expected, thirty-eight going on fifty, which he explained was a result of sleeping in a van for a year and a half.

Seth was co-operative and forthcoming. He admitted attending the Blueridge house party and stated that he had known nobody there. He explained how he'd gotten himself invited. "You see a bunch of people walking into a house carrying beer and whatnot, you just pick up on the vibe and swing along with 'em, right?" he said. "That's what we did. It's not against the law unless you refuse to leave when asked. When we were asked to leave, we did. No harm done."

Dion decided not to mention the stolen tequila. "You had a conversation with some people while you were there. Tell me about it."

"Ah, them," Seth said. "The big kid with the brush cut was razzing the smaller kid with the freckles about something. Don't ask me their names. So Paula butts in to find out what they're arguing about, mostly 'cause she wanted a toke of whatever they were passing between them, and Brush Cut says Freckles has a baby for sale, going cheap, ten thou. Paula says she'll buy it, since she's always wanted a baby, and next thing you know they're cutting a deal between 'em." He seemed amused, but when he saw that Dion wasn't, he gave a wide, apologetic grin. "They were just joking around, man."

"Strange kind of joke."

"They started it. Paula went along with it. Myself, I just stood back and watched. I'm not witty like she is."

"So was a deal struck between Paula and the two boys?"

"I think she bartered them down and said they'd have to include a passport in the price. So we could get the tyke back to Battersea."

"Battersea?"

"Being from another world makes you more interesting." Seth put on a British accent to go with the explanation. "Life is one big fantasyland, *innit*? We're troubadours. Travelling entertainers, mate. We liven up the party and in return we get to eat, drink, and be merry."

"How did the joke end?"

Canadian once more, Seth leaned forward and lowered his voice. "Frankly, I was getting a little worried. Maybe these guys were serious, and what were we getting ourselves into? I was going to say something polite and take Paula and go, when this really humongous Italian guy comes charging out on the back porch, asking who we were. So we basically hit the road at that point anyway."

"Any further contact with either of those two, the guy with the brush cut or the guy with freckles?"

"None," Seth said, and crossed his heart.

After Seth came Paula. She backed up everything her partner had said except for the chance that the conversation at the party was serious. The suggestion made her chuckle. "You can cross that out in your little book there," she said. "Me and those boys were totally horsing around." She gave a snort. "Wanting a baby. Me? One thing about Seth you gotta know, he always misses the punchline."

\* \* \*

Luna Mae Garland's disappearance was back to the drawing board, in Leith's mind. In an informal lunchtime meet at a diner on Lonsdale he went over the setback with JD and Dion. "It's not the first time rumours have messed us up. If we're writing off the kidnap for adoption as a false lead, where does that leave us?"

"Looking at the divorcees again," JD said. "Gemma and Zach. Time to shake things up. More questions, less sympathy."

Leith expected Dion to agree, as he seemed rife with doubts about the ex-couple and their involvement. But Dion was behaving in an unusually open-minded way, and he only murmured something about treading with care. He then added something more helpful. "Zachary's girlfriend, Chelsea Romanov. She answered a few questions, but didn't have much to say. We should talk to her again."

"And get Perry alone," JD said.

Leith looked at JD sitting next to Dion. They were both good cops. Intuitive. Dion was probably more so, but he was also trouble. If a land mine lay somewhere on the far reaches of his path, he was sure to go out of his way to step on it. JD was more circumspect, and though she complained a lot about, well, everything, she stuck to the rules. Teaming them up could be either a great idea or a regrettable mistake.

A few days ago JD had told Leith she thought Dion was a tool, and she really didn't like working with him. Leith didn't quite believe her. At least about the latter bit. He had a feeling the two were a good match when it came to drumming the pavement.

"You two give it a go," he said. "And keep me apprised."

"And you?" JD asked. "You don't look thrilled about whatever task you've assigned yourself."

He wasn't. "Millie Hartshorne," he said.

Kyler's mother. It was time to talk to her again about her dead son and that note he'd left behind.

* * *

It was raining as Leith returned to the Hartshorne home, and there was a tightness in his chest. Just past noon, yet the daylight seemed to be on the wane. Talking to next of kin in a murder investigation was always the worst box to tick off, but it had to be done.

On his first visit late last night to inform Millie Hartshorne her son was dead, she had been too drunk to fully understand. He hoped she would be sober today. The door swung open and the woman swung along with it. She gripped its jamb for stability as Leith attempted to reintroduce himself, and damn it, she was about as far from sober as she could get. "Thassomushfuckumin," she slurred.

He followed her inside and watched her collapse into an armchair. She was a squat woman with a greyish crew cut. She wore the same quilted housecoat that she'd had on last night, pink and plush. Behind her was a faux fireplace, its motor churning quietly. On the mantelpiece was a framed snapshot of Kyler. Beside her on a TV table was a mostly empty bottle of Crown Royal, and next to the bottle a tumbler containing an inch of liquid gold. She reached for the tumbler and her feet went up to a footstool, ankles crossed.

She cradled the drink in her lap and gazed sideways at the fireplace. The lights flickered and danced within plastic logs, and Leith could see that his presence was altogether forgotten.

He brought over a kitchen chair and placed himself in her line of vision, forcing her to speak to him, eye to eye. "I was here last night," he said. "And we talked a while. Do you remember?"

"Yessir. My boy, he's dead, you said."

She began to ramble about Kyler. Leith listened a moment before holding up a hand to slow her down. "Let's take this one step at a time, Millie."

"Who?"

Victim Services, Leith was thinking. He would have to get this woman some help. It wouldn't be enough, and it wouldn't last, but he would try. "So what's been going on in Kyler's life these days?" he asked. "What's he been up to? Has he talked to you at all about that?"

She looked at her hands in her lap, and her face brightened on finding a glass of Crown Royal there. Her favourite! She brought the tumbler to her mouth, but Leith reached out for it. "Let's put that aside for a minute, Millie, a'right?"

"S'okay," she assured him. "Just a little one."

He insisted, taking hold of the glass in her hand, struggling against what turned out to be a fierce grip. With the glass placed behind him, out of sight, he leaned toward her again. "I'm sorry. I know this is hard, but we should talk about Kyler. Did he help out around the house? Help you make dinner, clean up? Did you two have meals together, watch TV, talk?"

He wasn't sure how much Millie loved her son. She seemed to be broken up by his death, but she was also smashed. For all he knew, she was laughing inside. His efforts to ground her, to bring her back to a day-in-the-life of Kyler and Millie, seemed effective, as she blinked at him with a twinkle and for the first time spoke clearly. "Kyler likes to cook. Last week he made rattatwee." Her giggle was almost girlish. "'Get you healthy again, Mom,' he said. 'Get you back on your feet.'"

*Kyler*, *ratatouille*, and *healthy* didn't quite mesh, to Leith. But people never failed to surprise. Without warning Millie clambered from her chair and left the room. He watched her weave her way toward the back of the house, unsteady on her feet, touching walls. He worried that she would fall, pass out, or fetch herself a secret drink from a back room. But a moment later she returned with an object in hand. It looked like a glass angel, about the size and shape of a whisky decanter, except with wings. A gift from Kyler, she told him. "Isn't it beautiful?" she said, and almost dropped it.

Leith had jumped fast enough to seize it. He admired the angel before placing it safely on the mantelpiece. "Very nice. Did he often buy you presents?"

"Oh, little things. Not so beautiful like this, though. He knows I like my crystal."

"Looks expensive. Where did he get the money, d'you know?"

She was back in her chair. "'A man owes me a lotta money,' Ky said. 'Don't have to worry about anything anymore, Mom. We'll fix the car and we'll go to Disneyland, Mom. Just you and me.'"

"A man owes him money? Who's that?"

"I dunno. I know his car, though. I seen it drive by slow, and Ky was watching out the window, and he jumped up and got his boots on and went out, and I was so worried, 'cause it just didn't look right. And that's the last I seen him, my little boy."

"The car Kyler got into," Leith said. He was back on his kitchen chair, looking into Millie's watery, wandering eyes. She was slurring worse than ever now, and he had to tune in hard to make out her words. "Can you describe it for me?"

"Black, long," she said, with sudden clarity. "Four-door. We had one just like it when Ky was a baby. For sure a Caddy. Couldn't tell you the year."

Interesting.

They talked only a few minutes longer, as she had run out of useful information, and Leith was anxious to return to the detachment and get to work on this promising lead. Millie followed him down the hall to the front door. He told her he was going to get Victim Services to give her a call. Very nice people there, he told her. They can help you get through this.

She nodded, as if grateful, and like a good dog she stayed in place as he started down the steps. When he looked back she remained on the stoop with the door open, despite the chill, a dazed expression on her homely face. Her car sat in the driveway, the one that needed fixing, he supposed. The car would never take her and her son down to Disneyland, and the truth of it struck him with sudden and gut-wrenching force.

He returned to the woman in the entrance and put his arms around her, and she bawled against his chest like a child.

# NINETEEN

## WALLS

PERRY AND GEMMA VALE already knew about Kyler Hartshorne, so Dion couldn't watch them for reaction to his death. He and JD were at the Vale home, sitting at their dining room table, and as always the place was clean, glossy, fragrant. The last time Dion had seen Gemma was the day she'd dropped the juice jug, the day she'd learned Tiago was dead. She'd looked devastated then, but looked good now, the best he'd seen her so far. She was dressed nicely, her hair looked trimmed and poufed, and she smelled like a rose.

On the far side of the open living room/dining room Viviani Garland sat on the sofa, legs curled under her. She was reading a book and seemed to be minding her own business.

Dion explained to the Vales why he and JD were here, just a follow-up to the last discussion, with a few more questions and an update. From her place on the sofa, the clairvoyant wasn't minding her own business as much as she wanted them to think, he believed. She was listening and watching. Mostly she seemed to have an eye on JD. Maybe only because JD was a new face to her, or a female face. Or an interesting face.

"Last time we talked, you weren't sure about Vivi's custody arrangement," he told Gemma. He kept his voice low so the words didn't carry to the far side of the room, to the girl's ears. "Have you and Zachary worked it out?"

"He's not ready to fight about it quite yet, put it that way," Gemma said.

She was grasping Perry's hand like a lifeline. She gazed at him often, and her gaze was returned with affection. They looked like honeymooners. Dion wondered if their sex life was already on the road to recovery, and then felt bad for the thought. They were finding strength in each other, that's all, just as he was finding strength in Kate.

He recalled Perry's concerns about Vivi being alone with Zachary, the ugly, unspoken insinuation. He put the question to the couple now, again in a low voice. "Are you still having doubts about her safety?"

Perry hesitated, then shook his head no. Gemma seemed less willing to commit. She said instead, "I love Vivi." She'd almost shouted it out, as if all this murmuring was getting on her nerves. "She's all I've got left, and I don't want to lose that connection." She turned to the little girl at the far end of the long room and called out cheerfully, "I love you, baby. Why don't you go on downstairs like I asked you to, while we talk. This isn't stuff you want to hear, sweetie."

"I'm okay here, Gemma," Vivi called back. "I love you, too."

*Weird,* Dion thought. He caught JD's eye, and saw she was thinking the same. Love was a warm word to be thrown back and forth in this cold house.

Perry tapped the table, drawing Dion's gaze back to him. "You said you've got some news for us."

"The couple in the van," Gemma added.

JD spoke now, telling the Vales that the couple in the van had not panned out as a good lead. The conspiracy to kidnap Luna was likely nothing more than a bad joke shared between young people at a party. The van couple had been located, investigated, cleared. Sorry.

Dion saw that Perry didn't take the news well, though he looked more tired than crushed. Even his disappointment came across as obligatory. Maybe he'd lost hope from day one, and he saw the new developments as nothing more than his premonitions coming true.

Gemma was impossible to read because her hands were covering her face again. When she finally looked at Dion she looked weepy, but her voice was steel. "All the same, Tiago's done something, hasn't he? And Kyler. They were talking about kidnapping Luna. And Tiago … he couldn't live with himself. What has he done? You're not telling us everything. We're not going to get her back, are we?"

Instead of waiting for an answer, she leaned on Perry and began to cry.

Showy tears, in Dion's opinion. Maybe to give Gemma time out, JD stood and went to talk to Vivi, who had put down her book and was watching her approach. Dion watched, too. He saw Gemma crying, JD walking, Vivi observing. He saw Gemma jolt away from Perry, maybe aware that somebody had left the table, and turn to stare across at JD crouched down beside her daughter.

And Gemma was rising, knocking Perry's arm aside, crying out in anger, "Excuse me? What are you doing? Did I say you could talk to her? Leave her alone!"

Perry and Dion were also on their feet, and JD had risen from her crouch, turning in surprise. They were all standing except Vivi, who remained on the sofa, book in lap.

"I was just introducing myself," JD explained to Gemma. "Checking out what she's reading. No worries, Mrs. Vale."

Perry brought Gemma back down to her seat, and his arm went around her again. The squeeze he gave her looked to Dion more like restraint than solace. Maybe she was falling apart, and maybe Perry was working round the clock to keep her together.

Or was he afraid Gemma would blurt something out, something he didn't want said?

Gemma squared her shoulders and addressed JD, who was still at Vivi's side. "I'm sorry, Constable. I just thought — I just don't want her dragged into this, that's all."

JD held up her hands, a promise not to meddle. Dion saw her smile down at Vivi, and Vivi smile up at JD, and he thought how great it would be if those two could talk. But in private.

\* \* \*

In the passenger seat JD said, "Stop the car. I have to tell you something."

Dion pulled off Riverside Drive and parked near a path that accessed the Seymour. The river was calmer here, broadening toward the sea. When the engine was shut off, JD said, "That girl wants to say something, but she's afraid."

"She told you so?"

"I went over to say hello, asked what she was reading. She showed me her book. As I hunkered down to take a look, she said, 'I want to talk to you.' So quiet I hardly heard. Like it was a secret. I got the feeling it could be a problem for her if I told Gemma and Perry. And before I could answer, that's when Gemma started freaking out. So I stuck my business card into Vivi's book and closed it and gave it back to her. She saw. She knows what that business card means. What do I do if she calls me? I'm breaking all kinds of rules here. Am I going to get in big trouble?"

Dion wasn't sure. "It would be good if you could talk to her alone. Zachary is her primary caregiver, and he'll have the final say. He'll be more co-operative, I'm sure."

He restarted the car to get on with their second task, talking to Garland.

The man was looking as rough as Gemma was looking polished. He allowed them into his apartment and without ceremony slumped at the kitchen table, leaving them to find chairs and deliver their news. He nodded glumly when he heard that the Brits were a dead end. He then echoed what Gemma had said, though with some hesitation. "Still, it's pretty clear the boys were up to something. Kyler, at least. And Tia got himself involved somehow, though I'm sure it wasn't his fault. He was a good kid. He wouldn't do anything to hurt anyone. But why else would they kill themselves, if they hadn't done something to Luna?"

The image of Tiago sitting dead on the precipice was still sharp in Dion's mind. What had killed the teen, technically speaking, was too much liquor taken too fast by a body not properly primed for the stuff. But had he wanted to die? If so, wouldn't he have also swallowed a bunch of over-the-counter sleeping pills to go with the Scotch?

The bottom line was the boy had needed help, and who better to help than his father. Zachary had been wrapped up in his own problems, and he couldn't be blamed for that. But he could have met the police halfway, when Leith had asked permission to speak to Tiago alone.

JD said, "Mr. Garland —"

"Call me Zach, would you?"

"I've met Vivi, Zach. She's a lovely girl. I'm wondering if I could have a little chat with her, one-on-one. You know, sometimes children open up more outside the presence of their parents. She's clearly not responsible for any of this, so it would only be to find out if she knows anything that might help the investigation along. It would also be good to get an outsider's take on how she's doing."

In Tiago's case, Garland couldn't be blamed altogether for turning down this same request. Tiago could have been considered a suspect and needed that parental protection. Vivi was a different story, though. As JD said, the girl was in no jeopardy. Dion was confident that this time the father would consent.

"I'm sorry, I can't allow that," Garland said, and Dion blinked in surprise. "You can talk to her in my presence, yes. Alone, no."

JD nodded her understanding, but Dion lost patience and said, "Why? What's your reason this time?"

Garland jutted his chin out. "You want my reason? I'm her legal guardian. I know what's in her best interest. Being interrogated by cops is a hundred percent not, 'cause I know where it'll go from there. She'll say something, and you'll read into it some kind of lead, so you'll grill her further, and if I'm not there to keep tabs, I'll lose control of the situation. And when you finally get the guy and it ends up going to court, it'll go on for years, interview after interview, then preliminary inquiry, then trial, then retrial. I know how the system works. Slow, that's how. She'll be a teenager by the time it's all said and done, and have nothing left of her childhood. Okay? Kids shouldn't have to go through any of that. That good enough reason for you?"

"You don't think it would have been a good idea for us to have spoken to Tiago?" Dion put to him. "You don't think he might have had something he wanted to say, but couldn't because you were there? He refused counselling. His body language said he was afraid of talking in front of you. You think silence was in his best interest?"

Garland leapt to his feet and wagged a finger at Dion's face as he shouted, "You're not going to lay Tia's death at my feet, sir."

"No, but I'm sure not going to bullshit and say what you did was right," Dion shouted back, also on his feet. He had plenty more to add, but JD stepped in and called the whole thing off.

# TWENTY

## THE BRINK

EVERY TIME JD'S PHONE RANG, she anxiously checked its display. If there was no caller ID, she answered anyway, half hoping and half dreading that it would be Viviani Garland on the line. It never was. She tried to stop worrying about that quiet little girl in that awful house above the Seymour River, and focused instead on an exciting lead she'd turned up in the case of Robbie Clark.

She took her update to Leith at his desk. "Long black sedan," she told him. "You say Millie Hartshorne saw Kyler get into a Cadillac DeVille. Having personally seen Clark get into a car of similar general body type, I've checked further. Guess what he owns?"

Leith raised his brows. "A Cadillac DeVille."

"Way old, a '95er. But still shiny. What do we do? Haul him back in?"

"Not yet. Got anything else on him?"

With so much work to be done, JD was too restless to sit. The two cases, Luna Mae Garland and Tasha Aziz, were not bound as one, but had one thing in common, that being Kyler Hartshorne. With Hartshorne's death, he was not only the linchpin, but possibly a murder inquiry unto himself. And Kyler was now connected to Robbie Clark by a nice, fat, tangible link in the shape of a four-door sedan.

"Nothing," she said. "No criminal record. Clark has worked for the school district for ten years. Till now, no stain on his employee file. If he's been paying Kyler off for something, it would be good to have a go at his banking records. Maybe Kyler was blackmailing him over the weed? A school counsellor would get fired for that, for sure. Wouldn't he?"

"For sure," Leith said. "What about Kyler's goodbye note? Handwriting expert got any news for you?"

"Nothing definitive. But off the record, I think it's forged."

Again Leith's brows went up. "Why?"

JD had been waiting for this, the chance to gloat. "When Doug and Jim went looking for known samples of Kyler's writing, his mom gave them some letters he wrote home last year when he went on a school trip to the Island. I looked at those letters, and one thing I can tell you for sure is Kyler knows how to spell *sincerely*."

"He was stressed when he wrote the note. Could be a slip."

"Or could be a dumbass counsellor assuming the lug can't spell, and trying too hard for authenticity."

"Or that."

"Anyway, we'll know soon enough," JD said. She didn't have to add that a definitive *Yes, it's a forgery* from the document analyst would take Hartshorne's death from suicide straight to murder. "I'd say whatever Clark's done, it's a whole lot more serious than smoking pot."

Leith had guessed what she was referring to. "Tasha Aziz. Lean on that handwriting expert, JD. Expedite the report. See if you can get a sample of Clark's writing, too, in case she can match it up to the forgery. If that's what it turns out to be."

From what JD knew, reverse engineering a forged document was rarely possible, positively identifying the forger unlikely. She said so, then added, "But Robbie doesn't have to know that, does he?"

* * *

In the late afternoon Dion was summoned to Bosko's office, where he sat and waited for the sergeant to finish a phone call and say whatever he had to say. With all the trouble in the air, he expected the worst.

"I've received a complaint against you, Cal," Bosko said, his call ended and his expression grave. "Zachary Garland says you harassed and threatened him."

This was nowhere near the worst, but it wasn't good, either. "I *what*?"

Bosko checked his notes. "Slandered and insulted him, too."

"I didn't. I told him what was what."

"Sometimes it's best not to tell people what's what," Bosko said. "He's not going to pursue it, he tells me, as long as he gets an apology from you."

"An apology?"

"In writing."

"What am I supposed to say, sorry you're an ass-hole for putting your kids' lives at risk, not to mention hindering the investigation into your youngest child's abduction?"

"Something like that, except stop at *sorry*. And he's got every right to be present when his kids are inter-viewed. You know that. I expect better of you."

On a mental notepad Dion tried to script an apology that would satisfy both himself and Zachary Garland. Impossible. He looked at his watch. He was between tasks, and now was as good a time as ever. Cut this complaint at the bud before it bloomed into a problem. "I'll go tell him in person," he said. "Will that do?" Already he was up and standing in the doorway. "It'll be better in person. I can explain what the issue is and put this to bed."

"Here's an even better idea," Bosko said. "Write a note, let me vet it, and I'll have it delivered. He'll be glad to accept it. I doubt he's seriously up to a lawsuit."

Dion didn't want letters of apology on his service rec-ord. He was loving Zachary Garland less by the second, but he could fix this. "I think an apology in person will be good for both me and him."

When no objection came fast enough, he let the door swing shut and headed first to the squad room to grab his winter coat, then down to the parkade to sign out a car.

He knew the traffic pulse on the North Shore — which thoroughfares to avoid, which roundabout routes ended up being shortcuts — and in minutes he was outside Garland's apartment block. He was pulling the handbrake on his unmarked cruiser when he saw the man he was supposed to grovel to come jetting out of the building's foyer. Garland looked stressed. Late for work, maybe. He sometimes worked into the evening as a trainer at the boxing gym, and maybe this was the late shift he was heading to.

Dion considered stepping out of his car and hailing Garland, but too late. The man had trotted to the driver's side of a pickup parked at the curb, and only a sprint and tackle would stop him. No, this discussion would have to wait for another day.

As he pulled out, he saw Garland's truck wasn't swinging left along Marine Drive, as it should if he was going to the gym. Instead it was heading down Forbes toward Esplanade. Dion's preferred route back to the detachment would take him in the opposite direction, up Forbes to Keith. But downward would also get him there, no harm done. He drove, keeping Garland's tail lights in sight. Maybe the guy was out on some minor errand, like a grocery run. But the rush he was in, the sense of urgency, that had nothing to do with bread and milk.

They travelled in tandem down Esplanade and took the Low Level Road along the waterfront, with its pigeons and silos, train tracks and chain-link and mountains of coal. The Low Level became Cotton, and Cotton joined Main Street, and still Garland kept driving southbound. It was starting to look like his destination was Riverside Drive.

Dion understood the importance of team communication. Even an unplanned goose chase that would likely lead to nowhere but some supermarket parking lot needed to be flagged. He placed a hands-free call to Leith to let him know what he was doing.

"Probably nothing," he added, when he had Leith's interest. "But he seems to be heading to the Vales'. I thought maybe he was going to the Wholesale Club, but he just passed it this second. He's carrying on. I'll check it out and let you know."

"Yeah, you do that," Leith said.

Dion disconnected. Leith had sounded wary, like he assumed Dion was going to get into some kind of trouble. Irritating. Just because of one bad experience last fall? What would it take to prove he'd learned his lesson, had smartened up, and knew everything there was to know about officer safety?

"Give me a little credit …" he muttered, and he sped up, not to lose Garland's tail lights in traffic.

* * *

The documents analyst was more than happy to explain to JD why she felt Kyler Hartshorne's suicide note was a forgery. She leaned on the countertop in the Vancouver lab and pointed out the minuscule clues that could be found in the note. Clues that suggested to the trained eye that this was not penned by Kyler. She then pointed at one of Kyler's known samples, a science assignment about venomous insects, and said, "It's well written."

The prose, she meant, not the penmanship, which was a mess.

"Yes, because it was plagiarized," JD said. The teacher who had supplied the three pages of messy foolscap had told her so, as if plagiarism was a fact of life in her classroom. Didn't matter to JD, as long as the cheating hand that had put pen to paper belonged to Kyler.

The handwriting expert wasn't done, though, after her critical analysis of the venom project. She returned to where she'd left off, educating JD on the technicalities of forgery detection.

"No, I trust you're right," JD said. Again she was ignored, so she waited through the rest of the lesson in silence. Let the pro have her day, talking about upstrokes, hooks, and crossbars.

JD then asked about the known sample she'd provided of Robbie Clark's signature, scooped when he'd filled out paperwork following his pot-buying confession. What she wanted to know now was whether this passionate expert could match Clark's signature to the forgery. She found out soon enough that the expert could not.

Back at the detachment JD formulated a plan to present to the team on how to approach Clark and how to use this handwriting information — or misinformation, to be precise — to their best advantage.

\* \* \*

Dion was right in guessing Garland was headed to Riverside Drive. He had lost the truck in traffic, having got stuck at a murderously long red light, and by the time he arrived at the Vales' he found the pickup parked curbside, its driver nowhere in sight.

Maybe Viviani was the reason for Garland's fast trip out here. Had he been called because something was wrong, and raced over to help out?

Unsure what to do, Dion pulled into the adjacent boulevard and parked. It was none of his business where Garland went, or why. There was no restraining order at play here, and seeing as the estranged couple shared custody of Viviani, contact between them was inevitable.

From where he was parked he could see the face of the house that had been the hub of disaster since the evening of February 6, when Luna Mae had vanished from her crib. All quiet now. He rolled down his window to listen. Did he hear shouting? No, just the noise of the river floating up from below. Funny how river flow could sound like an angry mob. If he listened hard enough, he could almost make out the words.

He sighed and fidgeted. He considered going over, knocking on the door with a story. He'd say he was stopping by with an update, say, and slip in the question about Zach's visit. Why the impromptu drop-in? He then recalled the reason he'd gone to see Zach in the first place was to apologize. For harassment.

He called Leith again. "Garland's at the Vales'. No idea why. I'm just keeping an eye — oh!"

The Vale front door had burst open as he spoke, and a flurry of bodies had spilled out. He shouted at Leith as he pushed open his driver's door, "Garland and Perry Vale are fighting. Damn! Garland just slugged Vale, side of the head, pow. Vale's down." He paused, one foot out. "Wait. Garland was going to kick Vale, but Gemma pushed him away. I don't see Viviani anywhere. Looks like Vale's okay. He's up on his feet, and Garland's reaching out, looks like he wants to shake hands. Maybe it'll cool off now."

But it didn't cool off, and he gave Leith a final excited report: "Whoa, Vale's got Garland in a chokehold, and he's shaking him like a — I have to go help." He disconnected Leith's response and raced down the driveway, shouting, "Let him go, Perry, *now!*"

Perry let go, but only because he'd been judo flipped with a thud onto the welcome mat. Garland bounced on his feet, shaking out his shoulders as Gemma helped Perry up. Dion entered the fray and received a blow on the arm by one of Garland's air-jabs. When he'd recovered from a stagger, Gemma was shouting insults at her ex, Perry was knuckling blood off his lip but posturing for another round, and Zachary was winding up a fist for the knockout punch.

The fight was unfair: the skinny, middle-aged engineer facing off against the meaty boxer, and nobody was heeding Dion's commands to end it now. He approached Garland sidelong and seized his flexed arm. Garland shook him off and gave him a shove, then sprang out of reach, pointing at the Vales and crying, "They killed Luna."

"No, you killed Luna," Gemma bellowed. "You and your fucking stuffie obsession."

"It's not an obsession." Garland seemed to be choking on tears. "You hoarding jewellery is an obsession. And you don't know the first thing about being a mother."

Dion was sitting on the pavement after Garland's last shove, hurting all over. He wasn't going to tackle Garland again, not without backup. But as he struggled to his feet and tried to make the call, the skirmish ended. The Vales were supporting each other in their doorway, and Garland stood looking tearful and lost.

With Garland apparently defused, Dion apprached again. But the big man turned to him, eyes wide and bloodshot, chest heaving, and with a roar pushed past and raced away from the house, up the driveway. Not heading back to his vehicle, but swinging down toward the gateway that accessed the river below.

"*Goddamn it,*" Dion said. It was no stretch to imagine Garland meant to throw himself off the jumping rock, and he dashed after him, pounding down the steep metal-rung stairs in time to see Garland's heels scramble up toward the cliffs where Tiago had ended his life. He followed.

Atop the rock he came to a stop. Garland stood motionless by the flowers somebody had placed in memoriam on the brink overlooking the pool, the place Kyler Hartshorne had fallen to his death. He seemed to be staring at the swirling pool below.

"Garland." Dion worked to sound calm and in control, not angry and exhausted. He was advancing, too, but slowly. Step by cautious step.

Garland looked around. "What?"

"What are you doing?"

Pause. "I'm going to kill myself. What d'you think I'm doing?"

Another step closer. "Come on, Zach. That's not the answer. Let's talk it over."

"Stay where you are."

Dion stopped, leaving a distance of ten feet between them. He didn't believe Garland intended to kill himself. It was just words. The guy wanted sympathy. Wanted to be talked away from the ledge and forgiven for his screw-ups. But talking people off ledges wasn't something Dion knew much about. He felt trapped. Leith had been alerted and help was on its way, but what to do meanwhile? He couldn't leave Garland like this, and couldn't move closer. He tried to open a dialogue. "So what's going on, Zach? Why are you beating up on Perry and Gemma?"

"I've had it with the bitch, holding shit over my head like that. Can't make a move without her threatening to take Vivi. I'm going to end it, like now."

"It can't be that bad," Dion said. "You've got so much to live for." The words sounded flimsy in his own ears, and he feared Garland would jump if only to escape his rescuer's drivel. "C'mon. Let's talk about it."

"No. Go away."

"You know I can't do that."

"So do what you want."

There seemed nothing left to say. Dion had run out of drivel, and Garland continued to stare at the water below. But he wasn't jumping. Maybe he'd just painted himself into a corner by threatening to do so, and now he had no choice, if only for pride's sake.

Dion shifted his feet, praying Leith would arrive soon. Leith would know what to do.

But from the road above he heard only silence.

Garland inched closer to the brink. Dion lifted a helpless hand, then dropped it. He almost shouted out in anger, *Just do it, then, asshole.*

But he didn't. *What would Leith say if he was down here, negotiating with a madman who'd painted himself into a corner?*

Of course. Throw Garland a crown. "You gotta be strong, Zach," he called out with new conviction. "You really want to do this to Vivi? She needs you. Come away from that edge and talk to me."

*Bingo.*

He could see through Garland's hesitation. He could read his mind, every *Thank god* and *Fuck me* and *Don't let the bastard cop know he's won.* And finally, *Walk, don't run.*

Garland cleared his throat. He clapped his hands to his thighs in a show of resignation, and turned. Dion stepped back. Garland was powerful, unpredictable, stupid, and anything could set him off again. Dion could be picked up like a toy and heaved into the river. He'd end up dead, with Leith's parting words ringing in his ears: *Told you so.*

He saw that Garland was clearly in the mood to surrender, was heading this way, only delayed by his boot snagging a root. Garland would now head up the iron rungs to the safety of the street, as directed, and there would give up all those secrets he was harbouring. He'd tell Dion where Luna Mae was, dead or alive, and Dion would get congratulations on how well he'd handled the dicey situation.

Later, he realized he shouldn't have let his mind wander. If he had stayed in the moment, he would have thought twice when Garland's snagged boot tipped him off balance, toward the pool into which teenagers jumped when the river ran high. Even with the winter rainfall, the river was now running low. Rocky, ice-cold, and deadly — Garland would fall to certain death if Dion didn't run and grab him.

He should have predicted that if he took hold of Garland, Garland might take hold of him, and they'd both go over and be dashed to pieces on the rocks below.

It didn't happen that way, as it turned out, as Garland managed to grasp a sapling for anchor and pull himself aside, leaving Dion, still rushing toward what was now a void, to put on the brakes too late and plunge to certain death all on his own.

# TWENTY-ONE

## BATTLE SCARS

THE RAIN CAME DOWN in surges, beating the windshield, spattering on the shiny black road ahead. Leith was well on his way to the Vale home when he heard the dispatch: somebody had fallen off a rock bluff into the river. Based on the directions given, he knew which rock bluff it was. On listening further, he learned the fallen was apparently a cop, and the man who'd called in the fall was one Zachary Garland.

"Jesus," he shouted. He hit the siren and stepped on the gas.

He parked crookedly in the Vale driveway and grabbed the first aid kit from the trunk. He was met in the Vale driveway by Zach Garland, while Gemma and Perry stood by their front door. The three looked frayed and dazed. Leith told the Vales to stay put and direct the emergency crews when they arrived, then Zach led the way through the gate and down the iron steps, thumping and splashing down ahead of Leith in his heavy boots, *bang bang bang bang bang*, not detouring up to the jumping rock, but straight down to the riverbank, to the shallow pool that Dion had apparently fallen into.

It was an accident, Zach was saying, but Leith wasn't listening to the fine details. Cause didn't matter now — what mattered was effect, and a colleague who needed rescuing. Though from what Leith knew of the jumping rock, it wasn't going to be a rescue so much as a recovery mission.

The cold hit him as he reached the beach. This stretch of the Seymour was a chasm where darkness fell fast. Dimly he could see the water casually churning. Lazily munching up the body, he supposed. Rain pocked against him and the rocks and the river, water to water, dancing and dashing. His pants were wet at the knees, and only his parka protected his head and torso. That gritty stretch of beach over there would give him better reach, if it came to fishing out the body, but to get over there he had to wade from here. He stepped in and felt the ice snap around his ankles like electricity. The cobbles were large and slippery underfoot, making the few metres from shore to shore a gauntlet, but with much gasping, swearing, and arm wheeling, he made it.

Clambering onto the adjacent beach, he stared into the heart of the pool. Nothing. He dragged a wet palm down his wet face. Phone at his ear, he checked the emergency vehicles' ETA. The fire crew with its rescue expertise and equipment was on its way.

He peered, and now could see the body in the darkness. The body wasn't bobbing passively, but treading water and spluttering.

Too pissed off to be dead.

*I don't believe this.* He made a megaphone out of his hands. "Cal! Y'all right?"

The man in the pool seemed to be fighting with an adversary. No, he was shedding his coat to escape its drag. He thrashed his way toward Leith, made it to hip depth, and fell to his hands and knees, crawling through the shallows, following Leith's guiding voice. Leith stepped into the water and grasped his arm, pulling him up to where he could collapse across coarse sand.

But at these temperatures Leith knew relaxing was a bad idea. "C'mon now, sit up. Help's on the way. I was just planning what to wear to the funeral."

He removed his own parka, its shell wet but its lining dry, to wrap around Dion, and the rain pummelled him as he worked, plastering his hair and shirt and trousers in a hellishly uncomfortable shrink-wrap effect. The wind seemed to take pleasure doubling in strength as it whipped through the channel, snatching the last of his body heat.

But if he was uncomfortable, Dion was going to freeze to death if help didn't arrive soon. Leith crouched and managed to bully him into a sitting position — far from easy with the dead weight of a grown man — then snugged the parka around him as best he could. "Anything broken, d'you think?"

Dion winced, shivering violently. "F-f—" he said.

Speech, a good sign. Leith leaned closer. "What?"

Dion placed a palm on his own right leg. "F-f-f—"

"Fucking leg?"

Nod.

"You hurt your fucking leg?"

No nod this time. Leith ordered him again to stay sitting upright. "Listen. I hear sirens." It was wishful thinking and a bit of a bribe. All he heard was the wind and the chattering of Dion's teeth. The officer-down code had been broadcast, and fire and ambulance would be jumping to it. But it would take a few minutes still, and a few minutes was a long time for a wet and injured man to sit about in these temperatures. Leith turned to shout out to Zach to bring as many blankets as he could find, but Zach was gone.

He recalled the first aid kit he'd brought down and dropped on the beach, and had to traverse the cobble stones again to fetch it. The foil emergency blanket inside the kit was a neat packet. His fingers went numb as he gave the foil a snap into the wind to unfold it. Dion accepted the blanket indifferently. He wasn't shivering now. His dark eyes were open but he seemed faraway and no longer responded to questions.

Finally, sirens. The angels were descending.

Leith stood back as fire and rescue arrived and took over. He told them to be careful with the patient's right leg, which might be broken. He reclaimed his parka, and used the discarded emergency blanket as a shawl as he waded once more through the ice-cold water — almost an expert on the cobbles by now — and climbed the stairs behind the crew and their gurney. Up on the roadside, wet, dirty, and numb, he gave the paramedics as much information as he could about Dion's history. Which wasn't much. He realized he didn't even know an exact age. Thirty? Couldn't give next of kin either, or specific allergies, or health conditions. But it didn't matter. The ambulance was idling, ready for takeoff.

Leith told the medics to take care of his buddy for him.

They promised they would, and the ambulance departed.

Back in his car, engine turning over and heat dialed to max, he phoned JD and told her he was out of commission for a while, but he had some people who needed to be tracked down and questioned. Gemma, Perry, and Zach. He gave her the abridged version of all that had happened here by the river. JD asked how dead Cal was, exactly.

"Not quite," he told her. "Just needs thawing."

He promised he'd keep her posted, then disconnected and headed up Riverside Drive. Already he could feel a nasty cold working its way to his sinuses. Damn. Just what he needed to end a perfect day.

\* \* \*

JD had a picture in her mind of Zachary Garland as a desperate fugitive who had pushed a cop to his death and was now on the run. He wasn't at the Vales', she learned, when she called to tell the couple to stay there till she could talk to them, hopefully within the next hour. Neither was the fugitive at his apartment. Or wasn't answering his buzzer, anyway.

She was thinking about warrants, dragnets, and border alerts when she arrived back at the detachment and saw his silver pickup in the lot. And there was someone in the cab, sitting motionless at the wheel. For Pete's sake. While she'd been looking for him high and low, he'd been here all along.

The figure in the driver's seat was impossible to identify through the misted windows. JD double-parked and approached the vehicle obliquely. She imagined opening the door and finding either a gun pointed at her face or a blood-spattered Garland slumped over the steering wheel, brains blown out.

Thankfully, she found neither. The man appeared alive and well, looking straight ahead, and seemed to be eating. Only when she knocked on the glass did he turn and see her. His window scrolled down.

"Hi," he said. The sandwich in his hand looked like a fast-food sub loaded with cold cuts. But he was only eating by rote, JD realized, his eyes wild like a spooked horse. "I figured you'd want to talk," he said, as his jaws rolled through meat and bread like a conveyor-belt shredder. "It was an accident. Like I told that other guy, Leith."

"I tried calling you, Zach. You didn't answer."

"I was driving. Here."

"You could have returned my call."

"I forgot. I'm under a lot of pressure right now."

"Well, come inside."

In an interview room upstairs, he told her what had happened at the river. "All I did was go over to talk with Gemma."

"Yeah?" JD said. "Had a nice friendly chat with her and Perry, did you?"

He pulled a face as he met her unflinching eyes. "We kind of had words."

*Words* wasn't what JD would call it, from what Leith had told her. Wasn't there something about a chokehold, bodies down? But best to let Garland go on shellacking the story. Sometimes the gloss proved most interesting. "Go on."

"Then the young cop showed up."

"Dion."

"That's him. And I just kind of freaked out. Felt surrounded. I climbed up on the rock where my son died. Tiago. Some of the students had brought flowers, you know. Really nice." He shook his head. "Felt like ending it myself. Like I'm done with this fucking life. You know?"

JD told him she got it.

"The cop came after me," he said. "Sorry, I don't even remember his name."

"Dion."

"Right. Is he …"

"Dead? No."

"Thank god."

"Yeah. Go on."

"Me and him had a conversation, and he reminded me that Vivi needs me. Which she does. So I smartened up and turned back, but I must have tripped over a tree root or something." He gave his forehead a self-admonishing whack. "And he reached out to grab me, and then he kind of flew sideways and over he went."

JD had learned that Dion had hurt his knee, was being defrosted, and was otherwise fine. She found the idea of him flying through the air like a Frisbee kind of hilarious, now that he was out of danger. She looked forward to seeing him so she could tell him so.

"First thing I did was call 911," Garland said. "Then I headed for the steps to see if I could save him. But that's when the other cop showed up, Leith. I led the way to the beach, but then all of a sudden I couldn't face it. It was my fault for tripping, and I just felt so bad. I ran back to my truck and took off. I went to the gym and sat in the parking lot for a while. Then I realized you'd want me to give a statement, and headed to the detachment instead. Thought I'd just sit and wait till I got called in."

*And somewhere along the way picked up a foot-long sub*, JD thought. She wondered what had sent Dion out to Riverside Drive in the first place. How did he always manage to pinpoint trouble, and then get in the middle of it? "What were you arguing with Gemma and Perry about?"

Garland's eyes shifted now, JD noted. He was preparing his answer. "Viviani," he said. "First Gemma doesn't want her, then she does, and now it's like, 'I get sole custody, Zach, and you get visitation rights.'" He hadn't done a bad job of imitating his ex, and was now his angry self again. "Well, no, Gemma. She's my brother's kid. You're not even related. So fuck off. But it's like now that Luna's gone, she's decided she wants to have Vivi. It's not that she loves Vivi. She just likes making me dance to her tune."

His words had the ring of truth to them, JD believed. But there was also evasion. She asked him about the physical altercation, and he admitted some punches had been thrown. And yes, he was partly to blame for the fracas. Well, mostly to blame.

Beyond admitting his part in the fight, JD could get no more from Garland.

She released him, collected Shiomi, and headed out to Riverside Drive to get the Vales' version of events. Gemma and Perry were waiting for them, ready to talk. JD asked them about the skirmish. "We've heard Zach's side," she told them. "What's yours?"

The Vales' story struck JD as a few degrees more honest than Garland's. Perry described Garland as bullying, rude, and verbally abusive. Garland had thrown the first punch as Perry tried to escort him to the exit, he said, leading to a bit of a brawl on the doorstep.

Gemma pointed out the bruise on her husband's cheek. "He might even have a tooth knocked loose. Does it still feel wiggly, hun? Good thing half your friends are dentists."

"My teeth are fine," Perry said, stoically accepting his wife's caresses. "It's a split lip, Gem. That's all."

The couple's explanation of the fight parallelled Garland's, JD learned. The three of them had argued about Vivi's primary residence. "She'd be far better off with us," Gemma said. "We're in a good neighbourhood, and we're close to the school and all her friends. Zach just doesn't have the brains to accept it."

"What does Vivi think?"

"She loves it here."

"So you guys and Zach were arguing about where Vivi should live. I don't get it. What's the urgency? Why did Zach rush over here like his pants were on fire?"

Gemma shrugged. "We were talking on the phone about it, and ended up in a shouting match, so he came over to settle it face-to-face."

On some level, it seemed reasonable enough. JD thanked them, and she and Shiomi left.

In the vehicle on the way back to the city, Shiomi said, "That Perry guy is kind of proud of it, isn't he? I bet that split lip is his first battle scar ever. Want to bet how many selfies he'll take tonight?"

JD was wondering what the Vales weren't telling her, and whether it was the same thing that Garland wasn't. She said, "If Perry managed to get Zach in a chokehold, even for a few seconds, I'd say he's got something to be proud of."

"Got any battle scars yourself?" Shiomi asked, with a grin. "Shark bites?"

JD's battle scars were all inside and deeply personal, and she wasn't going to make light of them. "Nope," she said. "I'm too smart to swim with sharks."

Shiomi wasn't fazed. She showed JD a long, pearly line on the underside of her forearm. "First patrol," she explained. "I smartened up pretty fast after that."

"Blade?" JD guessed. "Lucky you got away with your life, Niko."

Thinking about close calls reminded JD of Cal, who'd survived a fall into the Seymour. What a dink, always stealing the spotlight. He was the free-falling cartoon character who just misses the trampoline, the bloody-nosed boxer reeling in circles. He was Buster Keaton walking against the wind. Couldn't be funnier, that guy. So why did she feel so blue?

* * *

Leith had changed into dry clothes and fortified himself with cold meds. He was standing in the glare of the hospital corridor, talking to the night-shift ward nurse about the state of Dion's health. Like everyone else, she seemed to take his scrape with death lightly, and Leith was starting to feel silly for having thought the worst.

"He'll live," the nurse told him. "He's got the lowest-grade hypothermia on the scale and a patellar contusion."

"Yikes!"

"Bruised kneecap," she said.

"Ah."

"And he's asleep, so unless it's super important, you'll have to wait till morning to talk to him. He'll be kept in for observation tonight to make sure the swelling goes down. Assuming it does, he'll be cleared out along with his breakfast tray."

Leith decided it wasn't super important to talk to Dion now, and rode down on the elevator. He was exiting the lobby toward the rear exit when he spotted a familiar figure standing to one side, the broad back and shoulders of Mike Bosko. Bosko was stooping slightly as he spoke to a slim young woman with long blond hair. Leith recognized the woman as he neared. Kate Ballantyne, Dion's girlfriend.

"Hey, Dave," Bosko said, straightening to his full height. "I dropped by to see Cal, but apparently that's not going to happen. Got any news for us?"

"Banged his knee, but otherwise fine," Leith said. "Can't get his statement till tomorrow morning, so I figure I'll take off for now."

"I actually did get to poke my head in and say hello," Kate told him. "But that's about all, as he was being tended to. I told him I'd be back in the morning."

So why was she hanging around now, at this hour? Why were both of them hanging around?

"I hear you saved his life," Kate added. "Not for the first time. Thanks, Dave."

She had a nice smile. Captivating. No wonder Dion was working hard to rebuild their relationship. "All part of the job," he heard himself reply in a blustery way. "Well, good night."

As the glass doors closed behind him, he paused to glance back, and saw that Bosko and Kate had gone back to whatever conversation he had interrupted.

Something wrong with the picture, though. Bosko listening instead of talking for a change. His head tilted, mouth shut. Strange. And what Kate had been talking about when Leith approached wasn't her lover's injured knee, but a much broader subject: India.

"Am I the only one who cares?" he said aloud as he returned to his vehicle. Then he remembered JD. Once in the driver's seat, he texted her with the update.

> **C will be OK. How many lives does he have left?**

JD texted back a minute later.

> **By my count 5.**

# TWENTY-TWO
## SEEING RED

*February 13*

DION WOKE IN a hospital room with a jolt. It was a sickening flashback, too much like the last time he'd opened his eyes to a new reality, patched together after a car crash, learning that Looch was dead and his own troubles were just beginning.

The flashback was gone as he blinked into the daylight and recalled where he was, and why. He'd fallen into the river, that's all. And Leith had fished him out again. So in the end he'd proven himself wrong, and a fall from the rock at this time of year was survivable after all.

He lay trying to firm up the series of events in his mind. He'd climbed the cliffs to convince Zachary Garland not to kill himself. Garland had stumbled but hadn't fallen.

He recalled some of what followed. Not the plunge itself, much. But rain coming down. Cold. Feeling sure he'd snapped his leg, worrying how a broken leg would affect his job. David Leith hovering over him like a wet, scowling angel, telling him to sit up. A silver wing spread out fluttering and crackling, protecting him from the biting wind. Then he must have blacked out.

He felt okay now, if fuzzy-headed. The leg didn't hurt, but maybe only because he had massive painkillers on board. He threw back the blankets to inspect his knee. A wrecked leg could lead to desk duty, sometimes for a long time. Sometimes forever.

A nurse appeared and drew the blankets back over him. "You're not going anywhere just yet," she said.

He braced for the news as he stared up at her. "Nothing serious, right?"

"Nothing serious," she told him, and described his bruised kneecap, and how walking might be touchy for a while. "Take it easy at the dance, that's all. No hip hop."

"Dance?"

She was Indian Canadian, and still had the overseas accent. "Your good friend Doug came by to see how you're doing. He said you'll be taking your sweetheart out to a shindig tomorrow. The Eagles dance? You look confused."

"Oh," he said. "That." The fundraising Valentine's Day dance he wouldn't be attending tomorrow. "I'm not going," he said. "You want the tickets?"

A breakfast tray arrived as the nurse turned down the offer, but Dion wasn't hungry. He tried flexing his knee, but the nurse stopped him. He wanted to leave, but she told him the physiotherapist would be up soon to talk to him. As she headed for the door, he stopped her with another question. He'd just recalled something he had to tell Leith — it was about Zachary Garland, and it was important. "Where's my phone?"

His water-resistant iPhone had been clipped to his belt when he'd gone in the river, and when it was brought to him he was happy to find it had survived the dousing as well. He made the call, and twenty minutes later was sitting in bed and telling Leith what he had overheard between Gemma and Zachary the evening before. Each had accused the other of killing Luna. Interesting, but that wasn't all. Down by the river Zachary had confessed his reason for wanting to throw himself into the river. Gemma was holding something over his head, he'd said. And she had threatened to take Vivi.

He then recalled maybe the most important and most puzzling clue of all. "Up at the house when they were arguing, Gemma told Zachary he had a stuffie obsession. What's a stuffie?"

"You don't know what stuffies are?" Leith asked, surprised. "Little plush toys. For kids."

"Oh."

"Bears, dogs, lizards, owls. Pretty well any animal you can think of, a stuffie's been made of it."

Dion tried to imagine a grown man — a boxing trainer, yet — collecting stuffed toys. Ridiculous. "Then Zachary said Gemma hoards jewellery," he said. "And that she's a bad mom."

"You know what it sounds like to me?" Leith said, as he jotted notes. He looked at Dion with a grin. "Sounds like they're running out of mud to throw. Anyway, good job. I'll put all this to Zach. Can you think of anything else?"

"That's it."

In the doorway Leith stopped for a last word. "Lucky you're out so soon. Tomorrow's Valentine's Day. Wouldn't want to miss out on that, right?"

Then he was gone. His words echoed the nurse's shindig remark, and Dion sat thinking about his plans for the day of romance. Taking Kate out, showing her a good time, reminding her of what a great, fun guy he was. Then proposing marriage.

The hospital breakfast tray still sat before him. A bowl of something with a lid on it. He picked up the spoon. It was important to eat, but he was a knot inside. He had to stay positive. Everything would be okay, and Kate wouldn't turn him down.

She couldn't turn him down. Where would he go from there?

He knocked off the lid and put it back again. His physio arrived, wanting to run him through the process of walking on his damaged leg without making it worse. He paid attention, as he needed to walk. Or to hell with walking; he needed to be ready to run.

\* \* \*

The Vales weren't pressing for assault charges to be laid, and Leith had not arrested Garland, but he had brought him in for a follow-up statement about the serious incident at the Vale home, focusing on the fragments of conversation Dion had shared.

He repeated the less damning fragments to Garland, saving the most serious — the accusations of murder — for later. Garland listened with a troubled scowl, thought it over, and finally said, "I guess the cat's out of the bag."

The recorder recorded, and Leith waited.

"Gemma's devious," Garland said. "Ever since our marriage started going south she's been on a mission, collecting evidence against me. Or what she decides is evidence. It started even before Luna was born. She used to think I was cheating on her, all the time. After Luna was born …"

His flattened hand demonstrated a sled going down a steep hill.

"And what made you tear over to Riverside Drive yesterday afternoon?"

"Vivi. I wanted to bring her home, and Gemma wanted to keep her for another week. That's all. Just stupid stuff."

Leith was beginning to think the scuffle between the parents was going to be a big pile of nothing. A make-work project for him and his team. A file-filler. Even the murder accusations were invented on the spot, the cruellest words the two could come up with on the spur of the moment. He knew about lovers' spats, how minor infractions get twisted into high treason.

But he couldn't let it go till he was sure. "What's she got on you, Zach?"

Garland looked shocked. "Got on me? Nothing."

"You told Constable Dion that Gemma is holding something over your head. In the same breath you said she's also threatening to take Vivi. I can't help putting the two together. What's she saying you've done?"

"What she's saying I've done and what I've done are two completely different animals," Garland snapped. "You get that, right?"

"I get that a lot."

"Good. Because I know where things like this can go." Garland seemed to pull in a deep breath, then blurted it out, the thing Leith had been expecting. "She's decided I molest my kids." His face twisted with disgust. "Which is so not true. No way, ever, would I have any inclination to do anything even remotely ... *ugh*."

"Has she made any formal allegations of this?"

"No. She's just always dangling it in front of me. Uses it to get her way. If you don't do this, I'll say that. She's ... she's a terrorist."

Done, Garland sat looking depressed.

"And you accused her of hoarding jewellery," Leith put to him. "What's that about?"

Garland hooted a laugh at the ceiling. "Jewellery? That's just the tip of the iceberg. Gold, diamonds, clothes, shoes, makeup, new kitchen counter, a night at the opera. Big reason our marriage fell apart, she's mistaken herself for a princess. There was never enough. Embarrassed about the house, the furniture, the car, her tennis racquet, Luna's stroller. *My* fucking hair embarrassed her."

"And your stuffie obsession?"

"I don't have a stuffie obsession," Garland shouted. "Luna loves her stuffies, as a normal healthy baby should. Gemma doesn't think children should get too attached to their toys. Hell knows why. She insisted on weaning Luna from her soother *way* too early. Gemma is a mean, vain woman, and a hypocrite. She didn't even love Luna, not deep down. What kind of mom lets her baby cry till she's blue in the face? I came home from work one day, before we divorced, and Luna's just wailing away in her crib, and Gemma is sitting in the bathroom, plucking her eyebrows or some damn thing. I go in and pick up Luna and comfort her. Gemma says you can't jump up every time a kid bawls. It spoils them. Fine, we each have our parenting style. I accept that. But soon as we're out in public, she's the perfect doting mom and I'm the useless bum of a dad. It's all about appearances, to Gemma. Being a parent isn't deep for her, like it is for me."

"But what have stuffies got to do with Luna's disappearance? Why would Gemma bring up a detail like that?"

"I guess in the same way I was bringing up that crappy vitamin-deficient baby food she'd kept shoving into the kid early on, before I threw it in the garbage and got a crate of the good stuff. I'm into fitness. Not the superficial kind, but the nuts and bolts of what makes us healthy human beings."

Leith decided he knew enough of this couple's personal war, and put to Garland the accusation he'd been saving for last. "Gemma says you killed Luna."

The short, sharp sentence caught Garland by surprise. When he answered, after all the shouting he'd done, his voice was almost small. "She blames me for Luna disappearing."

"And you blame her."

"I have more right to blame her than vice versa. She had Luna under her care when she was taken. But yes, we're both to blame. Not for the disappearance, but for acting like children."

Leith recalled day one of the investigation, how the ex-couple accused each other of kidnapping. But they had come around since then. They had accepted the darker truth — that Luna had been taken by persons unknown. Now they were reverting to blame of the more amorphous sort. *Whatever happened to my baby, if not for you, she'd still be here, alive and well.*

But if there was any truth behind the blaming, Leith had to know what it was. "Does she really think you hurt Luna? Why would she think that?"

"No, she doesn't think I hurt Luna. And it's not her fault, either. We're just being stupid, blowing off steam, looking for scapegoats."

Garland's demeanour had changed, Leith noticed. He sounded cautious now, feeling out his words before he released them. "We had a good talk this morning," he said. "On the phone. 'Cause last night was a wake-up call. We're working toward getting along better. For Vivi's sake. Didn't agree on much, in the end, but one thing we acknowledged is we both owe you guys an apology."

In fact he was starting to sound amazingly smart and mature, for a change. Not that it lasted. "And *I'm* apologizing to you right now, aren't I?" he exclaimed. "But will she? No way, because she's too busy admiring the latest diamond-studded bracelet Perry gave her." He grunted and lowered his face. "I'm sorry, there I go again. She says it's envy, and maybe it is. Maybe I don't like that I'm just a dumb jock and not a zillionaire engineer." He

sniffed and added, as if to himself, "But I'm better looking than him. At least I got that, right?"

True.

Next Leith talked to Chelsea Romanov. It wasn't the
first time he had asked her about the relationship between the divorcees, but today he asked more pointedly. Of the lot, Chelsea seemed the most straightforward
and the least invested in the family dynamics. But affected by the ordeal, Leith could tell. As he'd expected,
she was unable to tell him anything new or interesting
today. Gemma and Zach were tense around each other,
she said, and sharing custody was rough. But for Luna's
sake they had co-operated as best they knew how.

"Zach called her a mean, vain hypocrite," Leith quoted. "What d'you think? Do you agree?"

"No," Chelsea said. "Gemma's as good a parent and
as good a person as Zach is. He's just seeing her through
this lens of aggravation. And he does have a way of exaggerating his feelings. You know, he takes everything
to the extreme."

As if Leith needed to be told. "Did Luna Mae have a
favourite kind of toy?"

Chelsea cast down her eyes. "Sure," she said. "She
likes her fluffy animals. Has a whole bunch of them."

"Does she have a favourite?"

"The parrot, probably. Probably because of its colours. Zach told me this. Babies don't see in colour right
away, but when it starts to kick in, red stands out to
them most, so they may seem to gravitate toward it. And
eventually they're seeing all the primary colours, you
know. The parrot is very bright, of course. Lots of red."

"Was that toy, or any toy, a particular bone of contention between Gemma and Zach?"

"A bone of contention?" Chelsea rolled her eyes. "The parrot, sure. And the doggie, and the froggie, and the clothes she should wear, the styling of her hair, the food she should eat, the world she should or should not be exposed to. Everything's a bone of contention between those two."

"Must have been tough for you, being in the middle, kind of."

"Not really. Soon as Gemma's out of sight he relaxes. He knows the last thing I want to hear about is their little war."

"Is he a good dad?" Leith asked, knowing how biased the answer would be.

Her bias came out without hesitation or apology. "The best. He loves Luna immensely. He would throw himself off a cliff for her."

Or throw a cop off a cliff, anyway. "Did his love for Luna get in the way of the attention he gave to Vivi and Tia, d'you think? Make them feel left out?"

She shook her head. "He is — *was* — hyper aware of those two kids, and how this divorce and custody battle was affecting them. He made sure to spread his love around, make us all feel important and necessary. Zach used to be less vigilant, when Tia and Vivi had each other. But now that Tia's gone, he's focused on protecting Vivi. A really good dad."

"Does Zach tell you the kinds of things Gemma is accusing him of?"

Chelsea nodded. "He did, and they're totally untrue. Gemma maybe isn't lying so much as just really, really wrong. And they talked this morning, trying to come to terms. She called, and he answered. Big steps. I think they finally get it that they've got to grow up."

"That's always good," Leith said.

"For sure."

Next in line for Leith was Perry Vale.

Perry had a colourful bruise on his lower cheek and a small cut on the lip, now congealed. "Zach's a berserker," he said. "You know, if he at least tried to get along, Gemma would be able to cope with all she's lost. And she tries, but Zach doesn't. He comes barging in, stirring up trouble. This incident is really the last straw."

"So he barged in, no reason given?"

Unlike Garland, Perry seemed to carefully consider his words before speaking. "He'd come over to quarrel with Gem about Vivi," he said. "He had it fixed in his mind that the girl was better off with him. Or something along those lines."

"I thought the argument was less about Vivi and more about them blaming each other for what happened to Luna."

"It segued," said Perry, with some bitterness.

"They're now accusing each other of killing her."

"I don't know about Zach, but Gemma's lost hope for getting Luna back alive. It's tearing her apart. She's got me, of course, and she's got her friends, which she didn't have when she was with Zach. I've brought her into a strong social circle. Good women friends who get her out and about, keep her mind off things. But still, she wants to hold somebody responsible, and Zach's like the matador's cape wagging in front of her nose. She knows it's wrong to keep fighting over nothing, and she understands she owes you an apology. We all do."

Leith studied the engineer's face, which seemed more closed than usual. There was something he was sidestepping, and there was also fear.

Fear for his wife's state of mind, maybe that's all it was. "What's Gemma holding over Zach's head? Something to do with Vivi. Tell me about it."

"Nothing but suspicion," Perry said, tiredly. "Things you can't prove."

Was there a shadow of discontent in his attitude? Leith wondered if Perry was falling out of love with the woman he'd married. But moments later as Perry was leaving the room and Gemma entering, the two stopped in passing and embraced. It was a passionate hug. It was real.

With Perry gone, Gemma took her chair. She was slimmer yet fuller than Leith recalled from the beginning of the case. And prettier. He imagined Alison losing Izzy, how grief would drain and age her. Looking at Gemma now, he had doubts about Perry's claim that losing Luna was tearing her apart. She looked, well, perfectly intact.

After some small talk — her diamond-studded bracelet flashing under the fluorescents — Leith put to her the scuffle on the doorstep. "You three were really going at it. What was the problem?"

"I'm sorry we dragged you into our argument," she said. She didn't sound sorry. She sounded edgy. "I didn't realize we were under surveillance."

Leith gave her the half-truth he'd prepared in advance. "It wasn't surveillance. Constable Dion was heading out that way to talk to you, and happened to catch the action. He felt he had to step in."

She relaxed. "Yes, of course. I'm sorry. We must be hard work for you people. I'm genuinely sorry for that."

She was sounding sincere now. Leith thought about the many faces of Gemma Vale he'd seen so far, and wondered how far he could trust her. "Seems you and Zach were both accusing each other of killing Luna," he said. "Want to tell me about it?"

"The blame game. That's all it is. We're working through it. I called Zach this morning, and we faced some difficult truths. We realized we've got a lot of growing up to do. This won't happen again. I'll make sure of it. For your sake as well as ours."

"That's good to hear."

She nodded, and her eyes were drawn again to her bracelet.

But for one last question, Leith was done. "How does your new co-operative attitude affect your thoughts about Vivi's safety in Zach's home?"

She was giving the bracelet a partial turn, maybe to better catch the light. She came out of what looked like a daydream and gave him her full attention. "Yes, well, I might have jumped to conclusions unfairly. Maybe it's a cultural thing. When I was growing up, there was very little *hugging*, in my family. So it struck me as strange, how Zach would cuddle with the girls, Vivi and Luna. I'm sure I was overprotective. Still am. Probably always will be. But I'll try to be less so from now on. Unless and until I'm convinced I'm right. Which of course would be too late, as the damage would be done, as it always is. Am I right?"

Tragically, she was. "Where do you see things going forward with Vivi?"

"We'll have to work it out like adults. Because nothing matters except that girl and what makes her happy. Zach and I have no choice but to get along. She's all we've got left."

"What about P.E.I.? Is Zach still talking about moving?"

"Gosh no. He probably never meant it. Tactical manoeuvres. His way to wound."

Leith saw Gemma out. He watched her burrow against Perry's flank as they walked down the hall toward the exit, his arm around her. His hand clasped around her shoulder looked tight enough to leave bruises.

# TWENTY-THREE

## ROMANTICS

*February 14*

LAST NIGHT'S WIND had blown the rain off to the east, and Valentine's Day began with immaculate skies. Still dark, when Dion woke, but he could see the hint of blue beyond the partially drawn curtains. Kate was beside him, sound asleep. He watched her for a moment, planning. This was going to be her day, and he was going to make it good.

These days he was mostly staying in Kate's condo just off Mountain Highway. It wasn't a great setup. Her condo had too much stuff in it, making it chaotic and impractical. Had it always been like that? He didn't remember being bothered by Kate's disorderliness in the times they'd lived together. Either she'd gotten worse or he'd gotten fussier. But no matter. Once they committed to a shared life, they would combine their resources and move.

He already knew where to: the apartment tower where he'd lived, sometimes alone, sometimes with Kate, before the crash. He loved that place, high over the city. One bedroom and a den, not much larger than this condo, but nicer. She could have the den for her studio. They'd refurnish, do some clutter-busting, start fresh.

He sat on the side of the bed and stretched his hurt leg. Bruised and stiff, but already on the mend. He limped to the kitchen to make coffee, and brought the cups to bed in time for Kate to open her eyes. The coffee grew cold as they made love. Not their usual expedited working-day morning bang, but a Valentine's Day special. Not as *special* as he wanted it to be, with knee pain interfering, but a good one all the same. After breakfast they agreed that hiking the trails wasn't going to happen, and they strolled along the harbourfront instead, ending at the restaurant near the Quay where they had a table reserved for lunch.

They arrived early and had to wait for their table to clear. They sat at the bar, each with a glass of wine, and talked. He drove the conversation toward art. He'd done his homework, looking through the books on Kate's shelf and learning the key points of her world. Realism, impressionism, different mediums, all the big names. He wasn't going to pretend to be an overnight expert — that would stink of fraud — but it was enough to show interest, ask questions, listen to her answers. She seemed to enjoy this new side of him. She ordered another glass of wine.

While she was smoothing down her skirt he took a snapshot of her with his phone, then showed her when she asked to see. The lens had caught only motion, a cascade of her golden hair and the pattern of her blouse, with the bartender in the background pulling a face at someone. A bad shot, but he liked it, even if Kate thought it was a dud. He would add it to his folder of other duds on his computer, for his eyes only.

He told her of the plans he'd made for the rest of the day. After lunch they'd ride the SeaBus across to the city. They'd walk about downtown, if his leg co-operated, check out the Vancouver Art Gallery and shops. Then he'd take her dancing at the Roxy, have a lot of fun, then whenever they got tired they'd cab it home.

He didn't tell her of the highlight of the evening, the ring and the question that he'd ask as soon as the moment was right.

As it turned out, though, he couldn't wait. Finally shown to their table, more wine ordered, she was studying the menu and he was studying her. He reached out and touched her hand. Her smile was warm and happy. With their glasses of shiraz sparkling ruby red in front of them and a magical view of the inlet waters, the moment couldn't get any more perfect. Except for one detail. He'd forgotten the ring in his car's glove box. But did it really matter?

"Kate," he said, as if it had just occurred to him. "Let's get married!"

He beamed at her, and after only a beat — not even — she beamed back and said, "Well, hell ya!"

* * *

"Come on, it'll be fun," said Shiomi's miniaturized telephone voice in JD's ear as JD waited in line at the supermarket. "We've both got tickets. We're both single. You don't have to dance or anything like that. We'll just sit, get drunk, and people-watch. Maybe even get lucky."

Sitting, getting drunk at the Eagles hall, and people-watching did sound kind of all right, JD decided. A break from the job. A break from Tasha's voice. And maybe her heart of stone was softening under the force of Shiomi's insistence on friendship. Maybe it was time to yield an inch.

"Okay," she said. "I know I'll regret this, but I'll see you there."

"Fab! What'll you wear?"

JD looked down at her grungy runners. "Let's see. How about steel-toed boots, torn jeans, and a T-shirt with a rude slogan across it."

Shiomi laughed as if JD was kidding, and they disconnected.

JD *had* been kidding, but now that she'd said it, what a lark it would be if she showed up dressed exactly as she said. Get Shiomi to stop gnashing her perfect teeth and drop her jaw.

What would be a fitting novelty T-shirt for Valentine's Day? JD didn't have anything cheeky in her closet, but she did have connections to a goof who might. She found Doug Paley's home phone number in her contacts and gave him a call.

\* \* \*

"And look at this world," Leith told Alison over a light lunch, trying to cheer her up. She'd gotten her period and was feeling low, and he was clumsily trying to make her see the bright side of things. "It'll happen. But if it doesn't, at least we'll have less to worry about. "

He didn't mention that Ali's attitude to child-watching was a little looser than he'd wish. They both loved their daughter fiercely, but Ali believed the world was a generally good and safe place. Whereas he, as a cop, knew it wasn't.

"I get it," Alison told him. "There's a lot of bad out there. But don't forget it's also getting better. And don't forget you see the worst of the worst."

Leith reflected on the worst of the worst. Tasha Aziz, Luna Garland, Tia and Kyler, and what they had gone through in their final minutes. Every murder through the course of his career had left a gouge in his spirit, some deeper than others. Crimes against children were the worst. As Alison well knew, he was fairly gouged up by now.

"And you think every generation doesn't feel the same?" she was saying. "The world's coming to an end. 'The Eve of Destruction,' that song you used to sing in the shower way back when we first met …"

"I did not."

"Did so. Whenever you watched the news."

"It was a catchy tune."

"And heartfelt words. But a few eves have passed since, and we're still here, and the sky's still blue. All you can do is have faith. And if good people like you give up, that only leaves more room for the bad. Right?"

"For sure," he said.

But what if you've lost faith, and can't drum up more? If you've stopped believing in God, and don't trust the government, and sometimes don't trust your own values? Share your gloom with your wife on Valentine's Day, when all she wants is another child to round out the family? It might be doubling his dread, but it would be doubling her happiness, and what mattered more? Hands down, Alison's happiness won.

That left him with only one option — shut up and keep trying. There was definitely a bright side to that as well.

He smiled and gave the table a decisive thump with his fist. "You're right, that's the last you'll hear of my whining. Oh, hey!" He went to grab his wallet, pulled two dance tickets, a gift from Doug Paley, and tossed them on the table in front of her. "Almost forgot. How about this instead of the movies?"

Alison studied the tickets and gave him a smile of surprise and delight that warmed his heart. "That would be so much cooler, Dave!"

"Or a dreary flop."

"Or that. I'll bring my camera, get some people shots."

A babysitter had been arranged for their movie night out, so a last-minute change of plans would be easy enough to arrange. They would simply ask Suki to stay for four hours instead of three, in case the dance was so much fun they wanted to stay.

Unlikely. Neither of them was a smooth mover on the dance floor, or terrifically comfortable among strangers. It was social awkwardness that had drawn them together in the first place, two wallflowers at some-body's wedding. Four left feet that ended up tangled in bedsheets.

As Alison gathered dishes and headed for the kitch-en, Leith balled up a serviette and lobbed it at her back. She turned in surprise, and he said, "Love you."

Even the obvious had to be stated, once in a while.

# TWENTY-FOUR

## UNROMANTICS

DION WAS STARTING to understand the momentum of anger, as he walked alone in the night, his leg hurting. Like throwing punches, in anger you say things you shouldn't, behave badly, embarrass yourself, and even as you hear yourself doing it, you keep on slugging away. To accomplish what? Ease the pain. It did ease the pain, but only in the heat of the moment. Soon as the heat's gone, the cold moves in, and the pain is worse than ever.

He had said things to Kate today that he shouldn't have. He had behaved badly. He had embarrassed himself. Not in the restaurant, following the misunderstanding, when she had enlightened him with her *godawfully* gentle, "I'm sorry, I'm a little tipsy, and I thought you were kidding."

He hadn't responded then. The bad behaviour came afterward, when they were back in the apartment and he'd tried to keep busy with tidying up, doing the dishes, but couldn't stop interrogating her.

*Why? Why not?*

"It's too soon," she had said. "We're still getting to know each other again. You've been through so much. I'm not ready to commit to a stranger, and I don't think you are either."

"I'm totally ready," he had told her. Among other things. "I'm not a stranger. I'm back. I'm the guy you were always crazy about. No, I'm *better* than him. I've come a long way. How can you say no? We're made for each other. I'll treat you right, better than ever. Don't you want to go back to the way we were?"

She'd shocked him then by saying no, she didn't want to go back to the way they were. Because along with the good memories were the bad, which he must have forgotten. They'd both been unfaithful. They'd split up and got back together too many times to count. Didn't he recall the yelling and the tears? The moving in and moving out, the revenge fucks, the insults? Even if the crash hadn't happened, there was a good chance they'd have broken up anyway. Permanently. The writing was on the wall.

He didn't remember the writing on the wall. All he recalled was the laughter and good times, the parties, the feeling that his body fit with hers like two gorgeous jigsaw puzzle pieces.

*I'll be better at it now*, he had repeated.

*I know you will*, she'd said. *But let's give it some time.*

*How much time?* he had asked, and he recalled now, as he walked, that he hadn't asked the question in a sane, polite way, as he should have, but bellowed it at her, with some F-words attached. At which point she had opted out of the conversation, and he had put on his coat and left, slamming the door behind him.

The evening was supposed to have been like in the movies, lying face-to-face after epic sex, drowsily talking about their exciting future together. His vision was clear, even if hers wasn't. Step one, after marriage, would be to get back his old apartment where he had lived before the crash had splintered both their lives.

He was already on the tower's wait-list. Once in, he'd work his way up to the exact same unit on the tenth floor that overlooked the Burrard Inlet. Same view, same paths of sunlight and shadow tracking across floors and ceilings through the seasons. They would move in and re-equip, replacing the stuff he'd had to abandon when he boarded the Greyhound to head north last year. A new top-of-the-line barbecue, another king-sized bed. The best linens, dishes, furniture, appliances, stereo system. They would throw dinner parties, as they had before. Have friends over. Maybe get a dog.

Thinking back on what Kate had told him tonight, he knew she was right. They'd been madly in love 95 percent of the time, but their life had been rocky at times, too, with broken dishes, harsh words, cheating. Quite a lot of cheating. And maybe she was right that if they had gotten married, they'd have gotten divorced pretty quick, too, just like Zachary and Gemma.

But now he had grown up. He would have committed to her 100 percent, if she had said yes. Not her facetious *hell ya*, but the starry-eyed *oh yes, Cal* that he had been waiting for.

What added insult to injury was that he hadn't gotten it at first that she was joking. Only when he had stupidly sat back and shared the great news with the waitress, quite loudly — *We're getting married!* — had Kate realized he was serious. He'd then noticed the worried look on her face, even as the waitress congratulated them. Other diners had overheard and were also giving them warm smiles, one lady even blowing them a kiss. But his eyes had locked on Kate, because she was blushing. And he knew that blush. It wasn't happiness. It was stress.

When the waitress was gone and the other diners were minding their own business again, she had confessed. Sorry, she'd thought he was kidding.

"*Kidding?*" he had echoed across the table, the quietest shout in the world.

"Because we've only just met, really," she said.

"We've known each other forever."

"But everything's changed, hasn't it? We're both new people. It's like we have to get to know each other again, and that's kind of exciting, too, isn't it?"

A hundred and ten percent, he would have committed to her, if she had let him.

Walking aimlessly, he found himself on Third. He stopped when he realized he was outside the entrance to the Eagles hall where the Valentine's Day dance was taking place. When he opened the door to peek in, music issued out, tumbling down the staircase. His cheeks and ears were cold but his eyes were hot. He stood listening. Dated music, but it sounded seductive.

What was the best way to show Kate he was fine without her?

Have fun, that's what.

\* \* \*

The classic rock suited Leith. They were songs he still considered quite *now*, but were actually very *yesterday*, Ali informed him. He and Ali had been too shy to dance so far, but when the moment was right and the music slowed down, they would likely leave their drinks behind and shimmy their hips a bit. Till then, they sat side by side at the large banquet table, took in the milieu, and talked.

There was a good crowd here, but nobody they knew. Leith worried that Alison was secretly thinking this was the worst idea he'd had in a long time.

But she smiled at him, and he smiled at her. At least they had each other, and what else mattered?

For a few minutes the pressure to be romantic stifled their conversation. Then they were back to normal, talking over renovation plans. The rundown house they'd bought recently needed work, and the question was where to begin and how to budget the thing.

The trouble between them tonight began when Leith wondered aloud how Suki was doing with Izzy. At which point he learned that Alison had actually called a different babysitter in, since Suki couldn't stay longer than the three hours originally requested. But Suki had given Alison the name of a friend who also babysat. Shaylene.

"Shaylene?" Leith said. Then he realized he didn't know Suki by sight, and had assumed the dark-haired girl he'd given last-minute instructions to this evening was the one he had previously vetted and approved through Alison. "Shaylene who? How old is she? Has she taken the course?"

Alison admitted she didn't know if Shaylene had taken the babysitters' course. She knew nothing about the girl except that Suki had recommended her, and she trusted Suki.

"The recommendation of one teenager for another is not enough," Leith snapped. "You should have told me."

"So you could what, grill her? Run a criminal record check?"

*Possibly,* Leith thought.

"What are you doing?" Alison said. "Are you calling her?"

"Yes, I'm calling her."

"God."

The phone rang too many times for his liking before the unknown entity named Shaylene answered. He wanted to ask what the hell she had been doing for five long rings, but instead told her he was just checking in. Everything's fine, she told him. Izzy had woken and made a fuss, but after a bedtime story had fallen asleep again.

Leith told her to double-check the doors and windows, and Shaylene seemed to hesitate before promising yes, she would, sir, make sure everything was locked up nice and super tight.

He ended the call and told Alison, "She sounds like a flake."

"And now you're going to spend the rest of the night imagining her letting in bad boys or getting drunk and burning down the house," Alison said. "Better yet, you'll spend the rest of the night brooding over Picnic Day."

Picnic Day was their code for the event best not spoken about. It happened last summer, the Leiths being fairly new to the North Shore, taking a day out to visit the beaches of Stanley Park. He had gone to grab something from the car, and on his return had found Alison chatting with some school-aged children, and that Izzy had vanished off the planet.

Not vanished, actually, but she had toddled off down the sand and was blocked from his view by a group of sunbathers. By the time he had spotted her, she was all but striding into the waves.

Moments later she might have drowned. Or been kidnapped. Murdered. His heart still missed a beat whenever he recalled the moment.

Alison had felt bad about her carelessness, but not bad enough, and the event had left a scar on their relationship. A scar that should mend with time, except how could it with shit like this happening, putting a perfect stranger in charge of Izzy, without so much as a heads-up to the father?

And since Alison had a generally laid-back approach to child rearing, and since she was alone with Izzy most of the day, how could he trust that she wouldn't get distracted again? At the supermarket, say. Or leave the back door unlatched. Or what about when Izzy was a couple years older and ready to go play outside by herself? It wouldn't happen on Leith's watch. But Alison had grown up running wild on the beaches and back roads of Vancouver Island, and might assume Izzy should be granted the same freedom.

Freedom was great, until the unthinkable happened. And it only took the blink of an eye. And now she wanted a second child. If she couldn't keep tabs on one, how would she deal with two?

A love song played, "Just My Imagination," but husband and wife sat it out in silence. The silence began to work at Leith's conscience. He had overreacted, but couldn't apologize. He wanted to ask her to dance, but couldn't bring himself to speak. He'd spoiled the mood, and Alison looked remote and lonely. Picnic Day still hung between them, along with memories of the argument that followed. Unable to contain themselves, the shouting match in the car, forgetting that Izzy was there behind them picking up on the vibes until she burst into frightened wails.

Never would he shout at Alison like that again. Especially in front of Izzy. He thought about Gemma and Zachary and their custody battle, and he wondered how good they had been at protecting Luna from their anger.

Great way to introduce a child to the world, tearing her in two.

He looked across the room and did a double take. JD and Niko Shiomi had appeared, and were making their way through the crowd toward the bar. They seemed to be arguing. Shiomi was dazzling in red, dressed to kill, but JD was most decidedly not. And what did that say on her shirt?

"I'm with stupid," Alison said coldly.

Leith glanced at her. "What?"

\* \* \*

"Of course I'm mad," Niko said as they waited to order drinks. JD was only half listening. She had just spotted Leith and his wife, Alison, sitting on the sidelines. Leith looked depressed and Alison was aiming her camera at dancers. JD waved, and the couple waved back. She signalled to them that she'd just grab a drink and would join them. But maybe her sign language was too complicated, as Leith didn't look thrilled.

"I put effort into this —" Niko went on, and she skimmed her fingertips over the fabric of her sleek mini-dress. "And you show up like a finalist for ugliest bitch on the planet. And by the way, you get my vote."

JD smoothed the front of her shirt, the slogan Niko hadn't bothered reading. The shirt belonged to Doug Paley, who was a big man, and JD was twiggy, so it was a loose fit. Yet "I'm with stupid" and the pictogram finger were clear enough. Right now the finger was pointing to the person on her right. Which was Niko.

JD waved again at Leith, and pointed at her shirt, and pointed at Niko, but he was looking away and missed it. It was JD's turn to order a drink, and she asked the server for whatever dark beer they had on tap. "What does it matter how I dress?" she said. "The only one who should care is me, and I don't, long as I'm comfy. Are you, in those?"

"It's offensive to others." Shiomi stood taller than usual in platform shoes. She was almost as tall as JD. She ordered a pear cider. "It's disrespectful to wear jeans to a Valentine's Day dance. They shouldn't have let you in. You're such a cow."

The only person who had insulted JD so brazenly, ever, was her sister, and that was back in their teens. JD had learned then to give back in kind. "And you're stupid, I guess," she said.

"Huh? What's that supposed to mean?"

"Not much of a detective, either." Again JD smoothed the front of her shirt. This time Niko read the message and gave a shout of disgust. "Cow," she said again, and moved to JD's left.

"You asked what I would wear tonight, and I told you. And I always keep my word."

They took their drinks to join Leith and Alison. JD had to admire the efforts of whoever had organized this event — the hall was done up for glamour on a dollar-store budget. The long tables were draped with crepe paper cloths, and fake candles flickered next to vases of fake flowers. The lights were low, and a cheap projector spun blurry pink and blue hearts across the ceiling. Fortunately, the sound system was better than the projector, and did justice to the best-known Righteous Brothers song to ever hit the charts, a song that echoed its blue progressions through the large hall and was now busy pulling couples out to the floor.

It wasn't pulling Leith and his wife, though. JD had only met Alison a couple of times, and they hadn't talked much. She seemed to be a quiet woman, and Leith rarely spoke of her. But then he was a private kind of guy who liked to keep home and office separate. JD wondered what their home life was like. By the looks of it, not so jazzy.

"I now totally get why JD's single," Niko was telling Leith. "She thinks she's so smart and funny, but she's horrible, and any man with brains would run the other way."

JD batted her lashes. "You flatter me, Niko."

But she was a little worried. This was supposed to be a romantic night, at least for the Leiths. She and Shiomi crashing their party was probably a bit hellish for them. She sat thinking about Shiomi's dig about men running the other way. Hadn't JD said something along those lines to Dion, referring to Robbie Clark? Thoughts of Clark and his cowboy boots made her want to ask Leith if the search warrant he had applied for, asking to toss Clark's place, was looking promising.

But again, she was intruding on his sexy-romp day. She'd save it for tomorrow, when they were back in the office and back on the case.

She stole a look at Leith's profile as he turned to watch the MC drawing mid-show door prizes. He looked un-happy. He looked as if he might be wanting to say some-thing, too, but was holding his tongue. Alison and Niko on that end of the table were making small talk, liking each other's dresses or something. But on this end, nothing but awkward silence.

JD was about to say, *Well, it's been a blast*, ditch them all, and leave, when Shiomi said, "Oh my god, look who's here."

JD turned to look across the hall. Dion stood in the doorway and was looking around with curiosity. Or hostility. Or both.

* * *

It seemed to Dion that half the detachment had attended the Valentine's Day dance after all. Too late to back out, he walked over to join the gang at the long table with its paper covering, bowls of cinnamon hearts, plates of small sandwiches, candles flickering mechanically.

"Thought you were going to rip up your ticket and flush it," he said to JD as he sat.

"Like you predicted, I couldn't pass up the free food." She was munching through a handful of nacho chips to prove it. "And this loser couldn't get a man to take her out, so she begged me to keep her company. I'm too nice for my own good."

She had pointed to her left at Niko Shiomi, who looked like a winner to Dion. Niko was pointedly ignoring him. The way she ignored him was kind of exciting. Or would be if he wasn't so miserable.

Leith said, "So is Kate on her way?"

"Kate who?" Dion said with bravado.

He received a lot of stares, even from the aloof Niko. But so what? It was a table of detectives. Let them figure it out for themselves. The only non-detective here he had met only once before. Alison asked him how he was feeling after the big shock of falling off a cliff into the Seymour River in mid-February, and how his leg was doing.

"It wasn't a big deal," he said. "Leg's good, thanks."

JD said, "Cal's such a perfectionist. He had to test out how fatal the fall is for himself."

Alison smiled, but Leith didn't. Niko said, "And JD's such a clown, all she needs is a nose that honks and some floppy shoes."

Niko was only teasing, Dion realized, and JD only looked amused. Whatever game was going on between them, he didn't know and didn't care.

The music was loud, but the table of off-duty cops had gone quiet. Shiomi and JD remained at odds. Leith and his wife seemed to be as well. Dion looked down at his phone, which had somehow ended up in his hand. Motion woke the home screen, and Kate smiled up at him.

One love song had ended and another began with an orgasmic drum riff. "Excuse me, back in a minute," Alison said, and gathered her handbag and left the table, heading for the ladies' room.

When she was out of sight, Leith said to JD, "So the warrant's a no-go. Not enough to hang my hat on."

"What, a long black Cadillac's not enough?"

"Not without a tag number, or something more specific than colour."

JD shrugged. "Bet we wouldn't have found anything anyway. Clark's a smart cookie. He'd have gotten rid of the evidence. Which would be what, the handwriting sample of Kyler Hartshorne he'd used to copy from? Even if we found it, it wouldn't prove anything. But we've still got a tail on him. How long do we have?"

"Not long. Again, I couldn't make a case for extended surveillance."

JD grabbed more chips. "Waste of time. We'll have to get him in again, shake him up. Tell him we've identified the forgery as his. Try to get a confession before he cries foul."

Dion looked again at Kate's face on his phone screen. If he had any brains he'd call her and explain. He'd flipped out, but he was okay now. He started to punch out a text, but didn't know how to phrase it. All he'd done by storming out was prove her right, that he wasn't ready. He deleted the awkward message. Beside him Niko was swaying to the music, eyes closed.

"Still bothers me that Vivi hasn't called," JD was telling Leith. "There's something going on. Do you get the feeling either parent really wants Vivi around? So what's all the bickering really about?"

"I think they've wised up since their last dust-up," Leith said. "Still, I was thinking about it today, Zachary and Gemma. Something about the two of them …"

Dion scowled. Something about Zachary and Gemma had bothered him from the start, and he'd said so. A scent like crushed rose petals distracted him, and he looked down the table into Shiomi's eyes.

"Rings untrue like how?" JD asked Leith, but Dion was no longer paying attention. An oldie was playing, "Magnet and Steel." He gestured to Niko, indicating the dance floor with his thumb. Even with a sore knee he could manage a slow dance.

Niko leaned in and whispered something to JD, who rolled her eyes. Then she smiled at Dion and joined him under the pink and blue swirling heart show.

# TWENTY-FIVE

## WHEN THE DANCE ENDS

*February 15*

IN A MORNING MEETING with his core team of investigators, Leith tackled the issue he had been considering late last night, the shifting of his suspicions in the kidnap of Luna Mae Garland. It was a shift from the unknown to an inside job. His own conflict with Alison around the Picnic incident was the inspiration for his fresh thoughts on the case.

"I was thinking about the indivisible asset," he said. "I was thinking, what if my wife and I split up, and I wanted to move back to North Battleford and she wanted to move back to Parksville. Hardly what you'd call a commutable distance. What do we do about our child, then? We both love her, can't live without her. What do we do?"

"Get yourself a private jet, I guess," JD suggested.

"I can't afford one."

"Then you'll have to cut her in half." She carried on as he gave her a withering glance. "If that doesn't work for you, you'll have to settle in a location midway so you can easily share custody. And suck up the rest."

"What if compromise is impossible?" Leith said. "My wife has to be with her ailing parents, and I can't get a transfer."

"Then move her ailing parents in next door at your own expense," JD said. Her temper was shorter than usual. Maybe it was the spat she'd gotten into with Niko last night. He had heard the two women sniping, had heard Niko say something to JD that crossed the line.

"What's your point?" she added.

"My point is that I think whatever happened to Luna happened within the family. Things were reaching a crisis. Zach was threatening to take Luna to P.E.I. Neither parent can afford the ongoing court costs, especially Zach. Somebody here felt driven to take Luna. My bet is on Zach. He's impulsive, hostile. Maybe he took her in a fit of anger, and now he's got no way out. If so, either his poker mates are giving him a false alibi, or he has an accomplice."

"Chelsea," JD said. "If that's true, she has to be in on it."

Dion said, "I think both parents have done something to Luna."

Leith raised his brows at him. "You want to explain that?"

"I tried putting this to you before," Dion told him. Tersely. "I just couldn't frame it right."

"Try again."

Dion tried again. "I picked this up when we were letting Gemma and Zachary each know about the kidnap theory," he said. "Kyler and Tiago conspiring to sell Luna Mae to the Brits."

Leith well remembered the day and its dead-end theory. "Sure," he said. "You had doubts. You didn't believe Tia would harm Luna."

"I'm talking about how Gemma and Zachary had taken the news. Like I told you."

JD wasn't the only cranky one today, Leith was thinking. It was the failed romance, he'd bet, seeing as how Dion had been carrying on with Shiomi at last night's dance. Instead of Kate, as he should have been. "Yes?"

"I told you it was the ratio of their reactions," Dion said. "I wasn't sure what I meant, but I've pinned it down better. You were giving them potentially good news that maybe she's still alive, but you told them not to get their hopes up."

"Which both Gemma and Zach did."

"But it wasn't real. They were faking it."

Leith and the team waited for the ratio revelation to solidify as Dion struggled to find the right words. "They had honest gut reactions to start with," he said, using an open palm to demonstrate his point. "Then there was the gut reaction they thought they should be displaying." His other palm went out. "And the two didn't match up." He seemed unsure of where his hands should go now, and crossed his arms.

Leith wasn't getting the point, and he expected Dion to give up on his explanation. Large challenges didn't faze Dion much, but minor ones did. Like hello in the hallway, or expressing some of his more convoluted thought processes.

But Dion didn't give up. "So I'm Gemma," he said. "And I've got a secret. I know what really happened to Luna, and I know she's dead, and I know I'm responsible. Now you come along and tell me my son Tiago and a guy named Kyler have conspired to steal Luna and sell her to a nameless couple in a van. Right?"

"Right," Leith said.

"So, two things have just happened. One, you've told me something that I know you've got totally wrong, and two, you've just given me a couple of scapegoats. Tiago and Kyler. What do I do? First I have to get over the shock of being given all this wrong info. Then I have to pretend it's thrilled me. Then I realize I better look like this is actually the best news ever, because my daughter might be alive, when I know she isn't. Right? What it comes down to is I haven't had time to prepare. My thoughts are all over the map."

Whatever had spoiled Dion's mood earlier, misfired cupid's arrow or whatever, it was forgotten. He had warmed up to his telling. He was in his element, when his mind hit maximum velocity and all was well. But it wouldn't last, Leith knew. Wouldn't last longer than somebody around this table confessing they didn't get it.

"And I almost pulled it off." Dion was zealously still being Gemma. "Except I didn't get the ratio right. I was more shocked than thrilled. I spent too much time dealing with the news and working out what to do with it and not enough blindly thanking God that my baby might still be alive. I'm a fraud!"

He was looking at Leith as if he was the only one present. Leith wished he could reflect back a show of epiphany. But he couldn't. They were talking about the changing demeanour of a woman that had taken place over a few seconds, and he couldn't replay it in his mind, let alone make sense of whatever he should have seen.

But the pitch wasn't over. "And Zachary Garland was exactly the same," Dion concluded with a broad smile. "That nailed it for me. Neither of them could have kidnapped her, but they both know who did, and why, and they've been covering each other's ass since day one."

\* \* \*

JD listened. She really wasn't able to follow Dion's logic. She hadn't taken part in the early Gemma and Zachary interviews; she'd been more involved in the murder of Tasha Aziz. The two cases had been loosely connected by Tia Garland for a while, when it seemed possible he'd conspired with Kyler Hartshorne in taking Luna — Hartshorne who was also a suspect in Tasha's murder.

But with the baby-bartering link broken, there was nothing. Kyler and Tia weren't friends and had nothing in common except one conversation at a party, under the influence of whatever they'd been smoking or drinking.

Except there was something Dion had told her about Tia's nerdy pal, Oliver Walsh. Walsh had told Dion, following Tia's death, that he thought Kyler had corrupted Tia. Something about a hundred bucks and a shady hand signal. The comment had gone into the file and no further, but it continued to flash in JD's mind as interesting.

"I was thinking about Tiago and Kyler," she now told Leith and the other members in the team. "We have their relationship framed in our heads in a certain way. Tia's a nice kid, and Kyler's a few years older and a dirtbag. But friendship can take many forms."

She had earned a flicker of annoyance from Leith with the word *dirtbag*, and his annoyance annoyed her, since calling people what they were was about the only satisfaction she got out of this fucking job. She corrected herself. "Did I say dirtbag? I meant to say person of unwholesome character."

"Anyway," he said.

JD took a moment to arrange her thoughts. Thoughts that had been inspired by blessed Niko Shiomi. Shiomi wasn't in the room but was in JD's head, the nemesis she couldn't help but enjoy. Sometimes even bully-type relationships were better than no relationship at all, and maybe Tiago and Hartshorne were closer than anybody supposed.

"Whatever Hartshorne was up to with Robbie Clark," she said, "drugs, murder, blackmail, maybe Hartshorne had pulled Tia into it with him." She repeated what Oliver Walsh had said about funds and corruption. "I'm saying maybe that's what killed Tia. Whether he did it to himself or somebody else got to him. It's not quite off the table yet, is it? Tiago fell into bad company with Kyler, and died for it."

"It's a possibility," Leith said. "As you say, still on the table. See where you can take it, JD. Thanks."

With a few more housekeeping matters, the meeting ended.

The large window next to her desk was where JD did some of her best meditating. She looked across the city, between buildings that seemed to be clambering heavenward like magic beanstalks. Between the buildings a hard but muted light shone, illuminating mist flecks that gusted along sideways. Briefly she considered the afterlife and Ouija boards. Since she didn't believe in either, and Tia and Kyler weren't here to explain their own deaths, closure would have to come from this side of the great divide.

She needed to talk to Robbie Clark, but as Leith had told her, the fact that he drove a long black Cadillac was not grounds for a warrant. How to scare a judge into issuing one, then? Back at her cubicle, she reread Clark's statement. She followed up with a visit to Leith's desk.

"Clark admits he was buying weed from Kyler," she told him. "But I'd like to know if he has any information about amphetamine use among students. Recall last year that Riverside student who OD'd? We never did find out where she got the shit from. If Clark had dealings with Kyler, he might have insider info about other drugs making the rounds. If Clark isn't willing to come in of his own volition, I'd like a warrant to compel him."

"And while you're at it, mention you can prove he forged Kyler's note?" Leith said. "Afraid not, JD."

*Rats.* Well, at least she'd tried.

Leith was attempting to work at his computer, and JD studied his profile. On a more personal level, she wanted to ask him for advice about last night. The dance, and all the bad things that had spun off from it.

There had been fun moments, too, of course. Like taking Shiomi aside after "Magnet and Steel" and telling her to keep her sweaty paws off Cal Dion. Just because Cal and Kate were on the outs didn't give Shiomi an automatic in.

Shiomi had asked JD what century she had dropped out of, and said Cal was a grown-up and could make his own choices. The argument had escalated, with others at Team RCMP clearly listening in. JD had called Shiomi a tramp, which she considered a sweet turn-of-the-century compliment, and far too good for a whore like Shiomi. Shiomi's comeback was to call JD Rabbit Face.

The obvious reference to JD's lip scar was a low blow, but the lowest point of the night came when Dion finished his beer and walked out with the tramp on his arm — after what Niko had called JD for all the world to hear. By walking out with Niko he had told JD what she was worth to him, after all their years of friendship. Or quasi-friendship at least. What a charmer.

But what did she care? Karma would get them both.

Leith turned and looked at her. "What are you snickering about?"

"Thinking about karma getting Cal and Niko," JD said. "And you and Alison showing us your tango moves."

Leith flicked his fingers at her to buzz off, and turned back to his keyboard.

The one touching episode at the Eagles hall, JD thought as she made her way back to her desk, was Leith's jealousy. Some cruising Lothario had invited Alison out to the floor, leaving Leith and JD alone at the long table, nursing their drinks. Lothario and Alison swept through the strains of "Endless Love," and Leith pretended not to notice. Then "Suspicious Minds," when he pretended to notice but not care. Finally, as another smoking-hot love song began with no signs of the dancers unlocking, he had leapt from his seat, strode across the room, and taken over.

How stiff and self-conscious the Leiths were as they ballroom danced. But adorable. And so in love.

JD had not been swept off her feet by anyone last night. Maybe it was the T-shirt. Not that she would have accepted anyway. She liked dancing, but only to her own kind of music, and only alone. She had no intention of becoming anyone's valentine. Not in this lifetime.

* * *

Dion's knee needed exercise for a fast recovery, so he was using the fire stairs for a makeshift gym, climbing up and down. He was trying to understand the low feeling that always followed sharing his thoughts in group settings. Like the team meeting he'd just left. It was all part of striving for success, he guessed. Success at anything required taking risks, and for him an after-effect of risk-taking was this whump of depression as he obsessed over how much better he could have done.

It never lasted more than an hour or two, of course, and with each round he was getting better at dealing with it. He knew the drill. Don't fret, give it a while, let it pass.

This one lingered, though. He should have mulled it over further before declaring to the team that the mystery of Luna Mae Garland was a conspiracy between the parents. But what was done was done, and so what if he was proven wrong in the end? Not everybody could be right all the time.

He stumbled on one of the risers and swore. It worried him that his leg was getting worse instead of better. He blamed it on his rough night. Slow dancing with Shiomi, her body against his, Kate all but forgotten, himself all but certain where this dance would lead. Then instead of it going there, it had ended with him and Shiomi sitting at Denny's till past 2:00 a.m., talking, before going their separate ways.

Where had their passion gone? They had come so close, standing outside the lobby of her apartment building in the wind and rain, Niko fiddling with the fob to the apartment's front door. "I'm sorry, I can't do this," she had finally said.

Taking him by surprise, after all the slow-dance stroking and grinding.

He'd been flooded with relief. He'd made sure to look devastated. "Why?"

"'Cause I just feel so rotten," she said. "For saying what I said to JD."

"Saying what?"

"Didn't you hear? I called her Rabbit Face. Because of her mouth. I just blurted it out, and I totally, utterly despise myself. Fuck this. Looks like my bad conscience has totally wrecked my libido."

Dion had heard her remark at the dance, but hadn't associated it with JD's scar. Maybe because he no longer saw the scar as damage. In any case, JD had once told him she'd rather be insulted to her face than behind her back. He didn't think she'd lose sleep over it.

But Niko would. He recalled her fine black hair whipping around her face as she went on telling him what a thoughtless, loud-mouthed bitch she'd always been. He'd told her not to worry. Tell JD she was sorry, and JD wouldn't hold it against her.

They had almost parted ways then, but instead had ended up in the all-night restaurant with decafs, talking. About what, he couldn't remember. Nothing important, except for the brief discussion about Luna Garland.

Talking over the investigation with Niko had helped Dion pinpoint his ratio argument, which ultimately had caused him to go out on a limb today and share those thoughts with the team, which had led to this odd cocktail of feelings he couldn't seem to ditch.

A sharp pain jolted his kneecap and he gave a cry of rage. Pushing it too hard. His yell echoed against concrete and faded. He massaged the knee till the twinge eased. Then pulled in a breath and gave the stairs another go.

# TWENTY-SIX

# ZACCARDI

*February 16*

THE ZACCARDI INTERVIEWS, as JD called them, were scheduled for today. She had a sick sense of taking one step too close to the cliff's edge. What had she committed to, conspiring with Doug Paley and Jim Torr to lie, fudging over Brooke's rant in the bar that night?

*We're all going to get fired. Or worse.*

Not as long as they stuck to their guns, she comforted herself. After all, what were they doing wrong? Nothing except erring on the side of caution. Brooke had been emotional, and nobody at the table that night had wanted to hear her spew. Jim and Doug had more or less blocked their ears against her. And Ken Poole? She tried to picture him there. As far as she recalled, he had been talking with Jim Torr, so he wouldn't have heard Brooke's damning words. Something about murder.

No way Ken had caught it, JD decided. Good thing she hadn't found the right time to hook him into a private talk about that night, to figure out what he'd made of Brooke's comments. She would have set alarm bells going in his head. And he was an old vet on the force, loyal to its mandate. Had she put it to him, he might have dug deeper into his memories, recalled Brooke's words, and done something about it.

No, he hadn't heard, hadn't done anything about it. She wasn't even sure he was there when Brooke said what she'd said. He'd actually left before that, probably. Pulled on his coat, said good night, walked out.

Which in itself was strange, come to think of it. Ken didn't often come out for drinks, but when he did, he stayed for at least a few. Maybe Brooke's presence had been such a downer he'd decided to leave early.

But on the whole, JD chose to believe Poole wasn't a threat. She breathed deeply, sat back, closed her eyes, and worked on rewriting the data in her mind in preparation for the IHIT confrontation. Blur the lunatic's words, rearrange them.

She failed at blurring them, and they remained clear in her mind, Brooke's statement about something Dion had done. "He didn't just kill that man. He killed Looch. He killed Looch's beautiful, happy family. He killed me."

... *didn't just kill that man.*

What man?

The one o'clock alarm buzzed on her phone. With butterflies in her stomach, she went to give Bosko and two IHIT members from Surrey a bald-faced lie.

* * *

Dion's interview was easy and brief. Mike Bosko was sitting in, but not participating, and it was two IHIT guys who put the questions to him. How well did he know Brooke? Had Dion been in contact with her at all since Luciano Ferraro's death? Had he tracked her movements after she had left the Lower Mainland a year and a half ago?

He described it all again, as he had described it to Bosko once already. He had heard that Brooke was back in the city, heard she'd gone for drinks with Doug Paley and some others. Doug had later described her as unstable, possibly on something. Other than Doug's hearsay, he couldn't help, sorry.

The questions frightened him, but he was a pro at hiding his fear. Sit comfortably, maintain eye contact, speak low and slow. But don't overdo it. Some edginess was expected. They would attribute it to bad memories of the crash, the death of his closest friend, the gruelling road to recovery that followed. They would realize how painful this all was for him, dredging up the memories, talking about his dead friend's widow.

Bosko was only present as a mute witness on behalf of the North Shore members. A formality. He seemed not quite tuned in to the discussion, and his presence shouldn't have worried Dion. But it did.

It was a relief to be dismissed, and he left the room certain he'd aced the test. He walked along the hallway, smiling in the rebound from stress, and when Doug Paley approached, they stopped for a chat.

"Done with your grilling?" Paley asked. "Lightly seared on both sides?"

"Pretty well. Not fun."

"Coming to Rainey's to celebrate?"

"For sure," Dion said. "I could use a drink."

"Uh-huh," was all Paley said. Then went on his way. His final *uh-huh* had been icy, which wasn't like him. Cold and meaningful. Dion watched him go, wondering. He no longer felt like smiling. Just like that, the stress was back.

\* \* \*

When Dion arrived at Rainey's and brought his pint to the crew's table, JD, Doug Paley, and Jim Torr were already finishing a first round of drinks.

"Well, there he is," Paley cried. "The prodigal son. Take a load off, Cal. Tell us how it went for you. Nerve-wracking, isn't it, facing off with IHIT? Even if you've done nothing wrong. We're still shaking in our boots, can you tell?"

So Paley was back to playing Santa Claus, and now overdoing it. Dion took a chair and raised his pint in cheers, and couldn't help thinking that the faces around him seemed skewed. What was it? They were hiding something. Paley knew it showed, and covered it with an excuse that they were simply nerve-wracked. But it was more. JD's cold shoulder was nothing new, it was just her way, but the sullen gleam of anger in her eyes startled him. Jimmy Torr didn't like Dion, and vice versa, so his unfriendly demeanour was no problem. But even

Torr seemed different. Right now he was looking grim as he twisted his beer glass, and Dion knew a grim Torr was a worried Torr.

He shrugged at Paley's question. "There wasn't much I could tell them, other than what I heard from you. They told *me* something, though. They said you all met with Brooke that day."

"*Met* isn't the word I'd use," Paley said.

"More like *endured*," JD said.

"You and who else?" Dion asked. "Anybody join you?"

"Ken," Torr said. "Lil."

"Briefly," Paley clarified.

Dion adjusted the image in his head. This pub table, just after New Year's. JD, Doug, Jim, sitting around, Ken Poole and Lil Hart dropping by. Poole and Hart were regulars at Rainey's. Not *as* regular, but still it wasn't unusual they'd pop in.

He posed his next question casually. "Did you have anything interesting to tell IHIT?"

"Yeah," Paley said. "Brooke Zaccardi is mixed nuts."

"She cursed you to hell," JD said.

"What, for killing Looch?" Dion said, and suddenly he knew they were all blaming him for something. "For getting hit by a speeding car that shot out of nowhere? I didn't have a chance. She's going to curse me for having shitty luck?"

He hoped his show of surprise was convincing. Nothing surprised him these days. They were thinking Brooke was cursing him for the accident, but he knew it went deeper than that. She was cursing him for getting Looch in trouble, for what Dion had done that night, and she was back in North Van with her knowledge for only one reason — to expose him.

Instead, she had vanished. Directly after meeting with this bunch of cops and cursing him to hell, as JD said. But cursing must have been all Brooke had done. She hadn't spilled about the murder — otherwise he wouldn't be sitting here now, a free man. IHIT wouldn't have let him walk out of that room.

"What else did she say?" he asked them.

He saw a lot of shrugs, and no glances exchanged. They should have known better. One thing that spoke louder than exchanged glances was lack of exchanged glances.

"That's about it," JD said. "She complained that her life is the shits, and when we didn't burst into tears of sympathy, she got pissed off and left. I offered to drive her home, but she stormed out."

Never to be heard from again.

Dion had a hard time swallowing his beer. If that was all Brooke had said to this group that night, then why were they being so cagey? He wondered where Kenny Poole had been when she'd said whatever she'd said. And what Ken had done about it.

JD's phone burred, and she looked at the display. "Unknown caller." She answered, plugging her free ear against the pub noise. Then without warning scrambled from her chair and bolted for the exit. Whatever the caller was trying to tell her, she wanted to hear it without Rainey's rock and roll and hubbub drowning it out.

Dion stared after her, and a moment later grabbed his jacket. "Vivi got in touch," he said. He left Rainey's on JD's heels, but she was already gone.

\* \* \*

At the end of the day Leith was in Bosko's office, talking over the open cases — the Tasha Aziz homicide, the Luna Garland abduction, and the disappearance of Brooke Zaccardi.

The last was a file Leith had nothing to do with, except as it concerned the under-the-table investigation of Cal Dion, and he was hoping Bosko wouldn't pull him into this offshoot of the case.

Bosko went straight to it. "I'm concerned about this one," he said, after describing his participation in the IHIT interviews. JD, Paley, Torr, Ken Poole, Lil Hart. These were the last people on earth to see Brooke alive, apparently, so they had all been brought in and questioned. Dion had been interviewed as well, as he had been close to Brooke once upon a time. He'd also killed her husband and ruined her life. Not that it was put to him that way, but it was background and something IHIT felt necessary to cover.

None of the interviewees had shed light on Zaccardi's evaporation, Bosko told Leith. Not on what she had been doing visiting the North Shore that day, not what her plans were, not who might have wanted to harm her.

IHIT had gone away speculating that whatever had befallen the woman, it was likely related to her well-established drug habit. The investigators remained open to other theories, but following the interviews their focal point had shifted away from Brooke's North Shore visit in January and back to the dangerous life she lived on the Lower Mainland. With drugs came debt, and with debt, prostitution. Probably she had just been sucked down the same hole that destroyed so many.

Leith paid reluctant attention to Bosko's unwelcome recapping. Bosko seemed sharper than usual, less cheerful. Even a tad haggard. His trademark crumpled tie was badly knotted and his glasses, usually pristine, were smudged. "And your focal point is where?" Leith asked. Because even if IHIT didn't get it, he did. Zaccardi's disappearance was tied to Dion in some way, somehow, and he and Bosko were both worried.

Bosko nodded. "It was a telling interview, Dave. There's no question in my mind that Cal either knows what happened to Brooke, or he's somehow involved."

Leith said nothing.

"I'm getting to know him," Bosko said. "I think I know him better than he knows himself."

Leith kept his mouth closed, arms loosely crossed, ankle over knee. The allegation was serious. More serious than the vague unprovable murder he had Dion under observation for. That, for all Leith knew, could have been an accident. If Bosko was right, the removal of Zaccardi from the picture was about as serious as it got. A hit.

Bosko put Leith's thoughts into words. "Whatever Cal has gotten up to in Surrey, it could be some kind of misadventure. But I can't let it ride anymore. Now it's top of the pile. I'm going to have to share what I know with Surrey. It's out of my hands."

Leith's phone rang, and speak of the devil, Dion was breathlessly telling him something important. He said he wasn't positive, but he believed Vivi Garland had just contacted JD on her cell, and JD was heading to Riverside Drive to check out the situation. Dion was following, he said, and wanted backup ready to go.

A second call came in as Leith disconnected from Dion. JD. He was rising to action as she told him that she was en route to the Vale home. Not only had Vivi made contact at last, but the call had been cut off abruptly. JD didn't have to put it to words, for Leith. The strain in her voice said it all. She was seriously afraid for the little girl's well-being.

# TWENTY-SEVEN

# YELP

VIVI'S SOFT-SPOKEN words continued to ring in JD's ears as she pushed her car up Riverside Drive through darkness and rain, high beams on, fast as she dared go in a neighbourhood with so many joggers and kids.

She knew she was overreacting. Chances were Vivi was fine. She'd used the phone without permission, which was against house rules, and was being scolded for her naughtiness. That was all.

No, it wasn't all.

"I'm sorry I haven't called," Vivi had begun as JD rose from her seat at Rainey's and headed for a quieter place in order to catch every word. "I haven't had the chance," the girl said. "But Gemma is out now, shopping, and I need to talk to you about something."

"You can tell me now," JD had told her, backing into the swing doors, taking the call outside Rainey's, phone to ear, car keys in hand.

"They won't tell you. They say I'm lying. But Tia —"

The girl stopped cold, and JD heard why. A background noise, a door thudding shut. And now Vivi was whispering, "Oh no. She's come back. I have to —"

And then Gemma's voice, distant but growing louder with every stride, "Vivi, I told you, damn it —"

The girl squealed as if she'd been grabbed, the call disconnected, and JD had been racing to her car, pressing redial as she went. Nobody at the Vale home had picked up.

The trip took longer than she wanted. She had called Leith hands-free as she drove, telling him what was happening. He told her Dion had been in touch and was close behind her, and that more cars were on their way.

JD had failed Tia, and was damned if she'd fail Vivi now, too. She arrived at the home, her veins buzzing with anxiety. A sharp turn into the driveway, skidding on loose gravel, nearly hitting Gemma's Mazda that sat nosed against the garage door. She left her car and jogged to the front door, banged on it with her fist, too impatient for doorbells. "Gemma? Mrs. Vale? Police. Open up."

She heard voices inside. A muffled shouting? Like an angry person trying to bottle her frustration. Then the door flung open and Gemma stood dressed for the outdoors in a furry winter coat, hood dropped back, jeans, boots on her feet. She was flushed, blinking, irate. But not outwardly frantic. Not homicidal. "Yes?"

"I was talking to Vivi on the phone." Calm, unflustered, even polite, JD knew she came across as a whole lot more professional than she felt. "It sounded like she was in trouble. I don't know what this is all about, but I need to see her."

Gemma's eyes rolled back in an apology of sorts, implying this was nothing but a silly misunderstanding and she regretted JD's wasted trip. "Yes, Vivi *is* in trouble. She's not allowed to use the phone in my absence, and she knows it. That's all. We've talked it over and reached an understanding."

"Sure. Still, I need to see her. Once I've seen her, then we can talk about your house rules."

"I'm on my way out, actually. I'm sorry, but I need to get to the store before it closes. You can come back in a couple hours."

"Ma'am," JD barked, still professional but no longer polite. "If you won't let me in, I'll arrest you. You have to confirm for me that she's all right, then we'll talk, then I'll leave, then you can go get your groceries. Get it?"

The woman turned and walked back into her house, leaving the door wide. JD took the open door as permission to follow. With Vivi nowhere in sight, her hackles were starting to rise.

Down a half-flight of stairs toward the front of the house, Gemma had entered what looked like an office with a computer desk and leather sofa. She shut the door behind JD and sat at one end of the sofa, and JD assumed she was supposed to sit at the other.

But sitting down wasn't going to happen. "Look, Gemma —"

"No, you look," Gemma said. "I have to tell you this. Before you talk to Vivi. You have to understand something about that child. Did Zachary tell you she's a genius? Did he also mention she's a manipulator? No, I'm sure he didn't. We've both worked hard to protect her against herself. She likes Zach. She likes all men. But she doesn't like me. Sometimes I think she hates me. I don't know why. I've given her nothing but love all these years."

"Fine, we'll talk. Just as soon as I —"

*Thump.*

From somewhere on the other side of the house.

*Thump, thump.*

Like something softly but firmly hitting a window, sending faint reverberations through the structure.

"I locked her out on the balcony," Gemma cried, chasing after JD. It was a confession, blurted out to get ahead of the situation as JD launched from the office to track the noise to its source. "Just so I could talk to you and explain. Don't believe her. Don't believe a word she says. You know what we think, Perry and I? We think she took Luna, did something with her. We've been trying to protect her, but it's over. I've had enough." Anger now was mixed with self-pity. "Put it to her. Get the truth out of that little girl."

JD ignored the protests that followed her from room to room. She passed the dinner table, pulled back the drapes, and saw Vivi standing shivering, nose against the glass, as she gave it a final thump with her balled-up fist. Her eyes met JD's and widened in relief.

"Christ," JD said. She unlocked the sliding glass door and the noise of the river rushed in, along with the cold and cedar-scented air and one swift-footed little girl, not dressed for the elements, not dressed to be locked outside like this. Vivi flitted to safety at JD's side and from there stared up at Gemma.

With Vivi at her side, JD watched Gemma, trying to understand. The woman's face was flushed, but from what? The exertion of chasing a kid around the house, or shouting excuses? Or was it shame? Anger?

"I know it was the wrong thing to do," Gemma said, and her voice shook. "I know how it looks." She crouched to chide her daughter, and to JD it looked like bad play-acting. "But Vivi, I don't want you telling lies to the police. We've talked about it, haven't we?"

"It's not lies," Vivi said. She had grasped JD's arm. "It's what Tia saw."

JD looked from the girl to the mother, who was over-due for arrest and a reading of her rights. The woman looked shaken and depressed, like a mother who had done her best, only to be disappointed time and again. Gemma knelt and held her arms out to the girl. "Why are you doing this to me, Vivi? Tell me."

"You won't listen. I've told you over and over, and you won't listen."

Gemma stood again, looking defeated. Then swiftly, with a sob, she pulled open the sliding door and slipped outside. The door zipped shut as JD was still blinking in surprise.

She didn't blink for long. She threw the door open. The surrounding forest was blue in the dusky light, and Gemma stood leaning despondently against the railing. Was she going to do like Zach and threaten to jump? What was wrong with this crazy family? The house was built on a steep slope, and the distance from the deck to the forest floor below could easily be a killing fall.

But Gemma made no move to step onto the deck chair at her side and pitch herself overboard. Still in her furry coat, emotionally drained, all she wanted, she told JD over her shoulder, was a bit of goddamn privacy.

But privacy was not an option. JD had gone into suicide-prevention mode, even with no suicide threat per se. She told Gemma that she understood these were troubled times, and what they needed to do was first of all get Vivi warmed up. After that they should sit down and figure this out. She was so intent on talking sense into Gemma that she didn't notice Vivi slip past till the girl stood at Gemma's side, taking her mother's hand, looking up at her, trying to comfort her.

*Oh shit*, JD thought. But she shouldn't panic. She wanted to separate mother and child, but didn't want to set off a chain reaction by saying so. Backup was on the way. She'd ease the two apart diplomatically. But even that was uncalled for, it seemed. Gemma had crouched down once again to talk to Vivi in soft tones. No longer play-acting. Begging for forgiveness, it looked like. Even when Vivi nodded and the two of them hugged, JD decided to shut up and let them make peace.

Even when Gemma wrapped her arms around Vivi, and Vivi buried her face in the fur of Gemma's coat. But when Gemma rose, with the girl in her arms, and seated the girl on the railing, JD thought, *What?* "Hey," she said.

"Gemma —" Vivi yelped, clutching the fur.

"I love you so much, Vivi," Gemma said.

"Gemma, don't," JD said, lunging forward. The railing was cedar, green and slimy from perpetual shade and humidity, a terrible place to balance a child at the best of times. She grabbed at the woman's coat with her left hand, tried to catch Vivi's skinny arm with her right, but the girl's arm was wheeling, trying to counter the pull of gravity.

Vivi's scream was like a nail on glass. Outside a car was pulling up. Dion, at last. And thank god, Vivi had stopped yelping and seemed calm. Gemma had no intention of tossing the child over. No, she was clutching her in a bear hug. But why wasn't she heeding JD's whip-like warnings to back away from the railing and set the girl down?

Gemma continued to hold tight, and Vivi was silent, and JD had wrapped an arm around the woman's shoulder to manoeuvre her and her captive as a unit away from that slippery fucking railing. And she was winning, finally getting through to the woman. Gemma was moving with her, co-operating, toward the sliding door, easing her daughter's butt off the railing. JD heard the doorbell. She took a breath, knowing all would be okay — but her inhalation turned into a gasp of horror. *No!* The child was slithering sideways, so fast, so unbelievably fast. An arm thrust out, small fingers almost meeting JD's, and with a final scream Vivi disappeared over the edge.

\* \* \*

The scream ended abruptly but continued to drill at JD's ears. Maybe her imagination had filled in the distant crack of bracken and bones. She didn't look over the railing — it would be two seconds wasted — but told Gemma not to move a muscle, left her standing and sped through the house. She was out the front door, almost knocking Dion over as he tried the handle, pushing past him, telling him to call 911 and detain Gemma Vale, that Vivi had fallen from the balcony. "I'm going to find her. Go to the balcony and see if you can spot her for me. There's a lot of bush down there. Be my eyes."

She didn't know the property well, and a false turn doubled her back. A gate led to a stone path that spanned the home's north wall. The front yard was picture perfect, but out back the terrain was a brambly wilderness. The stone path ended and bushes surrounded her. And godforsaken darkness.

Her only flashlight was her phone, its light feeble, almost useless, but it revealed a path that switchbacked down the steep slope toward the river. She stopped to get her bearings, calling Vivi's name. She bushwhacked toward the base of the house. Enormous foundation pillars supported the structure and provided the framework for the covered balcony from which Vivi had fallen. Light emitted from the window above and JD was remotely aware of shifting shadows and voices above. A man's voice talking, a woman's wailing.

She called out Vivi's name again and was answered by silence.

She heard Dion hail her from above. She looked up and his silhouette shouted down that it was too dark, that he couldn't see anything. A moment later he called, "Gemma says there's a motion detector closer to the corner of the house down there. Try to activate it."

JD did as he told her. The light flooded on. Bushes, brambles, and tree trunks glowed, but no child. What had Vivi been wearing? Purple sweatshirt, grey tights, bare feet. JD squatted and peered. Visible ahead between the criss-cross of foliage she glimpsed purple. She waded toward the colour and found what she was looking for on the forest floor.

Vivi lay face up, an arm twisted unnaturally at her side. Still and lifeless as a rag doll.

JD could feel no pulse at the child's throat. Not at first. Then there it was, a healthy throb.

She told Vivi everything was going to be okay now, help was coming. The floodlight had timed out and switched off, but someone was approaching along the muddy path behind JD with a powerful light beam, and she heard a siren. She turned to signal a thumbs-up to the blinding, swaying light that marked Dion's approach, then turned back to Vivi and let out a long breath.

* * *

When fire and rescue arrived with their equipment bags and gurney, Dion left them with JD and made his way back to the house to attend to Gemma. The rain was falling again, heavy drops that smashed down, gathered into guzzling brooks, drizzled off the eaves of the Vale home in curtains. Gemma was on the sofa where he'd left her. She seemed to be in shock, talking to herself. He stood and listened. She was crying for her husband and her baby Luna, and she was crying about Vivi, who she thought was dead. She also seemed to think it was JD's fault, if Dion was understanding her right.

He didn't set Gemma straight. He didn't tell her that Vivi was alive. He didn't know what the status of the girl was, and whether she would live as long as the ambulance ride. The height she had fallen from was considerable, and the ground below peppered with boulders. Gemma was staring at him with anger, her mouth pale and her eyes bloodshot. "You cops always have to come along and fuck things up, don't you?" she said. "Why did she come here? Why did she kill my little girl?"

Dion watched her, thinking she was mad. He had tried to get from her what happened, but aside from her muttering and crying she had told him nothing. All he could do was wait. Leith was on his way and would take over. If Gemma didn't talk here, she would be arrested for questioning. If she refused to answer the questions, depending on what JD said, she could be charged.

He wondered if Gemma was right, that JD had somehow messed up, triggered an accident. He puffed out a breath of relief as he heard the front door open and Leith's voice, talking to Perry Vale, who must have arrived at the same time. Vale sounded upset and Leith was doing his best to calm him. Dion joined them.

"What happened?" Vale was saying. "Where's Vivi? Where's Gemma? What happened? Who did this?"

Gemma rushed to her husband's embrace. Her words were muffled, her face crushed against his jacket, but Dion caught much of what she said as he cajoled the story out of her. "She fell, Perry. I was trying to tell the policewoman about Vivi and her lies, and she wouldn't believe me. I got upset. I went out on the balcony to gather my thoughts, and Vivi came out and tried to comfort me. I picked her up and hugged her. That's all.

And the policewoman kept shouting at me, as if I was trying to harm Vivi, and then she started grabbing at me, and she knocked against me, and Vivi fell."

Outside the ambulance siren gave a loud whoop, then went speeding into the distance. JD would be accompanying the crew and staying with Vivi.

Dion had caught Leith's silent question, *Know anything about this?* and gave the silent answer, *Not a clue.* Leith made the decision then to guide Gemma to the dining room table to get a full statement. No reason to arrest her at this point, no need to warn her. Niko Shiomi had arrived meanwhile, to assist, and she was given the task of escorting Perry to another room, the office or wherever a door could be closed, and remaining with him there.

Gemma waited in a chair by the dining room table. She seemed stunned beyond words. Leith left her there and took Dion aside to get what little he knew.

"Vivi had just fallen," Dion told him. "JD told me to arrest Gemma, then rushed down to find Vivi. She didn't have time to talk and didn't say whose fault it was. I couldn't get anything useful out of Gemma. I got my flashlight out of the car and went down to the back of the house. JD had already found Vivi, and said she was alive. I don't know if she'll make it, though. Fire and rescue had arrived and I wanted to get back to Gemma and preserve the scene. All JD told me when I was down there is that Gemma had lifted Vivi onto the railing and the girl fell. She didn't say Gemma did anything wrong. She didn't say she was at fault herself, either."

"Clear as mud," Leith said. Back at the table, he took a chair across from Gemma, and Dion sat at the end of the table, recorder on, pen ready, and the clear-as-mud story began to clarify. Gemma had pulled herself together and now spoke slowly and clearly, though Dion heard shades of outrage in her voice. "I had gone out to the store for a few grocery items," she said. "But halfway there I recalled I'd forgotten my wallet in my other purse, and had to return home. When I walked in, I found Vivi on the phone, and she stared at me like I'd caught her with her hand in the cookie jar. Now you're going to think I'm paranoid."

"Go on," Leith said. "I'm listening."

Dion stopped writing to observe. JD's job was at stake, and he couldn't afford to miss the faintest twitch of deceit on this woman's face.

"Vivi heard me coming," Gemma said. "She set this up. She knew she wasn't to use the phone in my absence, and she knew I'd be angry. As soon as she heard my car in the drive, she got on that phone and made that call, and got the police on the line, and I fell for it. Just like she planned, I got mad and yelled at her. So she'd have it on record that I'm a monster."

"Why isn't she allowed to use the phone?"

"You'll find this hard to believe, but ever since Luna was born, Vivi's been trying to make trouble for me, just in quiet little ways. She tried turning Perry against me, and I'm sure she did her magic on Zach, too. After Luna disappeared, it got even stranger, and I think I know why."

Instead of explaining herself, she fell silent. She breathed through her nose, as if she didn't trust her own mouth. Finally she said, "It's horrible, but it's true. I think she took Luna."

"What makes you think that?"

Gemma was twisting a chunky gold ring round and round on her finger. "I have no proof, and I didn't accuse her of it, but I think she sensed that I suspected her, and that came between us. She started saying she wanted to speak to you, to the police. She explained very reasonably that she was going to tell you what I'd done, and she wouldn't say what, but I imagined she'd come up with something smart. And she's a sweet girl, and you'd believe her. But listen to me. I haven't done anything."

She was pleading with Leith to believe her.

"So you walked in, and she was on the phone. Did you take the phone, hang up?"

"I hardly remember. I shouted at her. Yes, I must have taken it from her, or she hung up on her own. It rang a moment later, but I let it go to voice mail."

She looked down at the table. "I even wonder … about … Tiago." Her hands crept to her face and she was forming a mask of fingers again. Dion asked her to take her hands away from her mouth, and she did as told. "Tiago was a good kid," she said. "He seemed happy with us, till lately. Perry and I both tried to talk to him, to find out what we'd done wrong, but he wouldn't say. And now it's so obvious to me. Vivi turned him against us, too."

Leith asked her to go on with her narrative about tonight.

"After I caught Vivi on the phone, we had another talk," Gemma said. "Vivi does this passive resistance thing. She'll listen, and pretend, and be nice, but she won't give an inch. Then the cop — Constable Temple, I mean — came to the door, knocked, and I could see where this was going. Vivi telling her lies before I had a chance to tell my side of the story. So I did it. I locked my daughter on the deck. Only for a moment, only so I could I explain myself. I let Constable Temple in, but before I could talk to her, Vivi banged on the glass. Constable Temple unlocked the sliding door, and Vivi came in, and I could see where it was going, how bad I looked. I went out on the deck. I was crying. Vivi came to my side. Whatever is wrong with her, I know it's not her fault. It's a disorder of some kind, emotional, mental, I don't know. And she is a lovable girl, and I do love her. I love her very much."

She described again the sequence as she'd told it to Perry. She had picked up Vivi to give her a hug, then JD had stepped in, and she was so pushy that she had jostled Gemma and made her lose her grip on Vivi, causing the fall.

Leith tried to wrangle more detail out of her, as he couldn't understand how Vivi could flip over the railing. Gemma admitted that in hugging Vivi she had rested her bottom on the railing, only for a moment. And that's when Constable Temple had reached out too aggressively and inadvertently knocked her arm, causing the fall.

Leith excused himself. He stood and went out to the balcony. Dion remained at the table with Gemma. He could see Leith looking at the patio furniture, the railing, leaning over and staring down.

Beside him, Gemma murmured to herself the usual lines. She couldn't believe it. Just couldn't believe this had happened. But mostly she was keeping an eye on Leith's inspection of the deck, Dion thought. He heard a ping that he recognized as a phone, and turned to see Leith answer. For nearly a minute Leith spoke to whoever it was, then he returned to the room and told Gemma, "We'll go downtown. Vivi's in intensive care. You and Perry can check up on her, see how she's doing. Zach's going to be there, too, so listen to me. You're all going to have to behave. And none of you will be seeing her without one of us in attendance."

Dion's eyes had been on Leith, but switched to Gemma at the words *intensive care*. And good thing, too, as he caught the jolt as she received the good news.

Vivi had survived.

He noted the ratio of reactions, just as before, when she'd been coping with unexpected good news. Less detectable this time, almost microscopic, but Gemma Vale's relief at the good news was preceded — he was almost sure of it — by a split second of horror.

# TWENTY-EIGHT

## BLACK AND BLUE

*February 17*

JD HAD TO WAIT till early the next day before she got her chance to speak. Nobody told her how Vivi was faring. Dead, for all she knew. Finally, Mike Bosko arrived with an internal investigations detective named Rafati. Her attendance tipped JD off that she could be in some kind of trouble.

The trouble she was in was worse than she imagined. An allegation that she herself had caused the accident, though Rafati wouldn't go into detail. She wanted to get JD's version first.

How had JD screwed up? She scoured her own narrative for procedural flaws as she spoke. She described receiving Vivi's phone call, its abrupt disconnection. She'd tried the number, received no answer. Raced to Riverside Drive while alerting Dave Leith.

She told of Gemma greeting her at the door, being hustled into an office, hearing her out. Heard a distant thumping. Followed the sound, found Vivi locked on the deck. Let her in. She described the conversation between the three of them, what she could remember of it. Gemma retreating to the deck, JD following, Vivi flitting to Gemma's side as if to comfort her.

She described the hug, the girl being lifted up. Vivi's cry of alarm, JD's own sense of panic. The situation had gone haywire so fast. Yes, she had shouted at Gemma to set the girl down. Was ignored. Insisted, put her hands on her, trying to pull woman and child away from the railing. Didn't see the actual fall, because Gemma had turned away from her, had somehow obscured the final, disastrous moment.

Rafati didn't seem to believe her.

JD couldn't believe that she wasn't believed. Never in her career had she been eyeballed by an agent of her own employer like she was a criminal. Bosko was no help, sitting there impassively, so JD put it to Rafati directly in her softest voice, stage one of outrage. "You think I'm lying? Why would I lie about it?"

Instead of apologizing like she should, Rafati went on to lead her through a detailed rehash of the story, beginning to end, sniffing out inconsistencies. *Don't take it personally*, JD told herself. *Just say it all again.*

But not taking it personally was easier said than done. She thought of Dion, and what he had been going through since that day in July when he'd crashed his car. He'd never been charged, but he didn't seem to be a free man, either. He *lived* this shadow of doubt every day.

When Rafati began a second rehash from a different angle, JD interrupted to ask, "What are you saying I've done wrong here?"

At which point Bosko pulled his chair closer to the table and said, "Is it possible you got it wrong, JD? Is it possible that when you grabbed Gemma, you knocked her off balance? Anything like that?"

"No fucking way. Gemma was in full control. It wasn't a hostage situation. She wasn't threatening to throw Vivi over. She was just hugging her in an incredibly dangerous place, and I felt it was imperative that I pull them both away from the railing. Gemma tried to shake me off, but we weren't even close to struggling. Are you saying I should have backed off?"

Rafati said, "You say you grabbed Vivi. At what point did you do that?"

JD couldn't pinpoint exactly when she had tried to reach past Gemma's bulk and get a grip on Vivi's flailing arm. It was an exasperating question, impossible to answer. "I don't know."

"Is it possible your contact with the child is what unbalanced her?"

"No. No way. No way at all."

Bosko and Rafati watched her. They were second-guessing her. She could feel it in her veins, the anger rising. Stage two of outrage. Her voice was no longer soft, but loud as brass. "I told you exactly what happened. Yes, it's my fault. I should have reacted faster when Vivi slipped past me and went to Gemma. But in my eyes Gemma wasn't a threat, and the safest thing to do was stay calm."

"Locking a nine-year-old out in the cold didn't seem threatening to you?" Rafati asked.

She had a point. But there was something more at play here than an investigator trying to untangle a confusing situation. The investigator had something solid. JD asked her what it was. "What's Gemma saying I did, exactly?"

Bosko told her what Gemma had said she did.

JD absorbed the accusation, reflected on it, then harnessed her anger and told Rafati and Bosko what she thought of Gemma Vale's version of events. In no polite terms.

Rafati, the internal investigations detective who was always on the lookout for snakes within their midst, watched her for tells.

\* \* \*

"Outside," said a cold, clear voice, and Dion looked up. JD was looking down at him at his desk. She was scowling, which meant her meeting hadn't gone well. He stood and followed her out, down the halls, through the front door, out into the fresh air.

Just past noon and already the day was closing in and the natural light was fading. It was too cold and wet to sit at the courtyard bench, so they walked to Lonsdale instead, up past shops and restaurants, and JD told him about the wringer she'd just been through.

"First Rafati suggests I'm no better than a rookie," she exclaimed. "Do I look green to you?"

"More like pink," he said. "Calm down. It's their job. It's your word against Gemma's, and they have to get at the truth."

"Then they accuse me of shit, like that crazy lady's telling the truth and I'm the liar. After all my years on the force. I'm now getting where you're coming from,

Cal, always under the gun. Doesn't mean I like you any better, but I get you."

JD's eyes were often dark brown, but sometimes they went black. They looked black to Dion now. "Why don't you like me?" he burst out. "What have I done? Is it 'cause of Niko? How is that any of your business anyway?"

"It's go nothing to do with you and Niko."

"Good, because there *is* nothing between me and Niko."

JD glared at him. "Would you fucking stick to the point? What did Gemma say about me? I got the boiled-down version. She says it's my fault. I want to hear every word that liar said about me."

"You know I can't share the details," Dion said. He didn't tell her that if Gemma Vale was lying about the fall, she was doing an excellent job of it.

"Of course you can't." JD made a snarling noise. "I hear Vivi's still in the ICU," she said. "Hasn't woken up yet. Coma. Maybe never will. And then what?"

"She'll wake up."

They walked a while before JD asked with less hostility, "What's it like, waking from a coma?"

"Gross." When Dion had surfaced after so many days under, he had wanted to dive back down again, sleep forever. Viviani had broken more bones than he had, but the doctors seemed to think there was no major head trauma. "Don't worry. She's going to wake up and tell the truth."

"But if she doesn't, you'll believe me, will you?"

"What d'you care if I believe you or not?"

JD shrugged, so Dion did, too. But he liked that JD was leaning on him. It felt great being on the safe side of trouble for a change.

"I guess I'm just hoping you'll back me, like I back you," she said.

He didn't recall her particularly backing him on anything. Maybe she meant it in the big picture sense. "Of course I will."

"You'll go out on a limb for me? Lie, cheat, steal, break me out of jail?"

This was sounding less big picture, and no longer felt great. He didn't want to be painted into corners or forced into making promises he couldn't keep. "Don't push it," he said.

JD wasn't interested in his answer anyway. "So what's she playing at, that bitch," she muttered, more to herself than Dion. She went on picking at her wound, complaining that she'd never been accused of shit like this, how she didn't deserve it.

Dion stopped listening. He wanted to take a picture of JD, because she'd taken to wearing a felt beret lately, and looked nice. The cap was crimson and the city was dark blue around her. But in her frame of mind, if he brought out his phone and pointed it at her, she'd grab it from his hands and break it. "Lying through her teeth," JD was saying. "Trying to blame me. What's up her sleeve? That's what I want to know."

Dion followed JD's line of sight up Lonsdale. He had been wondering the same thing about Gemma, what was up her sleeve. First the fear he'd seen flash in her eyes when she learned Vivi wasn't dead, and now this off-the-wall accusation.

He had a possible answer: Gemma had dropped Vivi deliberately, that's what. And instead of sticking to a more nebulous lie, like *Oh my god, I lost my grip*, she was trying to blame JD. Gemma's problem was she hadn't taken Vivi's possible survival into account, a live witness who would settle the question once and for all.

JD stopped by a grocery store that sold fresh-cut flowers at its frontage. Even in February the display was a riot of colours, attracting shoppers who were winter weary and looking for a hint of spring. She seemed unusually interested in the flowers, Dion noticed. Bright blooms wrapped in cellophane, hothouse roses and daisies and garish carnations.

"I recommend that one," she told him. She was pointing out a bouquet mostly in pinks and purples, with splashes of what had to be artificial blue. "It's got apology written all over it."

He was irritated. "Apologize to who? To Kate? For what? It's nothing. I proposed and she turned me down. I was a little upset, but I got over it. Next day I told her I'm fine with her decision, and we're still together, same as ever." The last three words sounded weak, so he added to the lie. "Nothing's changed except I'm getting a refund for the ring."

JD was watching him like he stank. "A little upset? On Valentine's Day you dumped Kate and jumped into Niko's bed. Like, wow."

"I told you, I didn't jump into Niko's bed."

"Okay, slithered."

He raised his voice. "I didn't get into her bed at all. I didn't even step into her apartment. We went for coffee and talked half the night. We talked. We did not sleep together."

JD studied him. "Truth?"

"Hundred percent. And I don't know why you care."

They both looked at the flowers. JD's mood hadn't improved. "You say nothing's changed," she said. "But you get all mopey when you say it. It's always all or nothing for you. If she won't marry you, it's over. You know how Kate will take that kind of pressure? She'll realize you're a loser and leave you in the dust."

Dion gave an angry shrug to say *You just can't win*. But JD was pushing off, so he grabbed the bouquet she'd recommended and stepped inside to pay for it. With flowers in hand, he followed her back to the station. They detoured to the parkade, where he placed the bundle of springtime cheer in his car.

"Good for you," JD said. Her voice rang out against cars and concrete. "You got the flowers, now all you gotta do is talk. Talk your face off. You're not going to get anywhere pretending nothing's wrong."

He beeped his car lock shut. "You're a relationship expert all of a sudden?"

She snorted. "Next to you, anyone's an expert."

It wasn't until they were in the stairwell climbing two flights that he came up with a snappy comeback to direct at her slim backside. "Fuck you."

"You wish," was her instant reply. She had always been snappier than him.

# TWENTY-NINE

## RELEASE

*February 18*

BY 4:00 A.M. LEITH had been sitting in a chair by
Vivi's bedside for over an hour. He'd been called in on
a false alarm. Which was probably his fault for being so
officious, telling hospital staff he wanted to be notified
the instant she opened her eyes.

Might have qualified that a bit, but it was too late for
fine tuning. The call had come, waking him and Alison,
and he had leapt from pyjamas into trousers, sweater,
boots, and with hair all on end like a madman he'd raced
over here, only to find the patient's eyes had opened for
a moment, but were no longer. She was sleeping. Wired
to machines, one arm in a cast and one leg in a splint, all
signals showing she was on the mend, but, yeah, asleep.

He didn't mind. The delight he felt for her recovery easily made up for the inconvenience. He sat and

listened to the night sounds of a hospital. Hospitals didn't bother him, maybe because he'd spent so much time in their wards and corridors since he was young, as relatives were born, or got sick, or died. One by one his grandparents had left him, and new cousins arrived. Then there were the casts to sign as friends broke their legs doing wheelies or falling off ladders.

Hospitals were rich reminders of emotion. Grief, laughter, boredom, thrills. Maybe he was accustomed to the place. Maybe it was just an extension of home.

He semi-dozed in his chair. As the room's natural light began to spill in through the window, he woke and saw Vivi's eyes were open and fixed on him. He straightened and smiled at her. Though she had to be disoriented and in pain, she smiled back.

The gratitude he saw in her smile was probably more generally directed to some saint of slim chances, but he accepted it as a personal hello. "Good morning," he said. "And welcome back."

\* \* \*

"Well, the truth is Gemma doesn't like kids," Vivi told Leith. "She just knows she's supposed to, so she acts like she does." She was seated upright and was holding a glass of water. Her voice was raspy and disjointed, but she was getting her story across well enough. Like Dion, she had a way of stating her gut feelings as though they were fact. But she had a right to be so bold, being only nine.

"How do you know that?" Leith asked. His digital recorder was getting it all down, but there was nothing like the face-to-face of real-time conversation. And this one had opened with a bombshell accusation.

Not that he was going to take Vivi's word for anything. What had Gemma called the child, according to JD? A manipulator. A mental case. Dangerous.

He thought back to what he'd seen as genuine grief in Gemma's face on the night Luna Mae had gone missing. No, Viviani was wrong in saying Gemma didn't like kids.

"I told you that Tia said I'm a seer, right?" Vivi said. "I think I know now what he meant. It's like I have X-ray vision into people's heads."

Wrong again. If Vivi had X-ray vision, she would see Leith didn't believe in ESP or crystal balls. He tried to sound like a believer. "And what do you see in Gemma's head?"

"She wishes Luna had never been born," Vivi told him. She said it with quiet regret, as though she didn't like speaking ill of Gemma, but had no choice. "She wishes she could just spend all her time fixing up the house and looking nice and throwing dinner parties for Perry's friends. She hates, like, dirt, and diapers, and babies crying. She especially hates it when Luna cries. It's like I can see her swearing at Luna really loud inside her head, but when I'm there she doesn't say it out loud, right? And then she gets even madder. But she acts really nice, especially to Luna, especially when people are around. And to me, too, and to Tia, when he was alive. It's like she just wishes in her head we were all gone."

Leith considered telling her she was wrong, that Gemma was under a lot of stress but that she loved her family deeply. Yet did he really know that was true?

And did he want to risk breaking the trust between himself and the girl?

And besides, after what Gemma had done to JD, a part of him wanted to see the woman fall from a great height. He said, "You know what I think? I think what you've got is better than magic. I think you're just uber perceptive."

"What's uber?"

"Super."

She considered that, watching him, sussing him out. Then she said, "Gemma didn't push me."

"Nobody's saying she did," Leith said. "What I understand happened is —"

But Vivi's hand went up to silence him. "She didn't push me," she said. "She just let go."

Just let go? This was a twist. Leith absorbed the statement. He sensed the fragility of the moment, was afraid to break it. Softly, he asked her, "How did she let go?"

Vivi reached out and gripped his arm in demonstration. She tugged, suspended his arm as high as she could over the bedclothes, and released. Deliberately. His arm fell to the mattress and lay there. "Like that," she said.

\* \* \*

Viviani went on to tell Leith that Gemma had let her fall because of what Tia had seen. Tia had told Vivi, and after his death she'd told both Zachary and Gemma. Because what he'd seen could help find Luna. But instead of talking about it, they'd gotten mad at her and said she was lying. Or Tia was lying. Or both kids were lying.

Leith got Vivi to start from the beginning, as far back as she wanted. She began with the day Luna Mae disappeared. "Gemma and Perry were having a dinner party with their friends," she said. "So they were busy, so I was playing with my friend Alexa, and Tia was at Oliver's house. But Tia had to go home to pick up his homework, and when he cycled to the driveway and looked down, that's when he saw."

She watched Leith keenly now, making sure he understood. "He saw them fighting, Gemma and Zachary, and they had Luna, and they were all yelling and screaming. And they were holding onto Luna, Tiago says, and trying to pull her in half."

Leith flinched. It was too much a reminder of him and Alison in the car on Picnic Day, shouting at each other, their anger escalating until Izzy in the car seat behind them interrupted with a heartbreaking howl, "*Don't, don't, don't.*" Which had shut them up fast.

From what Vivi was saying, though, Gemma and Zachary were too much in the zone to shut up. "What did Tia do when he saw them fighting like that?"

"Nothing. They stopped when they saw him, and told him to go away. He saw that Luna was okay, just scared, and he turned and left. He didn't tell me about it till after Luna was gone. He told me that it made him sick, seeing them fighting over her, not caring how she must feel. He said he couldn't sleep well after that, because he should have done something. We talked about it, and I told him it's not his fault. But I don't think he really believed me."

"Did Tia tell you he thought their arguing over Luna had something to do with her disappearance?"

"Oh no, he didn't think that. He was just mad at them. When he died, though, I told them what he'd told me, and I told them they should tell you about it, because it might help find Luna. But they didn't. So I said I would."

"How did they react to that?"

"Zachary just pretended like it wasn't true. Gemma said she'd kill me if I told."

She had quoted the startling words without drama.

"She really said that?" Leith asked.

"She didn't mean it, though. It's just like saying I'm so mad I could kill you."

Leith wasn't so sure. "And that's why you got in touch with Constable Temple."

Vivi nodded.

Leith also wasn't sure whether he should put this last question to Vivi. "The argument between Zach and Gemma might not have had anything to do with the disappearance. Why not just obey your mom? Why push her so hard, make her mad?"

Vivi looked surprised, and maybe disappointed with Leith and his dumb question. "I wouldn't have pushed Gemma except she called Tia a liar, when I know he's not. Why would she lie about him lying? I don't know. All I know is she knows something important, and so does Zach, and they should tell you what it is, because you're trying to find Luna. And they should stop telling me it's none of my business. It is my business. Luna's my sister, and I want to know where she is and if she's okay. Right?"

Leith couldn't argue with that.

# THIRTY

# FRACTURES

WHO TO BELIEVE? Leith needed to get to the bottom of what had really happened on the Riverside balcony yesterday. Viviani claimed Gemma had deliberately let her fall, and Gemma was adamant that it was JD's pushiness to blame.

Before interviewing Gemma he decided to get Dion's opinion. And he vowed to himself that for a change he would hear Cal out without contradicting him, give his intuition the respect it deserved.

He met Dion in the case room and opened the conversation by playing devil's advocate, suggesting that Vivi wasn't the little sweetheart she appeared to be, but a pint-sized psychopath and master manipulator. "What d'you think?" he asked, when he was done. "Anything's possible, right?"

Dion narrowed his eyes — maybe in thoughtfulness, maybe contempt.

"She just strikes me as a little unnaturally mature," Leith said.

Dion had read Gemma and Viviani's statements. He said, "What's so unnaturally mature about the conclusions she came to? They make good sense to me."

"Sure, but I still lean more toward Gemma. I don't prefer her, but I believe her."

"I'd trust Gemma as far as I can throw her," Dion said.

Vows forgotten, Leith said, "So you're going to go in there with your mind made up, are you, to hell with other possibilities?"

"I'm going to go in there looking for ways to trip her up."

"Good," Leith said with some heat. "You want to ask the questions, then? Go for it."

"Sure thing," Dion snapped.

"Good," Leith repeated. But no longer with heat. Dion would do a good job of it, he was sure. "You can do them all, in fact. I've got Zach lined up next, then Perry, and I've called Chelsea in as well. We're going to be here a while."

"Sure," Dion said again, this time without the snap, and his fingers tapped a nervous tattoo on the tabletop.

Leith's phone vibrated with a message. The detainee was ready.

* * *

Dion faced Gemma Vale, hoping he could trip her up as promised, and worried about failure. For JD he had to do his best.

"Do you think you're a good mom?" he began.

Gemma was dressed down today, in greys and blacks, and had gone easy on the bling. "I'm a very good mom," she said.

"You love your kids?"

"Of course I do."

"Luna, Vivi, Tia, you love them all equally?"

"In different ways, but yes."

"Earlier in the day, before Luna went missing, Tia saw you and Zachary fighting, is that right?"

"Vivi told you about that, did she?"

"She said Tia told her about it. She also said you got mad when she told you. You told her Tia was lying. So which is true?"

"Zachary and I were arguing. That's normal. Not very mature, but nothing extreme."

"But when Vivi put it to you, you told her Tia was lying. Why?"

"Vivi made it sound like it was a thing. It wasn't."

"He said you were tearing Luna in half."

"That's silly. It's a teenager's interpretation. Zach and I do our best not to argue in front of the kids, so seeing us shouting like that upset Tia more than it should have. Have you asked the neighbours if they've ever heard us fighting?"

"Was Luna crying?"

"A little upset, yes. Whining. Losing patience."

"Why do you say Tia's lying?"

"Don't forget my baby had just been taken from me," Gemma said, and her voice could have iced over a fast river. "Maybe I was a little distracted by that, hmm? It's kind of hard being the perfect parent when your heart is breaking in two."

"Must have been hard for Tiago, too."

"I'm aware of that."

"Why would he make up something like you and Zach yelling and screaming?"

"Not making up. Exaggerating. Kids are great at making horror stories out of nothing. Aren't we here to talk about Vivi's fall?"

"If you're such a good mom, why are you and Zach yelling and screaming over Luna?"

"Is there some kind of new law I'm not aware of against being imperfect?"

"Did you swear at Zach in front of Luna?"

"No, we never swear in front of Luna."

"Insulted each other? Called each other names? Made threats?"

She fell silent, staring at him, trying to figure him out. She was thinking, but he didn't want to give her the time. "Is Luna more important to you than your adopted kids?"

"*What?*"

"Telling Tia to mind his own business when all he wanted you to do was stop scaring Luna."

"That did *not* happen."

"Why did he make up stories about you?"

"Like I said —"

"You did say, and I don't believe you. I think he saw you and Zachary yelling and screaming, and Luna was in distress, and you were ignoring her needs, and he saw that as abuse, and that's why you're telling all these lies."

"It got nowhere near abuse, and I'm going to see to it that you lose your badge. This is illegal, what you're doing." She looked at Leith, who didn't jump to her defence.

"Do you feel responsible for Tia's death?" Dion asked.

"Yes," she cried. "I let Luna overshadow everything else. I neglected Tiago and his needs. Obviously. Are you going to throw me in jail now?"

She grabbed a tissue. He'd driven her to tears, but he didn't slow down. "Hard to be a good mom in a situation when your baby's gone missing."

"Yes, it sure the hell is."

"You've spent the last few years making sacrifices for the kids. Invested a lot of time into making them happy, right?"

"I *willingly* made sacrifices."

"Still, even Luna got on your nerves, didn't she?"

"Of course. All moms get frazzled."

"But you love her."

"Always and forever, more each day. I miss her desperately."

"As much as you miss Tiago?"

Gemma half rose from her seat in anger, but sat again when he didn't react. "You're a good mom," he said. "A great mom, would you say?"

"In the scale of things, I'm a great mom."

She was baring her teeth now. She looked frozen.

"Yelling and screaming would be kind of traumatizing to a baby, I'd think."

She laughed coldly. "You're trying to get me to admit to something I didn't do. We didn't yell and scream. We argued."

"But you're a good mom anyway."

"Damn you," she said.

"You do your best."

"As best as I humanly can."

"So why did you push Vivi?"

"I didn't *push* her."

She stopped, and tried again with a shift of emphasis. "I *didn't* push her. She *fell*. I was trying to set her down, and the policewoman was getting aggressive. She grabbed my arm, jostled me. I lost my grip."

Dion watched her for a long moment. He checked his notes, and looked at her again. "You're right, you didn't push Vivi. You let her fall. That's what Vivi says."

"Not true."

"Constable Temple was telling you to put her down, but you didn't. You turned away so she couldn't see. Instead of taking Vivi off the railing, you sat her there, held onto her, and when you knew she was tipping backward, you let her go."

"I was trying to set her down, but the constable knocked my arm."

Dion held his half-empty glass out to the side, suspended over the linoleum. "There's a difference between this slipping out of my fingers 'cause my arm got knocked and me doing this." He opened his hand and the glass dropped to the floor. It didn't break into pieces, as he'd hoped, but bounced, spun, and left a puddle. "Big difference," he said. "It's what sets an accident apart from attempted murder. You *let* her fall."

"You people are just protecting your own, that's what this is," Gemma said. She added that she needed a bathroom break.

While they waited Dion picked up the glass and mopped up the water with paper towels.

"Nice demo," Leith said. "Would have been more showy if it shattered, though."

A crack ran down the side of the glass in Dion's hand. He showed it to Leith. "Close enough."

Like the glass, he knew that Gemma Vale was cracked, if not shattered. A full breakdown would take another hour or so, but it was going to happen. He now felt sure of it.

* * *

Gemma Vale's confession wasn't the clean sweep Dion had hoped for, but by the end of it he knew JD was out of danger, Viviani would no longer be called a manipulative monster, and answers to the mystery of Luna Mae Garland's kidnap would surface.

He took what he knew and put it to Zachary Garland.

"Assault, conspiracy, obstruction," Garland said, echoing the charges he couldn't quite believe. "That makes it sound like we did it on purpose. But we didn't. It just happened."

"How did it just happen?" Dion asked.

The big man seemed to shrink in his chair, and for most of his story he addressed the tabletop in front of him. "I was late bringing Luna to Gemma that day," he said. "I'd forgotten something. Her favourite toy. I had to turn back. No big deal, ten, twenty minutes behind schedule. Got to Gemma's, and we're in the driveway, and I'm holding Luna, and first thing Gemma does is start screaming at me for being late. She says I do it on purpose."

He looked at Dion. "Well, excuse me, I'm trying my best here." He worked his fists open and closed, and carried on, again avoiding eye contact. "I guess I said a thing or two as well. And how many times have I told her not to swear in front of the kids? Gemma's got zero self-control, and she knows I can't stand it. So I kind of changed my mind about handing Luna over till we'd come to some kind of agreement about her behaviour, and Gemma kind of grabbed Luna's arm, and I kind of pulled away, and …"

Garland broke down. He cried in a noisy way. Long, dragging sobs, until finally it was Dion who needed a break. He left the room and walked up and down the corridor outside, feeling queasy. Leith joined him and asked if he was okay.

"My knee's sore. Needed a stretch."

Of course it wasn't the knee, but the feelings of dread stirred up by Garland's confession. It was the parallels he could see between Garland's stupidity and his own. Two lives falling apart through bad choices. Not just bad — *disastrous*.

On their return Garland was able to carry on. "Luna's shoulder was dislocated. We took her inside. I've dealt with a few dislocated joints in my life, and I was able to pop it back in quite easy. I don't know if you've ever dislocated your shoulder, but it hurts. Man, it hurts. And she was crying and wailing, but not as bad as I thought."

He paused to reflect, rubbing his own shoulder as if in sympathy. "Babies are more rubbery, I think," he continued. "They mend quicker. But all the same, I was going to take her straight to emerg. But then Gemma was walking her around in the living room and got her quieted down, and she said there was no need to take her in. I had my doubts, but I agreed that we'd just give her infants' Tylenol and see if she was okay without treatment. And I left. I got home. The guys came over. We popped some beer, and Chelsea made chips and stuff. But I couldn't stop thinking about Luna, how she was doing."

He stopped and seemed perilously close to tears again. Dion pushed the tissue box forward and told him to take his time.

"I really, really don't like phoning Gemma," Garland said. "'Cause she either doesn't pick up or she calls me names and hangs up on me. So I told the guys and Chelsea I had to go out, and I drove over there. I knew Gemma and Perry were having a dinner party, but I didn't care. I knocked on the door, said I wanted to just see Luna, just make sure she's okay, and … and Gemma was mad that I showed up, but she didn't want to make a scene in front of her fancy guests, so we went downstairs, and we found Luna in her crib, and she was … she was dead. Not breathing. Cold. We picked her up. Shook her. Couldn't revive her."

Garland seized more tissues. "I figured it had to be the meds. But how could it be? We hadn't given her more than recommended. Some kind of adverse reaction, I said, and Gemma then admitted it wasn't baby Tylenol she'd given her, because she couldn't find the bottle, but an adult Tylenol 2, but just half a tab. Can that do it?"

He had stopped to ask Dion the question. Dion said he didn't know. What he did know, because Gemma had told him so, was that she had given Luna a full tab, not a half. Crushed up and added to food.

"And I was freaking out at her," Garland went on. "And she was freaking out at me. I grabbed Luna to take her to emerg. I knew we'd be arrested and charged, and probably do time, but I didn't care. Gemma wouldn't let me take her. She was in a panic. Didn't want anybody knowing she was stupid enough to play tug of war with her own child, and then poison her with meds. We argued. And then she started blackmailing me with Vivi again. She said she'd bring up those allegations, and make sure they stuck. She knows how it would kill me to go to jail, and to lose Vivi. I gave in. I agreed to do it her way. She said we had to hide Luna's body and say she'd been abducted."

He looked at his own hands like he couldn't believe they were a part of him.

"Somehow we kept it together. Went back upstairs and outside so nobody could hear, and made a plan. I told her I'd go home, establish an alibi, then come over, go around back, take Luna. Then after a certain time Gemma would find her gone and sound the alarm. Then all we'd have to do is live with what we'd done for the rest of our lives."

He was silent so long that Dion thought he was done. "So you followed through with the plan, did you?"

Garland stared at him. "What? No, I didn't. Couldn't. Besides, I knew I'd get blamed for the kidnap unless I had a solid alibi. So I went back to my own get-together with the guys, and somebody else went and picked her up, and hid the ... the body. Till we could figure out where to hide ... it ... permanently."

"Who's the somebody else?"

"I know a guy." Garland ducked his face.

"A guy?" Dion said. "What guy? Name."

"I just know his first name. John. Johnny. Met him through the gym a while ago, and heard he'd do stuff for pay. Illegal stuff. So I gave him a call. Gave him directions. And he ... he got Luna, brought her to me. And I ... I took her and gave her a burial at sea."

"How did you manage that?"

"I have a boat. Just a little runaround. Took her out, way out into Indian Arm. Dropped her in."

"You have John's number?"

"No. I lost it."

"You called him from your cell?"

Pause. "Yes."

"So there'll be a record. How much did you pay Johnny?"

Another pause. "Five thousand."

"Your bank records will show it, right?"

A third pause was one too many, and Dion said, "D'you want to start again, Zach?"

Garland nodded.

"Who went and got Luna's body for you?"

Garland toppled forward like he'd been shot. Then he sat up and said, "Chelsea. But she only wanted to save my ass. She's a good person. The best. Please don't rough her up. We'll both co-operate all the way. Promise. But please, please, please be nice to her."

Leith said, "What did she do with Luna's body? We need to find her."

"You won't find her," Garland told him. "It's true what I said about Indian Arm. Except Chelsea is the one who did it. She took my runaround, and she did it for me."

Chelsea had been spoken to on the night of the disappearance, Dion recalled. But only briefly. If the team had tracked her through the night, they might have come to this point a lot sooner. But there had been no reason to think she hadn't been at the Forbes apartment all evening with Zach and his poker buddies. She'd been written off as a suspect on the spot.

He could understand how she had slipped out. She wasn't part of the poker game, wasn't watching hockey with the boys. She was just around, cleaning up, staying mostly in her bedroom. Listening to music, somebody had mentioned. She had performed a kind of sleight of hand. She had planted herself in their minds as present, and then she hadn't been. That simple.

"If I wasn't under constant scrutiny, I'd have done it myself, believe me," Garland said. "But she did it. After she got Luna, she went to work as always, and grocery shopping, and whatever else she had to do, until she had a chance to take the boat out. But in the end I'm the only guilty party. I did this. I got her to drop my sweet little baby into the ocean. I don't know where. I'm so sorry, Luna Mae. I'm so, so sorry."

Dion checked the time, and stepped outside to make a call. Had Chelsea Romanov arrived yet? She had been notified this morning to attend the detachment following her day's work, but so far hadn't arrived.

Maybe she'd got wind that the interviews had changed course, her boyfriend was in custody, and she would be charged for her role in the disappearance of Luna Garland. Maybe she'd been on her toes and ready to skip town all along.

# THIRTY-ONE

# DOUBLE DOSE

THE DAY WAS WELL OVER, but Dion volunteered to stay on and complete the interviews alone. Perry Vale and hopefully Chelsea Romanov, if she finally turned up. Leith had said they should put Perry over till tomorrow, as there was no urgency, now, with Luna's body likely lost forever at the bottom of the channel.

But Dion wanted to get Perry's perspective. Even if he didn't get the full story, he might fill in some of the blanks left by Gemma and Zach.

Leith had agreed, and gone home to his dinner table. Dion's dinner was a cafeteria sandwich, and now he was shaking hands with a punctual Perry Vale. "Thanks for coming."

"I wish I could say my pleasure. You've arrested Gemma."

"Yes. I'm sorry it's come to this."

Perry sat down, and before the recorder was switched on and the interview formally opened, he said, "I know she's dead."

"Who's dead?"

"Luna."

Dion looked at him in surprise. He hadn't considered that Perry could be a party to the crime. A terrible crime where a small child was torn in two — virtually — her body was disposed of like trash, and a ridiculous amount of police time was wasted in looking for her abductor. Was he going to have to read this man his rights as well? "You're aware of what happened the night of your dinner party?"

"I am now." Perry appeared gloomy and anxious, but didn't seem touched by fugitive fear. He went on to explain why. "Gem only told me about it yesterday morning," he said. "Over the breakfast table, before I went to work, before what happened to Vivi, her fall. Gem said she and Zachary are somehow responsible for Luna's disappearance. They both conspired to get rid of the body. And really that's all I know."

"Kind of a big disclosure."

"Huge. I couldn't believe my ears."

"But you didn't grill her for more details?"

"No. I needed to get to work."

Perry's devotion to his work seemed almost pathological to Dion. But career was life to some people. He couldn't throw stones. "Go on."

"I told her we'd talk it over after I got home. I didn't know all this would happen meanwhile — Vivi falling off the balcony, Gem's arrest. Which, by the way, I stand by her on that point. She would never do anything to hurt Vivi, or any child. Not intentionally."

"What happened the day Luna disappeared?"

"What I know now or what I knew then?"

"Both. Put yourself back in the day and go through it for me."

"Certainly. It was Sunday, my birthday weekend. I went to see a dear friend who's not well. I hear you fellows have browbeaten the truth out of him on that score and satisfied yourselves that yes, I was there, not busy kidnapping babies."

"We questioned him," Dion said.

Perry grimaced. "I'm sorry. I shouldn't be snippy."

"Don't worry about it."

"We were having people over that night. Important guests, people I wanted to impress. I needed it to be a success. I was home by four to get ready. Gem was busy in the kitchen, and Luna was playing in the living room. Vivi and Tia were out with their friends. I remember little Luna was being cantankerous. Gem said the baby was just tired. So that's fine. But it went on and on. The whimpering and wailing was starting to get to me. I needed to prepare for dinner, get in the mood, you know. I tried walking Luna, which usually quiets her. I took her down and put her in her crib, even tried singing to her, which she likes. But she kept whining. She seemed extra tired, but simply wouldn't fall asleep. I supposed she was teething again. I could hear Gem upstairs getting exasperated, banging dishes. She always takes on more than she can handle, and wanted dinner to be perfect. I brought Luna back upstairs, tried to keep her entertained, managed to calm Gem down. I put on some music and got dressed. The doorbell rang. My guests were arriving."

He pleated his brow in thought. "Once Luna was back downstairs in her crib, I could still hear her crying, off and on. More on than off. It was like she was never going to stop. So, oh yes, at some point I went down and gave her something to help her sleep. I'd forgotten about that."

He fell silent, and Dion could almost see the realization dawning on him. Perry clapped a palm to his cheek as he repeated his last statement. "I gave her something to help her sleep." His voice dropped to a whisper. "What have I done?"

Dion was wondering the same. "What did you give her to help her sleep?"

"Acetaminophen with codeine," Perry said. "Tylenol 2. Oh god. Is that what did it? But why? Gem's given Luna half an adult tab once before — before she found out it wasn't safe — to help with teething, and nothing bad happened."

Dion was no physician, but even he knew better than to give codeine to the very young. "How much did you give her?"

"Just one, mashed up with banana. I didn't tell Gem. She's since found out that babies shouldn't be given adult meds, so it's the new house rule, only infant Tylenol for Luna."

"So you not only broke the rule, but upped the dose."

"I wasn't thinking."

Dion wondered if he should tell Perry that the overdose had likely been a combined effort. In her statement, Gemma first claimed she had given Luna a single dose of baby Tylenol, but under pressure confessed she couldn't find the bottle and had resorted to an adult pill. Only half, mashed up and added to yogurt. Mango flavoured to disguise the bitterness. On further questioning she had stumbled on her own lies and admitted that once Perry was home and getting changed, and since Luna was still complaining, she had fed the child another half tab.

The math was easy. Over the space of several hours, Luna had been given two adult-strength painkillers. With codeine. In the best-case scenario, she could have gotten sick, maybe puked. But Luna wasn't a best-case scenario. Some small children couldn't metabolize the drug properly, and she was one of those rare cases. She had stopped breathing. She had died.

"Did you and Gemma talk about why Luna was crying so much?"

"Luna had taken a tumble and bumped her arm, Gem told me. Not a big deal. I asked if she'd given Luna anything for the pain, and she hadn't, as she couldn't find the bottle. Like I said, I thought the risk of breaking the rule, just this once, was negligible. I went behind Gem's back and I did what I did. I'm so sorry. I just thought poor Luna would feel better and get some much-needed sleep."

And sleep she did. Forever.

Perry was pushing tears back with his palms. "Gem blames herself," he said. "She'll never forgive me. I'll never forgive myself. It's all my fault."

He was only one codeine pill away from the truth, and had the right to know the rest, so Dion told him. While Perry had broken Gemma's rule about the meds, so had Gemma. Each had given Luna a whole codeine pill, not wanting a squalling child to ruin the night's special dinner.

"You know," Perry said. "I was going to talk her into coming here and telling the whole story when I got home from work today. I really was."

Dion believed him. His phone was silent. The message he was waiting for, news of Chelsea's arrest, still hadn't come through. She'd lost her nerve and run. Alerts had gone out to be on the lookout for her vehicle, and he didn't believe she'd get far.

Then he remembered that this wasn't the average fugitive they were after. Chelsea Romanov was a survivalist.

* * *

After Perry had gone back to his lonely home on Riverside Drive, Dion stayed at his desk and replayed in his mind the incident of Gemma and her juice jug, how it had smashed to the floor moments before he and Leith had buzzed her doorbell on their mission to talk to Tiago, who had been dead for hours, down by the river.

An ugly idea had been circling through his mind since he'd crouched down to pick up the broken glass. Had Gemma smashed the jug to explain away her tears?

Did she know Tia had gone down to the river in the middle of the night?

Had she known and done nothing about it? Heard him stirring, and opened her bedroom door in time to see him leaving, headed for the river? She could have put on her boots and coat and gone after him, but had chosen not to. Instead, she went back to bed, hating herself for praying he wouldn't come back.

In the morning, after Perry had gone to work, maybe she'd sat alone with what she knew, looking out at the rainforest into which Tia had disappeared. Then headlights appeared in her driveway and she knew the cops had arrived. Bad timing. She'd been sitting there feeling conflicted and sinful, and it would show on her face — the guilt and fear and self-pity. Maybe she got some pleasure from the sympathy she was receiving over Luna these days, but Tia's case would be different. People would blame her for Tia.

Her red eyes were a giveaway, and she knew the detectives would see how freshly distraught she was. And later, when they found Tia, they would wonder why. She needed a reason, and fast. Even a little reason. Like a broken jug.

He'd never prove it, not without her admission. And she'd never admit it. He wouldn't put it in a report or talk it over with the team, not even Leith. Especially not Leith. Because Leith would be right, that it was probably just what it looked like, a broken jug, and pursuing it would accomplish nothing. He should just forget it, really.

But he wouldn't. The thought would just keep turning in circles, going nowhere, till another one took its place.

# THIRTY-TWO

## SASAMAT LANE

IT WAS LATE IN THE DAY and the skies were dark, but Dion remained too restless to pack it in. With permission, he sprang Garland from lock-up to accompany him to the apartment Garland shared with Chelsea. Maybe something there would point to the missing woman's whereabouts. A co-operative Garland looked through closets and drawers, desks, bathroom counters, and cabinets, looking for clues. Dion stood by and waited.

"She's gone," Garland said. He looked stunned.

"How gone is she?" Dion asked.

"Her gear's missing."

"What d'you mean? Camping gear?"

Garland listed the stuff. Her backpack, her ultra-lightweight overnight equipment, which meant tent, sleeping bag, cooking utensils. Her iPod, her poncho. Even her favourite little photo album was missing.

"Does that mean she's taken to the hills?"

"Obviously."

"Did you know she was planning on running?"

"No, sir, I didn't."

"Which hill has she taken off to? Where do we start looking?"

Garland guffawed in a bleak way. He beckoned to Dion and in the hallway showed him a map of B.C. pinned to the wall. The map bristled with a dozen push-pins, some on the Island, many on the coast, and one on the north-eastern rim of the province, mid-Rockies. "Those are a few of the mountains she's conquered. I have no idea where she's gone. Could be one of these or someplace new."

"How's her state of mind?"

"Not good," Garland admitted. "It was horrible of me to ask her to do it. She cries a lot. She has nightmares."

Dion took a snapshot of the map. "Let's narrow it down," he said. "It's February. We can forget the Rockies and the Island. Starting from closest to home, which pins are most likely?"

Garland named a few spots where Chelsea could have gone to ground at this time of year. The Pemberton Valley, Stave Lake, out toward Bella Coola. "You know, there's just no end to the places a person could take off to."

Too true. Even narrowed down, Dion realized a manhunt was out of the question. He wondered instead about contacts. Chelsea had no close relatives. Her mother was dead, and her dad lived in Ontario. That left friends and associates, a list he hoped would be manageable. "Are there people she might go to when she's in trouble? Maybe somebody who's also into camping and might have gone with her?"

Garland depressed him further by producing a printout of names, fellow survivalists who had taken his course and remained in contact. "We're a pretty tight-knit group. She could have gone to any of 'em."

Dion pocketed the list.

"Then there's her godmom," Garland added.

"Her godmom? Who's that? Where does she live?"

"You know Deep Cove, Indian Arm, Sasamat Lane?"

"Sure."

"Her name's Faith," Garland said. "She's pretty old. She's got a funky little house up near the top. But I'd have to go with you. She's kind of blockaded the old driveway, and if you don't know what you're doing, you can get lost. Especially in the dark."

"She's blockaded her driveway?"

"She's an artist."

"You figure Chelsea might have gone to Faith for help?"

"Not sure, but that would be a good bet. At least Faith might have talked to her before she took off and could tell you where she's gone."

*Would have been nice if you'd said all this from the start,* Dion thought. He sat at Zachary's kitchen table to phone Leith, to advise him where he was headed and who he was headed there with. When Leith heard about the rugged setting and the mad artist, he told Dion to run her name first — and not to go alone. And that was an order.

Dion made some calls to run the name Faith James, and didn't get any flags. Not a gun fanatic or terrorist, apparently. He next called JD, who was also working late. He wanted JD as a partner because he didn't like her cold shoulder and wanted to make things good between them. Or find out what he'd done wrong, because it had to be more than the Shiomi incident.

"I'm busy," JD told him, when he had her on the line. "I'm working on Aziz."

"Put it on hold. I need you."

"Tasha needs me more. Get someone else."

"Okay," he said. "No problem. I'm better off with Jim or Sean anyway. It's way up Indian Arm. Might be some hiking involved."

"I don't quite get the connection there." She sounded irate.

"A guy," Dion said. "Muscle. Endurance."

The noise she made, maybe a laugh, pushed the phone from his ear. "I get what you're trying to do here," she said. "You're so transparent." Pause. "Give me an hour."

"I don't have an hour."

"So ten minutes," she said.

"Bring a flashlight."

Ten minutes later they met at the detachment parkade and set out in an SUV fit for the slippery back roads of the North Shore foothills. Dion drove and JD rode shotgun. Zachary, under arrest but not deemed a threat, sat in the back giving directions. With the heat pumping from the dash they left the dark city, sparkling with raindrops and lamplight, bound for a crazy woman's den in the wilderness above Deep Cove, looking for a distressed young woman on the run.

\* \* \*

Up on Sasamat Lane the temperature had dropped and light snow that would never make it to the lowlands lashed the windshield. Dion parked on the winding country road, as directed by Garland, and stepped out of the truck to join Garland and JD a stone's throw up a rough driveway. They were looking at the downed tree lying across its mouth. Faith James's blockade.

It was a conifer of some kind, four inches in diameter at most, and a child could step over it. No doubt blow-down from some long ago storm, and the homeowner for whatever reason had decided to leave it. "Exaggerate much?" he asked Garland.

A small car sat parked in the stub of the driveway, nosed against the downed tree, and Dion checked his notes. Sure enough, it was Chelsea's Kia. There was no other vehicle in sight.

"What does Faith drive?" JD asked Garland.

He couldn't say. "I don't know her too well," he said. "I've only been here once."

The ascending driveway was narrow, shrubby, and long, but hardly the wilderness trail Garland had warned them about. A few minutes of trudging and Dion could see the house, small and dark, built of planks and shakes, squatting unlit among the evergreens like a part of the forest floor. Snow glittered in the air and a peculiar noise that had reached him from the roadway grew louder as he and the others neared the building. He shone his flashlight around. The beam caught wind chimes made of scrap wood and metal that clattered, tinkled, and bonged from branches all around the front porch.

JD at his side said, "Maybe I've seen too many horror flicks, but I'm scared."

She was probably kidding, but maybe not. The three of them had come to a stop before the home's front door. "Who gets to knock?" Dion asked, and was relieved when Garland volunteered.

There was a long wait. Garland knocked again. Dion stood back, hand resting on the butt of his gun. They were in the middle of nowhere with forest all around, wind chimes banging at his nerves. He wouldn't be surprised if a witch opened the door, hollow-eyed and weird and armed with whatever witches were armed with. Curses and bolts of lightning.

Still no answer. JD had been looking around, and she called out, "Tracks."

They followed bootprints through a fine skiff of snow around the side of the house. It was a large tiered garden, dormant and soggy, backing onto forest, and at the far end Dion could see a mini gazebo of sorts, barely large enough for one person to crouch within.

A person sat on the gazebo's wooden steps. Candlelight flickered around her. It was Chelsea Romanov, and although she must have noted their presence, she didn't lose interest in the object she twirled between her fingers.

"Stay here with Zachary," Dion told JD. "I'll go talk to her."

He walked through darkness down the cobblestone path to the gazebo, which he saw now was more of a shrine, with a bronze Buddhist statue meditating in its centre, not the usual fat guy but a female figure. Sprigs of fake flowers and colourful bottles were placed before her, bowls of wooden fruit, candles of all shapes and sizes.

More wind chimes hung on the trees around the shrine, softly bonging.

Chelsea hadn't moved at his approach. She was dressed for winter in ski jacket, jeans, boots, toque, scarf. The object she held in her hand was a flower. Like the sprigs around her, the petals were artificial.

He said her name, and finally she looked up at him. Her expression didn't change. No smile, no frown. He looked around. A heavy-boughed cedar tree loomed behind the shrine, hundreds of years old, no doubt. Its tangled roots heaved up the soil around its base, and cradled between the tangles he could see a spot where the earth had been disturbed. Softened and mounded, patted down, sprinkled with dried flowers, circled with pebbles and sticks. A small stone gremlin with wings sat like a headstone. Or a guardian.

Dion sat next to Chelsea on the step and looked at the grave. When he looked at her again she acknowledged him with a small nod. She knew. In a moment he would have to make a phone call, and tell the team he had found Luna's final resting place.

* * *

Under pitch-dark skies, Leith winced as the LEDs blared into his eyes and streaked across the back section of the property. The ornate little structure with its Buddhist shrine lost its candlelit gravitas and became so much gaudy clutter. The tree roots that cradled the small grave seemed to swell and writhe as the lights were adjusted and fixed in place. Before exhumation could begin, measurements were taken and the scene recorded. The Forensics unit photographer was looking pleased as he framed the shrine in his viewfinder. As he'd mentioned, it wasn't often his scenes were so picturesque.

"So where's the crazy artist?" Leith asked Dion. "You said it's her godmother?"

"Chelsea's godmother, Faith James," Dion said. "We don't have any idea where she is. Chelsea said when she arrived here this afternoon Faith was out. She doesn't know where she went. What if Ms. James sees all these police vehicles surrounding her place when she arrives, and beats a fast retreat? Maybe she already has."

"Can't be helped," Leith said. "If so, she'll be back. So who knew about the grave, besides Chelsea?"

"Nobody. It's taken Garland completely by surprise. Chelsea didn't tell him what she'd done. She couldn't bear the idea of dropping the body in the ocean and brought her here instead. It's a place where she could visit, even if nobody else ever could. She kept it from Garland for his own sake. The less he knew the better, I guess is what she was thinking. But now he's got the body for a proper burial. He's taking it hard. I had a job keeping him away."

Behind them, closer to the house and watched over by JD, Zachary and Chelsea had been clinging to each other like frightened kids, but now stood in a loose embrace, a blanket around their shoulders against the chill. Leith signalled to JD, and she led the two away. They mustn't be here when the digging began. "You got a statement from Chelsea?" he asked Dion.

"A brief one. When she and Zachary were both called in to talk today she figured it was all over. She went into panic mode, she says. Packed her gear and thought she'd disappear for a while. But she wanted to ask Faith's advice, so she drove up here. Then found her not home, and came out back to wait by Luna's grave."

Leith shook his head and watched the Forensics team, suited up and masked, begin their meticulous, layer-by-layer uncovering of the body.

He waited for the smell to hit him. So far all he got was wet foliage, pine.

"Once we have the body we should clear out the vehicles," Dion said. "So Ms. James feels safe to return. You and I can remain."

"And Chelsea," Leith said.

They watched the team digging, removing soil to a sifter, the photographer on standby.

"We found her," one of the team called out, for Leith's benefit.

"Jesus!" he heard another say in a spontaneous outburst. Leith lowered a brow at the man's lack of control. Forensics folks had seen everything under the sun and should know not to say such things aloud.

The team huddled over the grave. They seemed excited or agitated, and he realized he'd better start bracing himself for a shock. Though what could be more shocking than the corpse of an infant? Dion seemed apprehensive, too, shoulders drawn up against the cold. The photographer grabbed some shots of the body and walked back to show on his camera's flip-screen what he'd captured.

Leith and Dion leaned together to peer at the image on the small screen. The baby was bundled in a white blanket, its face revealed in the flash. Instead of eyes it had black buttons. Instead of hair it had pink wool. Instead of skin it had brown burlap. The corpse was a doll.

"Jesus!" Leith said.

\* \* \*

As planned, the vehicles cleared out in the hope that Faith James would feel the coast was clear and return to her little house. Walk into the trap. Explain the doll in the grave.

But after half an hour, Leith had decided they weren't going to wait. With the backing of a telephone warrant, he directed Dion and JD to break into the home while he waited on its porch with Chelsea and Zach. Zach had wanted to stay, and Leith didn't see why he shouldn't.

"So go over the burial process again," he told Chelsea. "You're as surprised as we all are by this. I was under the impression you took part in placing the body in the ground."

"No," she said, wide-eyed. Even with the blanket over her shoulders she was shivering. "That night, like I said, I did what Zach asked me to do. I took Luna's body from her crib and I got away from there fast. But it was so much worse than I imagined. I was shaking so bad I could hardly operate my car. I brought Luna here and told Faith what had happened. She promised she would help me, and keep quiet about it. I told her I would be back to take the body as soon as I could the next day. But there was no time to talk right then. I had to get back to the apartment as fast as I could, and just pray I wasn't missed."

"The alibi," Garland said. "I did a bit of play-acting, too. Made the guys think she was still around, you know, pretended to chat with her down the hall."

Chelsea continued. "When I managed to get back here the next afternoon, Faith told me she had buried Luna out back. I was surprised. And relieved, too. It was just Faith taking care of me, as she always had when I was small. And I saw the grave, and it was so beautiful. What could I do? I decided this is where Luna would stay. We had a little service, Faith and I. I couldn't stop crying."

The front door behind Leith swung open. Dion had broken into the house at the back, and was letting him inside. Leith told Chelsea and Zach to stay in the enclosed sun porch, where they could sit down, warm up, and with a good view of the long driveway could watch for Faith James's return. There would be plenty of warning, since Faith would have to park at the roadway, climb over the tree, and hoof it up the drive on foot. If she came back at all.

"When you talk to her, be nice," Chelsea begged, an echo of Zachary's earlier plea on her behalf. "She's the best person on the planet, and anything she's done wrong, she did it for me. And I really don't want to say this, but she's not been herself, lately. I've been worried about her state of mind. But this doll thing ... now I'm actually scared for her."

Leith promised he would treat her godmother with respect. He then followed the sound of conversation into the home's dark interior. It was a pleasant, cluttered place that smelled of apple pie and cinnamon. Dion and JD were having a discussion somewhere within. Instead of flicking on lamps they were using flashlights to explore, trying not to alert the homeowner that her place was being invaded.

Leith found them in the kitchen excitedly going through food items and dishes like a couple of hungry marauders. Not looking to eat, but deciphering the clues.

"Jars of apple sauce," JD said, nose in a cupboard. "Arrowroot cookies."

Dion held up little plastic dishes. "Upstairs," he told Leith. "There's a crib. It looks like it's been slept in."

This is "Goldilocks and the Three Bears," Leith was thinking. Except the bears were doing the trespassing. He turned as Chelsea shouted out from the sun porch, "Faith's back. And she's got Luna. Oh my god. Luna's alive!"

# THIRTY-THREE

## FAITH

*February 21*

LEITH STOOD IN THE detachment's foyer with Luna in his arms as the cameras snicked. The baby was the talk of the town, a bit of a celebrity, and the press wanted to capitalize on her adorable smile.

Both JD and Dion had refused to take part in the photo shoot, so Leith had stepped up to the plate. The last two days had been a flurry of activity, a bit like a lead-up to a parade. Luna had undergone a battery of examinations and been declared healthy, happy, and well nourished. In short, about as alive and well as a person could be.

How had it happened? As Faith James explained her actions, Leith had quickly gathered that Chelsea was right to worry about her godmother's state of mind. Chelsea's theory was that Faith's dementia had accelerated when she was left with a baby. A dead baby she had to hide from the police. Once Chelsea left, Faith had started preparing for the funeral. She had filled a tub with warm water and gently washed the child's lifeless body, but soon realized the baby was in some distress. The poor thing was cool and waxy, and her breathing was so shallow. Faith didn't panic, though, she told Leith. She had seen more than a few youngsters through difficulties over the years. So she walked her, patted her, kept her warm. And when the baby revived, she had fed her.

Faith's slipping mind had lost sight of the big picture and focused on the small. But why bury the doll? As the baby slept, she recalled there was a body to bury. She dug a grave close to the spot she had laid her dog to rest last year. She was a bit foggy on what she was supposed to bury, exactly, but believed it was something that made Chelsea cry. Accordingly, she had buried the rag doll that had sat on a tiny rocker in the corner of her bedroom for years. "I made it for Chelsea when she was small."

Faith wasn't completely loopy. When lucid she understood that there had been some kind of terrible mix-up. When not lucid, on the other hand, she was convinced Luna was a young Chelsea and would be going home with her at the end of the day.

Which she wouldn't be.

Leith had spoken to the doctors who had examined Luna, and was told it wasn't unthinkable that the panicky parents would fail to detect flutters of life in their comatose baby and believe she was dead.

Leith couldn't guess what kind of sentences the parents would receive for the long lists of charges they were facing, but in the long run, once Zachary had done his time and taken enough anger management and parenting courses, he would likely receive sole custody of Viviani, and maybe even Luna. In the meantime, the children would be kept together in a foster home.

When the photo shoot was over, he said goodbye to Luna and went to visit Dion at his desk. After an extended weekend, the man was nose-first into his work, typing reports.

Leith dropped into the visitor's chair and said, "What are you working on?"

"Wrap-up on Gemma Vale."

Leith nodded. "You know, it's occurred to me there are way too many heights here in B.C. for people to drop off and get hurt. You being a case in point."

Dion's grunt as he typed said this wasn't a topic to be joked about.

"Think I'll put in a transfer request back to the flatlands while I still have a chance," Leith said. "It's a lot harder to fall to your death in Saskatchewan."

Dion looked up from his keyboard, startled. "Serious?"

Leith laughed. "Not serious. Yet."

Dion went back to work, and Leith took the hint and left him alone. But as he walked down the hall he continued to reflect on their short conversation and that startled look he'd been given. Was that dismay? If Dion didn't want him heading to Saskatchewan, that meant he needed him to stay on the North Shore. Why?

He put the question to Alison over the dinner table that night. She didn't know about Leith's low-key investigation into Dion's past, but she did know of the workaday tension between them. He had told her about their inability to see eye to eye more than once.

In answer to his question, which was only rhetorical, she told him he had a bad habit of overthinking things.

He denied it.

She insisted. "You think things to death. Maybe he simply likes you, and doesn't want to lose a friend."

"He doesn't *like* me," Leith told her. "I'm about his most unfavourite person in the world. That's why it's weird that it matters to him if I'd move to Saskatchewan."

"Okay then," Alison said, but only to herself, and served the salad.

# THIRTY-FOUR

## REVERB

*February 22*

THE MORNING WAS BRILLIANT, for a change. An abnormally azure February sky. JD sat on the bench outside the detachment on her lunch break thinking about Tasha Aziz, wondering if her killer would ever be caught. She sighed as Niko Shiomi took a seat at the other end of the bench. Niko had been avoiding JD since the Valentine's Day dance. Hopefully this wasn't going to turn into some heart-to-heart attempt at reconciliation.

"That was some crazy case," JD said. "Luna Garland. Not every day you exhume a rag doll. You should have been there, Niko. Wild."

She had opened the conversation on a friendly note so Niko didn't think the lip-scar insult bothered her. Which it didn't. The scar was ugly to some, but if a fairy came along offering to exchange the deformity for the puffiest rosebud kisser in the world, JD would say no thanks. The scar made her who she was — perfect as is.

Niko said, "Uh-huh," and nothing else for a few moments. Finally, she came out with it. "I'm sorry about what I said, JD. I say the stupidest things when I'm mad."

JD shrugged. "I really don't care. Really."

Niko smiled. "I respect your tough-as-nails exterior. But I know you're a honey within. Not to mention smart."

JD pulled a face.

"And so you won't mind me saying something," Niko babbled on. "Laying all my cards on the table about Cal."

"What about him?" JD stared at Niko, worried the *something* tied into the IHIT inquiries.

But it didn't. It was personal and inane. "You can tell just by looking at him that he's in the doghouse," Niko said. "When he and his girlfriend split, I'm moving in. I'm just saying 'cause I know you've got a crush on him, but I've got dibs. Okay?"

JD gave a hearty laugh. Then she stood to show how *over* this conversation was. "If I was looking for a boyfriend, he'd be the last number on my list. So be my guest."

She walked away, satisfied that she had laughed loud enough. She didn't doubt that Niko would get Cal, in the end. Fabulous. Those two deserved each other.

She was on Lonsdale, tracing the same route she had walked with Dion the other day. Her feelings for him had come full circle. She had started out years ago not liking him much. He'd been full of himself, a jerk, a womanizer, and well on his way to corruption, and one thing she couldn't stand was a corrupt cop.

She had begun to change her mind on his return from the north with his ego cut down to a manageable size, but now she was back to not liking him again. This time it was because of Brooke, reappearing and then disappearing, taking her allegations with her, and detectives coming and asking questions, as if JD had something to hide. Which she did, and shouldn't have, and now she couldn't fix it.

*I lied for you, and I can't even tell you so. Buzz off. Don't drag me into your dirt any further.*

She found herself looking at the flowers outside the same supermarket where Dion had bought the apology bouquet. Had the apology done its job? Probably not. Probably Niko was right about all of it.

Maybe she should warn Dion to watch out for Niko the man-eater. She caught sight of her face in the supermarket's window, and saw she was looking sulky. And ugly. Then she saw something hurl across the aisle inside the store, and she heard raised voices. The howls of rage sounded like an older woman. JD squinted to see past reflections and shadows.

A commotion. Several people shouting. A fight had broken out inside. She slipped in, cautiously, to assess the situation. It was a smallish store with five or six well-stocked aisles and a staff of approximately three. Two clerks stood near the entrance, one of them making a call on a cordless phone.

Now JD could see the assailant. A squat, middle-aged woman in a blue felt coat. She stood splay-legged down the bread aisle and was seizing packages at random, hamburger buns and Ritz Cracker boxes, and pelting them at some target that remained out of sight by the freezers.

JD decided that if buns were the weapon of choice, it was unlikely the woman was armed. But possibly she was defending herself, and the individual she was pelting had guns, knives, or bombs. She asked the clerk beside her what was going on.

"She just went nuts," the clerk said. "Started throwing things at a customer. I think he's hurt."

A glass jar smashed. A man shrieked.

"I'm a cop," JD told the clerks. "Have you called 911?"

"They say a car's on its way."

"I'll see what I can do."

She made her way down the aisle, calling out that she was police and commanding the woman in blue to cease her actions. Another jar exploded and JD could smell vinegar. Pickles. She could make out the woman's words now. "You bastard. You killed my son. You bastard." A metallic crack against floor tiles, a tin can likely, followed by a second. The man's screams rose an octave. The projectiles were getting serious, and JD had to move in before somebody's skull got split.

There was a brief detente as the small woman halted her assault and searched for something heavier to lob at her victim. She was stooping to pick up a three-litre can of diced tomatoes from a lower shelf when JD moved in. The man was out of sight but she could hear him scrambling and slithering to escape. His words were hard to make out, between gasps of pain, but he seemed to be denying his attacker's accusations. His voice sounded familiar.

JD placed a hand on the woman's arm, a warning at first, then a firm grasp, pulling her upright. The woman jerked, and JD braced for a backlash — if only the whack of a tin can — but was spared. The woman was pointing a shaking finger at the figure JD could clearly see now huddled in the corner. Robbie Clark's round face was flushed and tear-stained, and he had one knee clutched to his chest. "Why?" the woman asked, turning to JD. "Why did he kill my boy?"

"Let's talk about it," JD said. "But not here. Not like this. What's your name?"

"Millie." The woman smelled like distilled plums. She stared up into JD's face with watery, hurt eyes, but appeared to pull herself together. Mustering up her cocktail party manners from better days, maybe, she said, "Pleased to meet you. What — what did you say your name was?"

"I'm Jane," JD said.

With fragile souls she liked to give her name in its unabbreviated form. *Jane* created a faster bond than *JD*. Her wish to bond with Millie wasn't all goodness of heart. From what she'd read in reports and case notes she knew who this Millie was. Kyler Hartshorne's mom, who had provided Leith the breakthrough tip about the long black sedan.

"Jane," Millie pleaded, clutching JD's sleeve with one hand and again pointing at Robbie Clark with the other. "That man killed my son. I was coming in for my groceries, and I saw his car. I saw him park it on the street and get out and come in here, too. It's a Cadillac. Just like the one we used to have. A DeVille. It's the same car I saw outside my house. Ky got into that man's car, and he never came home. That man killed Ky."

Uniforms had arrived as Millie spoke. JD signalled at them to hang back while she continued calming Millie

Hartshorne. She began to explain to Millie that throwing things wasn't helping, but that everything was going to be okay now. The man would be spoken to. Whatever he had done would come to light, no worries.

Robbie Clark had gotten to his feet, JD saw. He was steadying himself against the freezer doors and taking stock of his injuries, and just when she thought she had Millie under control, the little woman caught sight of Clark and lunged for him again. A small can of condensed soup in each hand, she managed to fling one at his face with her left as JD seized her right.

Clark dodged the bullet and dropped back into a defensive curl.

"You killed Ky," Millie cried at him, hoarse with passion. "Bastard. I hope you rot in hell."

JD rotated Millie with some force and gave her a push toward the uniforms, who would rein her in. Once the human rocket launcher was gone, she went to crouch beside Clark and ask if he was okay.

He sat like a bewildered four-year-old who had fallen off his bike and couldn't believe the cruelty of the world. Blood trickled down his scalp, and he was starting to cry. Great choked sobs of the broken and humiliated. JD had a feeling that laying her hand on his shoulder would be a brilliant move, so she did.

She gave his shoulder a soothing rub, telling him an ambulance was on its way. Her touch seemed to spring a release valve, turning on all Clark's underground sprinklers. He turned to her and wept, "It wasn't supposed to happen like that, with the janitor. She was so beautiful. She always had a smile for me. I thought she liked me. I just wanted to show her that I liked her, too."

"All right," JD said. "All right." Still being his best friend, which was ironic, since she was his worst enemy. *No, actually, he has that one covered.* "Let's get you patched up, then we'll sit down and talk, okay?"

He let out a breathy shudder as he walked beside her to the cruiser waiting curbside. The shudder reminded her of a small child after a full-blown tantrum, who now only wants to suck his thumb and snuggle in Mom's lap.

She hoped his quest for absolution would survive the booking process, his discussion with a defence lawyer, and all the other formalities that tended to sap the life out of good intentions. She hoped he would still be sucking his thumb when they got down to the nitty-gritty of his full, warned statement, which wouldn't get underway till much later.

The delay worried her. But there were witnesses to his confession, the store clerks who had been watching and listening from the sidelines. He would get it pretty quickly, that he couldn't change his mind now, take back his words or claim coercion. He was sunk.

Once he was taken away, she walked back to the detachment. There was no elation in her heart. Just the reverberations of Millie Hartshorne's rage.

\* \* \*

Kate would be home soon, and Dion was at her condo, making dinner. A stir-fry and rice. Kate's favourite music was on the stereo. The apology flowers in their vase on the dining room table were holding up well, and he glanced at them now and then as he chopped vegetables. Strange, to give someone cut flowers as proof of love. Flowers once cut are dead, no matter how nice they look. Snipped from their lifeblood, bunched together, strangled by a ribbon, placed on display.

He understood now where the relationship was headed. He was trying too hard to be someone he wasn't, and when he tried talking to Kate, as JD advised, his words came out empty. If anything, all he was doing was scaring Kate off. The crash had destroyed his bullshit skills, which left him with little to say. JD told him to stop pretending, to be honest. To be honest, he would have to tell Kate he was gone and never coming back.

The bouquet was a gaudy reminder of failure. Looking at it, he couldn't breathe. The only right thing to do, to be fair to Kate and to himself, would be leave, burning his bridges behind him. He pulled the flowers dripping from the retro milk jug she had put them in and stuffed them headfirst in the kitchen trash bin. Then he turned up the music — something about love being a drawn sword, which it sure the fuck was — turned off the stove, picked up his jacket, and left.

# THIRTY-FIVE

## GHOSTS

*February 24*

AT DAY'S END the crew gathered at Rainey's to get the full story on Tasha Aziz. Present along with Leith were Dion, Niko, JD, Doug, and Jim. Everyone knew much of what Robbie Clark had done, but not the full story. It was up to Leith to pull the details together and fill in the gaps.

He told them about Clark heading to the school grounds to pick up his dime bag of weed from the hidey-hole, as arranged with Kyler Hartshorne. Clark had parked in the back, not in the front as he'd originally said. He had a cover story for his pot-buying trips, taking a folder with him, actually stepping into his office and shuffling papers around, before heading back to his car. There he'd seen Kyler prowling in the shadows, and it turned out Kyler had spotted him, too.

"There's some guesswork on Clark's part," Leith said. "But he thinks Kyler slashed Tasha's tire. Tasha told him she'd given Kyler the finger one day, after Kyler made overtures to her."

"The kind of overtures that deserve the finger," Shiomi guessed.

"Clark figures after jabbing her tire, Hartshorne hung around so he could see the look on her face when she discovered the flat. Clark comes upon Tasha as she finds her tire slashed. He's had his eye on her for a while, and here's his chance to swoop in and save the day. He offers to change her tire, and things seem to go well. She sets off her car alarm by mistake, and they have a laugh about that. She asks Clark what he teaches, and he tells her he's actually a counsellor. He seems to think this is a good segue into offering her counselling for the trauma of finding her tire flattened, and places a hand on her arm. He admits his timing was bad, and his hand might have been overly firm. She's startled, jerks back, fumbles with her keys, drops them. He realizes she's getting ready to sound the alarm again, this time for real. Which pisses him off."

JD said, "Women just don't know how to not give off the wrong signals, do they?"

"So he's pissed off," Leith repeated. "He apologizes, but she makes it clear she just wants to get in her car and go. He teases her by putting his boot on her keys as she tries to pick them up. He thinks he's being funny, and she thinks he's being a threat. She leaves the keys and begins to walk back toward the school. He goes after her — to apologize, he says — steps on her keys on the way and sees he's damaged them. He's getting angrier and more worried by the moment. He gives the keys a furious kick and sends them under the car. Sees Tasha is rummaging in her bag as she walks away. For her phone, he realizes. He races after her."

Leith paused. Robbie Clark's story was pathetic and probably true. He tried to be a charmer and ended up a menace, a killer, a source of untold sorrow.

"He catches up with her at the fence and again grabs her by the arm. He wants to talk and explain himself, but ends up shouting. She pushes him. He pushes back. She goes down, and he sees his career flushed down the toilet, maybe worse. Jail time. He starts to walk away but turns back as she's trying to get to her feet and gives her a kick in the stomach. Then leaves her there."

"One kick?" Paley asked.

"The autopsy confirms it. Clark says he couldn't believe it when he found out she had died from one kick. Maybe if he hadn't been wearing steel toe caps it would have ended better. But he ruptured her spleen, and she was too injured to get at her phone. She died within the hour."

Leith moved on to part two of the Tasha Aziz tragedy. "Kyler Hartshorne witnessed the attack. Instead of rushing to help Aziz, he used his knowledge to blackmail Robbie Clark. And that's where it got tangled. Hartshorne knew there's strength in numbers, and when he approached Clark with his first demand for cash, he lied and said he wasn't alone that night, that Tiago Garland had been with him. Which he wasn't, we know, because Tia had been at Oliver Walsh's place."

Dion added, "Walsh was able to confirm it through his journal."

Paley squinted. "Teen boy documents his day and who he's with? Sounds fishy to me. Can we trust this nerd?"

"He didn't write down that Tia was with him," Dion said. "But says he extrapolated from his notes that he and Tia had been hanging out on February first."

"*Extrapolated*," Jimmy Torr echoed. "Who says *extrapolated*?"

"Oliver Walsh, for one," Dion told him. "Just because your vocabulary —"

"Quiet," Leith said. "You want to hear this or not?"

JD said she didn't, really, but Leith finished anyway. "Robbie Clark was puzzled that Kyler and Tia were hanging around together, since he didn't think they were buddies, but he believed Kyler's lie that they were in it together. And was doubly convinced when Tia passed him in the hall and did this." He demonstrated the *I'm watching you* hand signal, pointing across the table at Dion.

Shiomi said, "I see where this is going. Robbie Clark killed both boys?"

"Unlikely. We're still pretty sure Tia died of an overdose. Maybe on purpose. Maybe the hundred bucks he gave Oliver was a going-away present. We may never know. The theory is Kyler bribed Tia to give Clark the warning. Tia likely wondered what it was all about, but everyone agrees he wouldn't have done it if he'd known it was linked with a serious crime. Is it the cause of his depression? I'm not sure."

JD said, "So Kyler invented a ghost accomplice."

"For backup," Leith agreed. "And to up the ante. And it worked. Clark felt trapped, knowing there were two witnesses, two blackmailers. He says he paid Kyler two thousand dollars for his silence."

"This'll end in tears," Shiomi said.

"It sure did. Tia's death was good news to Clark. Now he only had one blackmailer to deal with. And turns out Kyler was right to worry. When he approached Clark for a second installment — maybe Kyler wasn't even aware that Tia was dead at that point — Clark decided this had to end. He agreed to meet him, and chose the rock where Tia had died."

"I have a theory about that," JD said. "It was Clark's way of giving his blackmailers the finger, having them both die on the same spot."

"Could be," Leith agreed. "What we know is Clark drove past the Hartshorne home, intending to park farther along to avoid being seen, but Kyler had seen him cruise by and rushed out to join him. That was unlucky for Clark, as Kyler's mom saw the meet up and was able to identify Clark's vehicle. Clark agrees it was a mistake, using his own distinctive car. As he told me, he should have rented a damned Toyota. But he didn't. He took precautions, though. Parked some distance from the jumping rock, and insisted he and Kyler walk there separately. They met on the rock, as planned. Met by the flowers someone had put down in memory of Tia. They were supposed to talk about the terms and do the payoff. From that point it was easy for Clark. He gave Kyler a shove, planted the note, and took off."

And Kyler had fallen in the worst way, headfirst into the rocky shallows. Knocked out, he had drowned. Unlike Dion, who had landed feet first in the depths of the pool. Leith wrapped up the sordid tale. "Clark's forgery is going to help put him away, but really it's Millie who won the day for us."

"Three cheers for Millie," JD exclaimed, glass raised.

Everyone at the table except Leith raised a toast to Millie. He had sympathy for the woman, but wasn't ready to give her any medals. She'd raised Kyler to be the type of guy who'd watch a woman die instead of helping her. For that, Millie Hartshorne had to take some blame. It was just another layer of sadness to this case.

"Millie's been charged for assaulting Clark, by the way," he said. "I'm not sure it'll be a bad thing, for her. Crown says she'll plead. She won't get much of a rap, but she will get help. Which she needs."

"So Tia Garland is the only outstanding question," JD said. "Why did he do it?"

There would be no clear answer to that one, but the rumours circulating around the school about Tia kidnapping his own sister didn't help. But there was maybe a bigger picture, a global-sized depression. In looking through boxes of documents for evidence in the Luna Garland kidnapping, back when Tiago had been a suspect, Leith had come across an English essay the boy had submitted. It spoke of where the world was headed, which was down the tubes. The planet was dying, and the leaders weren't leading his generation to a better place. As far as Tia could see, the end was near.

If he'd listened to some classic rock songs, it might have given him some perspective on the world ending, Leith thought. Or maybe not. But Tia was getting negativity from all sides. The stress of Luna's disappearance.

Parents too busy with their own skirmishes to notice his troubles. Pile that on top of the usual conflicts that come with growing up. Boy oh boy, the kid had plenty reasons to be blue, Leith reflected. A whole world full of reasons.

* * *

The conversation lightened around Dion. A live band was setting up, which was new to Rainey's. The pub was celebrating some kind of anniversary, and chairs were cleared from around the karaoke stage for anybody who wanted to dance. He watched the band hooking up amps and adjusting mics, and reflected on Robbie Clark's crime, how it mirrored his own, in ways. Clark had been living in fear of two witnesses, just as he was. Clark's witnesses were both dead, but at least one of Dion's was still out there, a girl with pink hair, the loose end without a name. The other was Brooke, and she was still missing.

Dion knew why Brooke was missing. His guardian angel had offed her, that's why. Poole hadn't said so, but what else could it be? He and Poole hadn't spoken since confession day at the Quay, but their conversation played in a loop in his mind, winding his nerves tighter with every pass. He and Kate were officially split up again. So much for that parachute. Now there were warnings in the air, like Leith sending the *I'm watching you* signal his way tonight. Coincidence? Hardly.

The band started to play. They were into upbeat new-age rock and roll, and the set started off with a popular Imagine Dragons cover. A few couples got up to dance.

The light show rigged by the pub was small-scale but effective, splashing and twirling mutating colours over the bodies in motion. Between songs a free round of drinks was announced to celebrate Rainey's new direction.

Happy hour.

Niko Shiomi, sitting next to Dion, bumped his thigh with hers. "Wanna?" she said.

Dance, she meant, and that probably wasn't all. Looking at her, he recalled the rabbit-face comment she'd made to JD, and was suddenly so angry he forgot to breathe. He was angry at everybody. Even dead friends, like Looch and Brooke. He was angry at himself most of all.

There was only one person he wasn't angry at. Rabbit Face. And she was angry with him, and didn't have the good grace to tell him why.

He turned down Shiomi's offer and stood to say good night to the crew. Shiomi said, "Aw, Cal, don't be a sad sack. Stick around and keep me company. I'll buy you a drink. I'll buy you two."

JD had been watching them, and now leaned forward and made a show of lapping her tongue at something invisible clutched in her hand. A lollipop, ice cream cone, or somehting cruder. She looked ridiculous. "Guess what's for dessert," she hooted.

"Bitch," Shiomi said. She stood and leaned toward Dion, affixing the top button of her blouse. She left her coat hooked on her chair, evidence that she was coming back, and murmured to Dion as she brushed past him, "Hope you'll be here in thirty seconds."

He wouldn't be. He carried on with his plan to leave then, saying good night to everyone, and everyone wished him a good night in return, except JD. He wanted her to say good night most of all, and instead she turned away.

Out on the sidewalk under the awning he stood wondering how to catch some oblivion. Meds, alcohol, sex. Nothing worked. He was walking up Lonsdale wondering if opiates were the answer when he heard footfalls behind him, the clip-clop of heels. He turned to see Niko Shiomi shadowing him.

"I don't give up that easily," she called, grinning.

She wore a dark satiny coat and sparkling earrings. She camouflaged well against the glitter of city lights. His anger didn't blow off, but shifted into a different kind of energy. He needed Niko right now like morphine, and this time he wasn't going to say no. He held out his hand, and she ran to catch up.

# THIRTY-SIX

## KENNY

*February 29*

*WHAT A MONTH FROM HELL,* JD thought. And today topped it off. First Brooke Zaccardi's body had turned up mired in sludge and badly decomposed, and now Ken, found shot dead in his own apartment, body still warm.

In the morning Bosko had called an informational meeting for all those invested in the mystery of Zaccardi's disappearance. Along with JD, Leith and Dion had been invited to the boss's office, as well as the two others besides JD who had last seen Brooke at Rainey's in January, Jim Torr and Doug Paley. Lil Hart and Ken Poole, who had been at the pub only briefly on the evening of Brooke's visit, were the only ones not included, probably because they hadn't seen or heard anything of interest and were considered peripheral.

How peripheral was Ken Poole, really, JD now wondered.

Bosko had described the discovery of Zaccardi's body in his easygoing, plodding way. The same voice he would use to announce a staff barbecue or an annihilating meteor headed to earth, JD thought. The body had been spotted last night by a tugboat operator. Nowhere near North Van, where Zaccardi had last been seen alive, he said, nor Burnaby, where she lived. She had been found far afield, on the banks of the Fraser River in Surrey, down from the train tracks and close to the log booms. Within minutes of Highway 35A, in fact. A bad area. Lotta drugs, lotta crime. IHIT had attended. The body was recovered, and a fentanyl death was suspected. A bad fix or a deliberate overdose, who knew.

JD had stolen a glance at those around her as they absorbed the news. All except Bosko and Leith had been friendly with Brooke in better times. Neither man had met her, and to them she was just a name.

Of all those present, Dion had been closest to Brooke. Maybe not the most friction-free relationship, but it was Dion and Kate, Looch and Brooke, always together, the four musketeers. Yet of everyone here absorbing the news, it seemed to JD that he looked least affected. He looked distant. Indifferent, even.

Paley was shaking his head ponderously. "Well, I guess it's kinda what we expected, isn't it? Poor Brooke. I guess she's never been the same since ... well."

"This sucks," Torr cut in. "This just fuckin' sucks."

Bosko nodded approval at Torr's summation. "IHIT's linked up the location of her body to an anonymous tip that Surrey RCMP received last month. A caller reported seeing a late-model SUV parked near the same spot. She said a woman and two men were in the cab of the SUV, and seemed to be arguing. Following the tip, members cruised the road and walked the beaches, but didn't find anything suspicious, so the info was filed and forgotten. Now, with a body, IHIT's backtracked through the tips and pulled up the anonymous 911 call. The timing is right, and the caller's description of the woman in the vehicle fits. The two men haven't been identified."

"Anonymous caller," JD said. "Does IHIT have any leads on that person?"

"Not much so far," Bosko said. "Untraceable number, and since she wasn't a railroad employee or connected to the tugs, and since it's not an area where people hang about for the fun of it, she's probably an addict. Maybe party to another deal, maybe even connected to the suspects. Sounded middle-aged, raspy. Could have been a man disguising his voice as a woman, too."

JD saw Dion give his mouth a twist and look down at his knit fingers, and she realized his indifference was only a disciplined kind of self-containment.

But Brooke Zaccardi's grisly end was just the beginning of this grisly day. Night had since fallen and more bad news had come along. Horrific news. Death of a brother officer, even if JD wasn't close to this particular brother.

The rain was heavier than usual, and rivers coursed along the curb outside Poole's apartment building. JD switched off her windshield wipers and her headlights turned the falling water into a million comet flares. An ambulance was parked in front of her, but it took off, as she arrived, in silent mode. She left her vehicle, and since she had thoughtlessly come out in joggers, kangaroo jacket, and baseball cap, she was instantly soaked.

She climbed the steps to the building and a constable posted by the front entrance pulled the glass door open, allowing her in. She removed her wet cap, stuffed it in her pocket. They spoke briefly, commenting on the rain, then JD rode the elevator up to Poole's floor. Another constable was inside the open doorway, but the apartment was small, leaving no mystery of where to go from here.

She joined Leith and Mike Bosko in the living room. They seemed to cut their conversation short on her arrival. She didn't have to be told to keep her path confined, touch nothing. From the bedroom came voices, Ident examining the body, taking photographs.

The living room was semi-dark. Messy. Quiet. Leith told JD she shouldn't be here. He asked if she was okay. She said she was. Bosko was checking his voice mail, and his phone sounded like a buzzing insect in his palm. Otherwise no sounds but the rain blowing against the windowpane in a fluctuating hiss and patter and the soft clack-clack of Ken Poole's Felix-the-Cat clock.

An Ident member summoned Bosko, and he went to join them, leaving JD alone with Leith. She looked around at the shitty furniture, the TV's greasy screen, the beer cans and whisky bottles. So Kenny Poole hadn't cleaned up to avoid going out like a loser. Maybe he just didn't care. She asked Leith, "No question it was self-inflicted?"

"Looks that way."

"Note?"

He nodded. "About as basic as it gets. Says he didn't want to live anymore. Tired of life."

Kenny Poole had been a fixture at the detachment as far back as JD could remember. Friendly enough guy, kind of quiet, definitely an introvert. A perennial bachelor, as far as she knew. Joined the crew for drinks now and then but didn't have much to say. In his role as supervisor he'd always gotten along with the male recruits best, and JD was pretty sure she knew why.

Leith explained how the body had been discovered. Tonight a 911 call had come in from tenants on the other side of this unit's wall. They had heard something, more a repercussion than a gunshot. Why report it? Just sounded weird. Uniformed first responders were directed to Ken's door, got no answer when they pounded. Door was locked. Obtained the key from the building manager and found Poole in his bed, pistol loose in hand, silencer attached, brains and blood spattered across the wall. The handwritten note on the dresser described his weariness with life.

JD got a nod from Leith and went to check out the bedroom and body. She looked at Ken's bulk sprawled on the bed. He lay on top of the blankets, propped against pillows. Half-empty mickey on the nightstand. The room was cool, thermostat down. He wore boxer shorts and a tank top, and his face was turned away from JD in the doorway, toward the window, his last eyeful of the world chopped by venetian blinds.

She looked at the blood spatter and envisioned the firing of the gun. First she pictured it fired by Ken's own hand, then by somebody else's.

Random memories and concepts gathered in her mind. Ken leaving Rainey's in advance of Brooke. Brooke vanishing, then turning up dead, taking whatever revelations she had about Dion with her to the grave. And now Ken was gone, too. Silenced. She returned to the living room, said good night to Leith and Bosko, and left them dealing with the sad case of Kenny Poole. Open and shut, it seemed. Maybe.